E. Cory-Kin
Tel: 82679.

GW00838424

23 Ventnor Rd
Fortuneswell
Portland
Dorset DT5 1JE

ASANTE MAMSAPU

E. Cory-King

MINERVA PRESS
MONTREUX LONDON WASHINGTON

ASANTE MAMSAPU

Copyright © E. Cory-King 1995

All Rights Reserved.

No part of this book may be reproduced in any form,
by photocopying or by any electronic or mechanical means,
including information storage or retrieval systems,
without permission in writing from both the copyright owner
and the publisher of this book.

ISBN 1 85863 452 0

First Published 1995 by
MINERVA PRESS
1, Cromwell Place
London SW7 2JE

Printed in Great Britain by
B.W.D. Ltd., Northolt, Middlesex

DEDICATION

For Tanganyika, and the people who were there at the time…

ABOUT THE AUTHOR

Although I studied Social Anthropology in order to walk in my father's footsteps, marriage to an Englishman kept me in Britain, and our four children claimed my time instead. When they needed me no longer I began to write, and having been brought up in Tanganyika, having absorbed whatever it is that differentiates us 'bush children', I express what that country told me.

CONTENTS

PAPA HANSELE

On a day when the sun shone as hot as the day before, and the day before that on the deck of the *S.S. Tanganyika*, my mother picked me up to see the approaching coast of Dar es Salaam, "See the palm trees, real palm trees, darling." She pointed to a fringe of vegetation slowly expanding into single trunks with tousled branch heads. I watched, infected by her excitement, though at the age of two and a half the significance of palm trees, real or otherwise, passed over my head like the smoke blowing from the funnel.

"There he is, *ach Du lieber Gott!* Do you see Papa Hansele? Can you see that figure in white?"

Everything was dazzling: the reflection of the sun on the water made it shimmer, a few port buildings bounced rays from their roofs in an explosion of white light which made them dissolve in a haze of heat. The figure stood wavy in outline as if walking in air. It was difficult to look out of my eyes; set down on deck I could see even less.

My mother rooted to the spot began waving regularly, an upside down pendulum movement, and though I tugged at her hand she had forgotten about me. Bored, I ran off to find something more interesting, and was extricated from the barber's shop by a search party helping my frantic Mutti to find the child whom she wanted to wash, comb and dress prettily before our meeting with Papa Hansele.

Ships steaming into Dar es Salaam harbour in 1927 had to anchor offshore for fear of running aground. Papi, therefore, had to come on a motor launch that ferried passengers, friends and customs officials back and forth from the mainland. It was a long wait for those on board while a ladder was swung outward and lowered, dangling down the ship's side to trail in the wash and slap of the swell. A crewman on the launch held it, allowing the rest of the boat-load to swarm up the swinging steps.

It was when my father had at last reached the top, breathless and flushed, that my rehearsed greeting failed, for I found myself in the arms of a short, stocky man with cropped dark hair, and an open-necked shirt, the sleeves of which hung to his elbows. A thick leather belt kept up his white shorts terminating only centimetres from the long socks turned over at the knee. Brown leather ankle boots, tough soled and laced, were the only part of his attire familiar to me. Mine had been discarded at Genoa when my aunts replaced them with white calf leather shoes of the bar-and-button kind before our final parting.

The intervening seven months of separation since he had gone to Tanganyika to prepare a home for us, made him a total stranger.

Moments before our meeting he removed his slouch hat, and when my mother thrust me upon him, his stumpy pipe was hastily tucked into a pocket stem first, bowl protruding to vent the dying wisps of pungent tobacco.

"Na hallo!" he said looking at me with interest, blue eyes signalling a joke. "You must surely be my child with those short legs."

Having claimed me for his own, I realised that this was my Papa Hansele, and stopped the tears of apprehension. From that moment on we easily assumed our roles of father and daughter, and it would only be a short while before I knew he was in charge of our lives because when he said it was time to go, no remonstration on the part of Mutti, eyeing the ship's ladder with consternation, persuaded him to the contrary.

"Never!" she cried out, "I can't do it. My head is swimming already, I shall fall in the ocean if I take another step."

The waiting African launch crew took no notice of her protestations, one man pulled her gently onto the first step, the other guided her from behind, murmuring encouragement. Wedged between her helpers like a piece of white cheese in two slices of black Pumpernickel, she was propelled downwards to the launch; Papi went next, followed by another of the crew carrying me in his arms.

It was a close introduction to a truly black man, black to the roots of his hair, not like those artificially painted 'Africans' I had seen at the 'cross the equator' fancy dress party.

So, black people really did exist!

Once on shore, we were introduced to the waiting servants before they carried our cabin trunk and suitcases to the hotel.

"This is Idi, and here is Juma, I brought them to see the great metropolis of Dar es Salaam, the seat of our Government, and a few unmentionable amusements!" He translated his remark for their laughter.

"Jambo, habari bibi? Habari mtoto? (Hello, how are you lady?

How are you child?)" They greeted each of us in turn.

"Now," said my father, bending down to me, "you shall have your first Swahili lesson. Smile as they are doing, yes like that, a bit more, good. Now you're laughing that's even better. Then you merely reply, *'Jambo,'* to each."

"Jambo! Jambo!"

"Ehe! kumbe Bwana ana mtoto mzuri sana. (Indeed! the master has a very nice child.)" It sounded like one long exclamation.

BEGINNINGS

When my father had left Mannheim for Tanganyika, Mutti's relations had suggested that it was the last she would see of him but when he did not vanish into the African 'jungle' as prophesied and time came for her and her small daughter, myself, to follow from Genoa, there were even greater misgivings. How could she think of exposing such a young child to the heat, diseases, wild men, poisonous insects, and man-eating beasts of the tropics, they said. There would undoubtedly be dire consequences.

It was therefore tremendously exciting for her, not only to be with Papi but to find herself at last in the country they had thought so dreadful. I could tell by the way her voice sounded shrill, and her mood communicated itself to me.

After a day in the hotel, there was a train journey to Morogoro, a short car ride on a track with cooling shade trees; and then Papi exclaimed, "There it is! Our new bungalow which the *fundis* (skilled workers) managed to complete in time for your arrival."

We stopped at the side of a white building with a corrugated iron roof and, as if on command, seven men assembled in a row by its steps chanting the litany I had already learnt,

"Jambo! Jambo! Jambo!..."

My mother, prepared for anything unusual, smiled at everyone and I was encouraged to try my *Jambos* on them.

The house seemed not too unfamiliar being somewhat like the ship: the cabins were the four rooms in a row, the deck a broad, cement floored verandah which allowed me a run almost all the way round until I was stopped by the bathroom, and lavatory cubicle.

The ocean of flat land around us was covered by rows of cotton plants which ran up to the house like waves lapping on a red, sandy beach that would become our garden. The further shores of the Uluguru Mountains in the distance stood hazy above the bright green crop, and next day, there was the sun blazing as it would for that day, and the next and the next and the... And as for black men? They had already taken the place of the white because there were not many of the latter around.

Papi I didn't see much of, he was always riding away on a bicycle to "plant sisal". During the time when we used my father's camping gear until the arrival of the crates, Mutti busied herself training the servants in an endeavour, as she said, to make them as proficient as her maid had been at home. She would not rest, she told us, until a "European type household" had been established. To that end she was aided by Steere's *Handbook of the Swahili Language*.

"Guard yourself, I am going to hit you," she read out one morning. "Really, Hans! People don't do things like that, do they?"

"Ahem - mh - remember the book was published in 1875. Didn't you get a more recent phrase book?"

"No. *'Fanya hivi'*, that means 'do it like this'; those are exactly the words I need."

"Fanya hivi! Fanya hivi!" Papi mimicked her when he came home at the day's end. "Is she still waving the baton? Only Furtwängler does that to advantage," he whispered in an aside to me.

He called her activities "playing queen to her domain".

Being mistress of our household brought her contentment expressed in later writings when she professed to have liked Africa from the start: "Hans bought a plantation, 'Rusegwa', where he planted sisal and cotton. Our labour camp was not too far distant from our house, and Hans used to spend a couple of hours every evening after sundown there. He took much interest in the welfare, customs and dances of his Africans."

My father's enthusiasm exceeded hers: "I am not exaggerating if I say that East Africa and I became friends at once," he wrote, explaining how he had arrived in Mombasa in 1913 via London to work with the leading Austrian exporters of fabrics, Alois Schweiger & Co., also represented in Dar es Salaam. The goods were likely to have been made in the cotton mills run by his father near Vienna.

In May 1914 he left Mombasa for Dar where at the outbreak of war, and together with other Austrians, he joined the German *Schutztruppe* as a volunteer.

I soon knew about the war because Mohamadi, our chief boy, and Sefu, the head overseer, enjoyed special status due to their association with my father during the campaign. On his return to Tanganyika, he had wasted no time in being measured for comfortable shirts and trousers. In the Morogoro bazaar under a shady tree, he had found a tailor sewing with an idle outstretched leg, the other doing the work of two on the Singer treadle. The man was none other than his wartime adjutant, our Mohamadi, with a stiff knee due to a gun shot wound received the same day as my father's injury.

A great reunion followed, drawing a crowd of people to whom my father extolled the virtue of his ex-*Askari*. In return Mohamadi entertained them with the story of how the Bwana had saved many villagers from certain death when he followed and finally shot a soldier who had gone berserk, and was not only terrorising the countryside but had already killed a well-known hunter by the name of 'Selous'.

My father wrote: "The man fell on his back and I on top of him. At this moment he gave up all resistance, looked into my eyes - we faced each other at a very close range - and said, *'Basi Bwana nimekosa.* (Let it be, I have wronged.)' I was now waiting for my *askaris* whom I had heard running up. When they arrived and saw me lying upon Maganga covered partly in his blood, one of them put the muzzle of his rifle to his head and fired."

As mentioned above, the day Mohamadi was shot by the enemy but managed to limp into camp, Papi, who had become separated from him, received a bullet in his thigh. Unable to move, he lay near the Rovuma river where game came to drink every sunset. Hearing the animals during waking moments, he believed it inevitable that they would pick up his scent and devour him. Days later, Sefu organised a search party which he urged to keep looking until my father was found, delirious and dying of thirst.

As his orderly, he nursed my father until the suppurating wound was dried by the African sun. It was during the convalescence that Papi had taught him the three 'Rs'.

Whereas my mother never stopped talking about the life she had left behind, Papi's response was, "*Ach!* all that frippery!" Looking back at his repatriation, he wrote that the Vienna of 1920 was bleak and wet, his family like a "picture lacking sharp contours of reality" and Europe a place suitable for wiping off the geographic slate. Disillusioned, he could not wait to get back and when in 1926 the entry of former enemies was permitted, he was one of the first returning to Tanganyika to buy land for a plantation.

That which my parents professed to like about their newly adopted country I took for granted. My shadowy memories of Mannheim and aunties having faded, the house felt as though we had always lived in it. Rusegwa was my world and black people populated it in an accepted relationship of servants or labourers. Swahili became my second language as imperceptibly as I had learned my mother tongue, German. On meeting whites, I would try *Guten Tag* but as likely as not they were English, whereupon even the briefest of exchanges had to be conducted in the 'servants' language', to the embarrassment of Mutti.

The arrival of the packing cases was a great event marking the real occupation of the house. We loosened the Rosenthal china from the grasp of curly wood shavings, extricated my toy chimpanzee put to 'sleep' in the cane furniture, unearthed the black iron saucepans for the cook's little tattoo with their lids, and unwrapped the brass and silver, with the honour of their cleaning going to Mohamadi as senior servant.

Papi would not allow anyone but himself to unpack his books, a remainder, he told me, of a large library collected in the few years between the end of war and his escape back to Africa. They were German classics, literary magazines and some best-sellers.

"Come here," he called to me, "come and look at something beautiful. Not only your Mutti's clothes are pretty, look at this book for instance." He explained the refined look of *Anna Karenina's* watermarked cover and tooled spine. "You may help me, there are about two to three hundred books to put away. Not many," he added sadly.

I began passing them. "No, no not like that. You must be very careful. Always be kind to books."

There were a few for me too, fairy stories, and one *Peterschen's Mondfahrt* with the front cover showing the moon, a star-studded great bear and a fiddling beetle, the adventures of which would soon fill my fantasy world.

Papi, insisting on a minimum of clutter, had dissuaded my mother from bringing wardrobes and carpets, instead, one of the plantation carpenters changed the packing cases into storage units, and the camp mat weavers made our floor coverings.

One of Mutti's complaints being that life was too quiet, I could not understand why she prevented me from laying my hands on the object which could be relied upon to create merriment. All you needed was a handle, a few turns... and Mutti was upon me snatching it out of my hands,

"Darling, only Mutti is allowed to do it or else we shall have to stop the music altogether."

It was a cruel threat. *"Annemarie, Annemarie...,"* the current hit when we left Mannheim was my favourite tune. Idi or Juma, when they saw me dancing to the music, joined in but stopped immediately my mother's footsteps were heard, assuming an indifference as though gramophones were commonplace in their huts.

Another object I loved became important at six o'clock in the evening when the sun sank without warning. A very short dusk prevailed during which the "zee-zee-zee" whine of mosquitoes became audible, a sign that it was time for the servants to light the lamps. Our bronze table lamp from Mannheim invariably exuded that acrid smell given off by smoking oil wicks. I always waited for the moment when the red flames, shrouded in smoke, looked as though they would never stop licking the vulnerable glass funnel until, all at once, the light caught properly to defuse through the opaque shade onto limewashed walls, and the flat brush strokes on my mother's oil paintings which reflected its glow.

It was a series of rites translating into one word, 'Tanganyika', to be repeated as regularly as sunset.

After the lamp lighting, Idi and Juma went round the house to make sure that the secondary mosquito-proofed frames were secure against invaders, six-legged of course. The glazed windows stayed open. Armed with the flit-pump, the boys bombarded insects, with the exception, on Mutti's orders, of spiders who aided the process with their own method of weaving snares, and geckos who sat motionless, clinging to the wall or ceiling with their toes, until a passing insect made them dart to devour it.

The mosquito-nets, suspended on frames over our iron bedsteads brought out from Europe, had been lowered earlier for the 'flitting', causing a refreshing smell of paraffin to pervade the house.

It was also a signal for my supper, the only occasion on which I was allowed a choice of food, "I would like boiled egg, and - steamed chocolate pudding - and vanilla sauce."

"Couldn't you do without the sauce, darling?"

"No, I would really very much like to have some." Mutti always succumbed to politeness. We would be off to the kitchen building where I remained at the entrance knowing what would follow. She commenced preparing the sauce over the wood-fire stove which never stopped smoking.

"Watch what I am doing," she urged the cook. "Next time you can make it." Tears trickled down her face as she beat the whites, "Blow on the fire, cook. Can't you stop the smoke?"

"It does not want to."

"See, make the whites like this." She turned the plate upside down, showing him how the stiffened foam did not fall off, "You understand? This is how we do it in Europe." There was a pause for blowing her nose, red by now, "Juma, if the Bwana is back, give him his whisky and soda; Idi, bring the child's bath water." She was in full spate, satisfied only when servants looked equally busy.

By the time I said goodnight to my father, should he be at home, he was sitting by the bronze lamp the whisky at his side, a book in one hand, in the other a pipe which spread its aroma in wisps about him.

Lying under my white box of mosquito-netting, declared the safest place on earth by him - "Not even a lion would dare to get himself entangled in such human cunning" - Mutti read from one of the fairy tale books, leaving their characters to loom large in the shadows when she turned down the lantern to glow discreetly until morning.

As I grew to five, all other white children of that age and above disappeared to Britain for their education. On the rare occasions when one came to Rusegwa with parents invited to tea, there was the initial difficulty of the language barrier, but once overcome and just when the moment of wordless understanding would be reached, there was an inevitable interference by her ayah.

When I suggested 'hide and seek', she would have none of it, too lazy to follow her charge's movements. Water and sand were not permitted, what would her mistress say about a dirty party dress! My rope swing, a cushion draped over its 'U' end hanging from the tamarind was considered too dangerous. Jumping off logs, in which activity I was practised to the point of wishing to show off, she regarded as too boisterous for her ward.

I learnt that the constant fuss of British mothers about the state of their children's clothes had made ayahs assume that European children were expected to sit still like the china figure on our bookcase, a chubby girl in a swirling skirt that never moved.

Once a week a lorry loaded with sacks of maize meal chugged past the house on its way to the camp. Papi said the money from the cotton crop paid for the labourers' rations. Sefu, using a measure, distributed it to the waiting rows of men, women and children. In addition there was a ration of beans.

Should we happen to pass by the store hut on an afternoon's walk, I would hear the on-going banter.

"You, Masasa, miserable wretch! Why are you coming round for the second time? You can't even get a concubine to stay - are you pretending you've two?"

On Fridays, Papi sitting at a table on the verandah of the store paid out the week's wages, in front of him rows of shillings, cents, and workcards issued to labourers and filled in by the overseer for each day worked. Beside him once again stood Sefu, witnessing that every labourer got his dues. The rows of men were noisy with anticipation of a happy weekend: a Saturday stroll into the township of Morogoro, a new pair of shorts or a colourful cloth for their *bibi*, a drink at the rowdy *pombe* (native beer) stall.

Papi said the fairness of pay marked the difference between the planter who was chronically short of labourers and one who, like himself, had a surplus to hire to other plantations.

The camp women also earned money. Binti Salehe, strong and tall, made earthenware pots with a sheen like her skin which she kept oiled for beauty. Binti Sulemani sat with her legs stretched straight, the fast growing strip of raffia undulating over them as her hands wove the coloured strands in and out, for our mats. Mama Panya (Mother Rat) rolled ear studs worn by women who pretended they were more *pwani* (coastal), and therefore more sophisticated than those up-country folk.

Mutti constantly admired the artistry of the studs, until Mama and friends offered to make her some. There were three different sizes of hole, small at the top, medium, and large for the bottom of the lobe. Little girls had their ears pierced and a peg was inserted to keep the hole open. As the girls grew older, larger pegs were inserted for the required size, the studs reaching a diameter of up to four centimetres in the lowest position.

From the Morogoro shops the women bought matt paper, coloured yellow, green, mauve and red, as well as sheets of assorted tinsel. The paper was cut into strips, folded along the spine and tightly rolled between thumb and forefinger. Tiny pieces of contrasting paper or tinsel were inserted, bent over and re-inserted, at the will of the designer, to form what Mutti considered exquisitely delicate patterns reminiscent of Eastern mosaics.

One day, when my mother and I took our usual mid-morning drink on the verandah, latterly enhanced by the waving arms of prickly pear planted in tins standing on the new verandah parapet, our view was permanently changed by workers pulling up the dried cotton plants.

From some of our sisal grew poles which branched briefly, erupting with light green flowers, the future bulbils, which would eventually fall off their perch and root. It was these regrown in a nursery which were about to be planted out.

"Aha!" said Mutti, waving her cup in the direction of the labourers, "One change in progress, another still to come. What do you say to that, Putzimännchen?"

"What change?"

"We are going to buy a lorry, a Ford I think your father said."

"Will we be riding in it?"

"But of course, darling, I can tell you about something else that is coming, though not quite so soon." She was in an excited and informative mood.

"Is it going to be a bicycle for me?" Always keen to emulate my father I wanted to ride round with him.

"No, darling, you will have to wait for one until you're bigger." She became thoughtful for a moment, leading me to think that she was considering my age, then continued, "You see, Papi says we are losing money selling our sisal leaves to other plantations for processing, therefore he has ordered our own decorticator. Then, you see, the removal of the pulp from the fibre will be done by our people here at Rusegwa."

The Raspador machinery arrived in several large crates, with instructions about assembly, and fixture to a concrete base. We went to see Papi staking out the foundations which were to include the whole factory building situated down-wind from habitation. He said it would have to be partly open to allow air to carry off the stench of the sisal pulp expelled through a channel.

When all was ready, the 'A' Model Ford began the daily work of shuttling between the off-loading ramp at the factory, and the sisal pick-up points on the plantation where labourers cut, tied and stacked bundles of mature leaves.

After our four o'clock tea, when my parents flavoured theirs with slices of lime, while mine was diluted with tinned milk, there being no fresh available, my father rode off on his bicycle to relieve the lorry driver from duty.

Later it was our turn to go on Mutti's constitutional walk which terminated at his sisal pick-up point. Although I could just keep up with her, Idi accompanied us to carry me whenever I flagged, purposely sometimes because I liked to tease my mother by lifting his cap whenever I was sitting astride his shoulders.

Idi grew his hair in a peak above the forehead, believed by her to be a potential lice haven. Secondly, she regarded servants who went capless as rebellious ne'er-do-wells, and therefore expected 'retainers' to keep their heads covered.

In the searing heat of the afternoon, we walked on a rough track between rows of sisal looking as parallel as the strips in our plaited mats, and stretching as far as I could see. By the time we reached the lorry, the Uluguru Mountains had turned a deeper shade of blue in the oblique rays of the late sun, allowing my mother to remove her slouch hat, a signal that I, too, could hand her mine.

The change of light and air was sudden, as if a door had opened beyond which it was cooler, strong colours having changed to muted hues.

Mutti, having walked her energy off, sighed with contentment as she lifted me onto the box seat in the cab, climbing after me for a much needed rest. My father, too, looked relaxed because our arrival signalled the last sisal-run of the day. At the back of the lorry Idi and the loaders shuffled their seats to find comfort among the bundles of sisal which exuded a sour smell, dissipated in the wind once we started.

Contentment expressed itself in song, first from the labourers, then with my father joining in and urging us to sing. We rushed along at about twenty five miles an hour over the rough track, bumping but still singing and clapping while Papi, pipe in his mouth, beat the tune on the steering wheel. The sunset progressed quickly, played in reds, oranges, and pinks fading to grey, as the big ball rolled down beyond the horizon and all at once left us in the dark.

Papi set us down at the house or we went with him as far as the factory to off-load.

Imprinted still on my ears is one of the haunting tunes,

"*Zeze nalia, zeze nalia* ... (The bowed lute plays ...)"

There is also my memory of Papi, excited about a song we had learned that afternoon, alighting from the lorry and dancing in front of our house steps: *"Ma, mi-i - o, ma, mi-i - o, anipe ulezi wangu.* (Mother, mother, let her give me my nurturing.)"

"Come on, come on, dance, it's one two-three, one two-three!"

Mutti watched his cavorting with embarrassment.

"It's waltz time!" he shouted, "unbelievable, most unusual for local songs."

Sometimes we arrived back in time for a 'sundowner', finding my parents' friends already sitting on the verandah, where Mohamadi was serving them drinks.

On these occasions, Mutti changed into one of her white silk gowns, V-necked. The blousey tops always reached to a low waistline from which a short skirt hung in gathers or pleats. The shoes had a bar and button like mine but she wore silk stockings whereas I had socks.

My father called her "pretty", her black bobbed hair "boyish", I thought his first description might be right, but as to the second... how could he mistake my 'Mutti' for anything else!

Whisky and soda, sherry and vermouth or beer for the adults, orange juice and filter water for me, waiting for Idi to bring the dishes of freshly roasted monkey nuts which had already tickled my palate with their smell of nutty brown burning, wafting from the direction of the kitchen.

I knew that if Papi, who liked company, persuaded the guests to stay - "Lili I am sure would be delighted to test the cook's ability to repeat one of her dishes" - then Mohamadi might be persuaded to pay a visit to my bedside. We chatted about the visitors or he told me one of his *sungura* (br'er rabbit) tales. My parents were not aware of this arrangement nor, as I knew, would they have approved it.

As I grew to five and six, I realised that what was hanging between the legs of dogs, bullocks and little boys assumed a special significance in men. When he came to my bedside I would ask him to let me see and feel what he had there, but he refused saying it was not good for me, which aroused my curiosity even further.

As there was no one other than adults to listen to, I knew that white men talked about the price of cotton and sisal, the availability of labour, and debated the policies of the Government at Dar, whereas the ladies were boring in their endless complaints about servants, or their laments at not having their children 'out' with them.

I also knew that my father's great interest did not form a subject of their conversation. Of it he wrote: "I spent many evenings with my labourers in their camp, talking, singing and dancing... I started to learn about medical plants and their use. [At a later date] I participated in initiation ceremonies and I learned to make the African forget that I was not one of them. Here and there I learned things which were not yet found in literature. Whilst my labourers were working in the day time like those on other plantations, they were my teachers and co-members of secret and other societies in our spare time."

This happy association had terrible consequences for one of the factory hands, Bakari, whose daily job it was to clean the decorticator after it had been turned off.

"Look! Here comes the Bwana," he shouted to others as Papi turned the lorry for off-loading, "now we'll have some good laughter." In looking round, his hand slipped into the aperture for feeding leaves to the blades, still revolving though the machine was turned off. Papi saw the man being drawn in by his arm but by the time he reached him, it was severed.

It was a race against time to get him to the Morogoro Hospital before he could die of shock and blood loss.

On his return my father sat in his chair, sipping hot tea and lime which Mutti had laced with cognac.

"Lili, Bakari was in such a state of shock that when he gained consciousness at the back of the lorry, he felt no pain and did not know his arm was missing."

Papi's face did not allow me to ask questions, I imagined it had been like the processing of meat in our mincer, sinew and bits of meat entangled in the blades.

The accident cast gloom over the plantation for a while, but the visits made by Papi to the hospital until Bakari was well enough to go to his tribal home, allowed Mutti and me to shop more frequently in the Morogoro bazaar.

Built of mud bricks or corrugated iron with mat awnings to keep out the sun, the *dukas* (shops) stood one side open to the unmade road on which black would-be shoppers milled about. *Kikapus* (baskets) stayed balanced on women's and girls' heads, men swung them from the hand.

Much was made of greetings according to Arab formula which had penetrated from the coastal lands. Hordes of children played by the wayside or under trees where old people sat on the roots worn bare by human bottoms.

My mother, walking fast and with that air of purpose assumed by all white people as though important business never failed to be ahead of them, towed me by the hand. At the rear, Idi sauntered nonchalantly at the respectful distance expected of servants accompanying their mistress. He carried our *kikapu*.

White children being a subject of interest, there were always remarks being made about my physical prospects.

"Her legs are growing straight."

"They are like the centre pole of a hut."

"Look at her breasts. You can see they are going to be full."

"That bottom of hers, *tch-tch!"* An appreciative clicking of the tongue.

They spoke loudly, giggling after each sentence. Mutti was differently treated, some staring at her open-mouthed or volunteering information.

"She is that *bibi* from Rusegwa."

Another woman curious to explore my mother's response, greeted her, *"Jambo! Eh?"*

My mother did not hear.

"Mutti, the woman says hello."

"Oh, *Jambo*!"

The woman shook her head in disbelief, "Deaf! and with such a young child."

It was fortunate that Mutti was hard of hearing, Idi, though, found it difficult to keep a straight face.

Then came a period when Mutti became strangely excited, her voice sweet, one tone up in the way it sometimes climbed when she was overwrought.

"I have something nice to tell you, darling, Papi's brother, Uncle Julius is coming to visit us. He has two little girls like you."

"Are they coming?"

"No. Sorry, darling, they have to stay with their two different mummies."

This was no new idea. I knew about polygamy among the labourers who might have one young wife at Rusegwa but were also sending money to the older one who kept the family fields under cultivation in their tribal land.

My father volunteered further information, "He is a geologist, that is a man who tries to find gold or diamonds where he knows perfectly well there is only coal or iron!"

My parents were so excited about his coming and overawed by his wealth that I assumed he had found gold after all.

On arrival, Uncle Julius repaid the turmoil of preparations by being appreciative and charming towards us all, black and white alike. He was constantly giving things: to my mother he presented a convertible Morris Cowley and my aim in life became an unsupervised journey in its dicky seat.

His generosity stretched to teaching her to drive, first using the dirt tracks on the plantation until proficiency attained, the Morris was taken out on the main avenue of kapok trees.

Meeting the maize lorry on the narrow road, Mutti drew into the left and, at the moment when she wished to brake, stepped heavily on the accelerator instead. The convertible lurched forward into a kapok trunk with a sound of shattering glass intermingling with her screech followed by a rain of splinters from the windscreen.

Warm liquid trickled pleasantly over my face, Uncle Julius, with blood flowing from a hand, tried to pull me from under the glass while Mutti sat unscathed, staring at us with a look of disbelief which immobilised her.

Once again our lorry acted as ambulance. At the hospital a white nurse bandaged Uncle Julius' hand, stuck a plaster on my slash from hair-line to nose and across it, and told my mother that children had miraculous powers of healing.

The incident convinced Mutti she was dogged by bad luck. "A Beethoven-type pessimism, Lili," was what Papi called her attitude. Subsequently, she lost her confidence as a driver, the Morris was sold, and I lost the opportunity of a solo dicky ride. My scar healed quickly leaving a permanent pucker between the eyebrows, a cross look for the rest of my life. "Don't look so glum, darling, smile a little," became as commonplace as, "Don't forget to clean your teeth."

The sad day came when we had to say goodbye to uncle. Before he stepped into the hired Chevrolet, he paid the kitchen a visit to press a great deal of money into each servant's hands before returning to hug and kiss my mother and me, the tears welling in his eyes.

Tearing himself away to shake Papi's hand, he said, "Don't worry, Hans, I go to London now and I'll fix everything for the plantation."

His departure put an end to the frequency of dinner parties and sundowners where his charming manner had made him - Mutti said - the ladies' sweetheart, and she added that the house now felt like a desert, hot and bare with not a gay mirage on the horizon.

After breakfast on the day following my sixth birthday in 1930, Mutti announced, "Darling Putzimännchen! Now you are such a big girlie you can start school."

Was something entirely new about to happen? I was hopeful.

"Where?" I asked, remembering the photographs seen in officials' houses of uniformed children standing in front of imposing entrances.

She led me out onto the verandah where mosquito-proof framing had lately been installed. Half-way down where it widened to accommodate an entrance from the garden, she stopped at the chair and table made for my play activities.

"Here, at your favourite place," she handed me some primers sent by one of the aunts.

My schooling had begun.

At nine o'clock I was required to attend, looking longingly at the outside world of palms and bougainvillaea which now marked the garden, a colourful foreground to the shimmering Ulugurus. I hated the daily tuition, which grew in length in proportion to my age, quite apart from the constraint of having to sit still despite the heat. Then there was the shame in feeling foolish when a letter refused to reveal the sound it was supposed to make.

My aunts had adored me, my mother thought me the one and only "Putzimännchen", my father regarded mild precociousness as a possible sign of mental activity, the admiration of the straight-haired English ladies for the tumble of curls over my forehead never ceased and my large eyes were praised for revealing an enquiring nature. My self-esteem therefore was considerable, yet when it came to synthesising sound and fusing syllables, I faltered like the Ford Papi could not get started in the morning.

"It is naughty to run across the street in front of a tram."

"A policeman helps a lost child."

Such sentences were meaningless, but had the reading been about "Haroun al Rashid the Glorious in the city of Bagdad..." I could have fared better. There were Arabs trading in Morogoro, their women covered head to foot in black *bui-buis*, there was that dusty street of *dukas*, the smell of Indian spices, the yap of stray dogs, crying children, the noisy chatter of women dressed in those colourful *kangas* (cotton rectangles). Nothing would have been easier than to replace the crowd in the bazaar with characters out of my fairy tales.

Papi wrote of my tuition: "The ups and downs of these daily lessons only compared to heavy storms making navigation difficult." It was a reference to the arguments which marred every lesson.

He took no part in teaching but played with me sometimes, building Grecian temples with bricks, making Meccano models of windmills. There were hours of boredom too: Mohamadi occupied by the polishing of silver and brass, Idi engrossed in squaring sheets for ironing, the *shamba* (garden, plot of land) boy scraping dust round the beds of marigolds encircling indigenous cacti, the cook always stoking smoky fires, the monkey under the tamarind asleep in his box, the swing not a person to whom I could talk.

During one such period my mother's remark, "Darling, will you be quiet now, I want to write to Erna," was the last straw. I removed the purple glass container from its filigree stand in the sideboard, ran into the kitchen and, at the moment when the cook looked up from his squatting position by the stove, emptied its contents of pepper into his eyes. The resulting tears and sneezes would surely be entertaining. Instead the cook let out a bellow of pain which sent me running back into the house for cover. My mother passed me going in the opposite direction. The howling and crying continued. From my bedroom I could hear Mutti calling for cotton wool and warm water and, as I learned later, Juma had gone to fetch my father.

Hiding was one line of action, on the other hand the commotion was just what I had hoped for, the boredom gone, I would stand watching at the window, stubbornly. Gradually the noise died down. My father, whom I had expected to appear before me like a genie out of the fisherman's bottle, took his time. Relieved, I went to play in my room.

By lunchtime he was back, ignoring me and calling the servants to relate an event which they all agreed they had not seen. Then it was my turn.

"Did you throw the pepper?"

"Yes."

"Why?"

I could not explain. Wanting to see what would happen, thinking it might result in amusement, would not be acceptable reasons though they were the truth.

My father delivered a stern lecture,

"Such deeds can land you in prison, restitution will have to be made. You will pay the cook a sum of money each week for compensation."

He could not have devised a more difficult punishment. On each appointed day the shilling in my hand, I entered the kitchen where the servants stood in a line which I had to pass on my way to the end where the cook waited for my apologies with a kindly smile. It was deeply humiliating.

My father's activities increased considerably after Uncle Julius' departure when strangers began visiting our house.

"They want to sell us part or the whole of their plantation," Mutti told me.

My father wrote: "Julius had decided to turn his attention to Rusegwa. He wanted to organise a big sisal-producing company and had behind him influential and rich people in England whom he won over for his plan. He took options for the purchase of several sisal plantations situated in Morogoro and intended to bring in my estate."

The name 'Julius' rang in my ears. My parents were so anxious for news from him that, each time the runner returned from the Morogoro Post Office, Mutti snatched the letters from his hands hopeful that his might be among them.

As mail took about six weeks to reach us by sea and train, it was a long time after the initial shock waves had passed through the family in Vienna before a letter from Rudi Bienenfeld, Papi's brother-in-law informed us that Uncle Julius was dead. He had committed suicide in Constantinople.

There had been a sojourn at a sanatorium about which my parents knew nothing, to cure him of drug addiction. It had proved unsuccessful and he was thought to have gone on a drugs trail to Turkey. With his fortune squandered, his prospects gone, his love-life bound up with women drug abusers, he had given up. That was what Mutti read out from the letter.

My father was too shaken to comment, Mutti not only burst into tears but interspersed her grief with self accusations: "It's partly my fault, I remember putting his clean linen away in the boxes, you know how untidy he was - papers everywhere - and Idi not much help either." She stopped, her voice drowned in sobs. Regaining composure from blowing her nose and wiping her eyes she managed to say, "I found a syringe tucked between some of the things, I never thought of mentioning it to you because I asked Julius about it later..." She began crying again.

It was upsetting to see both my parents so distressed. The boys, discreet and not wishing to be present at a domestic scene, had disappeared from their tasks round the house rendering it unusually quiet.

"Well, what did he say?"

"He said it had fallen out of his tropical First Aid kit. He made a joke about snake bite. It was all so plausible at the time."

Although strangers stopped coming, plantation life seemed undisturbed.

At the back of the sisal factory rows and rows of white fibre on wire lines were drying like so many wigs in the sun; in the effluent channel the stinking green ooze continued to discharge itself with difficulty into the plain.

Papi said the sisal was growing well and Mutti and I walked everywhere keeping up with the Ford's more distant runs.

One morning life at Rusegwa ended, I was told we were about to leave, all of us! It was bad luck but we had no more money.

My father wrote of the precipitate events: "The sisal price dropped from £36 per ton in 1929 to £10 in 1930. At this price the production of sisal caused considerable loss which together with the debts on the factory forced me to close down. Perhaps it would have been possible to raise some money on existing valuable assets. I think that my nature was against the sad experience of going round and meeting with false smiles and excuses from those who were not involved in the depression."

Mutti put all those of our possessions not immediately needed into one of the rooms to be guarded by a trustworthy labourer. Papi closed the doors of the Raspador factory and, after paying out the labour force and giving any man who wished to follow him a train ticket, left with the Ford loaded with as much as it could carry.

Mutti's father had been a millionaire who had lost most of his wealth after World War One, the little she had inherited having been buried in sisal, she had no money either.

We followed my father a few days later by train, Mutti telling me we might soon be back, "When the sisal price goes up as it's sure to do, darling."

I was never to see Rusegwa again and, twenty years later, my mother would find that nobody knew anything about it.

THE BUSH

The shock of our sudden departure from the plantation must have been like the trauma of birth. We were in Rusegwa and, next, it was a very hot afternoon at Manyoni station from which Papi fetched us in the Ford. At the hotel the German owners welcomed us with smiles befitting their jovial and rotund looks.

"Hello! hello! What a little edition of your father you are. Come, little one, take my hand, we'll have a quick look round and then I send you orange juice and cake, coffee for your mamma and papa. Not so?"

Mutti's unhappy expression elicited an assurance that she could call upon the hotel staff to supply our every need.

"Just call 'boy!', one or the other of the *verdammten Dummköpfe* will hear you."

A glance in her direction showed me the expletive was kindly meant.

My mother, sinking into one of the khaki-covered easy chairs on the verandah, admitted she would give her life for a cup of tea and had to laugh when Papi remarked, "A noble sacrifice, Lili. I don't think your Teuton hostess would grasp its significance."

On the road in front of the hotel, fine sand stirred by the passing of an occasional lorry drifted through the mosquito-proofing, covering the coffee tables and German beer mats with a fine layer of dust. Nothing else was in sight, and when our servants returned from their purchases in the bazaar to mount the lorry, Papi said a hasty goodbye, promising us an escape from the desolate place as soon as possible.

Nevertheless, the experience of our stay was exciting, if not extraordinary. Waking to a high pitched squeal, I witnessed two white men in white coats dancing about in the courtyard as they overcame a pink animal that retaliated by squirting blood all over them.

There was also a room in the hotel which held an air of mystique after Mutti's instruction, "Never ever go in, darling, ladies do not enter."

I learnt it was 'The Bar', and who was constantly in it, though always behind a counter - presumably for protection - but a lady!

The brush with civilisation did not last long because my father came to fetch us a week later.

The lorry bumped its way along a sandy track, nothing in sight but savannah scrub: yellow grass, acacia bush, a few trees branching horizontally at the top for an 'umbrella' and twisting their limbs into a trunk lower down.

Despite Papi's avowed dislike of Europe, his enthusiastic accounts of rock-climbing escapades during Tyrolean holidays had filled my imagination. Mutti's amusing anecdotes of excursions to Switzerland and Holland, when she and her sisters habitually tormented their good-natured nanny, portrayed a happy European childhood. I hoped our so-called holiday, no lessons for a few weeks, absence from Rusegwa, might prove equally pleasant.

Sliding about in my seat with expectation, in the hope of catching the first glimpse of our new home, I failed to recognise it when Papi stopped in a clearing before a thatched wattle and daub hut.

Mohamadi, Idi, the cook and a new addition, a puppy 'Dachsi', emerged from another behind it to greet us. The low building could not be compared with the square mud-brick houses of the black traders in Morogoro township. Surely this was like one of those wartime *bandas* (temporary huts), Papi had talked about.

Mutti, undaunted, slipped into the old gear of ordering everybody about, "Cook, I want tea. Idi, hand the cases and *kikapus* of provisions down to Mohamadi who will know what to do with them. Now we will look at the house."

It comprised a verandah and two bedrooms, one leading off the other. Closing windows and doors would not be necessary, Papi explained, because we were now *porini*, in the bush, where no one would steal from us. A separate hut served as kitchen, another belonged to the boys and then there was the loo, where a deep excavation had been covered by sticks, leaving an appropriate gap. A box, with the right shape cut out of the top, stood balancing unsteadily on this platform, the hole aligned with the gap.

We would bath in the old tub placed in one or the other bedroom, the small verandah was to be the living room. We were back where we started, in camping mode or not quite, because Mutti had managed to pack some luxuries like brass trays and raffia mats, and Papi had brought some cases of his favourite books. Mine were there, too, but not the toys which my parents had decided I had outgrown.

Our surroundings enclosed us as a tyre fits a lorry wheel; we were the hub, then came bare ground round the hut, further off was the African scrub, a track to the front door being the only outlet valve. And above us? There was limitless freedom in the vast cloudless sky.

The labourers who had agreed to follow Papi were building themselves a camp somewhere in the bush out of sight.

"With a promised labour force," wrote my mother, "Hans found contract work with an Italian Count, who obtained the chief contract from the Government to build the railway construction Manyoni-Singida-Kinyangiri. Hans got two sections of many kilometres."

Those who obtained the others might as well have been ghosts for all we ever saw of them.

The cook prepared our meals over three stones like the women in our Rusegwa camp, except that they used humps made of clay. Their staple food, a stiff porridge, swelled and bubbled, squeaked and blew little explosions while it cooked in earthenware pots firmly wedged between the clay summits. Some women had two extra mounds, enabling two pots to be on the boil simultaneously, useful for cooking a relish of meat-stew or beans, or the seasonal wild spinach.

Our cook's stones were soon replaced by a wood stove not dissimilar in smoke emission from the iron cooker of Rusegwa. Its sides and centre wall, built of rubble, supported two sheets of tin cut from petrol *debes* beaten straight and placed horizontally, one above the other. The lower section provided the firing area with adjacent oven and the top the cooking surface. The only drawback, Mutti said, was that her Austrian gateaux looked more like German pancakes.

"Aha!" Papi exclaimed on seeing the first offering. "Your mother can preside again at her sacred tea hour - with cake." At Rusegwa, he was always teasing her about the act of pouring tea ceremoniously from a silver tea pot. It had been smuggled onto the lorry with the 'essentials', my mother defending her action by saying, "Well, it gives me pleasure and the child will not forget civilised living."

"Now see," he continued, "how we are going to be offered strudel and *Linzertorte* and she will go off like a Roman empress to make room for more."

Mutti's increasing habit of disappearing to the loo, after she had eaten, exasperated him. Both of us knew it was only to empty her stomach with the excuse that she was feeling nervous.

Although we had cake we had no bread, until a parcel arrived from Mannheim containing a tin of *Flörelin* yeast, but though Mutti was able to prove dough at the side of the stove, there was not enough heat to bake it.

Mohamadi, remembering wartime improvisation, suggested ant hills for an extra oven. They stood conveniently scattered throughout the scrub around us. Eventually after pick-axing and chiselling a hole in the side of one, the cook hammered a piece of tin horizontally into it to make a shelf under which he placed burning embers, stoked periodically from the kitchen fire, until the hole became extremely hot. When the dough was ready, he threw sand on the embers to stop them from flaming, in went the bread on the shelf and a sheet of tin across the opening. Hours later the loaf was done, risen by half only but bread nevertheless.

Another subject for Mutti's concern was meat: once a week the lorry went to Manyoni bringing back maize flour for the labourers and provisions for us, including fresh meat. It had to be beaten before being cooked and eaten within hours in case it turned putrid in the heat.

Life had not altered much for me. My father, who left early in the morning to start the labourers on their day's digging of what would soon be the permanent way, came walking out of the bush for a brief lunch and disappeared into it again for the afternoon. We saw him for tea and supper, after which he and my mother played patience or rummy, though more than often, he spent some part of the evening in the camp.

There was no longer an excuse to postpone lessons when a new batch of correspondence course arrived with the yeast parcel. In the afternoon, with Dachsi for company, we walked round a never-ending network of bush tracks, animal and human, leading nowhere. The world was ours. We could have walked on and on and on... When the sun warned us about its proposed dive over the horizon, we found our way home by turning our backs on it.

Following Papi's track brought us out on a swathe newly-cut through the bush, marked by stakes and promising to be a railway line. Weeks later, the earth removed from cuttings was accumulated to build embankments, our labourers transporting every sort of material, whether sand, stone or concrete in a *kerai*, a shallow iron bowl placed on the head, cushioned by a piece of twisted cloth or grass pad.

Hoes rose and fell in line, as if pulled by a magician's string, pickaxes thumped into the hard ground with a muffled "ump!" or gave a metallic ring when they hit rock. Hammer blows to shatter the latter were timed to fall one after another in a fast moving beat to the slower scritch-scratch of shovels. As soon as men stood together with the same task in hand they organised themselves into a line, one began to sing, others answered in chorus or they all sang in rhythm with their movements.

At mealtimes Papi la-laed the tunes, trying to get into the right key of a melody heard sung in natural harmonies that came to the workers' throats, he said, like Caruso's tunefulness after swallowing raw eggs.

"The cook has waited long enough to serve the meal," my mother complained, or, "you are not helping me to instil mealtime manners in your daughter."

"Tch!" - in mocking derision - "do as your mother says, my dear, and remember a Mannheimer bourgeois has no understanding of folk music." I felt flattered, the implication was clear, I was no "bourgeois" whatever that meant and therefore I did understand folk music.

Another point of conversation concerned the fact that our labourers could work, sing and laugh on a minimum meat diet which would have spelled starvation for a white labourer. On the subject of shooting game for the pot - or for pleasure - Papi expressed the view that taking life was a sign of primitivity. I took it for granted that, like my father, every ex-soldier having killed men would be reluctant to increase the score of dead by killing animals.

The prolonged absence of rain was making the ground as hard as ant hills, so that when the wet season did set in, heralded by strong winds, Papi sent men to scrape channels round our house. Not before time, because the day the rain reached us, it was a deluge, bucketing down, pouring through the excessively dry thatch and forming red rivulets outside, fortunately draining down the slight incline on which the house had been purposely built.

Our servants ran in from the kitchen with every utensil available, while Mutti and I removed the boxes containing the books to dry areas.

Fortunately the thatch became saturated, swollen stems closed ranks, leaving intermittent drips in an increasing gloom which necessitated the lighting of lamps.

Papi had not returned since the first clap of thunder rocked the clouds into spilling their moisture. Sefu running to the camp, by way of our house, told us that my father had sent all the labourers home to see to their ditches but - he gesticulated helplessness - knowing them, they had probably barred themselves inside their huts and gone to sleep.

The servants retreated to the kitchen. Idi was asked to bring us tea between downpours. Rain blew into the verandah and fell like a curtain of droplets across all our openings making the house cold and damp.

My mother worried about the non-appearance of Papi although it was more than likely that he might be sheltering in somebody's hut. When he returned briefly, it was like another gust of wind. He had come to fetch our spare blankets, bandages, lint and ointment. I heard him tell the cook to make sweet tea and keep the kettle on the boil, someone would be sent to fetch it. Then he was gone.

Mutti became agitated, "Your father, doesn't listen as usual! I told him to put on his pullover before catching cold, and of course he hasn't got a proper raincoat for this weather. Did you hear what is going on? You know my ears! What exactly did he say?"

I did not know either. Time wore on, the rain continued. At last news came with the men fetching the tea, that some huts had collapsed and injured the inmates. At that Mutti became quiet, busied herself moving the vessels to new drips, and asked me every now and then whether I could hear Papi coming.

He appeared after dark, driven home by exhaustion and hunger and telling us that, due to the unwillingness of some to dig ditches, there had been serious flooding resulting in the partial collapse of huts. People had to be dug out and treated for shock, although some dwellings had been saved with props taken from the debris of others.

Another problem was that of shelter because the homeless just sat miserably on their ruins, and those who still had a home had to be given assurances that when they opened the door they would not be overrun by a crowd. Reluctant men, he said, had to be flushed from their warm hearths to relieve others weary with rescue work, such as holding up collapsing roofs while centre poles were being pushed upright again.

He returned to the camp leaving me to imagine a scene of dead and injured lying in the dark, lit up occasionally by flashes of lightning, and disturbed by the thunder which bellowed all around us. Perhaps the dead were decapitated, their limbs severed. There would be the moaning, or screaming with pain... a dead baby floating away on a river of mud.

My father would not be drawn for information, not next day either when his manner remained curt, indicating that awful things had happened and no questions were to be asked.

Our own situation remained dismal, the floor damp, the carpets rolled up, boxes containing books and clothes pushed under a canvas sheet, and each morning the clouds still winning.

Our boys ran between kitchen and verandah with trays of covered dishes to keep the food hot, Mutti for once having to be grateful for every pot of tea, and any other favours we received at their hand.

Going to the loo was an ordeal. After what we had heard of collapsing structures, it was feasible that, with all the rain softening the ground, there was the danger that the walls, sticks and loo box might slide into the excrement-filled hole when we added our weight.

Increasingly unlike his jovial self, Papi confided that work on the construction was still impossible, not only because of the rain, but because several of the workers were dying.

"Dying! How awful, are the injuries that bad? Hans! You should let me see to them."

"No, no. It's not the injured, they are improving and anyway you can't go near them."

"Why? What, *um Gottes Willen,* is the matter?"

"I do not know. There are very sick people in the camp."

In the days that followed, I realised that something terrible was taking place when Mutti had to give away our cast-off clothing to keep patients warm, the cook continually brewed sweetened tea for them, and Idi was sent to buy all available chickens for making soup with rice. Whenever Papi came home, he reported that high fevers were raging through the camp with fatal results.

A fierce row broke out between my parents when my mother begged Papi not to go near this contagious-whatever infection but to call for medical help.

"Who exactly have you in mind?" he snapped at her.

"Isn't there some sort of hospital in Manyoni? Or a dispensary?"

"The people there promised help but nobody wants to come near the camp, now we are in quarantine."

Mutti was horrified, "And you are trying to be the doctor?"

"Who else, Lili?"

I heard them mention "epidemic". Papi explained to me that, in a way, it was like malaria because one person could infect another via an agent, except that this disease was affecting the labourers at a far faster rate and he did not know the carrier. Only Sefu, who had so far proved resistant to the infection and those who recovered quickly, were allowed to come to our house to fetch the pots of chicken-rice and tea. Keeping up the strength of the sick and the recuperating, Papi maintained, was his only weapon.

Whenever the noise of rain and wind decreased, high-pitched keening, eerie because we saw no sign of the mourners, rose from the direction of the camp.

Nothing deterred my mother from continuing with my education, until the day that I found myself in the lorry, wrapped in a blanket and propped up between my parents. My sudden lack of appetite, a slight cough and the onset of a temperature had only meant one thing to them.

That morning when I sat down to my school work feeling unwell, Idi had been sent to fetch my father. One look at me sufficed. He asked Mutti to pack immediately because he was going to take us to Manyoni.

On the way, the discussion centred round whether the hoteliers would take us should they have heard of the epidemic, and if not, was it not incumbent on my parents to tell them.

Parked on the damp road in front of the grey mosquito-proofed verandah, we waited anxiously for my father to return. Instead, it was the portly hotel lady who came down the two steps to greet us.

"Hello, hello! little one, papa says you are ill, and mamma? What does she think? Mm? *Komm, komm!*" She helped me off the lorry, up the steps, along the verandah to our old room, pulled back the cover on one of the beds and put me into it with my sandals on.

"Your Mutti will undress you, meanwhile I make you an orange juice, *ja?* A coffee for her, not so? And papa, perhaps whisky and soda? No? Well do not worry, both your beloved are in good hands." My father taking her at her word, made a quick turn-around back to the stricken camp. Much to everyone's relief except mine, I began to whoop next day.

A collection of *dukas,* one or the other attached to an Indian's compound, a hotel, a *boma* (administrative headquarters), the houses of a few administrators, and the African quarter, made up the town of Manyoni. It was served, medically, by a dispensary supervised by a Mr. Singh. My mother, at her wits' end, called him to have a look at my deteriorating condition. He came dressed in a grey suit and tie, carrying his insignia, the black bag.

"Is this your child, please?"

"Yes."

"Very good, very strong."

He closely scrutinised what was showing of me above the sheet, "She will not die. If you wish you may give hot bath one time in the morning. You give boiled rice one time a day. Then she recover soon. Very soon." I began a slight whoop. "Goodbye child." He looked at me sympathetically, less so at my mother. "You must not make fuss, Memsahib, with more children you get used to these quite normal conditions."

Even if considered 'normal' my illness was terrible. When I whooped, deprived of breath, asphyxiated by the spasm of my own throat muscles, I rushed to my mother, my hands clawing to grip her in a frantic effort to climb up her frame, gasping for the air I could not inhale. Her stricken face and gestures of helplessness did nothing to diminish my terror.

Weeks later and restored to health, I returned with Mutti to our house which stood basking in the sun as though it had never seen a drop of rain. My intervening illness had left me with a blurred memory of the epidemic. Papi never talked of it and I never found out how many had died, therefore nothing seemed more natural than the sight of our labourers back on the construction, moving earth like so many ants.

With the course books Aunt Gretl had sent *Maya the Bee* which became an addition to my fantasy world. It was but a step from her into the real one of insects that abounded around us. In damp weather swarms of termites, wings grown as if by magic, erupted from holes in the ground like jets of steam blowing almost into the beaks and mouths of waiting birds, frogs, lizards and small mammals.

The increase in termites resulted in many more cooling, sandy passages being built at the back of the book cases. Papi moved the shelving, destroyed their walk-ways but days later they were back, regrouped, rebuilding, and when we looked they were blatantly transporting tiny fragments of shelving or minute scraps of paper impossible to paste back.

That which was visible could be avoided, unseen dangers required a drill which I had learnt at Rusegwa: never put your hand into anything without first looking inside; never put your feet into shoes without first turning them upside down and thumping them on the floor; never go into a room or anywhere in the dark without a lantern; always look up when walking under a low branch; always look down as you walk anywhere to make sure there is no puff adder, black mamba or python on which you are about to step.

Danger ceased the moment I was in my bed and contained by the mosquito-net, tucked firmly under the mattress. A mouthful of net was neither cellulose, grass nor meat.

Being awakened by a bite was nothing frightening, mosquitoes sometimes found their way under the net. One night, however, a few bites woke me to a sight of black streaks silhouetted against the dim glow of the lantern. Dachsi who was supposed to guard me was not in his accustomed place on the mat.

"Mutti!"

I heard her get out of bed, there was a yell, "Au!" She seemed to be tripping. My father woke and asked what was the matter.

"I think it's *siafu* (driver ants), Hans."

"What? Impossible! The house is virtually new. Bring the lantern closer, Lili, where do you see *siafu*?"

"Here, look, on our bed. And here, Hans, up the wall. And here on the floor. *Au! Au!"*

"*Raus!* (Out!)" Papi shouted. "Get the child quickly." His urgent command warned of the danger.

My mother, face screwed up in pain and jumping from foot to foot, tore at my net, snatched me up and hopping over streams of marching ants, carried me out into the open. Dachsi was out already whimpering and running round in a circle, biting at ants buried in his tail. Papi had gone to waken the boys who, wrapped in their *shukas* (sheet/loincloth) and drunk with sleep, stepped right into the path of the oncoming ants, with resulting howls.

Finding an unoccupied spot under my window, we looked into my room, still lit by the night lantern, which now shone on heaps of ants engulfing beetles, cockroaches, centipedes, millipedes and scorpions, flushed from the boxes and the thatch. The tins of paraffin, under each foot of the fly-proof food-safe which stood in one corner, were filled with drowning ants over whose mass others were crawling to reach our provisions. My net was still being invaded in the hope of killing what they thought could not escape. I knew it was a death sometimes invited by relatives of an enfeebled or demented dependant, left tied up in bush country.

Papi told me of people who, fleeing their house, found themselves running out in the company of snakes that had been living in their roof! I did not know whether to laugh or cry, the invasion had been a shock and the night air struck cold through my flimsy pyjamas.

Before long, however, we were bedded in deck chairs brought from the store, a fire was crackling near by, its pungent smoke curling upward into the still night air.

Mohamadi, the cook, and Idi lay down near the fire, cocooned in their *shukas*, and we all found some sleep.

At daybreak the ants beat a retreat as if a trumpet had sounded, or more likely a signalled message had convinced the troops that the larder was finally empty. A few remains of creatures, hollow carapaces, feelers and wings, a lizard's tail, the skeleton of a mouse, were a horrible reminder of their fate.

During the following weeks the driver ants struck again. This time our servants tried heading off their columns with fire brands and hot ashes, rather a dangerous remedy considering the dry state of the thatch. Wherever a column was destroyed by heat, those ants still arriving on the spot regrouped and doggedly marched round the obstacle. There seemed to be millions upon millions, as many as there were thorns on the acacia scrub.

Curled up in a deck chair, I watched our servants by the light of the flames, leaping, yelling with pain or whooping with the exhilaration of mock battle.

"They are over here!"

"You should see them here!"

"Ah! Ah!"

"You jumped right in, heh - heh!"

My father watched that flames did not set fire to the house; Mutti, who lay exhausted in her deck chair, opened her eyes every now and then and called, "Hans! finished now?"

The sun's rays on my lids jolted me from the darkness of sleep into the light of day, I heard my parents calling me to see the ants withdraw. A retreat as orderly as their advance, they joined a column which made a long line leading out of the house into the straggly grass of the savannah, their scouts running ahead looking for the next prey. Some ran around disorientated, unable to comprehend that the foray was over, Idi's besom swept them off the premises.

Shiny rails were creeping up as far as my father's section, enabling train-loads of ballast to be distributed where the rail bed was completed. Next came wagons of metal sleepers and rails. The former were bedded into the ballast, each protruding end looking like a paw, claws dug into the ground for anchor.

Rails were off-loaded to the accompaniment of chanting; the head linesman called out a word, the gang workers answered, at first only to warm up for the task ahead, then for the real lift.

Once in action the men worked in sustained rhythm until the wagon was empty. The laying of the rails proceeded in similar manner.

On our walks we often watched the work. There were hammer blows, metal on metal, as the rail and sleeper were bolted for life. Papi explained that to accommodate heat expansion there were large gaps left between rails, causing the beat audible from inside a moving coach, "Da-da-da-daaa, da-da-da-daa..."

My greatest wish was to stand among the men, heaving and chanting with them. I wore the same type of shorts and shirt, I was as sturdy, could lift heavy boxes though only six, rising seven. My parents, I knew, would not allow it even if I had been older because it was not the done thing. It never occurred to me that being a girl was an even greater drawback than being white.

Before Papi's Manyoni section was completed, the ants called again. They were burnt out in a terrible massacre of red hot ashes. If only they had waited! Days later during a game of patience, Papi said, "I shall be going away to see about the next section at Singida."

"Oh? What is Singida like, Hans, a bigger place? Any Europeans?"

"Humph! There is a District Officer, an Assistant District Officer and of course there are some *dukas*. I'm afraid that without the appendage of our sisal plantation you will find nobody interested in whether or not you can make strudel, Lili."

He was leaving for some weeks to prepare a camp, leaving Mutti and me behind. The camp ceased to exist, the chuff and clank of work trains going up the line replaced hammering and singing, though otherwise the *pori* remained as before, a vast area of savannah in which we wandered every afternoon as lonely as if we had been two Bedouins in my story book desert.

NO WATER

When Papi came to pick us up we left the house to its fate.

Travelling through bush country over steaming elephant pats, only our servants sitting high on the load could see ears flapping above thickets. Gradually it thinned and became steppe in which knobs of rocks relieved what would otherwise have been an undulating yellow plain.

At Singida we picked up provisions, and some time later reached the new camp where to Mutti's surprise our house proved to be a larger edition with an integral bathroom. She took possession of it in the usual manner by ordering tea.

Papi explained that we had no water except for the amount brought from Singida, had we not noticed the boys filling our *debes*?

He had purposely sited the camp and house on a rise, below which a hillock of rocks and bushes looked noticeably greener. During that week, the digging labourers proved him right when water seeped into a well until they were knee-deep in mud. One side was stepped diagonally with the help of stones, and then the daily mayhem began caused by those coming up the muddy steps being nudged into spilling water by others over-anxious to descend, until Papi's guards organised orderly conduct.

The weight of water carried by the smallest girls pushed their tummy out, hollowing the back. The neck became elongated like a crane's, and the head wove back and forth in a struggle to keep the vessel balanced.

At dawn our water carrier had priority of draw after the churned mud of the previous day had settled, leaving the overnight seepage of fresh water. It was boiled and kept in bottles, and cooled in a tubby earthenware vessel shaped like a hollowed tomato with its top rolled down for a rim.

Vegetables, served as fresh salad because there were no lettuces, were washed in the bottled water with the addition of mild permanganate. Despite these precautions I started having diarrhoea, doubling up with tummy pains and then with bowel cramp as I ran back and forth to the 'thunder box', afraid I would not get there in time and nothing to expel when I reached it. The rusty enamel potty, long unused, was brought back and showed up the blood in the slime from my intestines, an indication of the dreaded dysentery.

Once again rice became my diet, over-cooked this time in order to 'bind', though it left my bowels so fast that it had no time to do its work. Dehydration set in, there was little to pass, and the spasms of contractions became so painful that I wanted to cry but could not even find the energy to screw up my face.

Papi carrying the proof of my illness in a small bottle set off for the Singida Hospital, taking me there was out of the question considering his monthly income only just bought food for the camp, our servants and ourselves.

He returned with high hopes; an entirely new drug had just arrived called *Yatren*, pills of gun-metal grey and almost as heavy as lead but they wrought a miraculous turn-about in my condition, after which the potty was finally thrown away.

With my return to normal life Idi decided to leave us, causing another atmosphere of doom. It prevailed whenever one of our servants felt that a return to his tribal lands and family outweighed financial considerations.

Before leaving for Singida on the *posho* (rations) lorry, he demanded the usual letter of recommendation.

"What shall I write about him, Lili?"

"He is stupid but outstandingly honest."

"You can't put things like that in a certificate."

"Say that he is a delightful worker until four in the afternoon.'

"*Aber* Lili! don't be so silly." Muttering about European women thinking a servant was an instrument of perpetual motion, he wrote his own verdict. It would get Idi a job wherever he applied, probably with an official who might pay better wages.

His successor was Karol, a Mgoni, from southern Tanganyika where during German occupation, Papi told me, the famous '*Maji-Maji* (Water-Water)' uprising had taken place. It had been a rebellion against all foreigners, fiercely waged in the belief that witch doctor concoctions would turn the enemy's bullets into harmless liquid. Against such an historical background Karol enjoyed an unearned respect.

My recovery allowed a resumption of our afternoon walks through a belt of bush to a vast countryside of steppe. On its gentle yellow crests stood the cattle looking like narrow boxes on legs, the

Wanyaturu's most valuable possessions. The tribe had slanting eyes, which my mother attributed to squinting for hours into the distance of glaring sunlight.

"Tell that to the Japanese!" was Papi's reply to the theory. "You might fare better remembering that cattle herding tribes have a different origin from that of the agricultural Bantu."

The herders, dressed in a piece of brown hide thrown over one shoulder, stood, one leg drawn up, foot on thigh, leaning for balance on a staff thwacked occasionally on the rump of a cow or poked at a goat. The 'statues' doggedly refused to understand Swahili and our calls of, *"Jambo!"*.

Their animals grazed near depressions of water reflecting the surrounding reeds, where the stench of cow dung fermenting in the mud, a sweetish odour, hung in the air. They remained raggedy bony even when rain put a verdant cover on the swampy ground, suddenly blooming with white and mauve flowers - like Mutti's Rusegwa petunias. A rare red pompom of florets on a long stem excited her when it was the only bright colour in a landscape of vast skies, yellow land and blazing blind sunlight.

Some months later, Papi announced the imminent arrival of an Italian engineer who would be drawing plans for bridges. A site for his house had been chosen some distance from ours, would I like to help him peg the ground plan?

To my joy I was allowed to carry a ball of sisal twine and the measuring stick, Papi supported no more than a pencil and piece of paper; Bwana of us all, he never carried a heavier load than a book. Behind us walked a labourer, mallet in hand and a bundle of pegs hanging from the shoulder.

After the line for the back wall had been pegged, Papi had us measuring three units of the stick along it at one corner, and four at right angles. We then placed the stick diagonally at exactly five units, adjusting the pegs until the 3x4x5 units triangle gave us a true right angle. Having learned the drill we measured the other corners, strung the twine to show inner walls, door openings, and the position of windows.

"Have you taken notice of all this, Jumatatu? I am teaching my child how to plan a house. We Europeans expect our women to know as much as men!"

I knew Papi was having a dig at me because he did not usually equate the two. Influenced by his male chauvinism I believed women were shrewish and irrational. Apart from such slight differences as genital organs, I thought myself to be almost a male, at any rate the equal of a white boy - though I had never met the real thing.

Unfortunately Mutti fell into the above mentioned female category when, on hearing that the Italian was bringing somebody who needed a lean-to for cooking, she remarked, "He must have a lady of uncertain status, a wife would have asked for a kitchen for her cook, I wonder what sort of 'little piece' she will turn out to be!"

Annoyed at her innuendoes and my giggles, my father said sharply, "Saying something like that is beneath your dignity, Lili."

The exchange made me look forward to her arrival; meanwhile the house still had to be built.

The scrub yielded only medium-sized sticks used by the local inhabitants for building their flat-roofed dwellings, therefore longer tree trunks had to be delivered to us by lorry.

The camp builders trimmed these with machetes, lopping off all the stumps except for two to form a fork at one end. They were dug into the ground, short ones to support horizontal poles at the top of walls, long ones to carry the ridge poles.

To make the walls, the scrub wood was dug into furrows, back-filled.

A few days later the skeleton of the house was fusing together, willing itself into life.

Shorn of thorn and leaf, thinner branches used horizontally to secure the framework were tied with strips of bark soaked in water for pliability. No nail was ever used because it would have fallen out the moment the green wood dried.

Viewed from our verandah the structure resembled a giant oblong basket with a square handle, with but one drawback, the holes in its sides. In this case, the future windows.

It was difficult to concentrate on my school work when the growth of the building was observable from our verandah. What fun it would be balancing on the poles across the walls, strips of bark held between my teeth, hands free to tie down poles spanning to the ridge, I could see myself doing it... bit of a wobble... whoops... but I would manage.

"Please, Mutti, can I go over for a short time to see how the house is getting on?" She consented provided I remained within sight.

The poles having been tied down as I had imagined, men were working on securing branches across them horizontally to form a lattice work for the pitched roof. Others brought trusses of reeds, one bobbing at each end of a pliable yoke.

I listened to the men's chaffing.

"Ngalinda, bring me a stick about twice my size."

"Eheee! a dwarf like you should be building hen cages!"

A young man, boasting of his strength, was told that his loads fitted him like a *toto* on a woman's back. Any reference to resemblance with women was an insult meant as a joke. Our labourers seemed to joke about females as much as Papi did.

Another day, the thatchers sat like frogs on the lattice roof, spreading the reeds, tier by tier, tying them down with lengths of bark until they reached the ridge where reed ends were intertwined and secured.

Finally the plasterers mixed loam with water underfoot and with a flick of the wrist, threw handfuls at the walls. Some pats adhered, some fell to the ground, and all with a sucking "worpf" sound - "worpf - worpf!" Once the mud stuck to the sticks and poles, the key was there for the remaining layers of clay. It was finished with a slip to give the walls their look of brown, unpolished leather, inside and out.

There was one sentence I longed to hear from the men, "The child wants to come up." But they obviously had no inkling of my longing to sit on the roof ridge. Neither could I ask for a favour which would have been denied their own children. There was no difference between my parents and these black adults when it came to spoiling fun.

This time our camp was happy, many of the workers having brought their families from the tribal areas. My mother admired the beautiful eyes of the infants, "A lively but innocent pool of umber surrounded by porcelain white, how I wish I had my oil paints."

Camp discipline, the duty of Sefu and his assistant overseers, included keeping it clean.

"Binti Mustafa, are you pregnant?"

"How dare you ask me when you see I'm carrying an infant on my back."

"Ehe! In that case you can sweep round your hut, and what about

inside? Is it wind that has left all those leaves at the door opening?"

"Mama yangu!" she wailed, "listen to his insults, my sisters."

They also acted as camp police to keep the peace, complaints being plentiful among householders: *"Eh! Eh!* look at that smoke always blowing into my hut." Addressing the neighbour: "Do you fetch firewood from the middle of a river?"

"Leave me alone, you're nothing but your mother's miscarriage!"

"And you resemble an empty water vessel," a reference possibly to the woman being childless.

"Who says you could attract a blind man?"

Such exchanges could lead to screeching protestations and enmity not conducive to camp community life. It was the pride of both Papi and Sefu that no litigation reached the court at Singida from our camp.

Saturday drunkenness being the scourge of family life despite the ruling that no native beer was allowed on the premises, there were dramatic scenes when an otherwise good man suddenly became the cruel husband. Accusations of infidelity were followed by wife beating in the drunken belief that the action proved virility. Only quick intervention by the overseers prevented lasting damage, their method being to talk the couple into an honourable truce.

When Musa viciously attacked a fellow worker, my father called the overseers and key witnesses to form a self-styled court, explained why the man should be punished, and all having agreed to its appropriateness, meted out a couple of clouts according to the heinousness of the crime.

It was not the last time that I heard him practise this method.

Bronchial infections, and malaria in particular were the curse of the labour force. When Kasenge's wife decided to call a soothsayer to find out why her husband was acting strangely, he turned out to be delirious as a result of a high temperature which Papi persuaded her could be treated with quinine.

Mutti helped by holding a surgery once a week, "I learnt first aid during the war," she told me, "and I might as well make use of my knowledge."

Four aluminium Tropical medicine chests the size of over-grown tea caddies, were the all important holders of her 'magical' potions. In addition there were the ointments procured gratis for the camp by Papi from the Singida Hospital dispenser.

The labourers whose cuts and bruises she soothed, spread the news of my mother's efficiency, causing an ever greater number of people from neighbouring homesteads to come to her with appalling conditions, such as cuts down to the bone made by pickaxe or hoe, multiple sores made by jigger infestation, huge boils, and eye infections.

Reeking bandages proved that they had attended hospital but preferred to suffer at home rather than walk the distance to Singida, knowing there would be a long wait before they were seen.

Mutti's treatments were simple: iodoform powder or ointment for wounds, its pungent smell, she remarked, unmistakably 'hospital'; iodine for superficial skin lacerations, abrasions and punctures, hurts that I dare not tell her about, fearful that the bottle might be brought out for a stinging dab. The Africans thought the contrary, the more the pain, the greater the efficacy of the lotion. She used acetic acid for drawing pus; heated poultices for boils, and dissolved boracic for bathing eyes.

On these days I was told, "Get on with the lessons. Remember not to come anywhere near the patients in case of infection." But before long she would shout, "Putzi! could you just hand me the tweezers," or whatever item she had forgotten.

Papi had once been a medical student who had fainted at his first operation, not from the sight of a bloody mess but because he had an exaggerated sense of smell. When the stream of patients became a flood, he was only too happy to call a halt, declaring that my mother's patients could take a lift to hospital in the *posho* lorry.

The hillock by the water hole was mysterious. It shimmered with vapour in the midday heat. When I asked Mutti whether I could climb on its rocks, her "*Aber* Putzimännchen! Of course not," confirmed my belief that there was something unholy living there. Therefore when its rocks were going to be blasted, I asked permission to watch the preparations hoping to see an apparition flee its home.

To make the required holes in the rocks, one man squatted on his haunches holding a cold chisel. His partner, selecting a sledgehammer of required weight, swung it over one shoulder with both hands and brought it to bear upon the much-splayed end, a clear ring proving a centred impact. The squatter then twisted the tool by a quarter turn and blow by blow, turn after turn, it was driven into the rock. Water might be poured down the hole though usually the man just spat.

It was melodious work, because the hammer blows emphasised the rhythm of the accompanying song:

"*Ya-nderule!*" Bang! Twist. Spit.
"*Ya-nderule!*" Bang! Twist.

Followed by: "*Wabwana wakubwa wa nderule ya,*
Wabwana wadogo wa nderule ya,
Wabwana wakubwa wa nderule ya,"

And a mighty blow,

"*Ya-a-a-a nderule!*" Whomp! Twist.

I waited with fascination for the hammer to miss and land instead on the squatter's skull, splinters of bone erupting from the cleft, the convoluted brain scattering in soft, white lumps on the smooth granite.

It never happened.

When the site was ready for blasting, Papi allowed me to hold the reel of fuse wire while he cut off required lengths, each to be forced into a detonating capsule which in turn was fitted into a stick of gelignite.

Under his slouch hat he sweated profusely with the toil of pushing fraying fuses into the tight necks of their silvery holders. Their length was all important: "This longer, this one shorter, that so much shorter. You see, they have to be graded according to my plan of running round among the boulders to set light to each fuse."

Mutti was always concerned about the number of fuses he proposed to light with no more reliable means than a box of matches before dashing for cover.

She and I were sent in the direction of Kinyangiri where, at a point in the road, we unfurled a red flag to stop lorries from proceeding further. An overseer did the same on the Singida side.

Tense with apprehension my mother peered through the heat haze. The vapour above the hillock was gyrating into its usual weird shapes. Suddenly, the hillock - bushes, rocks, earth - lifted into the air, then came the thuds of explosions. Showers of broken rock rained in the distance, a pall of dust gathered over the site, and it was only after some moments that we saw Papi making his way to the house.

He told us he had stumbled in trying to rush the last fuses.

Ignoring him Mutti said angrily, "Your father is no longer the slim youthful man I first knew, and he should accept the fact."

When the Italian brought his 'piece' accompanied by her brother, Mutti regretted the previous remark made about her because Dadaletch turned out to be a charming young Eritrean girl with high cheek-bones, emphasised by a kerchief tied over frizzy hair. A tall figure lent her nobility.

I spent hours in her company, ostensibly to help with housework which was my own taboo at home, the highlight of our acquaintance being the making of noodles.

Standing in her hot lean-to, my chest pressed against the plank which improvised as table, I put a handful of flour on a board, made a hollow and added two eggs. Curling my fingers into the cool mess I began to knead, the white of egg always running to another part of the board with a will of its own until, finally caught up in the flour and yolk, it lay still. The dough was stretched with a rolling bottle, and left to dry while Dadaletch gave me a drink of sherbet, ruby red, more a feast for the eye than the tongue.

Once sufficiently firm, she folded the dough and began slicing it, sending the pieces into a pot of salted water bubbling on her Primus. Suddenly, alive with the boiling, the pieces uncurled and bobbed around the pot in a mad dance, though not for long, because she kept fishing them out to dry off on a serviette.

Fried breadcrumbs strewn on noodles became my favourite dish though steamed chocolate pudding, not forgetting vanilla custard sauce, never lost their supremacy.

As my perception grew, my mother's repeated descriptions of fashionable shops in Mannheim, opera and theatre, picnics in beauty spots of the Rhineland, made me realise how much she missed these and her own set of friends. Most of all she mourned the loss of her sisters' company: Erna married and settled in Vienna, Gretl practising physiotherapy in Germany. Deprived of all these stimuli, her mood deteriorated steadily, often bordering on depression.

To make matters worse, she was no longer the black and white willy-wagtail (dark hair above a white dress) that I remembered from Morogoro. Deeply unhappy, worried about our lack of money, our mode of life, her 'psychological state' (as my father called it) robbed her of appetite, and the little she ate usually joined what lay beneath the thunder box.

Mutti's youth gone, she became emaciated and sallow-skinned, where Papi and I were sun-tanned. Her hair was badly cut by her own hand as she stood in front of the square of shaving mirror attempting to give herself a bob. Dressed in badly fitting clothes crowned by the slouch hat, she looked ill and dowdy. I did not see other white women for comparison but I knew something was wrong about Mutti, she was so unlike pictures of smiling girls advertising *Chlorodont* toothpaste in the German magazine we received occasionally.

My parents portrayed Europe as a Utopian world in which everybody was polite, diligent and cultured. Apparently evenings in both Vienna and Mannheim rang with arias such as Carmen's, "La la-lala-la, da dida dida..." People spent time in museums admiring Chinese and Meissen porcelain, art galleries bloomed with a mass of colour from Gauguins to Kokoschkas uplifting the beholder's soul.

Their conversation made me sense the hurt pride felt by Mutti as a result of our fall from the heights of being well-to-do planters to the depths of scratching a hand-to-mouth living from the railroad. Lost to us were our English speaking friends, the Administrators, the peak of white hierarchy; lost too for me was any association with white children. Papi's attitude could be summed up in his, "Lili, you still have a sunset to admire at the end of the day."

During one of these, on our way home, we saw smoke rising into the sky.

"A bush fire, Putzimännchen, let us walk faster." A change in the direction of the wind could envelop us in choking smoke, as we knew from experience.

Topping a rise, we came in view of our encampment at the end of which, to our horror, the engineer's house was aflame. Smoke billowed from it in puffs as if from the funnel of a locomotive. We could see a crowd of workers standing back which seemed strange because the usual method of fire-fighting was to tear the thatch from the roof.

I began to run towards the scene not to miss the excitement. Mutti shouting, "Wait, wait, be careful!" followed as best she could in the high-heeled shoes she always wore.

We were stopped by a messenger from Papi with orders not to proceed because the petrol cases stored near the house by the Engineer had caught fire and might explode.

My mother glanced anxiously in the direction of our house, too near to the other to be safe. Remembering something else she asked,

"Where is the *bibi* of the Bwana Salva?"

"Ehe! Bibi ya Bwana Salva?" he was hedging. "Our Bwana gave orders that nobody should go near the house." He turned to watch the sight of the dark smoke escaping in those peculiar puffs, "Your cook, Ramadhani, disobeyed him, ran through the flames and brought her out but she ran back, refusing to be rescued."

"What happened next?" Mutti's tears were ready to flow.

"He went into the house again and pulled her out. People had to hold her."

We stood undecided what to do, wishing to disobey orders like Ramadhani so that we could rush to help Dadaletch in her distress. On the other hand we knew my father never exaggerated danger.

A more ominous black cloud of smoke shot into the sky causing us to duck in anticipation of an explosion but instead it dissipated in the sunset.

As we waited a messenger brought permission for us to return home where we learnt that the intense heat of the burning stack of cases, containing two tins of petrol each, had melted the seal of the outlet caps, thereby releasing the fuel for free burning.

Dadaletch was missing. Nobody had seen her after the first few minutes of the rescue drama. Search parties of labourers found her hiding in a thicket like a gazelle and, as they said, equally difficult to catch. She was led back, badly shocked, collapsed into a chair on our verandah, and would not be consoled.

The Engineer, arriving back from work, maintained a hostile silence, breaking it only to ask for the house to be re-built before driving off with Dadaletch and her brother in the direction of Singida.

Mutti was furious, "Why should the man be so angry, Hans? What have we to do with it all?"

"Perhaps he had some of his bridge plans burnt."

"And where was her brother when she was attempting suicide? Nobody seems to have seen him at the time."

"I don't know, Lili, he was probably relieving himself, and thought it safer to stay where he was - some distance from the house."

"*Ach*, Hans you are impossible. Don't you see that there is something funny about the whole business?"

Given priority, a replica of the house soon stood in its place, but when the occupants returned, we were rejected. Their hostility was inexplicable, and in addition, the Engineer did not thank Ramadhani for saving Dadaletch's life. In the end Papi decided to give him a small sum of money, a token of the community's recognition of his bravery.

One morning we looked across to find our neighbours gone. Sadly the highlights of my week had vanished when Dadaletch turned her back on us and the vacuum had to be filled with the old routine. A cup of tea brought to the bedside by Karol was followed by a face wash with the silty water. An *amerikani* (calico) dress and pair of pants, or shirt worn with khaki shorts, and sandals, completed my outfit.

Breakfast was Mutti's test of how well her 'European-type' household was functioning. The white cloth must be spotless, the place settings had to line up in neat squares of cutlery, the main plate plumb in the centre, the side plate outside the perimeter, the napkin lined up with the fork. It never failed to draw Papi's jovial remarks, "How is the queen this morning? Have the troops polished their shoes?"

The more she fussed over a minor fault, the greater his teasing, "The royal toasted bread! What? None yet! It must be the fault of one of your subjects, or could it be the vagary of the stove in our primitive royal kitchen?"

We often laughed our way through a meal.

I liked our first course, pawpaw, a gondola with a yellow gondolier, namely the slice of lemon. Or we shared a mango, my parents each spooning the flesh from one of the two cheeks and I sucking the fibres of the stone in the centre slice, until it looked like a yellow head with tousled hair.

Cool Singida mornings made us enjoy cooked eggs and the heavy home-made bread. We drank tea with watery milk brought in our own bottles by the herdsman, watery by design because their cows were dry in the udder. Boiled for safety, it had a wafer-thin skin of cream which my mother tried to skim for shaking into butter, unsuccessfully.

Making curd cheese, by letting sour milk tied in a serviette drip its whey off during the night, resulted in a soft paste which we smeared on bread. Left to mature under a damp cloth in the hope of producing some sort of camembert, the result was a playground for maggots.

At nine o'clock I began work on the correspondence course, possibly designed for a patient in a children's hospital in Germany but not for a girl living in the East African savannah. Papi contributed to my education when anything was discussed, by maintaining that all ideas were acceptable so long as they were based on the logical steps of cause and effect. When describing his home life in Vienna he wrote, "We venerated logic and were averse to the concession that it could be blurred by emotion." That was precisely what was drummed into me.

In the evening I read or we played cards. If Papi became bored with his sparse hoard of German classics, he announced, "I am going to the camp."

"You have seen your labourers all day, how can you bear to be with these bush-folk again?"

"What a stupid remark. You know how keen you were to book your concert or theatre seat again and again in Mannheim."

"And you call your camp a concert hall?" Mutti mocked, becoming indignant when he replied, "Yes," with absolute sincerity.

These frequent harangues were painful, but being my father's greatest admirer, I sided with him: of course Papi was always right.

The construction being almost completed, my mother agonised about the next contract. Would Papi be able to secure another or were we going to be destitute?

Engrossed in finishing off the section, or attending to the lesser problems of his men and their families, or studying their customs, songs and dance for his recreation, he was unperturbed.

"Nobody has got the number of labourers I can offer. Don't worry, Lili, as long as they are needed, I shall be welcomed."

He was right. Within months we were moving again, nearer to Singida where there was a difficult section requiring a large labour force.

Aladdin had rubbed his lamp. On the day we moved, the lorry took us along the main road, turned off on a sandy track and there, before us, was our house except that it smelled new.

The cook built himself a stove from the *debes* brought with us; Mohamadi erected the beds; Karol unfurled mats, put up the ironing table for our meals and brought us tea; Papi went to see how the hut-builders were getting on; and Dachsi rolled in the light brown sand outside the house, in recognition that this was his new patch.

KEEPING THE HYENA FROM THE DOOR

The smell of smoke from hearth fires christening new roofs, and that of drying mud, pervaded the camp air. In our house there was a whiff as clean as that from my shirt after it had been under the *dhobi's* charcoal iron.

Our curtains fitted the new windows, the mats the new floors. The ornamental beaded belts and skirts of the Wanyaturu collected by Mutti were hung anew on the verandah walls, and the drums used for occasional tables fell over with Papi's tea as before, whenever his clumsiness sent them rolling.

Mutti was staking a 'garden' to be demarcated with euphorbia cuttings, obtainable from the wild or any Nyaturu cattle enclosure. Stems stuck in the ground looked as though they were waiting for leaves, not to be however, because they were succulents whose finger-like offshoots would take time to grow bushy. If one snapped, the white sap was said, by Mutti, to be as dangerous to the eyes as the spit of a mamba.

Sitting behind the verandah parapet at my lessons, I could just see over its top the camp spread below, and beyond it the railway embankment with a gap like that of a child's toothy grin. Papi explained that it was one of several sites needing a filling, namely, concrete piers and a bridge.

To draw their plans, a young Italian moved into a house built for him on our camp site. Being the youngest white person I had seen for a couple of years, I felt drawn to him and whenever my mother allowed me a visit, his servant prepared a glass of fresh orange juice and opened the tin of *Peak Freans* from which I could pick the choicest biscuits without reprimand.

My mouth full, I asked him in Swahili about the life led by his fellow countrymen in Lombardy, never tiring to hear about the teachers who meted out discipline in schools. If girls or boys disobeyed, "Ouch! Ouch!" my friend enacted the consequences. Burdened with difficult lessons, children had to study for hours, head down and, if after such toil they looked up through a window, they were rewarded by beautiful views of marble buildings with golden domes, towering into an azure sky which vaulted over dark green olive groves outside the city.

Our conversation was made difficult in respect of colour: there was only *eusi* for black, *eupe* for white, *ekundu* for red or pink. After that, *manjano,* the name for turmeric described yellow; *samawi*, the sky, was supposed to be blue; *manjani* or leaves, was green; *zambarau,* a fruit, denoted purple.

Our firm friendship came to an end when I discovered strings of beads behind one of his cushions. Thinking he had bought them for me to play with, I handed them back so that he in turn could present me with the gift. When he said they belonged to somebody else and looked guilty, I knew he must be having black women and told Mutti who stopped my visits.

Whenever it surfaced, the topic of 'black concubines' was discussed with innuendoes by my parents. Mutti, lowering her voice presumably for my benefit, nevertheless sounded off, "Disgusting, Hans! Unimaginable! Europeans paying off their black mistress before going on leave to Britain or Europe with every intention of making a suitable match! Ugh! And having found an unsuspecting white girl, preferably one with a little money or good family connections, marrying her. But not only that! They bring her back as a specimen, a sort of 'see what I have caught'."

"With regard to your verbal storm, Lili, Tanganyika is subject to the law of need and availability no less."

"How can you make a joke of such a matter?"

"But I am not joking."

"Despicable, and what about the black woman in this love triangle?"

My father thought Mutti's outburst nothing but a show of sentimental nonsense. His opinion can be gauged from his experience prior to 1914: "...very few men married and it was considered the normal situation to acquire, following native procedures of marriage, a native girl who after a short time, began to supervise the household. One paid bridewealth to her father and when she behaved badly, the father was cited and menaced with the demand for repayment, unless he taught his daughter better manners.

"It was the usual experience, especially up-country, to find a native woman in the house of a friend, playing the part of his wife in offering drinks; one conversed about weather and crops and when there was a bastard child, one had to admire it. Cases were known in which friends became enemies because of jealousy.

"A great number of men left their valuables in the care of native women when they were called up at the outbreak of war (1914), and I have not heard of a case where those who came back to the Colony after the war had to write off the entrusted property as a loss.

"Many of the women came to their 'Mabwana', sometimes years after the latter's arrival, when news of the return had reached them with delay. I know of pathetic cases in which the meeting between the man and his former love caused a major shock when he, perhaps now married and living with his European wife, did not recognise his former consort and had even forgotten her name. But there was never a scene because the woman delivered the gold watches and rings and returned satisfied to her home, the richer by a few shillings and a small collection of *kangas*. The bastard children, whose number was estimated at 500 in 1914, were always given to Missions after the first few years of age, the father paying a round sum for food, lodging and tuition until they learned a useful trade. Girls were married off to other half-castes."

Papi said there were still a great number of them in the Territory, about three hundred at one Mission alone.

Mutti, I could see, hardly believed her ears, "Do you mean there are that many half-caste children even these days?"

Papi withdrew his pipe, "Yes!"

My mother, round-eyed, hardly able to contain herself over the scandal, lowered her voice again and whispered, "British administrators, too?"

"Yes, and why not? You don't think everyone in the British administration is a eunuch, do you?"

My parents laughed and for the time being I had to content myself with guessing what the word meant.

My problem of having to stop visiting Luigi resolved itself with his speedy departure due to meagre construction profits.

Papi earned only two hundred shillings per month, an unending source of stress between my parents. Mutti planned the dismissal of a servant for the sake of buying clothes, my father would not hear of her proposal to do housework in the tropics.

We heard of impoverished whites whose food was being supplemented with maize or sorghum meal contributed by their black neighbours against promises of future payment, which neither party believed would be forthcoming. The same was said of white prospectors always on safari, searching for gold. Mutti described them as gentlemen looking for minerals with a pouch of tobacco and half a bottle of whisky. Their credit arrangement with a *duka*, made in the glow of an imaginary gold seam, led them to dream about it cracking open beneath their boots.

One day, my father returned from work and ordered that Ramadhani should prepare extra large meals. Mutti remonstrated that he was going over her head in household matters, Papi remained tight-lipped. For a while, an African appeared at the kitchen door at midday, carrying a set of tiered aluminium pots into which was dished a portion of our food. Mutti guessed that the recipient might be one of those prospectors. "I wonder if he will remember us when he finds his gold," she added wistfully.

Looking over the verandah wall, I could see in the distance the gradual erection of the bridge piers. One morning, however, they were gone, wiped from view. Mutti was equally perplexed at their vanishing trick and the boys stared wide-eyed and exclaimed, *"Kumbe!"*

Even before my father's return, Mohamadi brought the news that a flash flood had destroyed the almost completed bridge. It had rained "somewhere", causing a torrent to sweep downstream and, as Papi said at lunchtime, the removal of concrete structures by a minor rain storm not only proved their design inadequate but faced everybody with a race against time because the monsoon rains were imminent.

He divided the labour force into shifts, working from sunrise until midnight. Having to watch for another flash flood, he said, added to the existing problem of vigilance, one of making sure that Kilumbe or Zukuyo, Mapala or Kilangabana, Swale and Sengo and many more, did not jump into seeping water or creeping sand in order to start enlarging the second edition of foundations before wooden shuttering had been hammered down to stop a cave-in.

The race for time was taken up by the camp as a matter of challenge. I imagined an outpost waving a flag to the sound of a shrill whistle when he sighted the wall of water bearing down upon the unsuspecting men. Mutti too, caught up in the mood of urgency, wished to make her contribution, "Shall we take Papi his food every evening, Putzimännchen?"

Having never been out for a walk after dark, it promised to be an adventure. Karol carrying a lantern and the supper tray led the way, we, for once, happy to walk behind him.

No light showed in the camp as we passed, alive though it was with murmuring voices and muffled laughter ringing from inside the huts nearest to us. Acrid smoke from the preparation of the evening meal hung heavily on the night air and bats, shooting between the low trees, were attracted by the insects following our lamp.

Through tall grasses already sprung up round the damp river bed, we saw the pressure lamp hanging on a pole, its white light supplemented by lanterns dotted about the site like fireflies. Figures bent, straightened, shovelled sand out of the way, poured concrete, walking and working in company with their shadow. Their talk, hushed by the quietness of the night, undisturbed by crickets or frogs.

My father ate and drank with relish, showed us the progress in the foundations and, as usual, promised to be back "soon".

On our return, the night was filled again with normal noises, a continuum of squawks, hums and high-pitched sawings, interrupted by the occasional weird laugh of a hyena.

Damp weather brought an increase of insects, especially mosquitoes. Moths wheeled silently and unceasingly round the pressure lamp on the verandah, agonising to see because, in their contact with it, they would be singed, flapping their wings in a slowing rhythm until death made them lie still.

One type of weighty beetle with feathery feelers whined in on two frail wings popping out from heavy wing cases. Mutti and I could not bear the continual drone and "smack" as it hit the light, "thump" as it fell on its back on the ground buzzing angrily, rowing its six feet in the air to find the floor. When she caught it, to take outside behind the house, we were lucky if it lost itself in the grass, but if not, we were due more of the same performance.

Papi's boots protected his ankles. Unable to afford mosquito boots for ladies, we were bitten nightly and resorted to wrapping a sheet round our legs. It was too warm to cover the whole of our arms, which therefore had to suffer slaps when we saw a bottoms-up Anopheles likely to inject us with malarial parasites. If down, it was Culex and a mere nuisance.

Although we were taking quinine pills prophylactically, they did not stop us from getting malaria. My attacks started with shivers, despite the beads of sweat dropping off my curls. My bones felt as though, if a hand had been drawn across them, it would have been left blooded by their roughness. Mutti told me I looked grumpier than usual and asked where was my concentration? When I refused the offer of chocolate pudding, she pronounced her diagnosis, "Hans, our Putzimännchen is getting her annual fever."

"So! To bed then."

And there I stayed, through cycles of soaring temperatures at night, plummeting to opposite lows in the morning, until one or other of the quinine drugs caused a levelling out, followed by three days of convalescence. Disobeying these rules, my parents said, was signing a death warrant. There was no cure for Black Water Fever, the inevitable result of what they called 'neglected malaria'. There were those who, ignoring elementary rules, refused to go to bed and thought they could drown the mosquito parasite with whisky. The next thing was dark red urine, the 'black' in their 'water' and then they died as surely as the moths on our lamps.

My malaria came once a year for certain. Twice, said my parents, was acceptable, but regularly recurring bouts could be proof of a pernicious variety, or a sign that the parasites had retreated to inaccessible parts to weaken the body and place it at death's door.

When I fell victim to the latter condition, Papi once more went to buy medicine from the hospital. But, as the weeks passed and the malaria struck frequently though without a perceivable pattern, the quinine drugs appeared to be as ineffectual as his promises to reduce weight by eating less.

Papi said that he knew of a Mission doctor who saved Africans abandoned as incurable by the Government Hospital. He would leave a letter with a *duka* from which the Mission bought its provisions, in that way it might get there.

Missions, I thought, were the homes of those religious white people mistakenly trying to stop blacks from behaving according to their tribal customs. Papi had made jokes to that effect.

Mutti said that blacks from Missions behaved like slaves, servile, repeating their greetings like a dirge and bowing and curtseying like puppets. She preferred not to have a Christian house-boy, especially if he was going to refuse wearing the Mohammedan-style white cap or fez. She was obviously prepared to forget her prejudices when an answering note invited us to attend, and we set off in the lorry with our driver Omari.

Bound for the Lutheran Mission, situated far from the edges of Government influence, therefore a long way off, our lorry was loaded with some cases of petrol which would not be available at our destination. A basket of food for us and a bundle of bread and fruit belonging to the driver and his *turni-boi* (person who cranks engine), had been added to the load.

The sun rose to heat the day, the lorry churned up the dust in a rolling cloud behind us. On three sides the savannah stretched to the horizon, on the fourth, low hills were faintly visible in the distance. Yellow grass, dried thorn bush, and giant baobab trees, thick in girth and devoid of leaf, were indicative of the season's arid conditions which had followed the short rainy season.

After the plains came an escarpment along the crest of which we drove under an avenue of trees, clad in green leaves, amazingly close growing by comparison with the tiny blobs of green passing for leaves on the savannah's acacias which, therefore, let streaks of sunshine through like a sieve and provided a chequered pattern for animal camouflage.

The smell of hot oil from the engine began to diminish in the cooling influence of the shade. We came upon the Mission built of stone, as was the church and its spire, standing among tall trees on a deserted forecourt. It proved difficult to find a person until at last a door opened to my mother's persistent knocking, and a Nun beckoned us to enter an echoing waiting room, cold, quiet, so unlike the heat and bustle of the construction line.

Cold! That was the signal for the onset of a rising temperature, and the knowledge that once it had exceeded the human limit my skin would burn, my mind alternate between sleep and the need for diversion, a "Please, Mutti, read to me," with never enough stories to feed the fevered brain.

I consoled myself with the thought of meeting the man who might stop my malaria, but when ushered into his room, I was ignored, he looked through me as though I had been the windscreen.

Papi had painted such a favourable picture of my encounter with this Missionary, he would be nice, a wizard of cures, interested in me because doctors always like people with strange complaints. Instead, my mother seemed to attract all his attention. Unwell, disappointed, I turned to studying the alabaster figure of Christ nailed to a wooden cross hanging on the wall. I knew about religious art from Mutti's books, but this! How could anyone find enjoyment in looking at anything so cruelly nasty.

Shortly I heard the Doctor say, "Promise me you will try."

"Yes, yes!" Mutti answered, in a tone which I knew meant, "never".

The adults shook hands, the door shut on the controversial world behind us, and we stood looking from the height of the Mission hill at chequered patches of yellow and grey stretching to the distant blue hills. Never had I looked so far, nor seen such emptiness.

The *turni-boi* turned the starter handle, the engine fired, the only sound on the lonely forecourt.

We stopped somewhere down the avenue for lunch, my appetite already halved. Mutti and I sat in the cab, the other two at the back under a tree, convenient separation when we went to find a thick bush behind which to squat.

At the bottom of the escarpment, back in the shimmering heat, faint billows of smoke hung in the steaming sky. Omari pointed a stubbled chin in their direction, "A fire!" He looked ahead with studied indifference. It might have been thought he was approaching a cloud of rain but as we drew near, the swirling smoke and leaping flames made passage look impossible.

Where the fire had already been, smouldering tussocks radiated enough heat to bake bread. Stumps of bushes and umbrella trees were still alight, birds circled aimlessly in eddies of hot air, having lost their nests.

I was very frightened, the more so at the thought of the boxes of petrol at the back of us. Hadn't Papi warned of an explosion when the Engineer's house caught fire near his petrol dump? I was certain Mutti had forgotten all about them. Omari's expression did not invite comment.

The moment we entered the fire zone, he turned his head to sound a warning through the back window, and depressed the accelerator to the floorboards with his big flat foot. The lorry leapt forward adding its roar to the inferno of crackling and exploding flames, and careered at breakneck speed to beat the elements.

Mutti clasped me tightly as though the bolted door might open to shoot us into the open mouth of the fire dragons. The moment was truly terrifying: there was the proximity of an uncontrolled fire, the heat of the air which made it difficult to breathe, the smoke obliterating the road, lastly the sight of an antelope racing panic stricken first alongside the lorry and then threatening to cross the track in front of us. On the other hand, speed and danger combined to add a thrill.

Once past the fire, Omari stopped to give the engine a rest.

"I was flat on the floor," said the *turni,* appearing at the cab's side, "with a *kikapu* over my head." He mimicked his fear. Then going to the radiator, he pretended to unscrew the filler cap which we all knew should not be touched until the water had cooled. Grimacing, he blew on his fingers, waved them about in a show of having burnt himself, and danced up and down with sham pain, until we laughed to forget our ordeal.

On our arrival home, malaria put me to bed.

Papi asking Omari why he had not waited for the fire to pass before taking the lorry through its heat, received a sensible answer, "Waiting would have delayed us. That would have been bad for the sick *mtoto.*"

As for the consultation, the Doctor had told Mutti about a drug called *Esanofeles*, recently perfected in Italy. He had also been concerned about her emaciated look, she told my father, and given her advice on stimulating appetite in the tropics.

"Obviously not a Freudian. Well anyway, what did you have to pay?"

To his relief we had not been charged a cent, the *Esanofeles* would be dear enough ordered through a *duka.*

In due course it expelled my parasites, though with the side effect of my lips turning bluish, which Papi said was due to slight oxygen deficiency mentioned in the drug's leaflet.

By the time I had regained my health, Karol was afflicted with something called 'circumcision'. My father explained that he had suffered a conversion to Mohammedanism which necessitated an operation, after which we were to call him 'Shabani'.

My mother looked embarrassed when I asked for details, "Ach Putzimännchen, he is being cut, you know where."

"You know where" could only mean in one place. "Cut!" Surely not. If animals were cut in "you know where" it would mean they could no longer do all their acts properly. Apparently the operation was as irrevocable as cicatrization on faces, arms and legs, or the filing of teeth, in aid of tribal marking,

My previous curiosity about male organs was stirred, especially the "cut" variety. Overriding conscience, I asked one of the Mohammedan house-boys whether he would let me touch his genitals, promising him ten cents filched from change my mother had left on the table. He was annoyed at being asked to accept money but promised to come to my room before supper. An urge spurred me on despite certainty that if I were discovered, my father would mete out the clouts than his miscreant labourers received from him.

The man came as promised, let me feel his flaccid genitals and made a hasty retreat when my mother could be heard emerging from the kitchen with last minute orders for the evening meal.

It had been a satisfying experience enabling me to consider myself as knowledgeable as an adult, although circumcision remained a puzzle because nothing on the man was missing.

Shabani returned to work, looking as shiny as a ripe mango and, judging by Mutti's general remarks, that which had been lost was replaced by an improved character.

After the labourers' sustained efforts before the onset of the rains, my father bought the camp an ox for slaughter. It cropped the grass nearby, one *mtoto* in charge.

On a Saturday, glancing over the verandah parapet, I saw men dragging it along by its horns. It resisted with all its strength, stiffening its muscles, splaying its feet, shoved from behind and pulled from the front, reminiscent of the ants' methods.

My mind filled with the sensation of terror that must come at being trapped by enemies. The presentiment of being killed overwhelmed me on behalf of the beast.

The butchers stopped near the huts and brought the animal down by binding its feet so that it passed from view under the amount of human bodies bending over it. I felt the knife cutting through the dewlap, an excruciating pain like the one I had experienced when gravel entered a cut in my knee. My tears had come involuntarily then, even as now the ox would want to bellow. Before it could, the knife cut its throat, red terror turned to black, void, he was dead.

Both upset and fascinated, and knowing my mother was busy in the house, I took my hat and wandered out hoping that, if I approached the place of slaughter in a casual manner, no one would notice me.

Women had already gathered with their enamel bowls. The mood was festive, playfully they nudged each other out of the way and called for preferential treatment.

"You've known me long enough, Chumvi (Salt), don't give me the tail, *uhuh*?"

"Chumvi, I've three children, what about giving me portions for each of their fathers!" The joke provoked a cackle of laughter.

The skin had been peeled away from the top side of the carcass, one of the men was cutting out the tongue, another hacking into the skull for the brain. Looped entrails hanging from the slit stomach were being squeezed to empty their foul-smelling contents, causing the nearest bystanders to scatter with cries of disgust.

Flies, buzzing to claim their share, sent me hurrying home.

Feasting was to be accompanied by the drinking of native beer, brewed from sorghum by women who had gained Papi's permission, and there would be a *ngoma* (dance).

At sunset, the drummers repaired slack drum skins by passing the top back and forth over a fire. Taps of "boom-boom" every few moments allowed them to judge whether the drum was tuning for play. Petrol tins cut in half lengthwise accompanied the drums with a "rat-a-tat-tat" or "rat-ta-ta" beat, made by striking them with a stick.

I knew that after dark, when bellies had been warmed by meat and beer, a few drum rolls were enough to bring the first enthusiasts to the centre of the camp. With their appearance, the drummers started up in earnest, beating out a fast rhythm, increasingly irresistible to feet. Mine, under the ironing-cum-supper table, covered by a cloth three times its surface, could not be seen tapping an answer between its folds.

The Tilley lamp maintained a steady hiss, diffusing paraffin to the white-hot mantle. Insects whirred, whined, circled and inevitably died. By contrast our house-boys moved quietly in and out of the verandah, serving supper, during which my parents continued their usual talk about lack of news from relatives, the state of the construction, future job prospects, or compared their Mannheim life with that in Tanganyika so that I might learn that our prevailing circumstances were abnormal.

It was agonising to sit through the evening's routine knowing what we were missing. At last, satiated, my father asked Mutti whether she would like to watch the *ngoma*.

"We might as well. You would like it, too, wouldn't you, darling, just for a short while as it's really your bedtime." Always the same excuse! I had hoped for a prolonged stay. How wonderful it would be to run down to the camp to join the circle of dancers, but I knew such pleasures were not allowed and accepted my station.

We sat on chairs at the edge of the arena illuminated by the fire which showed the sweat glistening on the drummers' bodies, and their faces ecstatic with the power of rhythm exerted on the dancers. The latter, driven by the beat, swayed, bowed, shuffled and stamped to the added ring of leg bells or the rattle of maracas made of empty cans. It was compelling music.

Papi, by contrast with Mutti's dutiful interest, was fascinated, there was always somebody by his side teaching him the dance steps, explaining the songs, so that he could record his observations.

Next day, when my mother was out of sight, I practised the steps, striking the characteristic pose of a dancing woman, bottom out, breasts to the fore, if one had any. I raised my shoulders, rotated them so that the arms gyrated, rotated my hips until my bottom was swinging in rhythm to my upper limbs. Faster and faster, in one continuous movement, I swirled round Mutti's drums to the beat in my ears. Of course I could do it! Just as expertly as the little African children who stood with the onlookers but occasionally stepped forward to practise. After puberty they would be considered old enough to join the circle. I would never get that chance. Resignedly I sat down to continue with my lesson.

Once the bridges had been built with strengthened piers, and the 'paw' sleepers had been laid to take the rails, we saw the arrival of locomotives, pulling open trucks herded at the rear by a caboose. Cowcatchers featured prominently in front of the engines, not only for shoving off stray oxen but also wild animals stupefied at night by the glare of the powerful searchlight, throwing a silvered arrow over the rails.

Taking a walk on the rails, we balanced by holding hands, my mother in her high heels, toppling off every few steps, and if we attempted a sprint, Dachsi and Peter jumped and barked at us in high spirits. The latter, a camp mongrel, had been given to me in lieu of unaffordable toys. Papi would not tolerate us buying wild baby animals because it encouraged their trade.

Unfortunately Mutti's sympathy was wrung from her heart at the sight of newly-born dik-diks, offered for a few cents by a passing hunter. Being tiny antelopes, the babies looked like toys, or more like the breakable ceramics in Mutti's books. I was not allowed to handle them and just as well, because despite warm bottles placed under the grass bedding in a box, and feeds of diluted cow milk, they pined away hardly able to raise a head to lick liquid from her finger. It was painful to peer into their housing, hoping to find a sign of improvement and dreading to see a stiff body. My mother, I knew, could not stop the light in their large brown eyes from going out and I dreaded the inevitable.

"No more," she told the servants and to us she said sadly, "I have no luck with wild animals." In a different sense we thought her exceptionally lucky when, a few weeks later, she picked up a dark ribbon from behind one of the tin trunks - she was always warning me never to grasp anything without first looking - and withdrew her fingers hastily as a baby black mamba wriggled out of her grasp. She was not so lucky when she forgot to turn her shoe upside down and her foot came to a soft obstruction seeking shelter where it was dark and sweaty-cool.

This time she yelled, bringing Mohamadi at a trot, knowing that the *bibi* never flinched at the sight of a tarantula scuttling off her dress as she picked it up from the top of the tin trunk, or at the confrontation with a scorpion, uncurling itself from under a bag, then advancing menacingly tail-up towards her. Something must be seriously amiss.

It was a scorpion, but fortunately one of the big black variety, much less painful in sting than the red. The cook treated the sore spot with lime juice and cold compresses but her foot was so swollen and painful that it was several weeks before we resumed our walks.

Apart from the warnings I received constantly in order to avoid Mutti's experiences, the other raised finger concerned the sun - "Never go out without wearing your hat!" My eyes could be blinded for ever if I glanced at the adversary, and to expose my neck for a few minutes directly to it would result in a *Sonnenstich* (sunstroke) which literally translated meant "a stab from the sun", a final coup de grâce.

All this almost came true on the day my father was led home by Sefu, who had found him in a collapsed state, blinded, distraught with a hammering headache, running a high temperature and vomiting.

The attack struck him in the course of surveying some culverts at midday when the sun's rays beat down from the zenith directly onto his neck as he bent to measure.

Mutti kept sponging him with tepid water to reduce the temperature, at the same time feeding him sips of cold water to keep him, as she said, "from drying up". Judging by my own experience of a fever, the amount of linen being carried out of his bedroom meant that he was sweating continuously, and his moans, too, never ceased.

When nobody took any notice of me, I knew matters were serious, also by the way the servants hurried back and forth with the tepid water, the fresh sheets, a tin for the *Bwana* to vomit into, another for relieving himself. Silence hung over the kitchen normally buzzing with chatter.

I had heard of people dying from sunstroke, it was a possibility about which I could not ask Mutti, who always burst into tears at the mention of death. I waited for the worst to happen, the only clue to his improvement being a gradual reduction in her regurgitations after meals.

It was some weeks before he was well enough to go to work, wearing sun goggles and a white piece of cloth hanging from his hat to cover what my mother called his Achilles' heel.

There seemed to be a giraffe feeding-ground in an area of thorn scrub along the main road in the direction of Kinyangiri. We thought the animals the prettiest of all in the world and they knew it. Mutti said they had been declared 'Royal Game' and therefore could not be shot, the result being that they did not mind human beings.

On hearing our footsteps and voices, and despite the barking of Dachsi and Peter, they remained standing behind the branches of the tallest thorn trees, camouflaged until we became aware of the munching going on somewhere above our heads. Any attempt at approach was rejected by stately long strides in the opposite direction. Our gaze was met unflinchingly. I concluded that eye contact at that height was of no significance. The presence of a calf made us sort legs, because the adults tended to stand round it protectively while we discussed who was mother, father, brother or sister.

On a late afternoon a giraffe family kept us at one spot, admiring them until we turned for home, pulling Peter on a lead, I whistled for Dachsi. My mother called cajolingly, hoping to hear an answering yap and the crackling of dry twigs which preceded his bounding from the thorn scrub. We whistled and called, and stepped into the bushes to see if he had cornered a rat or skunk and therefore refused to obey.

Suddenly it dawned on me that something was wrong. An absolute silence reigned, not a bird twittered in the increasing dusk. The giraffes stood as still as statues, on the alert. If a wild animal had taken Dachsi, we were in mortal danger because its next meal was right there beside us, and if we constituted an obstacle, there was the possibility of our being attacked.

My mother's face betrayed her anxiety when she said, "We had better hurry home to see if Dachsi is there."

I could not talk, nor did I dare to look behind me, aware that something unseen might be following.

Leopards were renowned for their love of dog flesh, their method of attack being to leap on the prey's back. All that long walk home, the scrub thick on either side, I knew that the animal might be stalking us in the shadows. Dachsi had not been a big meal.

If it jumped, it would grab by the neck. My body knitted together with fear, my back, with its expanse of white shirt, seemed an open invitation for the animal to land on it.

My mother's increasing pace was another sign of her anxiety, and made it difficult for me to keep up.

However much my ears strained to catch the slightest sound of a breaking twig, the bush remained uncannily silent until at last we veered off down the path to our house.

Relief in reaching home safely diminished the anguish of finding Dachsi was not there. However much he had been a member of our family I was glad that the leopard had eaten him instead of me.

My mother's hobby of growing wild plants found new impetus when Binti Salehe from Rusegwa joined the camp and restarted her pottery trade.

The sizes required were never in stock because the other women had already bought all she could make. In the dark interior of her hut, damp lumps of clay beckoned with their sheen to have my fingers sunk into them.

Though Mutti was willing that I should watch and Binti Salehe agreed to let me, it was some time before she had fetched the special clay from some distant location. When her invitation came, I found her grinding clumps to fine earth on a stone.

Next day she was squatting before a board to finish a pot, her bowed head with its rows of plaited hair, shiny with oil, and the rolled ear studs with their patterns made of tin foil reflecting the light from the doorway.

For the next vessel she took a wet lump, stuck her thumb into the substance, then her fist and dextrously teased out the thick clay into thin walls which grew under her treatment into half a pot in no time. She kept her hands wet with slip, working new lumps into the sides so fast that the vessel seemed to expand of its own accord. Her hands kneaded, stroked, pinched, pulled, smoothed, from all angles, as the pot began to bulge in the middle, narrow at the neck and roll to a finish at the rim. The left hand flew about the inside of the pot, working to support the building up of the sides by the other. She used a knife for cutting off surplus clay, sticks for imprinting criss-cross and diamond patterns round the neck, and a pebble dipped in water, made slimy by the infusion of leaves from a vetch, to give the inside and outside a smoother finish.

The new pots, including my pinch bowl, were kept in an open sided grass-roofed outhouse to dry before being fired. Weeks later, when I was called to find my piece among the many fired pots, there was red-hot charcoal glowing round a depression in the ground, cleared to reveal a nest of objects that looked like dark brown eggs.

She poked them clear with a stick and when cooled, tested them with a flick of her forefinger. If they rang with a "ping" she was satisfied, if the sound was a dull "doom-m" they were smashed into shards.

After losing Dachsi, we preferred the rail track for our walks, my mother carrying a picnic *kikapu* to share with Papi when we met him at the loco halt for a lift back.

Usually the train rolled on until the caboose was level with us. The labourers stood along the track, waiting with their clanking implements to pile into the trucks with much shoving and shouts of pleasure at being transported home.

Once, however, the engine stopped next to us. My father, already in the cab with the driver, beckoned that I should come up onto the footplate. It was my dream come true, an invitation so unexpected that I hardly knew how to contain myself.

The first rung of the vertical steps being too high, I snatched at the handrail. Missing it, I took another lunge, held on with both hands and pulled myself up onto one knee, fearful that if I did not make a show of getting there my opportunity would be lost. I felt absolutely heady with excitement, determined to reach the goal above me.

"*Eh!*" I heard the African driver say, "where her legs are short, her arms are strong," and he pulled me up beside him.

Papi laughed, "She is my true heir."

A delay followed until everybody was aboard including Mutti in the caboose, then the brakes were released with a "whoosh!", the driver, allowing me to keep my hands on the start lever, opened up, the steam surged in great puffs from the side of the locomotive and the long connecting rod began to push the drive wheels.

As we gathered speed everything around me made a noise: the tender clanked as it snaked from side to side behind us, the footplate squealed with a motion resembling hair clippers moving across each other, the boiler roared and the wheel and wind noise combined to make speech inaudible.

My father motioned to me to get up at the side opposite the driver where there was an iron box, from which vantage point I could see the line ahead through a porthole. Not for long. Soon cinders were flying into my eyes, whereas the driver wisely sat to one side, avoiding the particles yet still able to observe the track.

When the fireman opened the door of the firebox, the roaring of the flames was quite frightening. Using a broad shovel, he threw in large pieces of coal such as I had never seen, and after adding logs for good measure, he moved the fuel to the back using an extra long poker.

Astride the footplate, one leg on the tender, therefore each jerking independently, the power of the steam transmitted itself in exhilarating sensations, increased by the terrific din which disturbed the senses. It was a wonderful feeling, fulfilling all my expectations of flying past the countryside on a roaring beast.

The pleasure ceased all too quickly as we approached the camp, wheels objecting noisily to the braking, where I could only remonstrate in silence at their having to stop at all. Going down the loco's steps was easier because I could jump off the end.

Usually I felt rebellious about greeting and thanking people because it was preceded by my parents' meaningful look, 'observe your manners'. This time I could not thank the driver enough,

"*Asante, Asante!* (Thank you!)"

Our poverty had a bearing upon our lives which I understood well. Papi was inclined to joke about our shortages in a good humoured way. My mother, ever depressed by them, gave way to her feelings by calling East Africa, "this God-forsaken monkey land" and when worked up, claimed her bile was rising in disgust over the misdemeanour of the servants who would not sweep the corners of the rooms properly, failed to clean drinking glasses to their required crystal transparency, could not cook without burning the food... The list grew in proportion to the depth of her depression.

Her stock-in-trade phrase repeated to any of the servants unfortunate enough to become her target was, "It is not the custom in Europe to do it like this."

At mealtimes, her despair expressed itself in disparaging remarks, "In my home, Anna the cook would have had something else ready to serve if the food had tasted as smoky as this."

"Did she have a wood stove?" Papi enquired.

My mother, unaware of the trap he was setting, answered, "Of course not!"

"Aha! Perhaps a flue, though?"

"You're right," she conceded, her bad temper visibly diminished with the memory of Anna's superior kitchen.

Sometimes, Papi met her outburst with teasing:

"Though mother is Queen of her domain,
From sweeping corners, she won't refrain,
Her subjects refusing to pay attention,
There's constant *matata* (trouble) and high tension."

Unfortunately, when Mutti's nerves reached cracking point, she could no longer laugh at herself, instead she shrieked at one of the servants, sometimes receiving a cheeky answer or a declaration of resignation. At that she became even more upset because he was likeable, and she had put in a deal of effort to train him to the standard of a 'butler'.

In fact, no one ever left unless he had already decided to do so before the fracas.

I hated the strife, more so if it occurred at mealtimes and my father became so angry that he left the table to compose himself. The ensuing silence weighed heavily. Mutti's tears ran into her handkerchief; the servants assuming expressionless faces like a Sphinx offered food, cleared away, hesitated over the half empty plate left by him, which I had to tell them to keep warm in the kitchen, my mother being unable to speak. I sat feeling helpless, consoling myself by taking unnecessary second helpings.

The shaving mirror in the bathroom, suspended at the right height for my parents, too high for me, was a drawback which was to prove to my advantage.

Mutti discovering that there was ringworm on my scalp, I was taken to the hospital in the hope that the purchase of a pot of ointment might be inexpensive.

On arrival, my father, trying to allay my expected fears, said, "Don't worry, there'll be a nice doctor to see you."

He was quite wrong. The memory of the last consultation having made me hope that more notice would be taken of me this time, I was looking forward to meeting him.

What happened next was a nightmare. When I returned to the lorry I was as bald as a baboon's bottom. The prelude to this act had been my mother's translation of the Doctor's words, "Darling! He says he's having to cut your hair, then after one or two weeks, you'll have your curls again and be a pretty girl." I felt absolutely stunned, could not even remember him cutting it - one of the African orderlies had probably done it with a cut-throat; neither could I find tears in my mental shock. Mutti, upset because, as she said, my chatter had ceased so abruptly, promised to make me a fashionable bonnet, at which suggestion, considering how much I was trying to be like a boy, I opened my mouth once to say, "No!"

Papi tried to console me with facts about hair growth. The roots were still there, I was not to worry, had I not seen baby mice often enough!

There was only one solution, I kept my topee on all day, despite threats from my mother that the hair would not grow without fresh air. One day, when she asked me to start using my brush and comb again, I realised that it could be left off.

On my birthday Mutti abandoned lessons and gave me a chocolate cake with butter-cream filling, my age traced on the top with ground peanut. Eight candles burnt round the plate briefly, as they had to last for Christmas and the next birthday.

The surprise presents were laid out on the damask tablecloth, in company with the cactus growing from Binti Salehe's pot: cakes on doilies cut from writing paper, a new *amerikani* shirt, a book sent by a relative, pencils and paper, an embroidered sachet for handkerchiefs, a home-made bag for school books, the awaited verse from my father:

"Birthday child, now so much older, grown alert,
Your mother forgets teaching, instead, sews you a shirt,
Works in the kitchen with special fare to bake,
Abandon your thumb, find C for comforter in C-ake."

It was typical of him to make a joke of my thumb sucking, the constant subject of attack, in vain however, as I craved for it as much as my bed when tired.

Mohamadi, smart in his freshly laundered caftan and white embroidered cap, acknowledged the festivity with a smiling nod in my direction and served afternoon tea. Papi, who conceded a prolonged stay, made us laugh by contrasting my sensible behaviour with that of the 'Cinderella syndrome' shown by Mutti in her high heeled shoes. He hoped that as I grew older my outlook would become more logical, less like that of silly females.

During 1932, my father told us that the future of the railway was becoming uncertain. Would it be built as far as Kinyangiri as intended? Some contractors spoke of having been promised new sections, others threw doubt on the Government's ability to spend money on a railroad that was merely a branch intended to open up a hinterland.

He said that his labour force, accustomed as it was to orderly life in an established camp, needed the certainty of full employment, else the danger might arise that the sort of rumours he had heard would cause it to disband, leaving him without a means of livelihood. Jobs for whites not under the aegis of the British Administration were scarce.

"My men are our chicken and rice. From tomorrow on, Lili, I'll start writing to plantation managers. I remember some names from our stay at Rusegwa. I can offer them a disciplined hard-working labour force."

Mutti was aghast, "Is it to be finished so soon? I thought we were promised another section. What if you can't find work?"

"We stay put."

"Where is the money coming from for our food?"

"Some of my labourers will stay with me. I'll contract them out for work."

Each time Omari returned from Singida without bringing mail, Mutti began to agitate all over again, "When this section is finished, Hans, we have nowhere to go, nothing to turn to and no money in the bank either."

"Yes, Lili, and no sign of heart attack, no cancer and not even a carbuncle on the toe!"

"*Ach*, Hans, nothing ever bothers you!"

He shrugged, "Force majeure."

Mutti of course only saw the blackened side of the cooking pot. We would surely be going elsewhere. Moving had become an accepted way of life for me. There were people in my books who wandered about in horse-drawn caravans, or sat loftily on camels bearing their tents from place to place. We, at least, had a lorry.

To escape her worries, my mother escalated the daily walks like an animal seeking a water-hole in the drought. We set out earlier in the full heat of the afternoon, hats still on, provisioned with a *kikapu*-ful of drink and cakes, walked the railroad further than before and, foot sore, rendezvoused with my father on his returning trains. By sunset, we were usually sitting on the slatted bench in the brake van, he and I enjoying another snack, Mutti too weary to eat, Peter too hot and tired from running circles round us to do anything but lie down with his head on his paws, tongue lolling back and forth, lungs pumping "hu-hu-hu" like the chuffing locomotive.

Late one afternoon when we joined my father already settled in the van, this time leading the short train of two open trucks, a lurch caused the juice to spill from our enamel mugs.

Immediately an alarming acceleration occurred, causing the van to rush forward, rattling to the vibration of speed. The noise of steel wheels on steel lines penetrated into the interior with an increasing roar. My father sprang up to look out, leaving us peering anxiously through the swinging door where we could see the line ahead seemingly flying toward and under us.

Papi clawing his way back from the platform shook his head, the caboose only had a brake on the side, used when it was left in sidings. He pulled out his pocket watch to gauge the speed by the length of time it took for the kilometre stones to flash by, convinced that we were already in contravention of the limit imposed on new sections. What plausible reason was there for the driver's action?

Unhooking the warning lantern from the side of the van and standing on the steps while clinging to the handrail, he leaned outwards as far as possible, to wave the 'red for danger' glow in the direction of the engine which, controlled by hand or possibly in the grip of a mechanical fault, seemed to answer his signal by a renewed burst of speed.

"They were certainly not drunk when I spoke to them," he told us, "perhaps gone berserk, hashish! Such cases do exist." His expression, normally untroubled and hardly ever changing, became angry.

"The driver could have had a heart attack, Hans, a stroke. He might have had an epileptic fit..." My mother was ready to list the worst of physical calamities.

"Don't be silly, Lili! There is the fireman, he may not be a medical orderly, but he can stop the locomotive in an emergency. No, either the men are in collusion or one has turfed the other off in a fit of anger."

Peter sensing trouble sat up nervously.

We raced past our camp lying in darkness except for the pressure lamp defining the location of our house. A new worry surfaced, what about the points at Singida? There was no guarantee that they had been left open. Would the runaway train shoot itself into a siding, crashing us into the buffers to cause a derailment?

What about other late work trains, coming back to Singida from the opposite direction? The station did not keep open for their arrival because, at each morning's departure, the working locos were told the time at which they could pass each other in the few sidings in existence.

Despite the anxiety, it was exhilarating to go so fast, a speed I had never before experienced, with the added fillip of unexpected danger.

Thundering through Singida Station, shut down for the night as predicted, our train was a spear loosed by a madman aiming at nothing in particular. When would it run out of steam? My father could not even see whether fuelling was taking place.

Looking at each other by the shadowy light of one lantern fastened to the wall, we sat prisoners of the brake van, but not of our imagination.

The train slowed down as quickly as it had gathered speed. Papi made for the steps, ready to jump and race back to the engine, but aborted his action for a patient wait while we drew steadily into a station, coming to a controlled halt with a minimum of brake wear. He jumped off and disappeared into the night, leaving us to descend the steps as fast as we could to the unknown ground below us, to await the next move. Above us the stars shone as coldly in the night as the rails had gleamed unmercifully during our ordeal. The terrain was quiet except for the noise - like intermittent loud breathing - from the stationary locomotive. Voices raised in argument reached our ears.

Out of the dark appeared a white turban, turning into the figure of a Sikh, surely the Station Master. He requested that the *Memsahib* and *mtoto* should follow him to a coach standing at a siding. We were in Puma, he said, not far from Singida.

Papi returned with the news that the driver denied responsibility. Something must have jammed, he and the fireman had wrestled with the levers all the way, and did not the Bwana notice how they had managed to gain control and bring the train safely to a standstill so that he, the *bibi* and *mtoto* were unharmed despite the machine's extraordinary wilfulness?

"Huh, huh!" my mother exclaimed derisively, "his girlfriend, no doubt, lives in Puma. What are you going to report about him?"

"Nothing. I can neither disprove his engine's caprice nor prove its driver's suspected wantonness."

"But, Hans, after all we went through, and having the responsibility for our small daughter!" my mother fumed.

"Never mind, Lili, let me tell you that tonight you can sleep in company with the Governor's ghost."

True to a point, because we were sitting in His Excellency's private coach, sidelined over night en route for Dar, and after sharing our picnic leftovers, I was bedded down on a seat and knew no more, until the servant of the thoughtful Sikh woke us with a cup of tea.

The up-line train, flagged down to give us a lift, arrived at our camp in time for breakfast, much to the amazement of the workers who expected my father to walk down from the direction of our house. Mohamadi met us on the verandah, having spent the night keeping guard as well as pumping up the light, thinking we would walk in at any moment.

Mounting worries about our future were diminished for my parents shortly before my father's contract terminated, keeping the hyena from our door.

The manager of a sisal plantation, situated on the Tanga to Moshi railway line, confirmed that he would welcome the arrival of additional labour. There would be a satisfactory rate of pay per man and, best of all, accommodation was available for us.

At last I knew where we were going. Better still, my mother was excited and visibly cheered at the prospect of our getting a bungalow.

ACCOMMODATION AVAILABLE

We were on our way, the Ford loaded so high that Mohamadi and Ramadhani had a clear view ahead, though it was more prudent for them to keep their heads down in the cold morning wind.

Mohamadi found his stiff knee a difficulty when climbing a loaded lorry. This time, however, with three of us in the cab, there was no room for him. His wife, Mama Panya, was going by train.

Our house, emptied of beds but still accommodating three chairs for breakfast, had been a sorry place. It held an air of expectancy, sadly misplaced, since we were about to leave it like the empty camp, to be demolished for firewood by our Wanyaturu neighbours.

I knew Mutti and Papi hoped to forget our past mode of living in the improved circumstances promised by the Manager. Their happy anticipation was proof of it and infectious.

The camp had been in similar mood for weeks, as each man had made arrangements for departure. Everyone had money, a rail ticket and a promise from the Bwana that, after arrival at our destination, the Gomba Sisal Estate at Makuyuni, he would set out within a couple of days for Morogoro to meet those wishing to join him for the new contract. Others, desirous of going home to their tribal area, could return at a later date.

Papi said it was an "*au revoir*". Mutti hailed the exodus as a "finale", believing, in her pessimistic forecast, that he would never see his labourers again.

"That will mean that our livelihood will be gone," she wailed. "How embarrassing, considering we will be taking one of the plantation houses on false pretences, so to say."

Shabani confirmed her worst fears by taking leave of us to go and see his relations at Mahenge.

To hide her disappointment she enquired how many he had.

"Two mothers, the great mother and the little, seven brothers, three born of the great mother, four born of the little."

"And are you born of her?"

"No, I am the child of her sister. She is dead."

"How many sisters have you?"

"Twelve."

"Twelve sisters!" she echoed unbelievingly, forgetting he was counting cousins.

Shabani, I could see, regarded her exclamation as complimentary. Smiling with all the creases that could move in the lower half of his face, he grunted, "*Ahu*! Truly!" and returned to his task of packing household linen in the metal tropical trunks.

We stopped at Babati, the place of *bati*, sheets of tin roofing on a few *dukas* and a rattling "ba-ba-ti, ba-ba-ti" in an unrelenting wind.

It was also the refuelling stop and I went to watch a tin of petrol being opened. There was a designated roundel to be pierced for the pouring, but it was the air hole in the opposite corner which had to be judged skilfully for size. If it was punched too small, the petrol spurted out in intermittent gushes without centralising down the funnel.

Continuing our way towards the lunch hour, the wind ceased, the day grew hotter, the Ford needed more stops to cool down and the savannah began shimmering, every distant thorn tree enveloped in white flames of heat haze. Mutti, always better at seeing antelopes standing merged with the criss-cross shadows of branches, maintained that her keen eye resulted from her artist training.

"I see things as they are, darling. Look, there is one near those rocks - not as they are supposed to be. There are greens and reds where you see only brown noses."

"Yes, and if you look hard enough," my father added with a chuckle, "it would be difficult sometimes to know where white ends and black begins."

"Your father is a very clever man, all brain, far above my capacity for thought."

I did not understand his remark either but nodded my head and smiled knowingly, thereby hoping to put myself onto his elevated position of intellectuality; I did so want to be like him.

When the sun drew the least amount of shadow round the lorry, we stopped for lunch. Mutti and I took Peter for a walk round the next bend, where a scatter of rocks provided a screen for us to relieve ourselves. On our return, Mohamadi and Ramadhani had spread a cloth on a rock with the picnic things balancing on every available flat surface. Papi was already tucking in.

"Did you find the right lavatory?" he enquired, and I sensing his remark was a cue for a joke, said, "What lavatory, Papi?"

"Didn't you see? This being a favourite halting place there are signs of human defecation, but also buck droppings concentrated on one spot, and some leopard faeces too."

My mother and I looked at each other with consternation, "Hans! And you let us go with Peter."

"All the better. How many times have I told you, nothing is safer than the desirable meat walking in company with the unpalatable."

My mother, in her happy mood, laughed at his insinuation and agreed to eat an extra half tartlet.

After the meal, we continued at the slow pace dictated by the overloaded lorry, until reaching a place where the road descended to the plains, Papi slipped into low gear and with the weight of the goods forcing a slightly faster run than acceptable to the transmission, we roared down the incline.

Lake Manyara, visible in the distance, spread itself along what Papi called the 'Rift Wall'. The intervening terrain teamed with herds of zebra, buffalo, and wildebeest. The view resembled a giant picnic cloth of faded green, blotched in brown and streaked with black and white stripes. It undulated as if blown by the wind when a herd moved as one body. My father stopped by the zebra foals which pricked up their ears, gave a backward kick to gain momentum and jumped over an imagined tuft of grass or ran behind their mothers. Although none of the animals took to their heels, the herd moved imperceptibly away.

Mutti remarked that the blue of the Rift Wall shimmered like Cinderella's ball gown. In that context the buffalo and wildebeest could have been the ugly sisters. The horns of the former resembled thick hair parted in the middle over a stupid face, the latter bore a long head on an ungainly body, humped in appearance.

By afternoon we reached the *dukas* on the outskirts of Arusha, overshadowed by the triangular mass of Mount Meru. My parents explained that it was an extinct volcano, absolutely dead, inwardly choked to death by lava and ashes.

"Don't be anxious," Papi said soothingly, remembering my nightmares after seeing a picture in some German newspapers of Etna caught in the act of erupting, "it is striking a pose with its cone shape. If you went round to its other side, you would only see a torso with its head blown off."

The mountain was only one of a number of new impressions gained from surroundings so different from Singida. Arusha grass was succulent, the many trees had leaves almost obese with greenness, red-roofed houses peered over high hedges (not euphorbia) and driveways provided a glimpse of flowers as colourful as the beads I so much loved.

The place was more like an over-coloured picture in a story book.

Papi turned into the driveway of a bungalow from which emerged the 'Mayonnaise' gentleman, his lady and their new edition, to give us a great welcome. They were old friends, but all I could remember of them was his talent to hold an olive oil can steady as it dripped on two raw egg yolks which he stirred until the mess became a delicious salad dressing.

That feeling of unreality returned once we were seated in easy chairs, my feet resting on woollen rugs, my gaze drawn through glazed windows to a garden where the lawn was as green as the cloth inside my hat. A white ceiling prevented my eyes from seeing the roof structure, and thereby the familiar creepy-crawlies that had inhabited ours.

After tea, we took the baby in her pram, and Peter on his lead, for a walk between rows of coffee bushes and tall trees which provided their necessary shade.

A broad, shallow stream formed the boundary of the Mayonnaises' small plantation. At the waterside were their tanks, pulping machine and drying trays for the preparation of beans for export. Our host became increasingly animated in his explanation of what, I assumed, was the method of harvesting, because he gesticulated in the direction of the coffee berries, hanging between dark green leaves like droplets of blood on the hair of the slaughtered ox.

Unable to follow the English conversation, I walked away to explore the river's edge, an overhanging bank of vegetation.

The sun reflected on the water in dots of light. Pebbles glinted like beads on the river bed but when I tried to pull them out, the water bit me with cold. Flurries surged over stones from which moss tossed about like the silken hair of the Asian women, not at all like Mutti's and mine which was as crinkly as the short waves made by insects moving in the shallows.

I had never seen such a river, never heard such gurglings. The many impressions were overwhelming: so much clear water in the river bed, on the opposite bank fat cattle grazing on land overgrown with green grass, the dung smelling sweet where it should have been stinking, ferns, foliage, berries, flowers beneath the trees... a world which did not belong to the savannah, my home.

Next morning, ready to set off, I shouted my rehearsed "Goodbye," Mutti gave the baby another "kissy", Papi shook the Mayonnaise gentleman's big hand, and the Ford headed out of Arusha back to the arid plains on the road to Moshi, which translated meant "smoke" or "steam".

Hidden from us in its "steam", I was told, was another mountain.

"Kilimanjaro is famous, darling. Its peak, Kibo, has snow on top, something nobody in Europe would believe and also there are supposed to be the spoors of a leopard imprinted in the ice."

"Your mother is right, never would I have dared to tell an old lady in Mannheim about snow in Africa, in case she called me a liar."

On entering Moshi, Mutti looked at the cloudy sky, "Sorry, darling, she will not reveal herself to us."

What did she mean? Kibo, a woman, drawing a white *kanga* across her face in that demure way practised by African girls? I imagined brown feet and splayed toes emerging from the bottom of the wall of mountain, most of which was not visible either.

Our friends had recommended a stop at a store-cum-cafe, owned by a white family renowned for selling ice cream. I knew it had been Mutti's favourite sweet and one, which she said should be sold in heaven, adding that she was an atheist given to making a pig of herself with a Peach Melba in the here and now. I could not remember its taste even if she had fed me on it in Mannheim.

Papi ordered three large portions in addition to tea and led the way to a table at the back.

Set before us, the delicacy looked as its name indicated, creamy but which was the 'ice'? My mother looked fondly at hers, gingerly removed the wafer, a small dollop clinging to its tip, and took a nibble.

I could not wait. The moment the heaped spoonful entered my mouth it burned like fire, sending sharp pains through my teeth. Involuntarily my hands came up to receive it back but remembering my manners, I kept the substance in my pouched cheeks and ran the length of the cafe, through the open door, to spit the ice cream into the road.

The laughter behind me was more hurtful than the pain, worst of all on my return I found that my mother, in her misplaced kindness, had motioned to the manager to send us another portion, which chagrin would not allow me to eat. Upset and sulking I left my parents to their tea. Peter sitting in the lorry would be a more sympathetic companion.

"Don't worry any more about the ice cream," I was told as we drove out of Moshi. My mother could be infuriatingly tactless.

"I don't care about anything!" Tears threatened the morning, worst of all I knew they were the hallmark of silly females. Hastily I composed my face.

Papi could be infuriating, too, when he kept his pipe fixed in the corner of his mouth, smiled superciliously and puffed wisps of smoke in a provoking manner. He was however in the best of moods, 'We'll be there soon. Well at least after lunch. Remember that by this evening you may be lying in bed in our new house.'

His remark made me forget to sulk in the regained excitement of expectation.

Mountains continued to fill the landscape, the Pares on our left, followed by a chain of blue Usambaras on the same side, winding into the distance. The familiar sight of a railway stayed with us on the right, until we crossed over it. The mountains, rail and road ran in parallel, the latter often neck to neck, as if chasing one another to a distant winning post, which Papi said was the port of Tanga on the coast.

After a roadside lunch, my parents became more excited at the sight of sisal fanning out on either side. Mohamadi and Ramadhani, too, came to life at the back, shouting greetings to labourers and asking them for the way to Mtarawanda, where Papi was to meet the assistant Manager.

We drove down an avenue and crossed narrow gauge rails, on which a miniature locomotive was hooked up to platform trucks being loaded with cone-shaped bundles of sisal, a row on each side, tips meeting so that when the pile was complete, it would slope inward and could not fall off in transit.

In an open space, flanked by mud brick outhouses, the Ford stopped in front of a white bungalow, almost wrapped in mosquito gauze so that it was impossible to see what was going on inside.

Was this our new home? No. When the lorry pulled up, a lady

came through the mosquito-proofed door. She had on a blue skirt, a blouse of dainty floral pattern and... flat brown shoes... obviously she was no slave to the fashion heels my mother found indispensable. Her excitement was ill concealed in the repeated greeting. I was lifted down, Mutti received a steadying hand, Papi a friendly handshake, the dog a pat on the head. Her small blonde and blue-eyed daughter marked the occasion with squeals of delight, as she ran in and out of the open door. It was nice to be so welcome.

"Come in, mind the step, though. How was your journey? You must be so tired, from Singida, wasn't it?"

On the verandah, her armchairs were instantly familiar, the same as those in the Manyoni Hotel?

"Would you like a wash?"

Before my mother could answer, her breathless questions continued, "Is your daughter hungry? Lotti is always hungry, aren't you, my sweet?"

Surely she expected an answer. "Yes, I am hungry," I said truthfully.

For a moment she was startled, "Oh! Well you see. We are waiting for my husband to return from the plantation. He will only be a few minutes, then we will have coffee."

Lotti constantly pulled at my arm, "*Komm, komm.*" Suddenly she ran through the front door towards a large man wearing khaki shirt, shorts and topee, knee length socks and heavy boots, and threw herself into his arms exclaiming, "*Vati! Vati!*" as though she had not seen him for weeks. Picking her up with a toss to the skies which started her giggling, he advanced to shake hands with us, prefacing each greeting with, "*Na ja! Na ja!*"

Now surely we would have that promised meal. But when would we be shown our house? Where was it? We had not seen another bungalow on our way through part of the plantation. Was it situated elsewhere? Would I really sleep in a house like Lotti's that night?

When the coffee pot was brought by a bareheaded servant - Mutti's disapproving glances plain to read - we sat down in the corner of the verandah at a table covered with an embroidered cloth, varied in colour as the fare that stood upon it. Did I want simnel bread or currant bun? Would I prefer chocolate cake or ruby jelly?

After our cups had been filled several times, the ladies talked about the shortage of groceries in Tanganyika by comparison with

Kenya, the fathers about the shortage of workers, Lotti continued to be messy with her jelly, and I waited for her mother to offer more chocolate cake.

Our host mentioned the price of sisal. It was picking up again, prospects were good, therefore the plantation's need for more labourers. My father could hope to earn well if he had brought enough of them, and by the way, where were they? He expressed surprise that we had not come with a convoy. Papi explained that he would be fetching them shortly, first he must settle his family in the new house.

At the mention of it, Mutti said it was time to go. Thanking our hosts for the lovely meal, she asked to be excused, there was the unpacking to be done.

"You must excuse me too," said Lotti's mother, flustered once more, "it is the little one's bathtime, Ernst will show you where everything is."

"I am sorry, I can't come with you," he said, "unfortunately I must go to the factory. It's shutting down time, you know how one gets landed with these jobs as assistant Manager! I'll get my head boy to take you over to the house."

My father called our servants, whistled for Peter and started the engine. Mutti and I sat in the cab, our eyes glued to the back of the head boy who, starting to walk in front of the lorry, motioned Papi to follow.

We proceeded at walking pace towards one of the outhouses. Stopping in front of it he handed my father a key.

"This?" Papi exclaimed, pointing at the mud brick building with corrugated iron roof, "is our house?"

"*Ndiyo* (Yes) Bwana."

We were out of the lorry in a moment. Papi opened the slatted door to reveal a passage giving access to four more. Crowding in behind him, we watched as he opened one after another, three on one side leading to storerooms, each lit by a window at that moment shuttered from the outside. The under part of the corrugated iron roof glinted in the light penetrating with our entry, on the cement floor, the remains of maize meal and mice droppings made their individual patterns.

When he opened the fourth door on the right, Mutti no longer able to contain herself, exclaimed, "*Mein Gott!*" It was a large empty chicken shack, obviously built onto the length of what had been the grain store. Its walls reached only four fifths up, the remaining space being filled with chicken wire stretched from one corner post to the next. Feathers were lodged everywhere, in the wire loops, on the uneven surfaces of the mud walls, on the spikes of the rough roof timbers and in the droppings on the floor.

We were struck dumb. Papi reacted first by asking our servants to bear witness. They looked over the room, shook their heads and clicked their tongues unbelievingly.

Mohamadi spoke on our behalf, "Bwana! The European who has given you this house is bad, very bad! He thinks you are willing to step in dirt to get the little he will offer you. He is a polecat who uses a ruse to get his chicken. His own hole stinks, therefore he knows no better."

Ramadhani, stretching his hand out towards the other man, brought it back with an elegant sweep, made as if he were tucking the former's image into his chest.

"We would not be capable of doing anything like this," the haughty tone implied that he was separating whites from blacks. "You know, Bwana, that in our village, when a stranger arrives, the women clean a hut for his occupation. This European is acting like a *mshenzi* (savage)." He could not have spoken more contemptuously.

"Basi, shauri imekwisha! (Let it be, the matter is finished!)" Papi's words were always final. Turning to us, he said, "We have no option but to ignore what has been a dirty trick in more ways than one. There is nowhere else for us to go at present. Lili, I suggest you get the boys to clean one room for tonight, and put up beds, the child surely would like to see her 'haiya popaiya' again."

Glancing at him, I saw the remark was not unkindly meant, only exceptional circumstances would cause him to mention my cloth comforter without disdain.

The boys set to work. My mother sprayed the floor with carbolic until what was supposed to be bedroom smelled like the latrines in the labourers' camps.

The third room had a cold water tap protruding high enough from the wall to allow our bath tub to be placed under it.

Fortunately a thunder box and bucket had been installed in one of the smaller stores in the back yard, the rest would serve as kitchen and boys' quarters.

It was getting late, lamps were lit, mingling the smell of burning wicks with that of disinfectant. The opened shutters permitted a flow of cooling air, together with an invasion of the inevitable flying insects, which made Mutti remark that she was beginning to feel more at home.

Papi, who sat in the lorry reading a book until darkness fell, told us he was going away for a while to have a look round the area.

"In the dark?" Mutti was incredulous, but he was already out of earshot and starting the lorry.

"Just like your father, he will probably find some African to talk to and return when the boys and I have finished all the work."

In the tap room, our table and chairs were being set up temporarily by Mohamadi who laid the table placing a jam sponge in the middle, a send-off present from the gracious lady at Arusha.

Ramadhani could be heard beating a petrol tin to straighten it for a stove top, supper was ready by the time Papi returned.

"This fry-up is excellent, isn't it, Hans? And hasn't Mohamadi prepared everything nicely in this room?" For once Mutti found praise.

In bed, thumb in mouth, the haiya-popaiya caressing my cheek, the cloth ends of the mosquito net tucked around me, and the hurricane lamp turned low, I felt safe and contented despite the colossal disappointment of finding the promised accommodation had turned out to be nothing but a store and chicken shack.

No renewed light of day, no stretch of the imagination, could change our quarters into a bungalow, unless Aladdin had invited himself to breakfast. It was eaten in the tap room after the signs of our morning wash had been removed, and even while we ate our cool pawpaw with a sprinkle of lemon juice and sugar, the corrugated iron began to heat up with the rising sun.

My parents' silence was oppressive, like the heat. At last Papi pushed his serviette to one side to voice his thoughts, "I have decided to go to Morogoro straight away. You will realise" - I was included in his glance, as always when matters were serious - "that nothing can be gained from delay. Our situation here is precarious without our workers, whose promised labour constitutes our only right to occupy this..." he indicated the building at large, "...miserable *kuku* (chicken) nest!"

"Straight after breakfast?" Mutti stopped eating her half slice of bread.

"Yes, straight away, as I said, I'll take Ramadhani, who at least repairs a puncture as skilfully as he fries eggs. Last night I arranged for a man to help out with the cleaning. I don't want you, Lili, to strain yourself in this heat."

Once he had decided on action, his apparent placidness could change rapidly.

With the help of a hired labourer, Ramadhani and Mohamadi cleared the remaining household effects from the lorry, reloading it with a box of provisions, cooking utensils, camp bed, bedding, mosquito net and a suitcase.

Mutti, glancing round the boxes stacked in the passage, demanded to know the duration of Papi's absence.

"About a week or two if the lorry doesn't give me trouble and the men don't make me wait for them at Morogoro. Mohamadi has packed my suitcase, has he? Now I must find a book or two to read at night."

"Hans," she called after him in a more cheerful tone, "do you think you could bring some of our old things from Rusegwa..."

"No! The transport of men is the priority. We have got too much as it is."

"Oh, you are impossible!" she turned away in exasperation. I knew how much she treasured some items left behind which had belonged to my grandmother. At Singida she had tried to fit the greatest number of things into the least number of containers, in fear that if she put them in another box, Papi would throw it off the lorry as unnecessary baggage.

By morning-tea time Papi and Ramadhani had gone, so had the unknown helper in whose place another presented himself at the door, left open in the hope, as Mutti said, that a kind cloud might blow a little breeze.

"*Jambo mama,* I have come to start work."

She looked him over critically, "Have you been employed by a European before?"

"No."

"There's hope," she said aside to me in German, "although his eyes shifted when he spoke to me. Mohamadi! Talk to this man will you, find out if he's all right."

We had decided on which storeroom would be my bedroom when Mohamadi returned with his assessment, "He is called 'Paulo', a member of the local Wasambaa, his relatives on the plantation would know him."

"Paulo, a Christian then?" Mutti was sceptical about his suitability.

"Yes, I think he is, but we do need another man to help you, the Bwana said so."

"You know yourself, Mohamadi, how these Mission boys look smart and work well but are cheeky."

Paulo who should have been waiting in the courtyard appeared at the door again. "*Mama,*" he shouted, "your servant is wrong, he says my name is Paulo, it isn't, my name is Rajabu."

His turn-around conversion to Mohammedanism made us laugh, "You have good ears and a fast brain," Mutti told him, "we will try you out as dhobi and house boy."

"I started this job yesterday," Rajabu replied cheekily, "the Bwana employed me!"

Mutti would not let me help in the unpacking. Instead, I found myself seated at the ironing table, cleared of breakfast and waiting to be my school desk. Addition and subtraction, another page in the work book, some writing; Mutti, too occupied to check my work, gave me the opportunity to read some favourite stories.

With the inner ear listening to Sheherezade unfolding her tales, I let the black and white illustrations change dimension. They grew into life-size in colour, allowing me to join Sinbad and his Roc. Any cloud formation I could see through the window resembled a genie puffing himself up to overshadow everything before he grew thinner, elongated and lastly dissipated, restoring the sky to its clear blue.

Despite the whip cracks of the roof expanding in the heat, the shrill commands - Mutti ordering her two combatants to battle with the dirt of the store - I stayed with my fairy tales of dwarfs and giants, the wicked witch fattening a child for the pot... Somewhat different from the beheading ceremony, conducted every Sunday morning at the back of the kitchen for ours. Once, I had stolen round to see how it was done: the cook bowed, as he did when praying during his Ramadhan fasting, then stretched a chicken's wings, placing a flat foot gently on the tips, lifted its head, elongated the neck by stroking downward on the crop, and after muttering "*Bismillahi*... (In the name of God...)" severed the head from the body with one stroke of the kitchen knife. The body and wings twitched convulsively while the neck was held down to drain the blood. At this moment I withdrew before he turned round to carry it back.

There had been no fearful struggle, no frenzied squawk. My mind was eased when the roasted bird was served with all limbs raised in a gesture of what looked like excruciating pain.

Of our neighbour there was no sign until weeks later, when a note was delivered by her garden boy, inviting us to morning coffee, and afterwards a lift to the Makuyuni *dukas*.

Mutti had borne humiliation too long. This was the last straw, she protested, the last tatty feather in malodorous droppings. Her indignation found full vent, "See, how false a person can become! Sugar sweet after all that treachery. Oh what a woman! Coffee, tête-à-tête, huh! I suppose she imagines we should be thankful to sit on her verandah under a proper ceiling, to discuss the price of disinfectant. As for that "Ernst", what a wet rag, all talk and no substance! And that poor Lise-Lotte, what will become of her with parents like that!"

Later she wrote a reply:

"Thank you for the invitation, which I am forced to decline because of the increased amount of cleaning. As for the lift to Makuyuni, I am afraid it is not possible for me to ride with you."

"*Ach* damn!" she said, "darling, pass me your rubber and I'll erase the stop."

The more she rubbed, the more obvious it became that it had been there. Thoroughly exasperated, she added the words, "...on Thursday."

With the lorry away, it fell to Rajabu to act the errand boy. Briefed in the evening, he left at dawn for the market at Makuyuni. Swinging a full *kikapu* on his return, he had to account for every item purchased because Mutti believed that shopping servants filched change. Papi always said, "And if? What does it matter if he buys himself a couple of *sigaretis*? What youngster in Europe would have passed by a confectioner without being tempted. Weren't you?"

Once the frantic efforts by my mother to create a sitting-room in the chicken shack, and my own less ambitious endeavours to keep up a semblance of lessons, were over for the day, we reverted to taking our afternoon walks with Peter. There was always the chance that we might see my father's lorry coming round a bend.

In the familiar surroundings, "Sisal, sisal and nothing but..." as Mutti said, the only redeeming feature was the avenue of trees which she explained had been planted in German times.

One afternoon before leaving the house, Peter barked, the lorry came rumbling over the murram, but Mutti, tears of relief running down her cheeks, was unable to meet it.

Feeling it was my duty to represent us both, I ran out, "Ramadhani *jambo*, hello Papi; have you had a good safari?"

He shook my hand, patted Peter, "Where is your mother?"

"Come in, Papi, come and see."

Mystified and slightly worried, he stepped into the passage, then turned right into the chicken shack - the moment for which we had been waiting.

"*Na ja wirklich!* (Well, really!)" he exclaimed, looking nonplussed.

The place was spotless, the chicken wire gleamed from its scrubbing. The beams relieved of feathers gave the place a church-like appearance. Lower down on one wall, my mother had draped her two silken shawls, embroidered and tasselled. Elsewhere on the brown finish, hung the blue, white and red bead ornaments from Singida. In one corner, a construction of four sisal poles and three petrol box ends, made a stand supporting grasses and wild flowers in cans. New mats were lying on the floor, new green cushion covers refurbished the camp chairs, matching newly-painted petrol cases for the books.

The drums were back as occasional tables, the play surface hidden under brass trays. In one corner the ironing table had reached the height of household fashion, covered with a lace cloth on which Mutti placed her experiment of growing a prickly pear indoors.

My father delighted Mutti with his unfeigned surprise. The change was unbelievable, he said, how was such transformation possible? She was to be complimented on her inventiveness.

Flattered and happy, she fussed over his lime tea, urging, "Hans, do have another mango tartlet, they are particularly tasty this time."

Seeing him leaning back against the cushions, stretching his legs after the cramped journey, eager to taste fresh tea and cakes, gave me a great sense of cosiness. We were all together again.

Papi had interesting news: our house at Rusegwa was unoccupied. Grass, growing everywhere as tall as the sisal, indicated that the plantation was still in the process of being sold to pay for his debts.

In the derelict camp, he found exactly what he was looking for, some of his men and their families waiting to be picked up. Among them, Sefu, who had reconnoitred the situation and finding the place empty, had suggested the temporary occupation in the knowledge that the Bwana was surely on his way to fetch them.

"I thought Sefu wanted to go home to get a wife, Hansele."

"That was the idea. He said that on arrival at Morogoro and seeing the number of labourers getting off, he didn't want to go home after all."

"Are our things still in one room?"

"Yes they are. In fact I gave some to the old man who is looking after them, in lieu of wages."

"*Ach Gott Liebchen,*" Mutti groaned, "I wonder what we have lost now."

"We really do not need most of that stuff; I will pick up a few useful items like your painting paraphernalia, on my next safari."

He had camped on the verandah while waiting for the news of his arrival to filter through. It brought in those waiting elsewhere, and their friends who were seeking work for better wages. The increased number necessitated the devising of a plan for transportation, hiring lorries being out of the question. Where would the money have come from?

On the day of departure and with the help of Sefu, the travellers were divided into batches. Lifting up as many of the women and children, together with their baggage, as could be accommodated on the back of the lorry, he drove to the next village on the road to Korogwe, leaving those left behind to start walking. Once he had set down one group, he returned to pick up another, giving preferential treatment to those lingering behind for legitimate reasons, while others walked as far as they could.

The total distance travelled, he reckoned, must have been about three hundred kilometres, the constant shuttling very trying, but his people had been marvellous, vying with each other to walk the furthest, singing as they marched, hailing him with jubilant cries when he stopped to pick them up, then singing their joy, standing packed together while the lorry slowly conveyed its overload to the next setting down post.

He tried to get everybody together by nightfall, when the camp fires were lit and the maize meal he had helped to buy on the way, was made into *ugali*.

"It was a real joy, Lili, interesting conversation, joking and laughter, until the 'camp' fell asleep. Next day it was the same all over again."

"Where are they all now, Hans?"

"Do you remember the river we crossed as we reached the plantation on the day of our arrival? We turned off just after it into the avenue that led us here. I looked at the area that night. It is an excellent place for our camp: near the main road, next to water and not on plantation land, which makes my labourers independent of the estate workforce. The people are there for the night, tomorrow they will start building their huts. I'll get one of the Indians in Makuyuni to deliver some centre poles."

From the next day onward I saw little of Papi until evening, when he was too tired to play card games.

Having been left to my own devices while the chicken shack was getting its treatment, independence meant rising and dressing without being prompted, choosing my own clothes and often eating breakfast with only Mohamadi in attendance. I even started lessons without coercion.

Freedom to act as I pleased brought the realisation that people in books had friends, but there were no flesh and blood companions of my age to keep me company. My parents seemed incapable of understanding my desires, fears, pleasures, hopes and excitements. It was the first moment of truth regarding my situation as a white child without playmates and, from that moment on, I wished fervently to meet children, preferably in a school setting.

Mutti was companionable to a degree. She did ask, "Don't you think so, darling?" But I learned that the phrase was rhetorical. My opinion was not really required because she assumed it must be the same as hers.

Papi treated me as his best apprentice in matters concerning life, as he saw it. The key to living, he would have me know, was analysis and logic.

"They are a tool for retaining equilibrium in all situations, emotion and sentimentality, as you can observe in your mother, lead to false assumptions."

"Have it your own way, Hans! Your daughter takes after you anyway, so she is quite safe."

"There you are, Lili, is that a rational argument?"

"Probably not, but facts are facts."

Such conversations had me confused. How logical was his argument and what about hers? He was nearly always right, in which case it was easy to side with him, on the other hand, he had taught me to be fair in attitude. "Tolerance is a sign of intelligence," he reiterated. "Intolerance is stupidity in disguise." Was it fair, then, to belittle my mother so often? It was so difficult to bear divided loyalty.

It must have been months later that Papi sprang a surprise on us one evening, "The camp is established and your house ready for occupation!"

Thrilled, my mother at once called the servants to plan a shuttle service of boxes with the help of the lorry, and expressed excitement to see his new architecture.

Papi shook his head, and fluttered his hands up and down in a calming gesture, "The occupation of the house can wait another day, it's only just drying out."

"No, no, I must go and look at it first thing tomorrow morning. Then I'll come back to pack. What do you say, Putzi? Isn't Papi clever to have a house ready for us so quickly?" Another one of her rhetorical questions needing no answer. Instead, I asked him where it was. On all our walks we had not come across a site where building was in progress, except in our camp.

"Aha, you will see!"

The thought of leaving was a relief. Remembering the house of the Mayonnaises, and Lotti's too, I was ashamed of the store and chicken shack. Mutti and the boys had made such an effort to make it look nice - and it was nice - but it was not what white people should be living in. My feelings were complicated by being ashamed of feeling ashamed, when I knew I should be appreciating my mother's efforts.

How exciting to be on the move again. Going where? I would know next day.

CHANGE OF GEAR

After breakfast I was allowed to join the lorry on its shuttle run to our house, the location of which remained a mystery

The new driver, Salim, was topped by a fez, and clothed in a dark blue jersey and khaki shorts. His enormous feet were clasped by the straps of rubber-tyre sandals, available wherever there was a man skilled in using a sharp knife to cut up old tyres and prepare the necessary thongs. Sitting very straight, his feet obliterating the pedals, he drove as if the controls needed heaving before they answered his hand. His stern face discouraged questions.

We went past the camp. No, Papi would not have had the house built in its vicinity, the 'Bwana' relationship dictated fair separation.

Further on, towards Makuyuni, Salim took a right turn between rows of sisal on a track ascending a hill and there, three-quarters of the way up, a good-sized mud and grass house looked like barring our way.

In the forecourt, we stopped in the shade of a tree, grown to look taller by one bare branch rearing into the sky. It resembled a raised arm, the rest of the 'figure' was in a green skirt formed by the swirl of foliage.

Papi emerged from the entrance between two poles supporting the thatch.

"Hello!" He was as officious as an Administrative Officer in charge of a *boma*, my mother would have said. "Welcome to your new house."

It was bigger than any of our previous ones, cool in the rising heat and exuding that familiar smell of fresh grass and drying clay. It felt like 'home'.

Chicken shack and grain store paled into insignificance against the sight of the dark mud finish of our walls, the two tree-trunks supporting the lofty thatch, a verandah running the length of the house, the low parapets allowing a view between poles supporting the overhanging roof.

Papi would not hear of me staying. I was to return to help my mother.

Abeam of the camp, Salim stopped. So suddenly that I thought he had forgotten something. Papi had told us that despite the formidable look, he was a gentle man, an ex-police driver, worth employing because of his excellent certificate of service. I was, therefore, all the more astonished to hear a command of, "Get out!" which left no room for disobedience.

As I jumped onto the running-board, he made a swiping movement, dislodging a spider from the cab's back wall. It landed on the roadside, crouched, disorientated for a moment, then ran in an ungainly fashion into the grass. Its body was the size of the Ford's petrol indicator dial, hairy as my teddy bear, equally yellowish-orange.

Seeing my consternation, Salim's face creased into smiles as he explained, "It's a b-i-ig spider that lives in trees to hunt birds. If it finds a nest of *totos*, the spider makes '*tchee*'." He straightened a forefinger to aim at an imaginary victim. "Then the birds cannot move while the spider sucks them dry, '*lh-sh*'."

I knew the sound effects were made to alleviate my shock of coming close to leaning on the predator, nevertheless for the rest of the journey I sat on the edge of the seat.

Tarantulas were allowed by Mutti to run unmolested across our floors because, as she claimed, they were catchers of cockroaches, but this killer, this monster with furry down, had a nightmarish quality!

Shaken, I gave my mother a lurid description of my encounter, but as so often, she was not to be impressed with monster tales.

After the last goods had been transported, we had tea under our own roof. The afternoon felt like one at Singida, the view from the door, though, was quite different: the shoulders of the Usambara Mountains, a shade of blue, nudged one another across the vista from left to right. At their feet lay a plain in which a river snaked towards the left in zigzags of bushy vegetation that would provide firewood for the camp women. At the bottom of the picture there was the avenue, the road vying with the more distant rail embankment.

The heat haze almost erased the outlines of the hills, but by the clear air of morning they seemed much nearer, near enough to be reached on an afternoon's walk and possibly touched? Papi's conversation about the Austrian Alps made me believe that mountains and rocks were entities, and so wholesome were they, that they drew the finest response from human beings. Strength of character could be gained from mountaineering, why not from just touching their massif?

Our increased accommodation revealed a lack of furniture which was remedied by the combined talents of Mutti and Saidi Kapota, camp carpenter and night watchman. Papi said he was a deposed chief, though I could not imagine him holding office because he was like a large clumsy animal, flat-footed under a broad frame surmounted by the blackest of faces, sprouting tufts from the chin.

His smile, which appeared frequently, rolled up and down around the mouth in unison with his facial folds. He always wore a long white shirt, hanging over his *shuka* draped around his middle. Unlike the other labourers, he had a white embroidered cap, perhaps a sign of his former elevated position.

When an item of furniture was needed, Mutti designed and Saidi constructed. Using petrol cases and sisal poles, he made frames for armchairs, she padded them with sisal fibre covered with the toughest cotton cloth.

Their pièce de résistance was a coffee table bearing outrigger shelves for cakes.

In fulfilment of his promise to those workers who had wished to go home before following him to Makuyuni, Papi set out once more with the lorry and Ramadhani to fetch the last batch from Morogoro.

Two weeks later when there was still no sign of him, Mutti began to worry, "Putzi, something has happened to your father, I am certain of it. I can see him trapped under a car. Ramadhani would not know how to send a telegram."

Hopeful that any distant whirl of dust might prove to be the approaching Ford, we took our walks in the direction of its return. Fortunately she was still sewing curtains and measuring the open spaces on the verandah for reed awnings, so that her anxiety surfaced mainly at teatime.

"Mohamadi, yes, only two cups." She sighed, "We are all waiting for the Bwana to come back, eh?"

Mohamadi, like me, knew that many of her questions were rhetorical. She found answers difficult to hear. One day in the third week Rajabu came in during our tea. "*Bibi,* the Bwana has returned!"

Mutti jumped up, "Where, where is he?"

"In the camp."

"Make fresh tea, Rajabu, bring the cake I made yesterday. Did you hear, Putzimännchen, Papi is back, still in the camp of course, the labourers always come first!"

When Peter barked we knew the Ford had arrived and to our surprise it was not only Papi and Ramadhani who got down from it but Shabani as well.

Excited by the surprise, we crowded round him, shook hands, asked the state of his health and the well-being of those many relatives. He seemed so pleased to be back that he had to wipe his eyes.

Papi was urged to have tea, while Mutti opened the boxes he had brought, containing all he had been prepared to salvage from Rusegwa: books, the Rosenthal dinner set, and the silver service canteen.

"You've no idea," he said, sinking into what Mutti called her 'club chairs', and shuffling his bottom and back into the comfort of her cushions, "what an extraordinary story I have to tell." He related how he had adopted his well-tried method of transportation, but somewhere between Turiani and Handeni the Ford's engine began to splutter and the more he depressed the accelerator, the less it fired. Not even the pushing of the lorry by his passengers revived it.

"You know how I hate machines with their stubborn independence, this time there was no doubt that the lorry reciprocated my dislike!"

Worried about his lack of cash, not to mention the distance from the nearest garage at Handeni should he have to pay for a tow, he began pacing up and down at the edge of the group of anxious onlookers peering at the engine, "A dying donkey and the water-hole not within walking distance."

Some practical labourers made a fire, supplying the only glow in the fast approaching night. It was lit up suddenly by the headlights of a car which passed by, stopped further on, and reversed. A large man, dislodging himself from it with difficulty, greeted him in an American accent, and offered the help of a mechanic if the lorry could be made to reach his camp.

That gave Papi the clue, the American was obviously on safari with one of the Big Game hunting firms based in Nairobi.

"You know what I mean, Lili? Those which specialise in procuring licences from the Government. All that nonsense about shooting a lion or two before breakfast, or an elephant after lunch."

"I know, Hans, you mean these millionaires with their entourage - were there some ladies?"

"No I am sorry to disappoint you, there was a legal wife."

"*Aber* Hans!"

"Anyway, to continue the story without descending to your interest level, the man offered me a lift, saying, 'By the way, Hemingway is my name.'"

"Yes, and then?"

"That's just the point: Hemingway! It sounded familiar, I remembered reading an article by an author of that name in the *Querschnitt* magazine."

"So?"

"So I asked him if he had heard of the author. Can you imagine my astonishment when he said, 'That's me.'"

"Really? How extraordinary, and in the middle of Tanganyika."

"Precisely, imagine meeting anybody truly interested in literature, but even more extraordinary, to meet him because of a broken-down lorry between Turiani and Handeni."

"Did you have a chance to talk to him?"

"Hemingway and his wife were exceedingly kind. They entertained me for no less than three days, and we had many interesting conversations. One of the lorries of the Safari Company pulled mine into Handeni, which otherwise would have cost me a little fortune. Finally we parted company, he to pursue his shooting, and my labourers and I to return to the prosaic ways of life."

Papi's return brought two changes, Rajabu had to give way to Shabani, and I found *Aus dem Leben eines Taugenichts* (*Life Of A Good-for-Nothing*) in that last box of books.

It introduced me to the concept of the *Wandervogel.* The youth who, with not a care in the world, makes a bundle of his belongings (in my case including the cloth comforter), carries it suspended over his shoulder on a stout stick, pulls a cheeky looking cap over his forehead, and sets out to travel the world on foot.

The more I read, the more I was filled with the desire to leave my parents and Tanganyika for a roaming life through Europe. Foxes would sniff at my toes at night while I slept rough among encircling roots. Rivers would wash me, springs quench my thirst, berries and mushrooms would invite me to eat them.

Climbing over mountain passes, far spires of cities glinted in my imagined sunshine. In the valleys below, towns beckoned with the sights of quaint streets and leaning houses. I was a young man, strong in limb, desirous of adventure.

The fantasies sparkled in my mind, but instead of bringing happiness, a lump of pain in the middle of my chest made itself felt whenever I thought about *'das Wandern'*.

I could not define it to myself nor to my parents who, I realised, became confronted by an increasingly stubborn, sullen, sometimes argumentative and ill-mannered child. I no longer wanted to be taught lessons, my surroundings stifled me.

Once the labourers started cutting sisal on a contract basis, my father earned enough money for us to be re-shod.

Makuyuni, "the place of the wild fig tree", a variety grown for avenues, had a railway station and a few *dukas*, but Korogwe, which in Papi's calculation was about thirty kilometres distant, had a good sized bazaar, even an hotel.

Its *dukas* opened out onto the main road, under the shade of trees whose roots sank into the banks of the Pangani river, and provided gnarled seats for those who had nothing to do, the old, the lazy, and children.

We walked into a Hindu cobbler's workshop, my mother bringing her worn shoes for him to copy.

"Can you make another pair like this one?"

"No bother! No bother!" He rocked his head from side to side, his acquiescing hands one beat behind the movement. Painfully thin, he sat with his legs pressed against the floor in a diamond shape. At the apex, his toes held a hide sole, leaving his hands free to sew it to the leather uppers with a curved needle, and tough cotton thread held in his teeth. From time to time he made it pliable with wax.

After we had chosen our tan leather, smelling like Peter when he was sweating, Papi and I had to place each foot on a page of the order hook, full of other people's footprints and their names.

The pencil tracing round my feet tickled, raising goose pimples of pleasure on my arms. I would have gladly gone to several cobblers for a repeat measuring.

Next to the cobbler was a tinsmith who made funnels, mugs and something Mutti would not buy for me despite repeated entreaties, a *koroboi*, a round container, the size of half a can of peas, closed at the top except for a hole in the middle on which the smith fixed a tiny tube for a wick.

Papi having agreed to being measured for shorts, we walked from one *duka* to the next until Mutti found a bale of khaki marked 'Stockport'.

"Here you are, Hans, the best!"

"I'll bring an old pair for the *fundi* next time we come."

"But we are here."

The Asian shopkeeper began unrolling the Stockport.

On the road, in front of the shop, a tailor sat at his Singer sewing machine, a tape round his neck, his feet flip-flopping the treadle. Near the sewing needle lay the shears, agape like a crocodile's mouth.

Although he looked busy, he was engrossed in playing a fish, a young African, fingering one of the shirts suspended from a string stretched between the *duka* and its neighbour.

"How much for this shirt?"

The tailor's feet continued their steady motion on the treadle.

"Eh! Fundi! How much?"

Like one of the boys casting his line for a tiddler in the Pangani, the tailor's body, in all but feet and hands, remained still.

The customer became aggressive, "You Indian! I am asking, how much for this shirt?"

The machine continued its whirr, the African turned to go.

"Three shillings, for you only!" The tailor had recovered from his dumb state.

"Two fifty!"

"Two seventy five. I've too much trade as it is. You see I am sewing all day, the price of goods is much cheaper here than at Husseni next door." The treadle began to whirr again.

The youth started counting coins, kept in a much used cloth extricated from the pocket of his shorts.

"I have only got two sixty seven ..." falteringly, "next week..."

"Give it to me!" The tailor had caught his fish. He inspected the money, and keeping the hanger, presented the man with his shirt as though it were a present.

By this time my parents, having settled their differences, were ready to buy the khaki, and then it started all over again - endless haggling!

The sun standing at zenith beat down on our hats, the air resembled the heat of our kitchen at the height of Ramadhani's activities. Papi suggested a rare treat, a cool drink at the hotel. On its verandah, it was a relief to take off my hat, to feel Mutti's lace handkerchief, kept for outings only, fanning my face and to know that the boy had been ordered to bring glasses, soda, a sliced lime, and a bowl of sugar. It was turning out to be a trip with an added party air.

Raucous laughter and shouts of, "Boy! *Lete* beer - *chapuchapu!*" interrupted the sultry stillness.

"Germans!"

I knew Papi meant, "No one else would make such a row!" They sat down heavily, scraping their chairs on the concrete floor and rocking the table.

"Nazis!" Papi mouthed.

My parents sometimes mentioned the name in connection with my mother's fears that her sister in Germany might suffer at their hands.

The hotel boy, wary of their rough manner, brought them bottles and glasses before serving us.

Mutti could teach these whites a thing or two, I thought, noticing how they slurped their beer, wiped their mouth with the back of the hand, glanced rudely in our direction.

One of them rose and approached our table, perhaps he knew my parents from bygone times. But no, he ignored my mother, bent low over my father, showing us a rude back and murmured something like, "*...herüber kommen...* (come over)." When Papi followed him, the conversation was inaudible, but I noticed his astonished and then embarrassed face. Its cooled tan began to colour red in anger.

He returned abruptly to our table, from which we had already risen, paid the hotel servant, who was hovering uncertainly in a doorway, and walked out, Mutti and I trying to keep step.

Silence reigned all the way to the lorry, all the way home. I did not dare to ask what had happened, possibly it was the thing that Mutti feared my aunt might experience.

Weeks later we fetched our shoes. My toes complained after their carefree life in sandals, on the other hand, laces and heavy leather soles were a replica of my father's new ones, I was proud of that.

Seeing the cobbler at work had given me the idea of making sandals with cloth-covered cardboard soles for my parents' Christmas present.

On the twenty fourth of December, Papi was prepared to stop work in consideration of my mother's wishes. He said it was all sentimental nonsense - setting aside a day of remembrance for a mythical birth! Mutti, despite professing to be irreligious, insisted on making it a special day so that our lives would not suffer monotony.

The garden boy was sent to search for a leafy wild bush to be planted in half a *debe*, draped in a piece of colourful cloth. I made cardboard ornaments to hang on the branches which dried so quickly that the birthday-cum-Christmas candle holders would not remain upright.

Towards evening we placed our surprise presents on the dining-room table, covered in what had been my grandmother's damask cloth. Even biscuits suddenly tried to be stars, or men, or rabbits in imitation of *Lebkuchen*, once sent by the aunts.

New socks, pants and sometimes a dress, gained in prettiness from the occasion, and Papi's envelope of coins seemed to glow.

We gave him *Springbok* pipe tobacco, sold in a draw-string yellow cotton bag.

Mohamadi looked embarrassed when he received his Christmas bonus. Shabani repeated his *asante* several times, his face expressing pleasure from the gleam in his eyes to the sheen of his teeth, in a smile that went on, and on. Ramadhani took his envelope as a right, he was always a haughty man, and the garden boy, being a mission convert, gave a sort of bow, and said, "*Asante* Bwana!" in a voice which made Papi say afterwards that he wanted to add, "Amen".

The fattest envelope went to Sefu, to whom Papi was grateful for looking after our labourers so well that he himself could take time off for his studies.

Our festivities could have been a happy time for me if only... If only there had been a playmate... If only I were going to school. If only I could have friends of my own age. I envisaged a group standing round me as their focal point, then laughter, chasing about, playing games, fun!

My mother was not to be relied upon for happiness, she was often in the middle of a migraine, or 'depressed', which made her jump out of bed in the morning, dress at lightning speed, and trip fast-footed into the kitchen for a general harangue of the servants, whose response was silent embarrassment, unless there was a newcomer who might retaliate angrily over her trivial accusations.

At breakfast my father observed, half teasingly, that it was a wonder the boys did not turn to stone at the approach of such a Medusa. The comparison was apt, her hair like mine tended to stick out in fuzzy bunches, not to be straightened by a comb.

A few tears ran down Mutti's face, she held her handkerchief to her nose and blurted out, "I am so sorry, but you know what it is like when I am expecting my... you know what I mean."

"The maiden is being demure."

"Hans, you are dreadful!"

On this occasion we laughed it off. All very well for my mother, always making excuses for her migraine, her depressions, her feelings of pessimism, but what about my side of life?

I am so lonely, was the thought I took to bed at night, when will I meet some white children?

There was no solution to my problem. I knew there were schools for whites in Kenya, one was said to exist somewhere in the Usambaras for very small children. Papi did not have the money to send me to any of them.

My home tuition on the verandah was increasingly interrupted by the arrival of Africans, carrying basket trays covered by cloth. A call from Papi, studying at the dining-room table, warned us to disappear into a bedroom, while the delivery was being made.

There followed murmured explanation, which I knew he was writing in his notebooks, then the silence of careful offloading, the sound of the material being placed on shelving, a quiet "*Kwa heri* (Goodbye)," and we were allowed back, the visitor already halfway down the hill.

Items made of clay and decorated with bits of straw, beads, or daubed with lime and ochre, some carved of wood, were the secret paraphernalia that we were not supposed to see or know about. It was hidden away behind curtains strung along the top of the petrol cases.

At mealtimes, my parents' conversation, which had changed from references to bridges and trains to encompass sisal and labourers, contained a new word, 'figurines'. It rang from the first bite of minced liver dumplings to the last of *Palatshinken*, pancakes filled with Mutti's sweetened cottage cheese.

'Figurines', I heard from my father, were used to teach boys and girls of a tribe what they needed to know about puberty and marriage. Songs accompanied the tuition. If he had learned a new tune, we tried it out, much to the annoyance of Mutti who reminded us of our table manners, secondly that we should not be singing African songs because of 'the servants'.

Whenever my parents looked at the exhibits and I approached, curtains would be drawn across. Stolen glances showed me that the figurines either had pronounced genitals or were moulded to portray an act of sex. My parents' anxiety to keep such matters from my gaze seemed typical of adults, silly, miscalculating my maturity, making a secret of facts I knew perfectly well.

The use of figurines, kept secret from Europeans, became the subject of Papi's study. He had stumbled upon this form of art, he said, because in his evening chats with the labourers he had listened to their talk and kept his to a minimum. Gradually he had picked up enough information to put pertinent questions, mostly answered with evasive tactics worthy of br'er rabbit. In time, when confidence had been established between the informant and himself, an introduction to the functionaries resulted, men and women who were the sculptors of the figurines.

Week after week, they were brought up the hill, filling box after box, until the verandah was a museum behind curtains.

Occasionally Papi called us to have a look at something passed for my gaze. Once it was a small figurine representing an orphan, its legs brought up from the torso to the side of the head in two curves like handles to a cup. "This emphasises material poverty by physical deficiency. You see, it could not even afford two separate arms and legs."

The empty eye sockets, staring sightless at the world, seemed to me to be even more expressive of its sad state.

"You see how 'simple' art is able to combine form and meaning in one clump of clay."

"Yes, Hansele, I think I follow you."

"Isn't it wonderful how abstract thought can be translated into concrete objects? The text for this figurine is didactic, an instruction to girl novices to be kind to orphans."

Such talk was not easy for me to follow. Mutti blamed Professor Freud for all Papi's theories - a box of his books travelled round with us. I did understand, however, why he was in such euphoric mood when he told us that literature received from London confirmed his suspicion of there being little known about sculptured figurines in Tanganyika.

It became commonplace to see an African seated at our dining-room table, giving Papi 'information' and being served tea and cakes.

One morning, to my surprise, I found Saidi Kapota's large figure occupying my chair. Days later Papi announced that Saidi was preparing him for a visit to the secret initiation ceremony of snake charmers.

Mutti asked sarcastically whether he would be winding pythons round his neck like some men did at *ngomas*.

"No, because that is only a sort of advertisement, the real purpose is to create a self-help group within the tribe. Of course the members do maintain that they can cure snake bite." Next day and for several to follow, he went away all day, with Saidi carrying his lunch *kikapu*.

This time Mutti asked somewhat anxiously whether he was coping with the snakes, but Papi only shrugged. He refused to be drawn for information.

In the following weeks, Saidi lumbered up the hill with trays of tablets made of clay, painted with ochre, soot and white clay, or python excrement. Papi explained to us how these were copies of the murals painted on the walls of the initiation hut he had visited. It was so secret that he had not even been allowed to take a lantern to have a proper look at them. Saidi, with his artistic hands, was making copies.

They depicted fantastic looking creatures, some open-mouthed, revealing white teeth set at odd intervals. Saidi being an old man with wide gaps, it was not surprising to me that he should paint in his own image. Mutti thought the tablets so artistic that she made copies of them on paper.

My father wanted to write a book about the art form to dispel the general belief of Europeans that Tanganyika had no more to offer than zigzags and dots on baskets and calabashes, and some coloured semicircles on Masai war shields. Having been trusted not to reveal anything, he said, the description of the unknown material would have to wait.

Meanwhile he continued to listen. At sunset when we were returning from our walk, he was in his bath, by seven he had called for the garden boy to light his way down to the camp.

"Hans, please do not be so late," was every evening's request.

"Yes, yes, Lili, the song has a jaded tune." He could hardly wait to go.

"*Ach*, Putzimännchen, your father is only interested in his natives and their customs."

Some of the news he gathered from these visits was interesting, since there was no other: which *bwana* on the plantation was hitting a labourer, the men's opinion as to whether the punishment was just; who was stealing bundles of sisal from whom when Sefu's back was turned; who was shirking work, who was really ill; what was in the letter written to Asumani by a scribe about his family in the tribal area, the usual demands for money? What was happening about the litigation over land belonging to Lipuga's first wife? Whose children were undergoing puberty rites?

Up on the hill, Mutti sewed, I read. The reed awnings, rolled up at dawn, were let down for the night, stopping the swarms of *dudus*. The pressure lamp's steady sizzle fried the air, outside, the crickets chirped supreme.

In the kitchen, the boys talked, or dozed, waiting to join their families in the camp.

At nine o'clock Mutti became irritable, grumbling that Papi, despite his love of Africans was keeping his servants on duty too long. "Have a look down the hill, Putzi."

Outside it was pitch dark or alight with moonshine. Full of creature noises, a squawk from a night bird, the haunting laugh of a hyena.

Sometime or other before ten, a moving point of light showed that the garden boy was on his way up, Papi we hoped, beside him. Or there was a surprise shout of, "*Chakula!* (Food!)" before we realised he had arrived.

Everything came to life, as in the tale of *Sleeping Beauty*: Peter barked with joy thumping a tail on the mat, things clattered in the kitchen; Mutti called for a soda, complaining in the same breath that he was extra late, how did he expect Ramadhani to keep the food warm or palatable?

Papi, in excellent humour, made a joke, then grumbled in turn about our having waited for him. He downed his soda in long, thirsty gulps. Mutti pumped up the lamp, then rushed out because the meal was not appearing fast enough. I heard her snapping at Shabani and Ramadhani like Peter when he found a mongoose that stood its ground.

The time of the *masika* (greater rains) was upon us, the new roof about to be christened. Grey clouds gathered daily until they culminated in an unprecedented thunderstorm. It began with rumbles echoing across the mountains at midday. Chebembe, with whom my father had been working at the table, was sent home, the other labourers would have read the signs in the sky and returned to camp. Mohamadi let down the awnings, increasing the darkness in the house so that he had to light lanterns.

Flashes from the lightning pierced through chinks in the reed matting which bulged with gusts of wind, and rattled as though about to be torn from the fastenings.

When the peals drew near, we started counting the interval between flash and bang to ascertain the distance of the storm. I was not to worry, Papi said, our tree would act as a lightning conductor, capturing any bolt before it could set light to the dry roof. That extended 'arm' was surely beckoning for the electricity's attention.

Mutti, having shut the newly acquired monkey in his cage on the trunk, commented that a lightning death would at least be fast.

An explosion of electrical charges in the sky above us made me hold my breath, then down came the rain, in sheets smelling sharp and fresh, tickling my nose and making me want to 'eat' it.

Around us the dry roof began leaking everywhere at once, Papi bellowed in the direction of the kitchen for utensils and the servants rushed in with all they could lay their hands on. Nevertheless we were driven to huddle in a corner, Peter on his mat and each of us wrapped in a blanket due to the sudden drop in temperature. Mohamadi shivered so much that he was sent back to the kitchen fire in case the cold weather was bringing on his malaria, as was often the case.

Hours later when the storm had spent itself, and the roof, having reached saturation, stopped leaking, the reed mats were raised to let a drying breeze blow through the house.

In the plain below us, a brown sea stretched to the mountains. It was unbelievable. Where the river had been, a torrent carrying uprooted vegetation could be heard roaring past the camp. On the Usambaras, a waterfall appeared where none had been, further on a brown gash showed a landslide.

Papi went to inspect the camp, which he reported was still above flood level, if it rose no further. He had ordered Salim to start ferrying drinking water from Mtarawanda.

In the following days, our workers heard of villages that had been swept away. Nobody knew what calamities had befallen people, in what to us, was but a distant view. Nobody went there, nobody from there came our way, devastation could only be judged by what came floating past.

Despite the initial horrid sights of dead animals, the flood plain became a blessing because as the water subsided, every man, woman and child went damming the sludge and planting rice. In the middle of each family's patch, a platform of sticks supported their boys and girls turned bird scarers.

My mother, usually conservative in her activities, nevertheless agreed that we should go for walks between the rice fields. Refusing to demean herself by wearing canvas shoes like mine, she squelched for miles in her high heeled courts, which kept being sucked into the silt, until weary of retrieving them, she walked barefoot. Having worn heels since her teens she could no longer place a foot straight on the ground, and her wobbles on tiptoe and near slides into the mud, had me laughing all the way.

The sight of Peter swimming forewarned us of deeper water ahead, when we might have to wade up to pants level, a difficulty for Mutti who would not hold her dress up any further than above the knee for decency's sake.

Before entering a field, demarcated by small dams, we shouted for permission to cross, worried that in the tall reeds we might not be recognised for humans before a stone was released from a catapult. It was like a journey from one frontier to another.

Eventually the season came to its end, the water subsided, the crops were harvested and we were able to resume our walks along the river, shrunk to fit its channel. It drained even further by the dry season, becoming but a series of connected pools.

The river exuded smell, like Peter, like Mucki the monkey, like us, like the Africans. It was like a creature alive, waiting only to well up or go into spate to provide renewed excitement. From where did it come without a *masika*?

My mother said, "From the mountains."

"But how?"

"From a spring."

How could water come from inside a mountain! Could one put a finger in the hole of a spring to stop the flow?

Whenever my mother turned for home, bidding me to whistle for

Peter often hunting a giant lizard or a mongoose, I would beg her to go a little further up-river. I knew that we would never walk far enough to solve the mystery, but logic, such as my father demanded, took no part in my longing to catch the river creature in the act of being born.

There was another phenomenon connected with rains, that I never understood.

Before going to bed, it sometimes fell to me to take Peter for his last call. During the rainy season, and particularly while the flood filled the plain, a full moon glinting on the water turned it into a vast mirror, though somewhat dulled. Added to this weird sight came the sound of myriads of glass bells tinkling, now faint, now loud on the night air. My mother could not hear it, my father, when asked what it was, answered, "Probably frogs."

They must form an orchestra, I thought, with a conductor, because at times the bells stopped tinkling as if commanded by a baton, or after absolute silence, they would start up together. Sometimes one group followed upon another. How could frogs make a sound as if glass was being struck by tiny metal rods?

My father's encounter with Hemingway was not his strangest. In the following year, returning from a rail trip to Tanga, he gave us an account of an evening spent with what he called "the best-known non-official in the Territory of Tanganyika", a retired Major with a model sisal plantation. The gentleman had invited him to the Tanga Club. It had been a delight to meet another European who was interested in the African's life rather than in his potential as a labourer.

My mother was impressed by another factor, "You actually visited the holiest of holies! and what was it like, to lunch in the Tanga Club?"

"No different to anywhere else, meat, potatoes and tinned vegetable."

"Hans, but you know what I mean!"

"Some people sat in chairs like all human beings."

"You never talk about the interesting things," she grumbled.

Some weeks later, Salim, going to Makuyuni for mail from my aunts, brought a letter from the Major. It was an invitation for Papi to travel with him to Lushoto in the Usambaras, with the aim of meeting the Government Secretary for Native Affairs, at the exclusive

Country Club.

The prospect of spending more hours discussing African life pleased my father enormously, whereas Mutti expressed her envy of his chance to visit a place frequented by the Governor, therefore surely furnished in European style.

Of the outing my father wrote: "We met Mr. Mitchell and spent a day with him. He showed great interest in my conversation, and when we were tired of talking, we three went fishing, i.e. the others fished, and I was looking at the concentration of these grown-up men, squandered on catching fish; what a boring hobby!"

Months later, a letter from the Dar es Salaam Secretariat made him exclaim with astonishment.

Mutti came running, "What is it? Has something happened to my sisters?"

"Always thinking the worst, Lili. No, not at all. Mr. Mitchell is engaging me for work, on the very loosest terms, as a consultant to his office. I am to do no more than send a copy of what I record about native customs."

She was jubilant, "At last, Hans, at last somebody is taking notice of your interesting studies."

"I don't know about payment, mind you. Nevertheless it probably signifies a change in my life's direction, and, it would be fair, I think, to say that I have turned Social Anthropologist."

TO OUST A DEVIL

Papi's pseudo-employment gave him the excuse of devoting his time entirely to social anthropology, which meant increasing Sefu's responsibility for the labourers.

Sefu was slim, tall, with delicate hands, a long face without the breadth of nose or thickness of lips associated with some Bantu tribes. His height was emphasised by long trousers worn to indicate his chief headman position. Mutti regarded him as an example of how intelligence and honesty could combine with a charming disposition to produce a self-assurance impossible not to respect.

The intensified studies doubled the number of informants, so that it was not only Saidi Kapota I found occupying my chair but also Shyza Kulwa, or Shigera Gusa, or Katoto Masolwa, or Mihambo, or Sungura Shilinde, and many others.

Papi found it difficult to concentrate in the dining-room where his open plan construction allowed the sound of my lessons to reach his ears.

Unfortunately mine were not the only interruptions.

"*Bibi,* the egg vendor has arrived."

"You know I've told you not to call me '*bibi*' any more. When we were at Arusha with our friends, the boys called her '*Mamsahib*'. "

"*Ndiyo*, Mamsapu."

"Oh, very well then. I'll come in a moment... Darling, read to yourself for a while. The servants don't seem to be able to test for the addled eggs, probably too lazy to put them in water."

At lunchtime, my father declared he'd had enough of her voice, "I shall build a temple, and remove myself."

"What do you mean, Hans?"

"An office, just a box of a *banda*. I'll get some men to start tomorrow so that I can escape the 'German sergeant major'."

The finished 'box', a hut with a shallow pitched roof, bow shaped windows, rolled reed matting fastened over each, had an arched doorway. On either side of it, the wall was stepped back to demarcate the porch, Papi's architectural fancy. It stood at the top of our hill, where the stony ground had prevented the growth of sisal. Mutti called it his 'Swiss Chalet', he insisted it was 'Greek'.

I saw him sometimes, shuffling a few dance steps on his way down from the 'temple', happy because he had written a Swahili poem, or learned the secrets of the 'Porcupine' mutual help society, or an initiation ceremony, or having been taught a charming melody.

Some of the workers singled out for questioning were reluctant to talk of sacred matters, such as ancestor worship, or were afraid of retribution in divulging the ingredients of black magic. Of them Papi wrote: "I often was able to fill out the dead interval between the first acquaintance, and the final trustful friendship with recitations of poems."

Finding they were appreciated, he also read them to the labourers on his evening visits to the camp:

"You clouds, migrating swiftly across an endless sky,
Take home with you my greetings, bless, as you hurry by.
Passing over homesteads, my old folks you must greet,
Where I go, I'm stranger to every town and street."

By the last verse of *Longing*, his migrant workers were in tears, he told us, their responsiveness touching, so that he was spurred to write more for their pleasure.

At lunchtimes I raced up the hill to call him from the temple, and one day on our return, a cruel fight was being waged near our kitchen. A wasp flew hither and thither in front of a tarantula to distract its attention. The spider, black in contrast to the yellow coat of the enemy, rocked back and forth on its many legs, attempting to catch it, but avoiding the sting as the wasp dived upon it. The combatants were so engrossed, that we, their growing audience, were disregarded.

It was perturbing to witness such ferocious emotion in insects. Ants killed in a dispassionate way by means of outnumbering the enemy. This was a personal battle, evidenced in the way each combatant devised his next move. I wanted to save them from destroying each other, Shabani restrained my hand from using the stick I had picked up, saying this was an important event not to be interfered with.

The wasp continued to harry the spider until the latter became too weary to move, at which moment, the insect dived upon its back to sink the sting between its black hairs. The spider's legs curled up as the poison paralysed it. Instead of flying off victoriously as I expected it to do, the wasp began tugging its victim away, but a third enemy, Shabani, captured both insects in a piece of rag, folded over upon itself to form a tiny bundle, and carried it off to the boys' quarters.

Papi explained that the drama took the right sequence. If the spider had killed the wasp, Shabani would not have bothered with it. "The spider represents an opponent. A man who wears the dead insects in an amulet strung from his neck, acquires the advantage gained by the wasp. The protection covers his family and his property. It is a magic insurance."

The paddy fields of the previous year's flood gave way to ridge and furrow cultivation which forced us to make detours, unless there was a ready-made path between the sweet potato and cassava plants.

Mutti was dragging an unwilling Peter on a lead to stop him from tearing through the *shambas*, when a familiar sound struck our ears, the beating of tins, used to scare birds from filching grain from sorghum fields, only this time the beat was louder.

Within moments we knew the reason for the urgency. A flock of birds fluttered and wheeled in the sky, where a dense cloud moved towards us obliterating the sun as a swarm of locusts flew only metres above our heads, with the corporate power of uncountable wings. Walking underneath the moving whirring canopy was eerie. It was unending and coming lower.

Peter yapped uneasily, my mother quickened her step with a terse, "We'd better hurry home."

Before we had gone a few paces, one flank veered from the main stream to descend upon everything around us. There was a rustle, like that of crinkling paper, plants swayed with their burden and keeled to the ground, the noise of jaws tearing through leaves was everywhere. Locusts massed on top of one another, crawled over each other, hopped with a "thwack!" in their eagerness to reach a green leaf.

I was terrified in case the thousands of bodies should clog up my nostrils and mouth to suffocate me, but fortunately we were of no interest to them, and though some were pushed into us by others, it was amazing how accurately they could miss us.

Hurrying back, we slithered on an unavoidable carpet of insects, horrible to squash underfoot. A few still circled the air, the rest had settled for the night. Before long, the entire camp turned out with every available utensil to catch and roast what was considered a delicious evening meal. There was a whooping and a whistling, a laughing and shouting, a running about as if it had been a festive occasion. It was in everyone's mind that, having lost a crop, there was compensation in gaining another.

Days later, when the locusts had chewed their fill, and the population had eaten their surfeit of them, the remainder took off in small swarms, leaving a barren plain except for the unchewable sisal leaves.

Not long after Papi's change of gear, a letter announcing the visit of a Government official to see about his terms of employment caused a happy stir.

"There you are, Lili, we are going to have somebody from the administration."

"You mean one of the *wabwana wakubwa* (important people) is coming?"

"I don't know how eminent! Not quite the Aide-de-Camp to the Governor, I should think," he teased.

"But how nice, Hans, an Englishman in our house again, after all this time since Rusegwa."

"You can paint him on the wall, a memento of the occasion!"

Mutti laughed happily. She baked her special sweet cheese tartlets, Mohamadi was asked to have his caftan white, and Ramadhani offered to stay, ensuring there would be instant hot water for tea.

During the afternoon, the tyres of a car crunched their way up hill on our dirt track, bringing the welcome gentleman for an all round handshake. I could tell from the tone of his conversation that he liked the situation of our house - much gesticulating in the direction of the mountains. The name 'Usambara' flew back and forth in a way, I imagined, an echo might have done. The flowers in front of the house aroused interest, the 'elephant ears' growing in half *debes* on the verandah parapet received a patronising pat. Notice was taken of the reed awnings, the method of stringing them up during the day drawing special attention.

Once we were seated round Saidi's tea table, the man looked up at the poles and cross beam carrying the roof, and asked my father to explain the construction. He "oh!-ed" and "ah!-ed" over the dwarf partition between verandah and dining-room, and even Mutti's old paintings met with his approval.

Despite the smattering of English my mother had taught me I could not follow the fast flowing talk. When addressed, my confusion increased, because though I could pick up the meaning of words, sentences were beyond my comprehension. "Aunt yoo lucky to halve yoor mummy to teech yoo?" flummoxed me.

After tea, the gentlemen left to go up the hill. I, upset that a language my parents could speak fluently should be as foreign to me as Kinyaturu, went to my room to regain my self-esteem by painting with some of my mother's water-colours, until later when the visit sounded like ending.

Orange and soda was being served, our guest declining the sherry especially bought for him. He seemed to have made instant friends of my parents, still waving from the verandah doorway as his car rattled downhill.

Years later, risen to the rank of Government Sociologist, Papi chanced to come across an early file in which a memo bearing his name caught his attention. It was the man's summing-up of his visit: "The family lives in very lowly circumstances, I suggest shillings 'x' would be sufficient." The sum mentioned was paltry. It ensured our continued poverty.

My father, oblivious of the insult perpetrated by the treacherous visitor, meanwhile hoped for a reasonable remuneration. After the first cheque arrived, any hopes of my going to school were dashed.

In addition, another educational disadvantage cropped up when my correspondence course had to be abandoned. "Can't stand this Nazi praise of the Teutonic race," my mother complained, adding vehemently, "let the devil take them!"

"Na, na, Lili! be glad you can say things like that without being liquidated."

This was the German 'thing' again. Was it that which was worrying my mother about Aunt Erna and Gretl?

From then onwards I was left with the old books, and her memory of what she had been taught in primary school, a situation which made me lose all interest.

"Let her read books," Papi said soothingly when Mutti was near tears of frustration.

Schiller, Goethe, Dostoyevsky, all had their turn in my hands, their themes beyond my comprehension, their phraseology an acute pleasure. Gaining facility in language opened doors of which one was verbal chess.

To my mother's remark, "You must learn, otherwise you will remain uneducated, think of your cousin Erika in Germany and how clever she is." I replied, "But you don't like Germany."

"That's for different reasons."

"What reasons?"

My mother registered the sort of disgust shown when an addled egg is mistakenly cracked into a bowl containing fresh ones. She added a theatrical shiver, like a pinch of salt.

"We must get on with the lesson, darling."

"But you haven't said why."

The first sign of irritation crept into her voice, "Darling, that's enough questioning, be a good girlie and find the dictation jotter."

"Why must I find the jotter? You haven't explained about Erika being clever in a place you don't like."

She looked confused, like Shabani when she told him that in Europe servants wore black dresses.

"Well then," propitiatorily, "shall we do drawing instead?"

"Why?"

I knew it was checkmate - a grand slam. This game was endless and certain of a win, the attainment of one move ahead, a goal in itself.

Back at the dining-table again, school books spread before me, pencil twiddled idly in an unwilling hand, I felt as confined as Mucki, whose "ching-ching!" chain made the only noise in an eventless day, unless he broke into his "Huh-huh! Huh!" call at the approach of a vendor whom he greeted with screeching, baring of teeth, raising of eyebrows and bobbing. He made a better 'watch monkey' than Peter a watchdog, thereby making us take notice of his agitated dashing to and fro during an early afternoon when no one was expected, and the servants were not about.

His calls became terrified screams, echoed by my mother who had dashed out to investigate, followed by Peter's howls merging with both. She returned at a run with a swarm of bees after her, the expression on her face that of an animal pursued.

"Schnell, raus! (Quickly, out!)"

I joined her headlong flight through the back door, instantly aware that it was a life-death situation. We ran without a backward glance past the empty kitchen, through the sisal along a contour line, which provided a path of sorts. I in front, and she somehow managing to give her high heeled shoes wings. The bees stopped following, but we kept running, knowing how vulnerable we were in our cotton clothes, a target for thousands of angry stings which could turn us into poisoned pincushions in seconds.

When we reached the camp, Mutti, gasping for breath and forced to walking pace, panted her repeated thankfulness to fate, "How grateful I am that Hans was not - huh! - huh! - with us. He is so heavy in his gait." Being the time of day for families to take an indoor siesta, we roused Mama Panya to explain our plight. Resolute as always, she hauled out two chairs, bade us have a rest in the shade, and went to a neighbour with a convalescing husband to persuade him to reconnoitre the situation at our house.

Hours later, when he declared it safe for our return, we found Mucki dead, stretched in human attitude full length on the ground, a vivid reminder of what we might have looked like. Of Peter there was no sign until much later when he appeared dripping wet, obviously having saved himself by reaching the river. It took a long time for Mutti to remove his stings.

The killers remained swarmed together in possession of the top branches, a few lookouts buzzing to safeguard their new home.

"What will your father say?" my mother muttered repeatedly, "what will he say to this catastrophe!"

"How foolish!" was what he said. "What a narrow escape! How silly of you to take flight, Lili! Running is guaranteed to attract the swarm in its vindictive mood. Why didn't you jump on the beds and pull the mosquito net down?"

Mutti defended our action hotly, "Hans! If you had had bees in your hair, you wouldn't have been able to think so straight either!'

He conceded that we had acted in blind terror - on the spur of the moment, nevertheless illogically.

I will never again follow Mutti blindly, I promised myself, I'll always...

A honey gatherer who had heard the news offered help and brought bundles of green sticks for action. The awnings were lowered, lamps lit in the darkened house and my mother and I remained indoors as though besieged by the alarming smell of smoke filtering through the reeds.

Papi provided the details later, "You see, Nkasiwa sat up-wind, adding more and more green wood to a fire which made a billowing cloud of smoke. Nothing else was necessary, simple ideas always work best. After a while the bees, bemused by smoke, made a grumbling noise, some flew up from the tree, circling about as if to spy out the terrain. The noise increased alarmingly as more joined in, like old women undecided what to do. I was afraid that the approach of sunset might make them look at our roof for night shelter, but no! Suddenly the whole swarm marshalled itself half a metre above the tree, and flew off in one concerted action as if by command."

That night in bed, remembering my anthropomorphic Maya, the gentlest of bees, I wondered why ours had acted so ferociously.

"Because they were an East African killer strain. You just happened to get in their way," was Papi's explanation when he said good night.

Both white magic for curing, and black for cursing, were served by concoctions of vegetation. Papi having obtained permission from a sick man's family to accompany their 'doctor' on his walks in search of the required plants, set off on a stop-and-dig, or stop-and-cut, tour.

"What's happened to the patient?" Mutti asked, after the last of his walkabouts.

"He is up and down, I've decided to leave them to it in case his condition worsens."

"But Hans, surely we could give him quinine or aspirin, or something."

"No, his malaise is only partly physical, the rest lies in his belief that either he has neglected his ancestors or is the subject of a black magic vendetta. Therefore leaving him to the cures administered by his doctor is the only hope for recovery."

The first report of the use of medical plants, having brought a reply from Mr. Mitchell's secretary indicating the Government's interest, Papi organised a foot safari to the foothills of the Usambaras where he would establish a base camp for forages with his informants. Tin trunks and newspapers would serve as plant presses, Shabani as factotum, and a few labourers gladly offered to porter.

"*Ach*, darling," Mutti looked sadly down the hill where the column of men was turning right into the avenue, "nothing interesting for us in this God-forsaken-monkey-land!" She was proved wrong when a bearer brought a note from Papi. "A *banda* is being built here for my use, ready in a week, you can then follow with the child."

Her eyes lit up, "Darling, at last we are going on safari too, and we'll be able to stay with Papi during his investigations, won't that be nice?"

A week later we were on our way, led by one of the porters carrying the food *kikapu*, followed by another with a tin trunk containing bedding and clothes.

The path led through old plantations of rubber trees, which Mutti said had been planted in German times when they hoped to tap latex, however, the sap was found to be inferior. The trees were now being used for building poles.

After the forest, the terrain widened out into sloping grassland becoming steeper when we followed a stream between shoulders of hills. The picnic lunch was short, Mutti being as keen to keep climbing to reach Papi's *banda* as I was to show off how several hours of walking were not tiring me out.

By the time we reached Veruni, a small village situated on a saddle of foothills which defied our approach until we had climbed the steepest, the late afternoon had turned chilly. Smoke curled from the hut roofs in wisps, reminding our noses that something more than sandwiches was welcome.

It had been a long walk, the last section agonising for my blistered feet. Mutti, by contrast, tripped along in her high heels like a doe antelope on its dainty hooves, showing no sign of abrasion.

Papi, standing in the doorway of his *banda* to greet us, called for tea and to our surprise poured it. Mutti praised the cake baked by Shabani in his makeshift stove, refrained from unpacking her contribution, a Wiener strudel, and voiced her relief to hear that we were to enjoy hot food and a bath.

During the meal we heard that there was a surprise in store, a special sort of *ngoma* due to take place days later. Too weary for enthusiasm, I longed for nothing but my bed. There was none!

Instead, four forked sticks, dug into the floor of the tiny side verandah, others placed criss-crosswise, and some gunny bags laid on the frame, formed the lumpy substitute, though once the mosquito net had been lowered from the rafters, sleep came easily within its cosy confines.

In the morning, Papi went off to meet with villagers, leaving us to have a holiday from lessons. Years later he wrote: "I enjoyed every bit of life, for instance when I lived for weeks at Veruni, in a little grass hut... and participated in initiation ceremonies, collected medical plants and became an unobtrusive member of the community."

At breakfast on the verandah, we looked out onto a flank of hill where the night's mist was being torn by the rising heat. Presently, goats distributed themselves on the slopes, smoke curled from banana groves among which the tips of grass roofs showed above curving leaves. Mutti wished she had brought her paints.

On the evening of the *ngoma*, villagers hurried by, shouting their conversation as they drew further apart, perhaps the way in which communication was possible from hill to hill.

An acrid smell drifted across from the village where spears of flames were visible at the back of a palisade. It was time to go, Shabani carried our folding chairs to a place behind some women sitting on the yard floor, their menfolk stood talking in groups, somewhat aloof.

While the drums were being tuned, my father explained that we were about to witness a *Ngoma ya Shaitani* (Dance of Demons), a method of treating psychiatric disorders, mostly suffered by women.

The drummer struck up a fast tempo, one beat of the left hand to two of the right, "boom-ta-ta, boom ta-ta!" his accompanist syncopated the beat on the smaller drum. In the middle of the yard, and wrapped in a red *kanga*, huddled the possessed woman facing her 'doctor', grandly sitting on a chair and already gyrating his upper body behung with beads and iron bells, to the "cha-cha-cha" of a seed-filled gourd. His feathered headgear terminated in a bobbing leopard tail. The seance had begun.

Each demon previously exorcised had a signature tune, to which his ex-victim reacted by shaking violently before breaking into a frenzied dance, aided by rhythmic clapping.

It was a wild scene of ecstatic movement, though in the dim light of the fire and a few lanterns hung on poles, I could only see the whites of the women's' eyes and teeth as their faces grimaced in the pain of re-enacting their spirit's power over them.

The driving beat of the drums throbbed in my ears, resonated in my bones from skull to toe, until I too felt light-headed and ready to dance. My mother watched the *ngoma* with a look of embarrassment, I could see she felt out of place, Papi was too busy listening to an informant to notice my squirming.

Exhausted, the dancers sat down, except the possessed woman who had not stirred until the redoubled efforts of the drummers made her shake and cry shrilly, while her doctor bobbed, swirled his arms, and sang to challenge her demon to reveal himself.

I heard Papi's informant telling him that her convulsions and inarticulate cries were the manifestation of her demon's possession of her.

The drums throbbed unbearably, the excitement of the onlookers mounted, until a final "boom!" - silence. In the stillness, the doctor questioned the woman to ascertain her demon's name, which must have been forthcoming because he seized one of her arms, pulled a knife from his loincloth, slashed the air with it a few times, and with everyone gasping in horror, prepared to cut or stab her.

I was not at all sure whether he was acting or serious, until he sank the tip into her arm, and began sucking at the blood and spitting it out. There was no doubting his belief that he was ousting a devil.

The woman, relieved of her spasms, sat up looking dazed but normal. The onlookers registered a moment of relief before the drums started to accompany the women's resumed dancing. Using the change in mood, my mother thanked the nearest bystanders and made her excuses, the *mtoto* was tired and must go home. I was glad to be led from the intense scene and even more relieved to climb under my mosquito net where sleep easily possessed me.

Mutti and I went home after a week to return another time for a brief visit. Nearing journey's end, the *banda* by the stream, we were met by a group of older children dressed in grass skirts, bodies daubed in lime except for eyes, nose and lips. They began to sing and sway, refusing to let us pass. Just as the situation threatened to become unpleasant, Papi came down to greet us. "Give them a few cents," he shouted.

Mutti scattered her change to their delight and we were allowed to proceed. He explained that they were male novices attending puberty circumcision rites, which permitted them to give short performances in return for money.

Seeing males in skirts destroyed any notion I had harboured that my own might detract from the masculine virtues of which I felt so proud.

Trunks packed to capacity with pressed plants, notebooks full, my father eventually returned, feeling he had gained much from studying another culture and writing down fact.

'Writing down' had become keywords in our household. Ceremonies, songs, names of plants and their uses, figurines, everything was being recorded on paper for posterity. I felt left out of the activity until one night, unable to sleep, I called Mutti to tell her I intended to record African tales, having noticed how the servants hardly looked up at my entry into the kitchen when they were spinning these yarns.

She agreed to my asking whether they would tell them to me, obviously thinking that my project was an opportunity to have me practise my faulty German orthography. I would write, she would correct, finally the work could be copied into my best exercise book.

On Papi's departure for his camp evening, Mohamadi came to let himself slide onto a mat on the verandah, in which position he could rest his stiff knee. On our carved stool inlaid with beads, I sat waiting, pencil poised.

"*Palikuwa* (There was once) a king and his wicked cat..."

His voice promised the excitement of an unlikely tale. I scribbled the German translation into my mother's old diaries, my mind racing ahead on the options he would offer to keep the pestilential cat under control.

Presently the pencil drooped, the paper slipped off my lap, I leaned forward catching every turn of event in the plot until the moment the spell was broken when Mohamadi stopped.

"Tomorrow," he said, raising himself with difficulty by means of the healthy leg, "tomorrow I will continue the tale."

After his departure, I tried to record the story thus far. His expressive phrases jumped around in my mind, the narrative ran before my eyes like the proverbial hare I was soon to meet in seven other tales, but the word-picture reached no further than the pencil, where it met with a hand too slow to transmit thought to paper.

Having seen Papi dictate letters to my mother, I asked whether she would let me do the same. When she agreed, I took up his stance, hands locked behind my back, walked up and down several times, hard at thought, and said, "Please write 'Foreword'."

She complied.

"Now take this down. 'I am recording these stories so that when I grow up...'"

Having given a brief introduction, I asked her to date it. She wrote, "Makuyuni, 21.4.34." It would shortly be my tenth birthday, high time I felt, that I should be following in my father's footsteps.

Mohamadi's stories continued for weeks, because like Sheherezade, he stopped at crucial moments with excuses - "I must warm up the supper plates."

He was followed by Shabani, another born storyteller whose accentuated, "*Palikuwa...*", accompanied by rolling eyes, made us laugh before he had even started to describe the machination of his hares and tortoises. His stories ended with adages such as, "Beware high spirits, they may land you in a ditch."

Along the Tanga line, a spate of competitive *ngomas* was sweeping the sisal plantations, bringing groups who followed their favourite leader of the *Ngoma ya bati* (Dance of the tins) wherever it was being staged.

Empty petrol tins placed on their side, played by means of sticks, provided the beat. The songs of labourers from different tribal areas were the basis for new words and refrains. The dancing steps too, were borrowed.

Papi attended, because anything that spelled music drew him like water to drought-ridden soil. I went to absorb the excitement of the occasion.

At the first thrash of the tins, young men started the dance, showing off a pair of sunglasses, white Bata shoes, or a rakishly-worn straw hat, to the girls, who shortly allowed themselves to be persuaded to join the circle. Older men followed, and then women with their ridge-and-furrow plaited hair, oiled to glisten in the sun, swaying their straight shoulders as if hung from one hanger centred in the head. Grandmothers too had their fun, baring their tops to swing breasts empty as shrunken gourds.

Papi wrote appreciatively: "It may be observed that the African is still singing and dancing up to an age at which we know only to groan."

Our expectations of the *mwangi's* (dance leader) prowess made him dance exultantly. Helped by shrill blows on his whistle to the beat, he brandished a fly switch to exhort the dancers to wilder expressions of movement, sometimes singling out a person in front of whom he gave his all.

His bare upper body glistened with sweat, his thigh and calf muscles bulged with the effort of cavorting. Knees bent and legs astride, an attitude which lent him ferocity, he scattered the nearest bystanders when he broke out of the ring, his passing breath as hot as a dragon's. The man-ness of the man was like the maleness of a lion - I had only seen one in a picture book - but I felt it stirring me.

One of the dance leaders became a hot favourite with our camp. He had a particularly fine physique, enhanced by a dazzling smile. I found myself infatuated by him, no doubt as were my black sisters. My erotic feelings were new and embarrassing, hot in places, urgent, driving me to see him again and again, so that every ruse had to be used in getting one of my parents to take me to attend his *ngoma*. When my 'eroticism' (a word I had picked up from Papi) showed no sign of allowing me to return to a former equilibrium, I realised that I was growing older. Diagnosis, I learnt, did not make it any more comfortable.

My feelings about the sexes could be so conflicting. On the one hand, I wanted to be a man, self-assured, in command, above the giggly, demure and come-hither stance of the African girls, above the femininity and illogicality, as I perceived it, of my mother. On the other, I was in sympathy with white or black females and suffered a wave of anger if I heard the latter beaten on a Saturday night.

When males started stirring my feelings because I was a girl, the certainty that I was almost a boy was destroyed. Worse was to come.

A letter, hand-delivered by the garden boy, contained a straight forward proposal of marriage, with a final line which I knew to be sincerely meant, though it had a European ring about it, "You are my sweetheart, whom I will cherish to the end of my life."

It was from Sefu.

A compliment had been paid in that the proposal was sent to me rather than my parents. I felt flattered, then deeply disturbed when the implication of marriage began to dawn on me. After all, I was still a child. Finding myself desired as though womanhood with its physical attributes had been reached, meant that he thought me eligible for intercourse.

It was a charming letter from a family friend, requiring a reply which would not hurt him. How was I to handle the situation? Papi was not beyond asking his advice, Mutti talked to him openly, I had been taught to show him unerring respect.

When I consulted my parents they suggested I could decline the offer on grounds that, according to my people's customs, I still had to attend school and would not be of marriageable age for some time.

My reply, given to the same messenger, was an invitation to discuss the matter at my parent's bedroom window after dark, it was the only place where I could stand on my own ground this side of a wall. He, for his part, could look as though in passing by the house he had stopped to greet me.

Mid-evening, Peter's bark sent me hurrying to the appointed place to see the fez and familiar face of my suitor appearing from the shadows of the overhanging thatch.

I made my speech of thanks while he groped for my hand, conveniently kept from his reach by the wall. By the time I had explained the reasons for my having to decline his offer, he looked so crestfallen, that my own hand shot out in a gesture of friendship. He took it in a loose grip, absentmindedly, as though he was looking within himself, seeing what had been there all along.

He knows I cannot marry him, I thought, of course, he's far too intelligent not to have known. Perhaps he felt obliged to write the letter because he wants to marry and I, being the daughter of his greatest friend, am first in line.

During the ensuing silence, he turned his face away near to tears. Although the task of having to refuse him had looked difficult from the start, it had become doubly upsetting.

This was not an offer, the declining of which might tear the heart-strings of a young man in one of Papi's German classics. This concerned the rejection of a black friend by a white girl. Whatever the excuse I made, the unspoken barrier of race came between us as surely as the bedroom wall, and it hurt me as much as him.

The moonless night absorbed his figure when he went, no one therefore could have been witness to a scene which, I knew, had been sad in the worst possible sense.

By dint of Mohamadi's special position in our family, my parents suggested that his daughter Mwana Idi, one year my senior, might come up the hill occasionally to keep me company.

Having helped her to get past Peter, she stood rooted to my bedroom floor, unwilling to lower a body, which I was pleased to note, was increasing steadily in girth leaving me her slimmer companion.

Nothing I had interested her nor was there a game she agreed to play.

Mutti always came to our rescue with a tray of tea and cakes, placed on a stool so that we could both squat to share the one common activity of eating and drinking.

Her indifference to childish activities was explained the day I saw her elevated to a status I had but shortly declined, that of the marriage bed, where the new blankets were to smell of their Manchester origin, and the white of her pillows only just outdid the sheen of her anointed shoulders.

Weeks before, Mohamadi had informed us that his daughter's first menstruation had taken place, she would no longer come to play because she was confined to a hut, where women would perform the necessary puberty rites. Judging by all I had heard from Papi, that meant the use of clay figurines and didactic songs, to teach her about bodily functions, and the accepted behaviour towards men, in particular her future husband, none other than - Sefu!

Six weeks later, Mutti and I, having been invited to the wedding, witnessed her emergence. Carried on the shoulders of some camp women, like a queen termite, the ululating procession wound in and out of the shade trees. It was an important occasion, marriage of the senior overseer, and the camp watched in subdued manner until they reached the door of a new hut. Here the women bunched together with renewed excitement, in an effort to squeeze the bride through the narrow entrance, like so many termites with an oversized egg.

In the ensuing hubbub, I heard my name called to go and see her. She was sitting on the only piece of furniture, a wooden bed with slatted head- and footboard, made by Mr. Singh in Makuyuni.

Pressing the customary gift of money into her hand, I complimented her, "Your satin dress and the new *kangas* are very nice, Mwana Idi. Your pillows, sheets and blankets are very smart."

She responded with her fixed smile which in a moon-like face made the narrow eyes disappear, opening again only momentarily for the next donor's gift.

Walking out through the low doorway, I thought of how strange it was that, after me, Sefu had chosen her, and by way of an arranged marriage had paid many shillings of bridewealth in lieu of cattle. How could Sefu, such a sensitive and clever man, contemplate living with a mere lump of indifference?

On returning to my mother, watching from the comfort of a chair, she remarked, "All finished yet? *Na ja*, a small malheur, not so?"

The camp men stood idly round, secondary to the occasion, knowing it belonged to the women, of whom the young ran to each other imparting titbits of gossip amidst peals of laughter. Older ones suckled babies, admonished children, exchanged ribaldry.

"Salimaaaa!"

"*A-ndiyo-o.*"

"You are behaving as though you were about to consummate your marriage."

"Huh?"

"Yet you sit here with your TWO children."

"*Eh-eh-eh!* ...you whore Binti Kuzaza (mispronunciation of *kuzaa*, to procreate). What do you know about it!"

I glanced at my mother, glad of her partial deafness.

Another woman joined in. "Do you see Bibi Ndege (bird) over there, she had better run off if she wants... she'll never have one with her husband."

"*Ehe!* Who would have her - a goat with an empty belly on four sticks."

It was difficult to stop laughing even when, as a white girl, I should not find lewd jokes funny.

An extra flurry of excitement made us ask what was going on.

"She has been found to be a virgin."

It was nothing like the stir in the crowd caused by the appearance of the bridegroom, Sefu was dressed in a white shirt, grey tie, grey lounge suit and black shoes. He looked like a rich man striding towards the new hut with business in hand, rather than pleasure.

Popular with the men, they called to him, "May you be blessed! May your seed be many!" before he disappeared into the marriage hut, from which ululating women ran past him to a respectful distance. From there, every now and then, one dashed back to pretend she was peering between the frame and its ill fitting door.

After a while an ear-piercing, "Ululului-lulu!" rang out, taken up by every woman in the camp to a shrill crescendo.

"He has made the marriage," we were told.

It was also the signal for drinking and feasting to begin. The sour smell of millet beer was borne to us on a flurry of hot air, stirring the men into lining up with their mugs. Mama Panya and her helpers brought out large, earthenware vessels, from which the beer would be ladled in half coconut shells with wooden handles.

Sweetmeats, like doughnuts, were offered from shallow woven trays covered with their hat-like lids. We took one each, and left the gathering, knowing that we would not see Bibi Idi again until the chores of fetching wood and water, shopping in the market at Makuyuni, cooking, cleaning, and washing clothes on the stones of the river, had its effect on her waddle.

Although Sefu controlled all the business of the contract labour scheme, my father sometimes visited the plantation Manager at Gomba, to check that his men's work was satisfactory. From such a meeting he returned hot, tore off his slouch hat, called for a soda, let himself sink heavily into an armchair, and contrary to his normal manner, asked whether Mutti wanted to hear some news.

"But Hans! You know very well that in this God-forsaken place, there never is any."

"I've got some. We are moving!"

"Again?" Her look was a plea for remission from such a fate. "Where to?" in a voice of despair.

"Expecting the worst as usual!" he said teasingly. "Well, I heard from the Manager, the house in Mtarawanda is becoming vacant."

"Why?" She was being unusually laconic.

"Either Karimji Jiwanji the plantation owner is cutting down on his European personnel, or our assistant Manager and family have been recalled by the Nazi government. I have heard of a number of Germans suddenly leaving for home, possibly because they have not fulfilled the regime's expectation of their secret service in Tanganyika."

"And good riddance! I hope they enjoy this regime to which they pay such lip service, 'Our wonderful fatherland! Our great Führer!' Huh! Let them find out what reality is when they get there."

Finally spent, she remembered the subject of the conversation, "Yes Hansele, you said?"

"I said, that the house in Mtarawanda is going to be vacant."

"Really? You mean... you mean... we are moving into it?"

She was flabbergasted. Then recovering herself, "So when are they going? When can we move in? We must clean the place first of course, I must go into the kitchen and tell our boys at once."

Fate acted strangely. Within a matter of weeks, my parents took possession of the furnished bungalow from which the assistant Manager had once sent us to the Chicken Shack, still there, standing a few hundred metres away on the edge of the open ground forming the approach to what was now, our house!

ASANTE MAMSAPU

The bungalow in the direction of which we had refused to look, a sort of forbidden custard apple, during our short stay in the chicken shack, had become the promised accommodation after all.

I plumped into one of its easy chairs, wood frame furniture made by Sikhs. Their workshop in Korogwe had smelled of stacked reddish planks of hardwood from Usambara timber mills.

Mutti, true to the routine of every move, was hanging pictures and securing ornaments with the help of Mohamadi. "Bare walls, Putzi, warn a guest of a boring visit, decorated ones give him something to look at, an invitation to feel animated," she had once remarked.

Trotting back and forth, Papi sorted books, retrieved bits of plants fallen out of their pressing pages, unpacked his figurines which allowed me a forbidden glimpse.

The conventional dining-room table was a reminder that lessons would resume next day, possibly relieved by the characters from the newly arrived *Jungle Book*. Mowgli had temporarily usurped my father as role model.

"Darling, come down, it makes me giddy to see you so far up the guava. Let Katoto the garden boy pick the fruit for you," was Mutti's reaction to my imitation of Mowgli's monkey-like ability.

I swung from branch to branch, hoping the sight might aggravate her nerves, sending her back to the house.

Sunburned but without his scragginess, I reached for the fruits while keeping a wary eye on 'Kaa', in my reality the possibility of being confronted by a venomous boomslang.

"Are you going to listen and come down?"

"No!"

Disobedience spelled freedom, my body felt as if it had sloughed a skin, a sensation akin to shedding socks on a hot day.

"I am going," she announced as if expecting a navel cord to drag me after her.

My elation persisted, I imagined the three miserable pawpaw trees in the yard changed into jungle, where a chair could be fashioned from branches, a hammock from bark strips, a toothbrush from a fibrous twig like those used by Africans.

My game lasted until the realisation of loneliness struck. If only

Mowgli were there to play with me, if only I could go to school. If only... A longing for companionship pervaded my body, intense, turning into an ache, I knew it only too well because it was becoming more frequent.

"The Mamsapu says it is time for your *skooli*," Mohamadi called up quietly.

My self-pity had dispelled Mowgli's image, I conceded that lessons might be better than nothing, and followed him in.

Notwithstanding one problem, I was about to find another. The lavatory pit was covered by a cement slab, and on arrival, it had been a pleasure to sit on its box without see-sawing on uneven poles, but as I moved off, there was an eye-flicker of movement under the rim. Cockroaches! A colony of them.

Katoto washed the box with carbolic, sprinkled some on the floor, and poured the rest down the hole.

Although Mutti assured me that nobody liked carbolic, least of all cockroaches who had therefore surely packed up and gone to prettier places, I could still see somebody's feeler testing the air. However much fairy tale animals and insects had filled the vacuum of my loneliness, I did not want their kind near my unseeing end, which had to do the sitting while I waited fearfully for the tickle of antennae, or the sensation of crawling legs.

They liked their newly-cleaned quarters, increased in numbers, and on approach could be heard scuttling to danker hide-outs, a noise my mother hailed as an 'all clear' for sitting down.

It was an awkward situation, because despite inner voices which tried to persuade me that those in the lavatory box meant no harm, I was terrified.

"They live in their world, like peasants in Europe working in fields spread with cow dung," was Papi's attempt to calm my fears.

Comparison made it no easier to sit over the hole, until my permanent constipation released me from having to try. Mutti agreed to the new potty being kept in the corner, and it was then that we discovered my tapeworm, the purging of which involved a counting of segments culminating in seeing an expulsion of the head. Making sure there was no regeneration within, my intestine only showed up the next inhabitants, round worm, and by the time that parasite had been eliminated, my potty had become commonplace again.

The other invasion of our 'European' type household posed no problem.

In one of the outhouses a concrete mould supplied by an outside tank provided a bath, watched every evening by bat families, somnolent in the roof during the day. Emitting high-pitched squeaks as they pushed one another through gaps in the ceiling to get at the insects who were always making for the light, they winged back and forth, each trying to regain a foothold meanwhile occupied by rivals also shoving each other off. It was endless amusement as I lay soaking.

A sign of our re-instatement as members of the white community came in an invitation from an architect to spend a few days with his family at Mkuzi in the Usambaras beyond Lushoto. Papi had felt instant rapport with him at their chance meeting in the exclusive club.

The lorry took us through Mombo and into the mountains on a road carved from the terrain. Where I had expected forests like those in the Alps of my fantasies, there was only a scrub-like growth down to the empty stream bed.

The Ford chugged upward, begging to draw breath on an increasingly steep gradient. When Papi obligingly stopped where the road widened, my long-sought desire was fulfilled. Putting my cheek against the hot pebbly wall of a cutting, and my arms on its rough earth and protruding rocks, I waited for that inner strength to take hold of me. It did, with such heat, the sun having beaten down on it all midday, that I sprang back. There was no doubting the pulsating power of the mass.

On the other side of the single track road, the terrain fell away so steeply that the river bed was out of sight. Papi, being on the blind side, asked me to warn him should I see a vehicle approaching round the bend. Mutti had turned yellow and incapable of speech with what he called the 'Chinese phase' of mountain sickness, and the *turni boi's* face, usually framed in the cab's oval window, had disappeared, leaving only his fingers clutching at the sides, his nails white with the pressure, until we reached Lushoto where the lorry had to be refuelled.

Recovering, Mutti remarked on how the grass was a pleasant green, not like the brash colour of the fleshy sisal leaves, and their rapier thorn tips. The temperature too, was mild, had we come to a place sub-tropical?

"The area's fertility has attracted German settlement, they have named the next valley Jägersthal (Valley of the huntsman), reminiscent of feathered hats and leather breeches."

"In that case let us go on, I don't want to meet any of them, however nice it is here."

Everything German had become wicked in her eyes - they were all devils, monsters, beasts. I could not fathom how she equated her attitude with her origin, not to mention mine. Hadn't she told me jokingly how I was a 'half-caste', half German, half Austrian. The architect's family were Swiss, exempt from blemish.

"Look at the fireplace, Putzi, lovely, an example of good design, and these carpets," Mutti lowered her voice during a quiet moment after our arrival, "have come from Europe!" There was parquet flooring, exposed stone on walls, a flushing W.C., taps flowing with hot water from somewhere, electric light. It seemed to me that we had found favour with millionaires.

Our hostess grew her own vegetables, even lettuces, not to mention raspberries, eaten in muesli with cream. There was a granny as well, who minded her own business until it came to matters pertaining to her granddaughter. The two were closely linked, not only by love but by their common natures. Even I could see that the mother was merely a spare wheel.

"Come along your bath is ready," she called at six o'clock.

"I am playing."

"Stop at once and come to have your bath!"

"But I am playing!"

Granny to the rescue, "Precious, finish your game, then you and Oma will have another bit of play with your fishy in the bath, yes?"

My mother would have said, "If you don't come now, your water will be cold," and knowing how right she was, the choice was simple.

There was something else different about this household, our hostess preferred doing everything herself apart from digging the garden. Without servants, the house seemed lifeless. No sound of floors being cleaned at dawn, no furniture scraping the floor, no shaking of mats, no discreet, "*Hodi?* (May I enter?)" from a servant bringing tea to the bedside, and no chatter in the kitchen.

Morning sounds absent, the day seemed even more dreary when I looked out to find wisps of mist hanging from the rock heads surrounding the valley. A fine drizzle, fine as the sugar my mother obtained from grinding the granular sort with a bottle - castor for her cinnamon doughnuts - made it cold enough for us to borrow pullovers.

Long before going to Mkuzi, maize cobs and beef steaks had become impossible foods for Mutti, who was in need of dental treatment. "I can't afford new teeth," was her excuse for eating less because of her gaps.

After my father had gone home, persuaded that our hosts would like to have us a week longer, there was a letter from him, informing Mutti that arrangements had been made for her to visit a dentist nun in a nearby Mission. Our host immediately put his car at our disposal.

The convent was situated on a ridge, from which there was an extensive view of distant lands on the hazy plains. Did the nuns long for the kind of life people led there, I wondered, or did they look down upon them, in more senses than one? Novels portrayed them as strangely aloof women, lonely, kneeling in prayer on flagstones, murmuring words in the silence provided by thick walls like those of the Mission we had visited at Singida.

All my surmises were to be proved wrong. Just as we were being driven up an avenue, a bell must have rung in the little tower above the long white building on our left, because out of it streamed children of all ages and colour from burnt umber, sienna, café au lait, to beige, white, and black. By sheer chance we had come upon one of the Missions looking after the bastard children my father had described.

My mother stared in disbelief, "What lovely children, Half-castes!" Her face registered wonder that wicked behaviour should yield such success. "Putzimännchen, look at that sweet little one. And how healthy they all look. There is one with straight hair, and there with crinkly, and all so neatly dressed."

The younger children waved, the older ones smiled at the passing car of visitors, the shepherding nun gave us a friendly nod.

Our driver explained that the Mission was involved in all aspects of their lives, not only education, "The Nuns arrange their marriages. It is difficult sometimes because the European father has to be consulted. If he is married to a white woman, the Mission has to be careful that she doesn't get to hear about it."

Mutti snorted in disgust, "So that is what goes on - think of all one doesn't know about!"

But her disgust changed to apprehension the further we drove up hill, "You know, Putzi, these old nuns left Europe years ago, probably before anaesthetics were used, I mean, with these black people you can pull out a tooth without so much as an 'ouch!'. They're all so impassive in the face of pain."

At the surgery we were welcomed by an African clad in white, and asked to sit in a room, bare except for chairs, and that ugly crucifix. How could nuns be allowed a half naked art form, I wondered.

A whispered conversation focused our attention on a door through which came a figure swathed in so much white habit that only the face was visible, young, rosy, smiling with pink lips revealing gleaming teeth. Charmed, my mother was led away to the dental chair.

On our return that afternoon, I was shocked to find that my Mutti, who had entered the surgery looking her emaciated but friendly self, had turned into a woman who could not even broaden her mouth in a grin, had sunken cheeks, and looked ninety.

Back at Mkuzi, she wrapped a silk scarf round her head, brought one end over her mouth and tucked it back under her head-dress on the opposite side. In this disguise she remained for some months while her gums healed, only lifting the material slightly to one side during her pap meals.

When my father came to fetch us, it was a relief to be going back to Mtarawanda after the strangeness of the mountain valley, so different climatically, my parents' friends so European in lifestyle, the ladies' talk about cooking, so boring, and *Racker* (rascal) too young for a playmate.

The only time that conversation came alive was when Papi had been there, and one evening in front of the log fire, both men had stretched their relative length of leg. Papi lit his pipe, our host a cigar, and between the first deep draws he mentioned that the Government did not care whether the buildings in Tanganyika were thrown together using a load of sun-dried bricks, or were built more substantially to an architect's design.

Papi told him he had forgotten the African.

"What do you mean?"

"It's his country, and he builds from experience, light and not durable, therefore easily replaced. A new hut is a clean hut. Why should the Government wish to introduce innovation?"

"I am not talking of domestic architecture, Hans, but of larger buildings."

"Well then, we should ask the black man what he wants."

"What! One of these coolie-like individuals working on a plantation?"

"Yes. Although you are a worthy architect, you are only adapting your European-Swiss ideas to the Tanganyika conditions. Why not tap the artistic concepts of the natives?"

"Artistic?"

Knowing his way of thinking, I could see that Papi had steered the conversation round to arguing his case with examples from his collection. It was equally clear that the architect thought it impossible to get a straight answer from a black man, least of all, an opinion on form.

On the descent to Mombo fortunately for Mutti, the passenger side was next to the mountain slope. She sat in glum silence, in purdah.

Just as the engine seemed to be enjoying its reduced workload the brakes faded, and the Ford gathered speed. There was a roar as Papi rapidly changed down, thereby retrieving the situation from getting out of control. Heaving on the handbrake, he slowed the lorry sufficiently for the *turni* to place a rock forward of a back wheel, bringing us to a stop.

Mutti, forgetting herself, swept her shawl aside, "Do you want us to get out and start walking?"

"Be quiet, Lili. *Turni boi*, load some stones, and leave the tailgate down. When I shout, '*Haya!* (Action!)', jump off to place one in front of a wheel."

I was told to get down onto the floor and take hold of the handbrake. Satisfying himself that I had the strength to heave on it, we set off in low gear.

Whenever the oil smelled hot, I pulled on the brake, the wheels locked, the Ford skidded in the ruts, Papi shouted, "*Haya!*" and the *turni* skipped alongside with his rock to chock a wheel.

From Mombo onwards being on the flat, the tension remaining in the foot brake was sufficient to get us back.

My involvement comprised pride and pleasure in being a driver's assistant, halfway there to my ardent wish of being allowed to drive the vehicle. The *turni,* however, lay exhausted at the back.

Months later, gums healed, my mother fetched her new teeth which gave her more agony than the extraction of the old. Each meal was a tussle, she refusing food, my father trying persuasion, and I wondering how far similar behaviour in *Racker* would have been condoned.

Teeth and Mutti were reconciled by the time the plantation manager invited us to lunch, a great honour due in part to our acceptability now we were living in a bungalow. We were not to come in the lorry, the black estate limousine would be sent with the uniformed driver. My mother looked forward to riding on leather upholstery. Papi braced himself for several hours of small talk. "The whirring of a mill's water-wheel to the accompaniment of bird twitter," he called it.

We stayed for tea, after which the inevitable question, "How are you placed for labour?" led to an invitation to look over the sisal factory, situated at sufficient distance from the house not to offend ear or nose.

In the machine shed, the roar from the open door of a furnace, similar to the firebox of a locomotive, warned us to stand aside. The boiler hummed, the oil sizzled, drive belts slapped each time their joints passed over a wheel, "schlapp - whopp!" The European engineer shouted greetings. He was wearing khaki dungarees - I longed to have a pair myself in which the pockets could be filled with spanners - his black helper was in blue, almost indistinguishable from his skin in the darkness of the inner shed. Oily rags oozed from his pockets, he held a can with a straight spout like a stork's beak, through which oil was infused into the working parts as if the bird was feeding its young.

As we walked to the adjacent shed, a small locomotive was bringing in a row of clanking wagons, carrying the day's last loads of sisal bundles, and labourers lucky to have cadged the lift. I heard the wags shouting, "This lot's for Tungu who always says, 'I've finished.'"

"Here come the whites, he can keep the machines running for them."

And then the Jeremiah, "We'll be late, didn't I say the sun would set before my stomach could stop grumbling."

There were such men among all groups of workers, including those whose laughter was infectious. But I had also heard them change mood very quickly at the sight of an unpopular overseer.

The bundles were thrown onto a conveyor belt, workers slashed their bonds to arrange the leaves as they moved inexorably towards the decorticator. Like an animal in agony, there was a high-pitched screech when its blades scraped the pulp off the fibre.

Water sloshed inside the end of the decorticator, washing the pulp which foamed away as reeking slime in a gully. The fibre emerged dripping wet, yellow-white, to be collected and hung over wire lines in the sun like so many tresses of hair.

The baling shed was in an uproar to finish, last hanks were being compressed into their jute jackets belted by clinking metal bands until the surplus was snipped, stencils of origin and consignment sloshed on their side.

By the time we had said our *kwa heri*, the first workers were setting off for camp, the limousine ready to take us home.

The occasional parcels from Germany, no longer containing school material, brought newspapers in Gothic script, headlines up to six centimetres high, printed in menacing black.

I was told that they were not interesting for me, although my parents discussed their articles with increasing heat. The mention of Hitler-Goebbels-Göring, like the "da-da-da" of rail wheels, accompanied their talk monotonously. The word 'Jew' assumed new meaning. My parents were partly of Jewish origin, I knew, and had read that big noses and small chins remained as tell-tale features of these people, crinkly hair having been picked up somewhere on their wanderings. Some Jews still practised their religion, we did not. We also did not follow the Roman Catholic faith brought into Papi's family by his mother.

The whole subject was ammunition for his humour. He compared the two faiths with African ancestor worship, the former epitomised by the veneration of a spiritual 'father', robed and enthroned in heaven, while the other venerable had his spiritual seat up a tree.

Regarding Germans, Mutti's logic took a header, when, after calling them wicked, she also conveniently and unashamedly forgot she was one. Every anecdote connected with Europe became prefixed with the phrase, "We in Vienna..."

She lied convincingly, "*Ach ja!* The Prater? Beautiful, isn't it?"

Papi looked uncomfortable, knowing she had only spent forty eight hours in Austria while visiting his parents, but she had no such misgivings. Forced sparkle came to her eyes when speaking of the icy magnificence of Tyrolean mountains. Wagner made way for Lehar and Strauss, forgotten was Siegfried and Brünnhilde, the Danube triumphed over her beloved Rhine.

I was totally ashamed of her. My parents, hitherto, had set an example of honesty and truthfulness, the abandonment of which, I had been taught, would split the pillars of civilisation, and if virtues ceased, there would be the nothingness prevailing between the stars of the universe. Moreover I was being drawn into the lie, insofar that all I had been taught about Germany's wonderful culture had to be forgotten. Apparently I was to be ashamed of my German ancestry, though when faced with the question of where I had been born, it had to be admitted that by unfortunate miscalculation it happened to be at Mannheim - to an Austrian father, of course.

Papi, in turn, was inordinately proud of being Viennese. I felt a bastard, not because of race, but culture and nationality, and when my parents talked of "half Jews" and "three-quarter Jews", although it was laughable, there was an added loss of identity when I wondered what the other fraction was supposed to be.

My feelings did not affect anyone, on the contrary, Papi's became elated when he made another of his discoveries.

Kasungu, a plant growing in the Usambaras, he told us, could produce milk in the human breast. He had it tested on volunteering women of varying ages. They had laughed when he told them of the difficulty some white women had with suckling babies. One grandmother showed him the white fluid she could express from her wizened breasts, a young one who had not borne a child did the same. All agreed that, once a child was born, it was even easier to increase the milk supply with *kasungu.*

My father's reports of these findings must have raised interest in Mr. Mitchell's office, because an invitation arrived for him to show his plant collection to the resident Botanist of the East African Agricultural Research Station at Amani, situated in another part of the mountain chain.

A late afternoon under misty skies saw us to its rest-house, standing on a windswept ridge. Once more we experienced the cold of mountain temperatures, compensated, said Mutti, by the luxuries offered in the accommodation, indoor cooker, electric light and W.C.

Next day we heard from Papi that the botanist had recognised the milk medicine for Brassica jucca D.C., and would be helping him to identify the other plants brought in the metal boxes.

Meanwhile Mutti found herself the centre of hospitable interest.

Every day spelled a round of morning teas, at which our various hostesses made us feel like honoured guests. It was an entirely new world, to which the Ford had transported us like a magic carpet.

Beautiful gardens greeted us on our every walk to the scattered bungalows of the Amani scientists.

I knew that before we left their driveways there would be a conducted tour between arches of thorny bougainvillaea, glowing with their paper-like lanterns of flowers. I would be asked to admire the velvet of violets, to pronounce "snapdragon", or "marigold", difficult for my German tongue, and at worst, "Cape mesembryanthemum".

In the spacious sitting-rooms there was more to admire: copper trays on carved Indian tables supported Buddhas with green belly-folds of jade, porcelain figures of shepherdesses looked after ivory or ebony elephants, from a seventeen centimetre bull down to the two centimetre calf whose tail was not long enough for another to hold.

Multi-patterned Persian rugs adorned the walls, and an elephant's mounted foot with five horny nails often was the doorstopper. On the floors, snarling leopard heads lay at the front end of sprawling skins. Repugnant objects - how would humans look similarly disembowelled, de-boned, heads stuffed, chins resting on the floor?

At each morning tea party, I admired the ladies' fashionable clothes, which, Mutti explained, were bought on their frequent trips "home", where they shopped in "Bond Street" and "Regent Street".

"We, by comparison," she told Papi, "look like people from the *porini*."

"It's novel," was his curt answer.

Our invitations extended to dinner parties, at which everything, except the powdered nose of our hostess, shone. Whisky and brandy decanters scintillated, soda-making gadgets poured sparkling water, polished occasional tables reflected ashtrays and cigarette boxes. At dinner, the white table linen and starched serviettes aided the glint of silver cutlery and cut crystal. The white of caftans on the servants offset their red cummerbunds, and by the end of the evening our host's face had a sheen as well, having had his glass replenished rather frequently.

It was all splendid, in some ways intimidating, considering how we lived at Mtarawanda. Oh well! I told myself, when I began to feel ashamed of our state, this is only what your mother and father were used to in their parental homes, so pretend you have lived in luxury all your life, and act like it. I was quick to pass the salt and pepper, sugar cubes, and milk for coffee, waited patiently for the hostess to cease talking and notice that I might like another chocolate, sat upright at table, arms off, held my cutlery as taught, and kept my mouth shut.

My clothes did not really matter as there was no one with whom to compare myself, although I exchanged glances with children via their photos, the real thing long since having been sent 'home' to school.

In the absence of understanding what was being said, I amused myself by watching. For instance, there was the coffee-making ceremony: a glass percolator having been brought in reverently by one of their sashed servants, it was placed over a spirit flame. The noises made by the boiling water were very undignified. Once we had received our toy cup of mocha, the Turkish Delight was passed round with words like "*veeloo hevon*".

Shortly, I knew, my mother would signal with her eyes that I might offer to pass round the cigarette box, and if required, could even strike matches to provide the necessary flames. It gave me something to do in an evening when, once dinner was over, I would have to look suitably bright, even if the hour drew to midnight.

Unlike the treeless road to Lushoto, we had come through virgin forest before arriving at Amani. With leisure on our hands, Mutti suggested taking a walk into it. Past the laboratories, through the botanical section of the research station, and we were back on the main road, under trees grown to giant proportions. Away from the windy ridges, it was warm and wet, the ground vegetation lush, the leaves of our 'elephant ears' so large that the animals would have been proud to possess a pair.

The further we walked the gloomier it became, the soft light of day in the mountains shut out by foliage dripping audibly from overnight moisture. There was a prevailing smell of mould, worse than the one exuded by Papi's herbarium.

Apprehensive of meeting a large animal, an elephant for instance - the Mayonnaise gentleman had spoken of hunting safaris shooting big game in Meru's virgin forest - we turned back, relieved to see sunlight at the end of the forest tunnel. On either side, the leaf mould teemed with its own population, centipedes scuttled from under bits of mouldy bark, ants ran about on their errands, stag beetles lumbered over fallen leaves, spiders lurked in large nets beaded with drops from above, and frogs, indistinguishable from the leaf on which they found camouflage, waited to shoot a tongue at a passing insect on the wing.

A scream, heart-rending, stopped us in midstride, surely something had taken something else by the throat. The sound came from the forest canopy where spaces between foliage were windows to the scudding clouds. After following my gaze, Mutti sat down on a stump, "Arrrh! I feel dizzy."

Knowing I had to convince my brain of what was moving and who was stationary, I continued to look. Something large was sitting on a branch. It had a ruffle of white hair round a face with a beard, and was wearing a black and white cape over hunched shoulders.

"It's a colobus! He only needs a *meerschaum* to complete the picture." Mutti, recovered, tried to keep her eye on the monkey instead of the clouds, "You know, Putzi, the old 'men' are protected by the Government, remember the hunters who offered us their skins and whom Papi threatened with the police?" I remembered that she couldn't be deterred from taking their pathetic baby monkey.

Our last 'morning tea' was taken at the invitation of a lady who kept open house with the proviso that her guests had to drink cocoa. It was tasty, especially when served with biscuits, crisp and collared in ruffled paper contained in a tin reminiscent of Luigi's.

Another pleasure was trying out the few English words I had learned to say when asked, "Would you like to go to school?" That morning I had answered once more, "Yes thank you, I would like to go." The 'like' spoken with just enough emphasis not to sound rude, though my inclination was to shout, "Yes! I like!"

The questioner gave me a long and serious look, had my answer been wrong? "Good girl!" She smiled disarmingly. No, obviously it had been all right.

Peter went wild with pleasure at our return, I only noticed that Mutti's zinnias were curling up with dryness, that the late afternoon heat was oppressive, that reddish-brown dust lay everywhere, our house looked empty, a place awaiting a consignment of 'European' household goods, and worst of all there was the old loo box! At Amani there had been the W.C., the lid of which, after several days' inspection, could be trusted to remain insect free.

Next morning I woke to the realisation that Amani was of the past. After breakfast came the usual admonition, "Could you bring your books, you are late today."

Even the act of picking them up was anathema. What was there in them that I would want to know?

"No," I said flatly.

She insisted that although she could understand a continuation of holiday mood, nevertheless we had to get back to work.

"No!"

She pleaded, I refused. She threatened permanent stupidity if I did not return to learning, and enlightenment if I did. I was to be thankful for a lovely holiday, would I not respond by showing willingness to make a start? She appealed to my logic, my sense of fair play, "You're so much like your father, you must see wisdom in what I am saying."

I had the deaf ear of despondency, nothing would stir me into lifting a pencil. Left sitting at the table, the hopelessness of my situation struck home, more so considering I could not improve it. My bed being the only refuge, I threw myself upon it, tears came, then uncontrollable spasms of weeping.

Mutti rushed in, "Tell me what is the matter, *um Gottes Willen...* tell me."

I warded her off with my hands, desperately clearing space around myself to gasp for air. The dog came in to put his head on my bed, wagged his tail slowly, and looked at me with sad eyes which made me sob even more vehemently.

Unable to help, my mother left, declaring she would return later, "When you have finished."

Finished what? I wondered.

On his return at lunchtime I heard Papi's voice, "Stop fussing, Lili, let her find her own equilibrium." His words had the desired effect. After sleeping off my outburst, resolve returned to make the best of life. I was almost eleven and a half, an age for sensibleness, what about that bit of logic - and Mutti might make me a dress for Christmas. Had I myself not several good ideas for presents? A pouch for Papi's matches because he never could remember where he had put them; that box in which we had bought the translucent Japanese tea set would make...

Equanimity found, there only remained one bit of trouble, my puffy eyes, my red snuffy nose, what would the servants think to see me in a state more characteristic of my mother?

Life went on, lessons, walks, adult books to read, a game of cards after supper. Mutti tried to replace her zinnias with plants brought from Amani, Papi sat for hours cross-referencing his medicinal plants.

A letter from the architect's wife offered a temporary diversion; if agreeable, they would fetch me for a week's visit to Mkuzi.

My first experience of being away from my parents. I relished the thought. At Mkuzi I found the guest-house had been prepared for me as though I had been an adult. Oma was looking after a new addition to the family, *Racker* had gone to boarding school, nothing else had changed. Muesli was as good as before, the morning mist as cold as ever, the women perhaps more reconciled over the easy-going baby, the stone fire-place and parquet flooring still looked representative of superior design.

Despite the pleasure of being allotted a status, my mood seemed to be dipping, my skin felt like prickly pear, my mind out of focus. Several times during the coming days, my nerves seemed to be bucking like a Muscat donkey being driven too close to a thorn bush.

On one of my runs up to the guest-house, warm liquid trickled down my thigh, inspection showed my pants to be saturated with blood. I began to cry, how awkward it all was, just here at Mkuzi when I wanted to act like an adolescent. A knock on the door stopped my snivelling. It was my hostess, and taking in the situation at a glance, she said, "Don't worry, I have plenty of sanitary towels, just wait a few minutes, I'll bring you some." Her matter-of-fact attitude calmed me, she obviously thought I had menstruated before, and was upset over having forgotten to take a supply of towels. To be regarded as an old-timer! It showed I was making the right impression.

She returned with the packet, "It's always happening to me, invariably when I go anywhere these are forgotten. Here, if you need more let me know, I've plenty in the cupboard after the pregnancy."

Once she had left, I put one between my legs, only to discover that there was nothing with which to keep it up. Should I ask her? No, my ignorance might be detected. What did African girls do? I had heard of grass pads, old bits of *kanga*, how were those kept up? There was no string in the room, not a safety pin. In desperation, I took the belt off a dress, threaded it through the ends of the towel and tied it round my middle under my clothes. Loose garments were not in vogue in the Ladies Journals at Amani, but the sun having emerged from the morning mists, I could pretend that ventilation was welcome.

The discomfort of the large size towels made me sit as much as possible. Sore, immobilised, bored, I felt angry. This was what being a girl was doing to me. If I had been a real boy, I wouldn't be handicapped. My host, sensing frustration, offered to give me a bit of exercise by taking me fishing.

"Come along," he called on the next afternoon, "I'll show you where I have stocked the stream - in the hope of being rewarded!" How could he be so cruel? How could he put a baby fish in the water in the hope of catching it another day? Unable to protest, when he was being kind, I followed his striding figure to the stream.

It was an idyllic place. There were pools reflecting the sky and the reeds, tall and deeply green. The banks were cropped like the ones at Arusha, making them as smooth as a mushroom.

We walked up and down. He, in all his fishing regalia, cap, jacket and waders, whipped his line onto the water, stood rooted, gazing with determination at the spot where he willed a fish to bite. "No, not this time." He reeled in, on we went to some other magical spot, "Here is where I always get one." It was endless until he began to get impatient, swearing in Swiss-German.

Meanwhile the walking was causing the towel to chafe my inner thighs until they burnt with hell's own fire.

In his presence it was impossible to walk with my legs slightly apart, the only relief I could gain being from his frequent stops, when I could sit on the wettest part of the bank feeling the soothing cool penetrating to the soreness. It was an incredibly long nightmare including the bit of fishing I was asked to do.

He cast the line and handed me the rod. There was a movement, the line was being tugged. Fortunately, he snatched it from my hands and began hauling in. I watched the terror of the fish, screwing in 'S' curves as it was being lifted through the air. There was the final macabre dance of wriggling and snapping in the net, then the passing into death, eyes glazing over. Dreadful! Dreadful!

As if all this was not enough the architect, glowing with triumph, suggested, "Shall we try one more reach for luck, huh?" Off we marched up-stream in the opposite direction to the house. I slowed my step so that behind his back my tears could not be seen, not sure myself whether they were shed for the fish or to relieve my extreme discomfort. Black girls never complained, never seemed sore, nor hampered...

Another catch, and the immediate change in temperature when the sun rolled behind the rim of the valley, decided the architect to turn back for home.

"Come, we will get my wife to make you a lovely supper," he promised. Passing at the kitchen window, he held the cadavers high in triumph, "For supper, half each," he called, "you have no idea how much our young guest and I have enjoyed ourselves."

A business trip enabled him to hand me over to my mother at Mombo some days later.

"Hello Mutti! How's Peter?"

"Hello my Putzi."

My assumed adulthood waned in the first moments of reunion. The holiday had proved I could be a grown-up, could she not see how increased experiences had made me older? Rebellion surged again.

We reviewed our mutual holiday, I relating my trouble with periods, and countering her regret at not being to hand, with an airy, "I wasn't having a baby!"

Our wait was prolonged by the delayed *Nenda Mbiyo* (Go Fast), the motor Sentinel. That was its polite name. Our workers called it *malaya*, the 'prostitute' who could be stopped along the line with the wave of a hand for attention.

As unavoidable as my next period, and more certain of date, were the lessons which began the very next day. I turned the pages of the familiar books, looked with distaste at the Gothic script, picked up my pen, dipped it in the ink bottle - light blue was more friendly than black - and began to write up my holiday in Mkuzi: "I put myself under the shower every morning (a cold one), took quinine every day and still sucked my thumb."

Weeks later, in the middle of my self-imposed writing period, Mutti using the time for a letter to her sisters, my father entered holding the morning's mail. He pulled a letter out of a buff coloured envelope, read it, and looked up registering such surprise, that it could only portend matters extraordinary.

"Yes Hans?" my mother asked eagerly.

"The Government has..." he began, "no, I'd better translate for our daughter."

"The Government has considered your case and awarded your daughter a bursary, enabling her to attend the Arusha School, Arusha, as from the term commencing May 1936."

No blue Masai spear landing from a red sky could have astonished me more. My parents admitted that they had known of the behind-the-scenes activities since our visit to Amani. One of the ladies had made it her crusade to get me to a school.

Another surprise followed shortly in the form of the School Prospectus. A booklet of shiny cream-coloured paper, it smelled like the glue on envelope flaps, and contained photos tinged green by printing. The frontispiece showed an imposing building, a double storey over a pillared entrance, flanked by ground floor extensions. There was a picture of older children sitting in a classroom, ones of children playing tennis, hockey and football, another showing juniors lining up alongside a swimming pool. On the middle page printed in italic were the words FEES and beneath, "Payable in advance to the Headmaster".

Papi read from the booklet, "Shs.240/- per term for boarding, Shs.90/- for tuition, which is" - he calculated - "Shs.330/- per term altogether. Fortunately we won't have to worry about that."

On the last page was a "List of Clothing Required By Girls".

My parents drew breath audibly, my mother began reading the names of items, Papi translating where necessary.

"Three khaki gym dresses,
Four pairs khaki knickers,
One white topee, one old hat,
Five vests or combinations,
Three pairs of stockings for Sunday and evening wear."

When the thirty-fourth and last item had been read, my parents stared at each other in disbelief, Papi concluding, "But getting all that is impossible!"

My mother, for once the more practical, replied, "They don't want every item straight away, Hans. In time we shall get it together for her."

He looked relieved, "Then, Lili, I think it is in place to write a letter of thanks, a sort of '*Asante Mamsapu* (thank you lady)', don't you think?"

I had little part in what was being said, a stirring in my stomach, a fluttering as if fledglings were stretching their wings, rendered me speechless.

The moment had arrived! Fulfilment of a desire growing year by year until it had become an urge suffusing my being. Translated into simple words... I could not wait to go!

TURDS

Particles of smoke blowing past the carriages flew into my eyes, lodged in my bushy hair, but failed to drive me from one of the observation platforms on the train.

The footplates, sliding over each other, added a steady squeak to the wheels' familiar rhythm, "dadda-da-da", against the fainter beat up ahead, "chagga-chagga". All three making up a tune which made me jiggle this way and that.

Mutti, I knew, was resting after the rush of the last days, before things really did have to be packed in the cabin trunk. She looked washed out, like a khaki shirt beaten too often on the river's rocks, and in addition was so tearful that I was ashamed of her.

It was not the only reason for my remaining on the platform. Elation had reached a point when it had to fly with the same wind that was now taking my breath away, a storm of feelings. Holding on to the top rail of the safety gate, I chanted, "*Ich gehe zur Schule!* (I am going to school!)"

Any misgiving I might have had was dispelled by what Papi had told my mother consolingly, each time she burst into tears at the thought of my leaving. "Lili, do remember she will be back in the holidays. You're not giving her away in marriage." He was happy that I was going where children should spend part of their lives. Even Mohamadi admitted that he had thought my mother's tuition not very helpful of late, it was time for me to go to a *skooli*.

Any notion of returning could not have been further from my mind. My being was in turmoil, leaving only one clear vision, life had reached a stage when everything was about to change totally, irrevocably. It was difficult to grasp except for the reality of the journey, scenically, rows upon rows of sisal, followed by plains of yellow-dry grass, and clumps of acacia, growing as far as the foot of the blue mountains, above them the sky with its own trail of puffy clouds.

Mutti appeared, swaying in the gangway, "Darling!" she shouted, "Come in now it's lunchtime."

I shook my head.

"But you must have something to eat."

That was impossible, my disappointment having been too great when she brought the picnic basket. My father had eaten in the Dining Car on the occasion of his journey to Tanga, why couldn't we? She said there wasn't the money. It would have been the highlight of our trip to be in proximity of those bottles of Tomato Ketchup and Worcester Sauce, visible from the platform on the day we fetched him from Makuyuni Station.

Towards afternoon, my hair stiff, and my eyes streaming from smoke, I capitulated to a belated lunch, glad to find an excuse to come in. Mutti tried to hide her tears with a trembling smile, opened the *kikapu*, extracted a tin of sardines, inserted the tab into the key, and began winding with unusual clumsiness, spilling oil on the upholstery which immediately lost its pleasant leather smell.

Never had fish seemed so foul. Ashamed that we should be the cause of a stink about to be drawn along the draughty corridors into the compartments occupied by other Europeans, I ran back to the observation platform, refusing to return.

Why did my mother have to behave in such an insensitive manner, not to mention the fact that her thoughtlessness was leaving me hungry. I turned my face to the wind to cry in culmination of over-excitement, lack of food, and general exhaustion.

At her next visit, finding I had opened the gate and sat huddled on one of the steps, she exclaimed in alarm, "Darling, for God's sake don't sit there!"

But when I turned to ask a provocative, "Why not?" she was laughing.

"It doesn't become you. You're looking like one of Papi's puberty novitiates in reverse, you've got a sooty face. Come in, I'll wipe it."

We agreed that if she threw the tin of sardines out of the window, I would be willing to wash, and eat what remained of the lunch.

At Arusha Station our train slowed, screeching to a standstill. There was a moment of silence during which the sandwiches in my stomach turned into heavy dough balls. Mutti gathered up our belongings. "We are here," she said as if pronouncing sentence.

The Mayonnaise gentleman revealed his Mediterranean origin by greeting us with a kiss for my Mutti's hand, an encouraging hug for me. His 'Lady' was waiting at home to serve a meal which, when we came to eat it, dissolved my dough balls.

My impatience to see the school had to be curbed in favour of hearsay. "Lili, I'm not sure what goes on there. You know the girls are in one wing and the boys in the other. Well...!" She gave a little giggle behind her hand, and looked at me as though I should expect the devil. It sounded really exciting.

In the morning, after Messrs Goker Govind (as advertised in the Prospectus) had taken measurements for two gym dresses in best Stockport khaki at five shillings each, and one uniform dress in white drill for ten, we were driven to the school.

Sitting in the back of the car, Mutti in nervous conversation with Mayonnaise, I could feel my mounting excitement like cold breezes blowing down my neck. This, I thought, is the last journey before entry into a land of happiness.

A dirt road, but leafy approach, brought us round an oval flower-bed of cannas to the pillared entrance of the Arusha School, which looked even more imposing in the soft morning sun than its printed photo had implied in the harsh light of our Makuyuni day.

Behind us, as my mother and I mounted the shallow steps, the darker mass of Mount Meru stood offering a small crater lip to the sky.

My future headmaster was representative of the mountain, big, broad, and to be respected. I would shortly learn to call him "Big Sir". Unlike Meru, he was not a spent force but more like magma in spate which, combined with Welsh charm (I learnt later) made me like him immediately.

After a greeting in English, he stepped out of the office. Behind his vacated seat someone made eyes at us from a glass-fronted bookcase. Was that really me?

I heard, "Caulbety, wilyoo!" It was the first time the teacher - pupil tone had come to my ears.

A pretty girl of my age came to show me round the school with embarrassing results, because I could not understand her English, and when she tried Swahili, it was what Papi called 'kitchen', enough for ordering soup but not for explaining how to make it.

The classroom doors being shut as we passed, I still had not seen another child by the time she left me sitting on the bare verandah floor which ran round the girls' quadrangle, a sort of cloistered area, repeated for the boys, on the other side of the entrance block.

What was I supposed to do? Suddenly the euphoria was gone. Mutti by now had surely returned to her friends in the familiar coffee plantation, but I was here after many years of longing for a school, dangling my legs in the deep ditch which served as a drain.

After a while swing doors flew open, letting through - fortunately - a boy. I was interested in meeting a white one. Perhaps he had been sent to take me to a classroom. Relieved, and attempting a bit of coquetry, I flashed a smile with the phrase my mother had taught me never to omit at a first meeting with the English, "How do you do?"

At that he was startled, murmured something in reply and fled. Perhaps he was shy, I said to myself, remembering passages in books, "Shyly he took her hand..."

After him came a number of boys, who approached me with a "How do you do!"

Each time I replied with the same formula, they laughed uproariously and ran back, it seemed to be a signal for the next to appear. Perhaps another form of greeting might be better. I tried the Swahili *jambo*, whereupon the situation deteriorated when all the boys filed back to say their version, followed by foul mouthed Swahili phrases which shocked me into silence.

This! This was what white boys were like. Uncouth louts. I turned from them, upset that my friendly overtures should have been rejected.

A little later a bigger boy showed some interest by asking me my surname.

At last somebody decent enough to ask a question, and one I could understand. Smiling with relief, I obliged. It was a name to be proud of, twelve letters long and suspected of having been derived from a similar sounding village near the Austro-Czechoslovakian border.

The boy's eyes took on a gleam, reminiscent of fighting dogs attacking Peter. His voice, charged with hatred, exploded as he mispronounced the last eight letters, and spat out the Swahili, "Chooni! (At the place of turds!)"

Dismayed beyond measure I looked away, there was no black boy in the whole of Tanganyika so rude. This supposedly was another example of his less worthy counterpart, the young European male. In Swahili I said, "You are very bad, go!" in a voice I might have used to an insolent African.

That incensed him, "Choo...! Choo...! Choo...!" he yelled, triumphant to have the last word, which hung like stench in the air behind his retreating figure.

Next day I was placed in Standard four in the same class as the boy. The girls were quite friendly, especially a Senior, Laura, more woman than girl and beautiful, who was prepared to help out with German that she had learned in a school in southern Tanganyika.

At our farewell on the platform, Mutti's small face constantly disappeared behind a handkerchief, too saturated to absorb more tears.

She would just have to get along without me was my reaction. And this outburst! And her shabbiness! I was pleased to be rid of her. Papi by contrast had merely wished me bon voyage, he never kissed me of course, both of us knowing it would be effeminate. Striking a theatrical pose, ridicule glinting in his eyes, he had chanted some silly verses about, "Now the darling daughter goes, mother's got a runny nose..."

We had laughed as the train pulled out of Makuyuni, Mutti and I waving to him and Katoto, at that moment exchanging farewells with the rowdy third-class passengers leaning from their carriage windows.

At Arusha Station, I resolved to be a copy of my father. I would work hard, become equally clever, as calm and logical... Mutti still standing on the observation platform, a forlorn figure, was waving her handkerchief.

The resolve was difficult to put into practice since little of what was said, and less of what was written on the blackboard made sense. The sums were beyond my capability, the teachers' words 'double *Kinyaturu',* I felt isolated from the voices around me, bored with the inner ones I knew too well.

And how did one go about playing with others? How did one interact with children? At morning break, after the distribution of oranges, young girls brought out marbles to roll and capture from each other. It reminded me of our workers' game, for which thirty-two holes were scooped out of the ground, pebbles, cowrie shells or seeds being used for counters. The men's hands flew over the area, picking up here and putting down there, until I supposed that the aim was to avoid landing in an empty hole.

Older girls sat against the verandah pillars, sunning themselves, combed their pretty hair, admired themselves in mirrors, exclaiming in horror at blemishes only they could detect. They talked in the lowered voice of secrecy, paged in magazines, and exchanged colourful cards of men and women called 'Film Stars', frequently pressed to their bosom and kissed before changing hands. They giggled at length and vindictively, I thought, whenever I caught them looking in my direction.

I possessed nothing to exchange, nothing with which younger ones would have wanted to play, and sat around on the concrete in a mood of hopelessness.

Nobody wanted to chat to me in servant language, house boys were not employed. Almost overnight the world of blacks had been replaced by hostile whites. The ache I had experienced in longing to go to school, returned amplified, but more defused, like getting malaria. Having read about those *Wandervögel*, who despite the joys of traversing beautiful European countryside, still longed for home, I recognised my state for what it was, homesickness.

My mother's weekly letters vividly portrayed the old life: "Ramadhani returned with a new wife, 'Ariga', however he sometimes sits in the kitchen like an infuriated beast. His mood is better at the moment but last week it was catastrophic. Ariga was unfaithful, he ran after her early in the morning as far as the assistant Engineer's house, thrashed her there and then, and amidst puffing and blowing, brought her back to his side of the boys' quarters. Next day he found a letter in her box from a lover at Pongwe, conveyed to the dear lady by Sefu, as he learned later."

She added that it took all Papi's tactful intervention to stop bloodshed between the men, otherwise old friends. Furthermore Papi had had to tell the servants that his Government job was merely the "relish on the maize porridge" and that with my going to school, the money wasn't there to pay for all their wages.

Mohamadi, Shabani and Ramadhani had agreed to a cut.

She was now hoeing every afternoon like an African *bibi*, to keep the weeds down, and carried jugfuls of water to stop the newly-planted zinnias from wilting.

How glad I was not to be at home, party to the constant money worries, in fact I was just beginning to find a glimmer of understanding in what was being said, "Don't rub out mistakes, write the word again!" reiterated by the mistress known as Mama Chui (leopardess), an ex-missionary, more cat-purr than scratch.

She dressed immaculately in thinnest cotton probably dating back to the English summers in the garden of her employer's estate, where she had tutored "gurls" in a middle class milieu. Her lank greying hair, drawn into a bun at the nape of the neck, contrasted with thick brown eyebrows behind glasses. Striding along the cloister verandahs in brogues (they bloomed into court shoes with curved heels, on special occasions), she was an incongruous figure, the top all delicate flower patterns, at the bottom end, the lace-up leather shoes clomping. Otherwise, she was a passable adult, except when it came to the slightest overstepping of respect on the part of the boys, when her spear-like eyes bored through them leaving their insolence limply impaled.

On my twelfth birthday, a tin arrived with a melted chocolate cake, 'congratulations' written in peanuts by contrast with those I had observed, which had candles spiked with iced precision. Mutti's best wishes accompanied a report of Papi's work. There had been a letter of dismissal from the Government, followed by one asking him to collect ten cases of botanical specimens relating to poisons, and the one said to produce milk.

Taking it for granted that the first letter was from an over-zealous clerk, she and Papi were off to the foothills of the Usambaras, with tent and provisions, and accompanied by 'doctors' whose use of the poisons *mfeike* and *kioki* (*Catha edulis forsk*, and *Girendenia Condesata wedd*) was a Black Magic secret. The cases were to be shipped to an Oxford professor wishing to conduct a laboratory analysis.

Mountains! - But no! - that life was no longer for me. I was pledged to learn, had even begun to enjoy myself. Returning from one of the afternoon games, exhausted but content to have used up my energy, which always felt like dynamite waiting for the fuse to be lit, I was met by a group of girls trailing behind their messenger, "Laura wants you, you'd better hurry." They herded me to the locker-room, perhaps to share in my surprise.

Laura, long eyelashes like so many ants' legs, hair cascading to shoulders supporting, to my envy, an adult bosom, stood with her companions, staring at me with interest.

"Open your locker!"

I went to my bedside clothes box to fetch the key, the need for which had seemed strange from the start, since nothing in our houses had ever been locked.

Opening my locker, there! A rogue soap dish. The two halves, mismatched, looked as though they were about to allow a hatchling to escape.

A whistle of disbelief escaped from the lips of the Seniors. Everybody looked at me with astonishment, and I at them. Something showed in the pools of their eyes, stabbing at me in accusation.

"No! - No!" I shouted, too upset at what I read there, to find words for my defence.

"*Ja! - Ja! Du bist ein Dieb, nicht wahr?* (You're a thief, aren't you?)" Laura mocked, smirking with the pleasure of a bully. "You took Bo's soap dish out of her locker, and put it in your own, somebody saw you."

My throat contracted, breathing became difficult, my head felt swollen, fit to burst. The allegation was heinous. I tried to argue my innocence, Laura pointed out the foolproof evidence to the contrary.

Unable to bear the calumny, I rushed to the refuge of my bed, where embittered outrage began to set off a spasm of uncontrollable sobs, interspersed with gasps for air. Never had anyone called me a thief, or liar, because such epithets did not apply to me. I would run from such injustice, but where?

The slur to my honour felt like a slash in my soul, worst of all, word of the incident went round the school, so that pencils, pens, rubbers and rulers were hidden under desk lids with a glance in my direction.

School, which I had thought would bring undying friendships, a 'strudel-for-ever' place, turned out to be a rotten egg.

There was no relief from the teasing and tormenting, for which a life with adults had not prepared me. My parents, receiving blow by blow accounts of my struggle to survive the cruel tongues, were spared the mention of my nickname.

My mother seemed unperturbed about my predicament, Papi's work filled her pages instead. He was investigating 'Rite de Passage', attending boys' initiation and circumcision ceremonies based on rebirth into manhood.

I remembered his conversation at mealtimes; novices had to crawl through tunnels of thorn bush, representing the trauma of birth, at the end of which the helping hands of simulated midwives pulled them free. One of the boys would have his tummy smeared with red earth, or real blood from a chicken or goat, with a bit of their intestine placed on the area of his navel in imitation of the cord. Later, each boy was carried away on somebody's back in pretence of being an infant.

It was child's play by comparison with the initiation I was undergoing!

Imperceptibly, as my command of English increased, it was the clearing of mists from the Usambaras. I was not the only foreigner in the school. There were Afrikaners, Cypriots, Danes, English, Eurasians, French, Greeks, Germans, Italians, Seychellois, and Swedes, of whom some, like me, attempted to catch up on education, and a small number had not even experienced it consistently.

"I have an indescribable fear that I learn too little," I wrote home, "and that in a while it will be too late to catch up, it's all so confusing."

Papi, answering in one of his rare letters, told me that I was entering the age of quakes, that the buildings of my mind would shake, fit to be heard in Mtarawanda. Furthermore I should recognise that my sum total of understanding was undergoing change, registered by my fear of knowing too little, and shortly I would start worrying about being too insignificant.

"It's my personal view," he wrote, "that one always remains alone, that sharing one's inner life with others is impossible - and perhaps just as well. We live next to one another, not with one another."

His last sentence was very moving, it sounded like the opinion of one adult expressed to another, with a ring of resignation about it.

But I did need to share something with my peers. I needed to ask what they thought about the purpose of existence? Was it there to make me suffer a wave of emotion, when the stillness of dusk gave the playing-field another dimension? Or was existence for making friends, improving knowledge, winning approbation? The questions remained with me like the faint whine of mosquitoes. If I slapped one down, there was guaranteed to be another making the same annoying sound.

Big Sir was not only a headmaster, but an ex-missionary turned minister. He was also a tenor, a husband, father, mechanic and, so I heard, a friend to many local people in need of advice.

This big man, a strand of brown hair always stealing over a high forehead to an oval face, distinguished himself by wearing grey flannel shorts, not seen on any other male in the territory.

Oozing authority, as well as compassion, his lessons were

fascinating even when the subject was arithmetic.

"Does anyone know how long ago paper money was used?" There were guesses spanning from Queen Victoria to the 1918 armistice. I knew better, "Please Sir, Kublai Khan had paper money."

"Very good! and who was Marco Polo then?"

"Please Sir, he was a man selling things, he travelled from Ven-Ven-"

"Venice?"

"Yes, to stay at the palace of Kublai Khan, and came back with silk material." I rambled on, relating what I had read in one of my father's books.

"Very good indeed!"

Big Sir turned to the board to divide Shs.36/55 by five.

Behind his back the children turned to stare at me in disbelief. When he left the classroom, the boys began their teasing.

"Choo... has recovered from being constipated in er..." Francis pointed to his head.

"She's got diarrhoea instead, you know, words, words!" Jake blew a raspberry.

"Shut up! Take your filthy talk to the bushes if that is what you need." Susie came to my rescue.

Before long I had climbed to the top of the class for general knowledge.

"Ask Choo... sorry, I mean...!"

As well as that, my feet were planted on various rungs of the ladder in other subjects, and I was going up. Writing utensils found their way back to desktops, pupils turned to me for extra information, so that the approach of the holidays brought the spectre of spending a few weeks without my new friends, whose male element was already reviewing favourite pastimes.

"When I get home, I'll drive the V8 again, you know what a good sound comes out of that engine, doum-doum-doum, into first gear, grr-um, and vrrrmmm, off!" - from John.

Some of us gathered round to hear more. Francis obliged, "Yea, I know, we've only got a Ford box-body. Last rains we got stuck in black cotton soil 'cause dad wouldn't put on chains before he got into the *mbuga*. He can be real cussed, you know! I had to put the jack on a woodblock shoved in the mud... jacked up each wheel in turn, before we could put the chains on."

"What happened next?" The boys, familiar with these situations, loved to hear the story told again.

"A real almighty kerfuffle! While dad sat at the wheel shouting, 'Bloody car, bloody mud, bloody wogs, bloody God damn everything!' the wogs and me pushed. You know, '*Karambe ho! Karambe ho!*' and all that! It was a heck of a noise, with more of them pushing by the minute - if you meet one wog in the bush, there'll be half a dozen others near - but they got us out. Bloody well, God damn!"

These tales made me so envious. "How did you learn?" I asked him.

"You see, Choo... all you have to do is watch your dad and take over when he agrees. Mind you if you'd mine," he rolled his eyes, "perhaps it'd be better if you gave a few cents to your driver."

He, like me, had probably never seen a woman driving on her own, and considering that I was a girl - not in mind, of course - my chances of pushing an accelerator were nil.

The other hobby was shooting. Lions fell at their feet, holed in the heart. Bull elephants were pursued according to their tell-tale steaming dung until they charged, whereupon dad would dispatch them with one bullet from a big calibre gun. Rhinos chased and dented their lorries as easily as Ramadhani bent petrol tins.

Girls looked forward to sewing: dresses, underwear embroidered with French knots. The Greeks cooked, bringing back soft biscuit buttons rolled in icing sugar, which made a dust-storm in the mouth, like the little devils playing round the corners of our house. The English from southern Tanganyika swam, provided the crocodiles remained at the other end of their lake.

During the last days of term a girl, slim, blonde, and pale from her stay in England, asked whether I could spend a week of the holidays with her in the Usambaras, up from Korogwe.

Mutti's welcome at Makuyuni was tinged with tears of relief. The Ford bumped us home, offloading me to a tumultuous welcome from Peter and his new mate, Buyum, an Airedale. Shaking hands with our servants felt strange after being removed from contact with black people, and the sight of Papi was a shock, I had forgotten how short he was, and fat.

Sefu was there too, "*Jambo*, Mamsapu Mdogo (Junior Lady), *habari gani?* (how are you?)"

We exchanged news of Mwana Idi's new baby girl. Later I heard from Mutti, how, despite the arrival of the offspring, she was being unfaithful. Sefu had sent her packing several times, back to Mama Panya and Mohamadi, with a demand for the return of his money, a declaration of divorce.

After a few days at home I began to feel that there was something queer about the ideas and expressions of Mutti and 'Vati', as she had begun to call him in her letters, telling me that with my advancing years, it was time to adopt a more adult form of 'father'.

Their characters were radically different from those of the school community, whose ethos I had begun to absorb. I sensed that in my ordeal of the bully-fire, the tempering had produced a slightly different metal. Severance from my parents' world had begun, that was why the other at Arusha was accepting me. Or was it?

Before boredom provided time for further reflection, Josie and her parents came to fetch me.

The adults introduced themselves; Mohamadi served tea. The mother, tall and blonde, praised the cakes; the father, an ex-army major with an appropriate moustache, smoked a pipe with mine. Views were exchanged, then it was time to go, Mutti putting on a brave face at my premature departure.

The mountain road after Korogwe, narrow, hardly frequented judging by the tufts of grass growing on the ridged middle, ended in a clearing high up in the virgin forest, where a few whitewashed buildings looked lost in the secondary vegetation.

The car stopped in front of a bungalow, built on a high cement foundation, we mounted steps to a verandah, and there, apart from sleeping, we stayed for the rest of the week, amusing ourselves with board-games, books, and puzzles between meals.

The house held us captive, yet from it, a vista of valleys, slopes of tropical forest, thick with those hardwood trees, asked for exploration, perhaps confrontation with animals and birds, as strange as at Amani. But when I suggested a walk, Josie's mother opened her eyes wide in consternation, exclaiming in her warm throaty voice, "Darling! There is nowhere to go. Sweetie, you are not in London now, you know, with Regent's Park at your doorstep."

"Couldn't we go with you?" I asked, desperate to move the quantities of food eaten in boredom.

"But darling, I am working, and you wouldn't like it where I go, an office..." she made a deprecatory gesture. "I'll tell you what though," her eyes lit with pleasurable thought, "next time I'm in Arusha for half-term, I'll take you both to Nairobi to see a film."

Nairobi! I had heard of licentiousness, orgies of drunkenness, indulged in by some whites in Kenya. A trip there promised excitement though it would have to wait.

Mohamadi served Mutti's finest cashew-crumble and guava tartlets on our return. Josie and I, munching and silent, heard Vati talk about his studies, and her father disclose his directorship of the Bantu Educational Cinema Experiment (B.E.K.E.), which was attempting to make films for blacks about such subjects as soil erosion, infant health, hookworm, cattle disease...

My mother fortunately pushed the tartlets in our direction.

"You see, Hans," - I could tell her dad was warming to Vati's "Very interesting," - "the Government is quite keen to dress up these old subjects, especially as it's had no success in teaching the Africans to learn new ways."

Vati responded by telling him that Africans did their own teaching not only by visual means but also by the use of song.

"Now that is most interesting." Josie's father was impressed. "One of our remits has been to study the mental concentration of black audiences. We're in an unknown field here, therefore the work is experimental, able to incorporate innovation."

"And do you play a film star?" Mutti asked of Josie's mother, having heard only half of what had been discussed.

"Goodness no, Lili, I wish I were, instead of keeping B.E.K.E.'s accounts."

The major could not be stopped. "Tell me more about this singing, Hans. Our biggest snag so far has been the silence after the instructor's dialogue. The film might be showing successful crop rotation, but the whir of the projector draws more attention than the agricultural message."

Josie fidgeting with disinterest, and Vati mentioning African songs - he would probably expect me to sing an example with him - made me ask whether we could go and see the new kitten.

An innocent remark by Josie on our return to school could set Jake off, "Do you know, Choo... sings wog songs during her holidays."

Packing the cabin trunk for my return was an ill-concealed pleasure. I left, knowing that Vati was scanning the weekly post for a letter from the Director, who was asking his boss in London to release funds for my father's employment.

Back at school, I heard the Seniors relating their holiday conquests in whispers, "...he... it was gorgeous... cross... damn likely." They showed each other bits of letters, exclaiming, "Hell what sauce!" Giggled, threatened, "Sock him one next time!" or admired, "I'll be jiggered, he dared!" They laughed, tossing their heads to make the curls fly, lifting their legs in kicks of exuberance like those zebra. Of me they took no notice, I had become a nonentity.

Little Sir our standard master, a geographer at heart, missionary by choice, and teacher by profession, guarded his most cherished possession, making it available to only those whom he could trust to turn the large and magnificently coloured pages of green, yellow and brown - a rare spot of white here and there - framed by a brightly printed blue: it was his Atlas.

His religious fervour was such that it precluded him from becoming riled. He battled with his own indignation, tried to curb his anger, until human nature winning over principles made him leave the room to save someone from a wrung neck.

When we followed his enthusiastic descriptions of the earth's convoluted crust, when he let us feel the frustrations of the doldrums, the exhilaration of the trade winds, terrified some of us with talk of the unpredictable nature of volcanoes, it became impossible to desist from joking.

"Please Sir, will Meru erupt?"

"No, it has blown its top and has a caldera like Ngorongoro."

"What about Kilimanjaro, Sir?"

"It will erupt again, sometime in the future."

"Will you be at the top, Sir, to make your observations?"

A furious glance was supposed to silence me, his frown deepened to ditch proportions. "No, because it won't happen in my lifetime."

"Don't they feel earthquakes in heaven, Sir?"

The ditch became a crevasse.

Little Sir and Mama Chui had been up the mountain in an exercise of mind over matter, she had told us, for what had begun as a walk through coffee plantations, virgin forest, and then twenty foot high heaths, had ended in dragging one foot after another in the refined atmosphere of Kibo, the snow-covered summit.

"There was peace beyond understanding as we stood looking at clouds below us in the sunrise," Chui intoned. Little Sir had been more interested in the steam rising from the crater.

The boys asked whether Mama Chui had noticed the legendary leopard spoor in the ice, and laughed surreptitiously when she questioned its existence.

In Little Sir's lessons on Hygiene and Elementary Science, the discussion of fly foot pads gave rise to so much mirth, that he threatened, "If you are not going to listen, you will not be allowed lessons this afternoon, you'll hoe the school garden instead."

He knew our every minute need of education, not necessarily recognised by some boys. "Who wants to be like these D.C. wallahs sitting in the *boma*, sending poor wogs to prison for not paying bloody poll tax."

"Look at my dad, he didn't go to school for too long, but he can do everything. He's been a car mechanic, planter, gold digger, game ranger, and he's pretty good with the natives. An occasional 'wallop!' you know what I mean, and they'll do anything for him."

Some tales had a different ring, "Things got so bad, we started eating maize meal."

"You're telling me! We only got meat when dad afforded cartridges."

Some boasted of hardened feet because at one point in their lives their parents could not afford shoes. Others admitted to having been helped by blacks who allowed their parents credit on beans, maize and milk, when repayment was unlikely.

Despite such kindness, my friends despised blacks, excepting their own servants and labourers, of whom there were glowing reports of faithfulness and diligence.

I recognised that it would serve no purpose to tell the children of initiation ceremonies, expressive figurines, melodious songs, or the pulsing rhythm of the *bati*. Derision would have met any mention of Papi's opinion, that the African had a culture worth studying.

Although I was striving to learn, there was no resisting the urge to tease Little Sir's earnestness. "Could you tell me the date, please Sir, when Henry the Eighth married his seventh wife?"

"You know perfectly well there were only six."

"If he stopped at six, why couldn't he have stopped at five, or four, Sir?"

The more my cheek expanded, the greater was the laughter in the class, and with such forays into subtle insolence, and consequent success as class jester, in addition to a fearlessness of adults one of whom I had almost become before time, I gained a self-assurance which earned me the improved nickname of 'Cocky'. It provided the chance to pay some people back.

My parents were pleased to hear the teasing had been reversed, their fortunes, too, looked like changing. "On Saturday a letter arrived from the Director of B.E.K.E.," wrote my mother, "asking Vati whether he would like to be his assistant for one or two months."

Once a year parents brought sandwiches and cakes to help us host the inter-school sports for the children of three other nations.

The largest contingent, the Greeks from Moshi, ran their legs off as though they were defending the Olympic tradition.

The Afrikaners, their parents farmed the plains on the other side of Meru, looked like adults, but numbered a handful. Broad, freckled, and smiling, they never managed to lift themselves over the high jump.

The Germans from Oldeani were disciplined, aloof, and triumphant.

Unease filled me at the thought of my affinity with them, considering my friends looked askance on their regimented behaviour, and had been warned not to get into an argy-bargy.

When the teams mounted their lorries at sunset, cheered by our "Hip-hip-hurrays!", the leader of the Afrikaners turned to Big Sir with an invitation, "Headmaster, yous must breeng your best soccer teem, man, to play wid us, we expect yous pronto!"

In due course the day came, giving some of us girls a chance to go as cheer supporters. We travelled standing in the back of the hired lorry, holding on to its raised sides, thrilled to be on an outing.

The other side of Meru was as dramatic as Vati's "torso with head blown off" had led me to believe. There was the mountain, not only headless, but with most of its middle blown out. A crumpled image of its former tectonic heyday.

Stopping by a shack, we saw the opposing side assemble, the arid plain being the playing-field.

Eddie our goalie took one look, "Jesus Christ Almighty, they have got a mixed team!" The girls, buxom as the boys were stocky, could only be distinguished by longer hair. During the game, it was difficult to know whom to cheer on.

On our return journey, the late afternoon breeze whipping curls off my face and song from my mouth, I saw the undulating grassland rolling interminably to the western horizon of pink and purple, beyond which must lie the smoking mountain Oldonyo Lengai.

It was a volcanic landscape, some hillocks covered in grass had been vents, I imagined. A desolate place, uninhabited, therefore as lonely as I knew Tanganyika could be. And so still out there, where there was no tree to bend in a breeze. So still and so enormous, beyond human scale, too full of emanations touching me from the past, and - possibly - of the future, I could not absorb them, it was too soul sore. I wanted to cry out, "Hold it! hold it in!" It was dreadful, an experience which moved through every bit of me. Like encountering somebody reaching out for an amount of comfort I could not provide.

The sun sank quickly, as it always did once it had inclined too far towards the rim of the visible world, shutting away images for the night. The children continued singing, the lorry driver switched on his headlamps, warning us to duck under the boughs of the avenue leading back into Arusha.

My father's seconded employment with B.E.K.E. at Vugiri enabled me to take a lift in Josie's chauffeur driven limousine at the start of the next holiday.

I found a short-term home, wild plants in *debes* for the verandah, signs of a garden round the house on its enormous plinth, and learned from Vati that the German design was meant to keep rooms cool and undesirable tribesmen out. Vugiri had been a German sanatorium.

The place was in full swing, counting four white men, three wives, servants, black camera crews and support staff.

He was in great fettle, enjoying the rehearsal of black employees in their most melodious songs, recorded for background music. Actors, especially actresses, he said, were difficult to find. When they made a filmlet to show why maize meal should not be given to young infants, the chosen mother, sitting with the baby on her lap, bawling for the life-taking gruel, hid her face behind her hands and giggled just as the camera rolled. "Women are years behind their men in sophistication of the mind, steeped in tribal customs. Offered the minimum of schooling, they miss the recipe for an elastic horizon."

In contrast to his enthusiasm and concentration, I did not know where to focus mine, Josie having gone away with her mother.

In the afternoons when we took the dogs out, I walked past the impenetrable forest, realising that even out in the open we were trapped in the loneliness of vast regions, mountains untrodden, valleys allowing the eye to travel and travel, not an interruption in sight except perhaps for a buzzard, and the clouds, if any, hanging like forgotten linen in the sky.

It was such an enormous canvas, overwhelming, plucking self-importance from me, drawing me into its own need which I could not satisfy.

The experience was so disturbing that I broke the silence by asking Mutti to tell me the tittle-tattle she had promised. "Oh that! But you have reminded me of something else. Remember Vati's encounter with Hemingway? The architect sent us his latest book, *Green Hills of Africa*. You are in it. Vati is called Kandiski, has bandy legs, Tyrolean hat and leather breeches, and is supposed to have said that you are like the Heinz Tomato Ketchup on the daily food. What do you say to that!"

I was nonplussed. Later reading the relevant pages, I thought Mr. Hemingway had summed up my father nicely - apart from the caricatured figure.

Each day made me more homesick in reverse for the Arusha School. I longed for my friends, my tormentors even. Never again do I want to feel so lonely, I said to myself. Inactivity made me deeply unhappy. How did black children cope? Their life was organised by the big divide, before and after puberty. Their childhood was short, the girls doing what I had never done, helped their mother, the boys herded goats or calves, fished, or roamed to trap birds and small animals, something I hoped never to do. Suddenly these 'play' activities ceased, replaced by initiation rites and circumcision. Bang, hey presto! they became adults overnight! The girls pushed into marriage, and child bearing, the boys into man's work, and male sexual activity. Did they not long to get away to explore the world?

They had little chance. How many could read, and if they did, where was the literature in their own language to fire the mind as Vati's books had fuelled mine.

In the following week, the B.E.K.E. box-body brought up a letter for Vati, a Government directive advising him to proceed to Sukumaland for anthropological research after termination of the film work. An offer of salary would follow.

Mutti was over the moon, "Hans, how marvellous!"

"The lion-kill before he has charged."

"But Hans, the Government is actually offering you a post!"

"Sort of," he conceded. "We'll see what else is in the offing."

"Money! A fixed salary!" Mutti's voice rose with happiness.

"Have you not noticed an omission?"

She looked blank, "What?"

"Accommodation!"

"*Ach so!* We can keep our house at Mtarawanda, can't we?" Her jubilation was gone.

"Mm, for a while only."

What of my opinion? Not another chicken shack!

COCKY

Before leaving, Vati accompanied the B.E.K.E. director on a tour to show the new batch of films, incorporating African music and light-hearted dialogue for tuition by entertainment.

Mutti wrote of her loneliness. I sympathised with her, in my mind's eye the old sanatorium stood empty, on the verandah its ghosts of past German consumptives coughing discreetly as she went by with the dogs.

There was one consolation when Vati's return via Arusha enabled her to take the train to meet him.

"B.E.K.E. is closing in May," I heard him tell the Mayonnaises at our family tea, "despite excellent reception from the Africans wherever we showed the films. Crowds waited to see the *sinema.*"

"What did the District Officers think, Hans?"

"Some welcomed the new era of the instructional film, others - you know the benign smile of the Administration when it is totally disinterested - heard only the laughter, the delight of people hearing for the first time their own songs recorded, and wondered how entertainment could possibly be a way of instructing."

"Do you think that films, music, etc. for the improvement of this territory could be considered by the Administration?"

"I doubt it. The Governor in Dar isn't interested, and B.E.K.E.'s funds are finished."

"What a pity," the 'Lady' remarked. "All those songs which Lili tells me your little band recorded, what'll happen to them, a record or two? Trala!"

Vati rose to her taunt, "Not quite. But yes, you really don't know what a rich culture of music in form of harmonious songs and varied dance rhythms exist all around us. The European ear tends to hear the drum beat and the European brain thinks it is just a 'noise'. It is the same with the songs, the refrain is heard as a monotonous chant, and the harmony is lost in the prejudice. One day, African music will be 'discovered'."

"Oh really, Hans!" She sounded piqued. "You're full of strange notions, aren't you, dear? I'm sure Lili, like me, can only make out the same old 'bang-bang" on the drums, and the rather monotonous 'ho hos' that accompany what you call 'song'."

Vati would not let her get away with that, a lecture was in the air. I left the room quickly to find the baby and its ayah before becoming involved.

What strange notions white people had about the blacks living around them! I was to find more of that shortly.

At the school, Saturdays were marked by the concession of being allowed a walk into the town to buy necessities. Older boys found them particularly pressing, in reality they gathered somewhere for a "cig", claiming behind the teachers' backs that it was their birthright to be "smoking, drinking men."

Girls had to go out in groups, a gross injustice I thought. When I challenged the matron, Miss Vanecock, about this rule, she answered, "Because of the natives - you know." "You know" being a euphemistic phrase.

The local tribe was fierce-looking. The men's hair, ochre-plastered and ending in a pigtail, could have been mistaken for a warrior's helmet. Their sole apparel was a piece of hide fastened over one shoulder, leaving the side open for freedom of gait, and each man carried a glinting spear.

Those of warrior status, whether demonstrating an ability to defend themselves, or in sheer exuberance, were in the habit of walking through Arusha on a Saturday, brandishing their weapon. At the same time, they made noisy remarks about anything and everyone crossing their path, including us, an effective method of clearing shoppers out of their way.

I could see it was brash but good-humoured behaviour.

On our first visit to Arusha, Vati had told us about the deep-seated problem of these Wameru. At some time in their history they had begun to dress and behave like the Maasai, had developed a Maasai dialect but in fact were of Bantu origin. They adopted a bravura behaviour to prove to themselves that they should earn the respect normally attributed to the former tribe.

Our girls when walking past them, behaved like goats confronted by a lynx. Seeing no danger in their presence, I went up town by myself whenever pocket money stretched to buying a tin of condensed milk.

Like the boys, I walked openly down the drive of the school. Why not? My friends warned me that I would be detected, and when I was, Miss Vanecock assembled a sort of court martial, three lady teachers, demanding an assurance that there was neither boy nor man meeting me clandestinely at my destination. If there was none, why was I going out alone? The attraction of condensed milk was understood, but - "Haven't you thought of what might happen to you, dear, with all those wild Wameru about?"

"What, for instance?" silenced them.

The ensuing row involved the whole upper school, first because the shopping rights of girls were to be limited. I argued that differences in application of rules according to sex could not be tolerated. It was 'Cocky' cheek, but I felt outraged, insisting that if I was in danger from the Wameru, so was any boy, only more so, because there had been an incident when one of the Big Boys had tried to race his bicycle through their ranks, and another had leered at them, almost causing a warrior to throw a spear in fury.

The staff agreed to settle the matter in a move towards equality, in future both girls and boys were to be accompanied by a teacher.

In reality the boys were not required to be in the shadow of theirs! Little Sir was seen aimlessly walking round the *dukas*, just being sort of 'up town' for their protection, and the old derogatory phrases came flying my way. "It's all your bloody fault, Ch..., who in the hell do you think you are, telling the teachers somebody upset a bloody wog?"

Night descended on our quadrangle like a *buibui* (the black cover for Moslem women) shot with hot stars. If the moon added its illumination, there was no need for artificial light.

Already quietened by the aura of such beauty, the older children went to the Library for what the Prospectus called "school quiet time, Music and Prayer".

As none of us had records, we hoped Little Sir would bring his Kreisler Sonata or one of the more up-tempo Brandenburg Concertos to set our sandalled feet tapping a silent rhythm, accompanied by bowing on imaginary violins on the part of the boys. His beetling brows did nothing to suppress them, but sometimes, despite the tomfoolery, the school ethos won us over into feeling a communion of goodwill, filled with resolutions to do better, become worthy, so that the toughest among us was touched to love all things around him for half an hour.

On the polished hardwood shelves of the cupboards which comprised the 'library', lay specimens of shells, stones, a bird's nest, a snake's sloughed skin, and a few books. The *Billabong* series only came to my notice after I had mastered enough English to read them. Zane Grey was never on the shelves, I had to reserve my turn among his avid readers. After the Australian outback, I fell under his spell, riding the range, preserving the good by eliminating the rotten. My former yearnings to climb the craggy Alps were superseded by an overwhelming desire to become a tough cowboy, "keen as the wind, clean as the rain, promising as the sun at dawn, fierce as its rays at noon, kind as its farewell at sunset, humble as the quiet night," to mis-quote the "cowboy's prayer".

Outwardly Susie and I imitated our heroes by wearing scarves, inwardly I determined to fulfil all the virtues and strength of character demanded in a decent man of the Wild West, transposed to African conditions. In particular this was to be applied to friendship - to the bitter end! And to enemies - sock 'em, slug 'em, look them in the eye real cold-like and don't flinch, they will give way like all coyotes! Hyenas! Adopting ideas and character roles was fun, especially when they grafted easily onto my parents' ethics.

I came to realise that it was not the ability to read which constituted the difference between Africans and myself, but the types of books available to each of us. The fact was our mutual 'Rift Valley', a rift bottom apart, because Basewitz, Schiller, Mary Grant Bruce, or Zane Grey had influenced me by way of their books, but African children only had school readers, and if theirs were like ours, well!

"One day" - in Vati's words - one day my favourite books would be translated into Swahili, as I had translated Swahili stories into German. One day, the Rift Valley floor might rise again to the top of its walls to make us all level. The idea was obvious though no one seemed to entertain it.

My friends whom, in the idiom of Zane Grey, I valued more than any 'critter' on earth, graded like the rings in a pool made by a diving frog, Susie being at the point of entry. She was easygoing until roused, when a "You blasted fool!" came my way. Together we cursed the school, inwardly knowing how much we loved it. We swapped knowledge and she wore my dresses, though with difficulty, being taller, and full bosomed where I could not fill a brassière.

My Greek friends were alabaster like the famous sculptures with missing limbs I had seen in Mutti's art books. Tessi was particularly good-looking, dainty of feature and limb, like a dik-dik and as difficult to rear, always suffering physical setbacks.

They struggled to master tenses, "Cocky, what is this expression, 'I should have had...'"

They cried when lessons were too difficult, it was pitiful, because they were so earnest about everything. In time they learned to laugh with us, and over their exaggerated prudery which made them change their garments at lightning speed to avoid being seen naked. The rest of us had no body shame, 'b squared' and 'black cats' were standard schoolgirl slang.

Our friendship was bonded by silent outrage that our non-British parents should suffer the ignominy of unspoken second-class citizenship, when the mandatory nature of Tanganyika Territory made all whites foreigners.

Some British pupils copied their elders' attitudes by asking the Cypriot girl, "Did your father come from the Ituri forest?" that being the home of the Pigmies, mistakenly thought to be among the most primitive people on earth.

The joke about Starky whose children were "Two white, two black and one khaki" was levelled at the Eurasians.

Mama Chui's advice, "Sticks and stones will break my bones but words can never hurt me," was inept. She did not see the figure sobbing in a corner after having been compared with 'charcoal'.

It aroused my fiercest loyalties, loyalty to friends was absolute, I thought nothing could shake it.

A parting of the ways among loyal friends was occurring at home. Before my parents set off in the Ford for Vati's anthropological work in Sukumaland, I heard that our household had been divided, part left at Mtarawanda in the care of Ramadhani and Ariga with their new baby. Mohamadi had elected to stay with his wife Mama Panya to till their land, Rajabu, the mission boy turned Mohammedan, being re-engaged in his place.

Though the Government was prepared to pay travelling expenses, the monthly salary was insufficient, it would still have to be augmented by the sisal contract run by Sefu.

On their way through Arusha, not knowing where they would be staying at journey's end, Mutti had complained, "We can't go on with this safari life forever, packing and unpacking. Horrible!"

"Na, na, Lili, don't exaggerate, there will probably be an empty rest-house somewhere not occupied by a visiting High Court Judge on circuit duty."

"Pah! Do you really think we would get a Judge's place? They are reserved for the senior personnel. And for how long, Hans, do we have to live this hand-to-mouth, live-out-of-packing-cases existence?" She looked out of the Mayonnaises' guest-house window at the sagging lorry.

My father, knowing there were no answers, went out of the room.

I was happy to have a permanent 'home' at the school, removed from their life, Mutti's continuing depressions, my father's unrelenting pursuit of his interests. On their departure, I waved goodbye gladly. Shabani was holding Buyum, by now a seasoned traveller, and the monkey, having refused to get lost in the Vugiri forest, clambered restlessly over the luggage.

Vati, I knew, was hurrying to Singida to beat the big rains, but though the P.W.D. had assured him that there were no reports of trouble on the roads, he found them closed for fourteen days.

Mutti's letter described their mood: "*Ach*, I am so fed up, we could have sat in our comfortable house at Mtarawanda for a little longer, instead of the ubiquitous rest-house." She was, however, mollified by the D.O.'s. invitation to a sundowner. "He's a quiet gentleman, difficult to stir into conversation. Otherwise, he is most engaging, a handsome, elegant and tall figure of a man with greying hair."

The letter continued, "Shabani is, as always, losing his head, you know how he acts due to being near a town. When we returned at half past eight, he had gone to Singida leaving Rajabu with a message for me, that he had peeled and cooked a few potatoes and didn't know what else to do for supper. The short of it was that Vati laid the table, Rajabu made a fire, and your gracious mother cooked a meal. You can imagine what Shabani received on his not very sober home-coming, a good clout from your father."

Presently, due to the continuing closure of roads, Vati decided to take the lorry and all its passengers by rail, but there was another hold-up.

"On Tuesday we were already sitting in our compartment, that is, the lorry on a truck, the boys deep in conversation with the world of ladies in their carriage, the dogs and monkey with us, when hurried steps announced the arrival of the District Officer with telegram in hand. It was from the P.C. Dodoma asking him to wait for sanction by the Secretariat at Dar before writing out our rail warrant."

The D.C.'s unsuspected calibre was shown by a spirited reply to his superior that if nothing further was heard in twenty four hours, he would issue the warrant.

"I felt terribly angry right down in my stomach," continued her letter. "More unpacking and packing, in addition to a few more days' stay when Vati has had enough. However there was nothing we could do except put a brave face on it."

How embarrassing it must have been for the handsome gentleman to offload my parents. I could also envisage the station master's agitation, "This no good, this against regulations. The train you are now delaying, *Bwana*." Even on D.O.'s orders, Sikhs spoke their mind.

Wasn't I lucky to be at school?

Arusha was on the 'Cape to Cairo' route, imaginary for the time being because its various links were not yet forged. Nevertheless it gave the place a significance adopted by the New Arusha Hotel, which proclaimed its importance in a similar notice. And there was something else.

"Cocky, you should see the dining-room!"

"Why?"

"Round the walls..."

"Well, what is there?"

"Ah!" they exclaimed with reverence, like old Africans remembering. "*E-he*! In the time of the Wadatchi (Germans) there was a man, Emini Pasha ..."

I offered to go and see for myself.

"Not much chance of that, the owner is a real *simba*. We've tried when we wanted a drink. You'd never get in without a grown-up."

There was more gossip. In her time the lion-like owner was said to have thrown out any misbehaving drunk, rowdy American come to Tanganyika to shoot off his mouth as well as elephants, and ladies who conducted themselves beyond the bounds of locally accepted decency. Officials who mistook her premises for their Cambridge or Oxford boozing haunts were dismissed with clawed paws.

She ran her hotel flawlessly, the table linen was of the whitest, cuisine of the best, house boys drilled to military precision, guests' wishes paramount, and yet beneath those efficient claws we found her motherliness allowed our school to use the hotel swimming pool.

Kindness, though, could not be presumed upon too long. Big Sir ringing the bell at the Senior table to command our silence was about to announce a relevant surprise.

"I know," murmured somebody, "we are going to have more classrooms."

"No!" said Big Sir, who could be sitting in his office and still hear a person making for the passion-fruit creeper on the other side of his wall, didn't I know it? "No, we are going to build a swimming pool, you and I, the staff, and all our many friends."

A gasp of surprise was followed by whispers, "How?" "We'll have to collect money." "No, it'll just be a big tank - you can get canvas to put in a big hole."

"Don't be daft!"

"Shut up yourself, your mouth's too big."

Fortunately Big Sir couldn't help but smile. He went on to tell us that boys would do the digging and girls the carrying of stones for the foundations.

"Do you know, this is just like the time my dad was building our house," Garry remarked. "He wanted sun-dried bricks but mum insisted on stones and, whew! Were they God-damn difficult to get! Dad had to go in for dynamiting clumps of rocks, real dangerous when you light the fuse. Fizz! Bang! Whoosh! And if you aren't out of the way, gone!"

"I know all about it," I said proudly.

"You, Cocky?"

"Yes, my father..."

"Get away! You'd be lucky if death recognised you as human."

Boys never listened however much I tried to make manly conversation. To get their ear you had to have the femininity of Tessi, with whom every boy was in love, so that she received letters by the kilo.

Eventually when a hole of sorts had been dug, we were subject to another surprise.

"We have been asked to stage *The Tempest* as a contribution to the funds," Mama Chui announced with undisguised pride. "It'll be staged at the New Arusha Hotel."

My wish to see its mysterious dining-room was about to be

fulfilled, however, when the actors were chosen I was overlooked.

"Just a minute all of you," Chui called out, "I must admit that I completely forgot Caliban." She looked me straight in the eye defying refusal. The class began to laugh - cruelly they could see similarities - and I nodded assent, it seemed my only chance.

On the day of the dress rehearsal we were allowed entry. Below the slightly raised lounge which was to become our stage was the dining-room, wood-panelled and parquet-floored, and round the top of the walls? There were large friezes, edge to edge, depicting the volcanoes of the Rift Valley, a breathtaking sight.

Umbrella trees in the foreground, hills and craters painted in blue and green against skies of translucent white, presented a sweeping panorama on three walls, sufficiently three-dimensional to make me feel like an eagle flying through the immeasurable skies to enjoy the view. There was a smell of beeswax on hardwood combining with the freshness of what I imagined was cool rain and mist sweeping from the volcanic cones.

"Cocky!" I heard Susie - far away as though in the waters of her crocodile lake - "stop staring. Do you know how they got painted? Apparently a man came to stay who had no job, couldn't pay the bill, so he did the friezes instead."

"What was his name?"

"I think he wasn't too pleased about his work, probably signed a few scratch marks in the corners. I wouldn't go asking either if I were you, you'll probably get a sarcastic answer."

On the evening of our play, I had no eye for pictures.

"C'mon, Cocky Caliban get into your box cave," Ariel called down the hotel passage, where bedrooms had been allocated to us for changing. He could not wait to act his hair-pulling, and kicking of my behind, far beyond any measure Shakespeare had envisaged.

"The spirit torments me: O! - Oh! - Ouch!" I shrieked in real pain, to the delight of the Arusha audience. Ariel, of course, earned an ovation for "Full Fathom Five...". I, in my gunny-bag costume, charcoal smeared on my face, could only outdo him by hopping in toad fashion along the stage front, clawing the air for imagined help.

When the work of building the swimming pool was put in the hands of a contractor, I listened for the labourers' songs, the clanking of tools, the "vumm-vumm" of lorries bringing sand, cement and ballast, but nothing happened, the site looked derelict, the half-dug hole round which we had deposited our stones remained fenced off.

To my disappointment, it was all done during the holidays. The unmentioned rule made sure that we should live in a school-world where Africans did not exist. Perhaps the measure was taken in the belief that one of the boys would have called a labourer a *mpumbavu* (dunce), with the inevitable result of a furore.

After one month of safari my parents arrived at their destination, a rest-house (without a W.C.). Mutti wrote: "It's quite nice here, a real *pori*, plenty of rocks, stones all round us but unfortunately no flowers, therefore to the horror of your father, I have arranged acacia thorns in my 'vases'.

"The Sultan or *Ntemi* as he is called here, is a giant figure of a man, quite likeable and clever too. His district is very large, plenty of poll tax to collect. Up to now there has been a *ngoma* every evening called *mpuwa*. People stand around the drummer in a static circle, in one third of which the men jump in the air clapping their hands, the women stand bowed respectfully in the other, humming in accompaniment. The third segment is occupied by children."

What did they do? Probably copied their adults, lucky bastards! I thought, in my school lingo.

"There's plenty of *pombe*, you can imagine how I like that! The rest-house is not particularly big but we will be comfortable in it all together. We have already ordered you a bed, I shall make the mattress.

"Things look bad as far as obtaining eggs is concerned. Today I ordered a basket of vegetables per week to be sent by train from the garden of a retired white couple at Singida. Everything will be in running order by the time you arrive."

Exams would be thrust upon us before then for the benefit of our teachers. "Has many strong points but needs to curb a tendency to indiscretion", read one of their remarks on a previous report.

After exams there were only two questions we asked each other, "How many days to the hols?" and "What work are you going to show on Speech Day?"

Susie would exhibit a set of table-mats embroidered with lake fish, Tessi was cross-stitching a tray cloth, the boys invariably presented their letter holders, grumbling that cigarette cases were more suited to their needs.

My cut-out elephant, stumpy-legged, was like the one in Shabani's story describing a drought during which the animals stamped their feet round a dried well to make the waters come.

"*Likitu, likitu, panga pita maji atshwe! panga pita maji atshwe, atshwe!*" they chanted.

When I drew his eye, he looked at me the wiser for his experience. He had been chosen by tortoise to stand guard. The cunning rabbit had offered him honey, whereupon he allowed himself to be tied to the nearest tree in case he went wild with the pleasure of eating. The rabbit then helped himself to as much of the water as he wished to draw.

The other cut-outs, a giraffe, leopard, and colobus monkey, joined the elephant standing under a baobab three. In making the card animals, an energy seemed to pass from me to the paper imbuing it with life, my hands worked of their own accord, a creation of sorts was taking place.

On Speech Day, sitting in the dining hall with attending parents, we ranged from children of five to young men and women about to realise their dream of becoming garage mechanics and typists.

Big Sir, handsomely tall in a black gown, made his speech ring with both sadness and laughter, allowing us a range of feelings before the moment when one of the pile of prize books might, or might not, fall into our hands.

Towards the end of the ceremony I heard my name called. "It's you, go on, Cocky," my friends urged. Reaching the table, almost bare apart from trophies, I found the gloved hand of the P.C.'s, wife.

"Lovely animals, so original, dear."

Turning from receiving my book, I saw my tormentors clapping, genuinely. A quick glance at the flyleaf of the book showed a label inscribed 'Hobby Prize'. Triumph was like eating chocolate pudding. Next year, I said to myself, I want more.

When the rains ceased, roads became passable, our exams finished, and Speech Day was but a memory, came the moment of departure from school.

Feeling the early breeze, cold, blowing down the slopes of Meru, I stood waiting for the transport which would take us to Dodoma, the crossroads of central Tanganyika.

The roped trunks stood ready, Big Sir counted heads, and

Travelling Warrants, Little Sir tried to shake off a few juniors clinging to his hand to bid him farewell, probably at the instigation of one of the older pupils enjoying the sight of his smiling but embarrassed face.

Chui and the matron shepherded the smallest boys and girls, reminding them to retain their blazers and topees at least until they were penned in the Ford box-body to be driven ahead of us by Big Sir.

Once the lorry arrived, the luggage was secured on the cab's rack or stowed under the wooden benches running round the sides, before we were allowed to clamber aboard under the canvas awning.

"Shove off, Cocky!" I was told by one of the seasoned travellers.

"F... off, get away from me!" said the other along whose side I had brushed. Places continued to be fiercely contested.

"Shut your gob, and move your arse," Susie was instantly successful with boys. I was envious of her handling skills.

After the tuck box had been placed across the back, the tail gate came up, and the canvas flap was fastened down over it to stop the dust.

Little Sir, clutching his slouch hat with the guinea fowl feather, climbed up beside the driver, Big Sir waved from his Ford-ful of kids, we cheered and waved to the children awaiting other forms of transport, then huddled closer in the nippy air as the driver crashed the gears to drive us out of Arusha onto the great north road, except that we were going south on it.

The baby zebra were still kicking their legs in high spirits as we passed through the plains, on our right the shimmering soda slit of Lake Manyara against the dark blue of the rift wall - how stupid of Hemingway to talk of *Green Hills of Africa*.

The boys proved as good at recognising types of buck as they were in arguing about makes of cars, "That's a Thomson's," alternated with, "Here comes a Dodge."

Conversation became animated about Pienaar's Heights. What was so important about them I asked, forgetting about the time that Vati had mentioned how popular it was with travellers.

The sight of smoke promised food when we stopped behind Big Sir's parked car. The tuck box was handed down, he shouted, "Egg, bully or cheese!" and breathing the heavy noon air, and an occasional lungful of the *turni's* smoke, drifting from where the fire was being stirred under a huge sooty kettle, we munched gratefully, and drank from the big enamelled mugs.

Back in the lorry, a couple of boys held a competition, "Ah urp! tea excellent Bwana, you give fine dinna, Sir."

"Brr-urp! Oh yes Sir, bully extra good food." They burped away in imitation of the *duka* community.

"If you don't stop," said Susie after a while, "I am going to puke on you, ourragh!" she retched alarmingly.

When we descended to traverse the arid plain burning with a heat reminiscent of passing through the bushfire, smaller children fell asleep, sprawling loose-limbed on blazers in the centre of the lorry.

Towards afternoon we entered Dodoma, sandy, arid, a desert town by comparison with Arusha.

The small hotel, reflecting blinding light from its whitewashed walls, was asleep, the nearby station equally deserted.

One contingent of children swarmed into the hotel to use the lavatories while the driver of the next transport was shouting, "*Upesi! Upesi!* (Make haste!)" at his *turni*, and thereby obliquely at his school passengers. Known to be irascible, he commanded respect, so that even the boys greeted him with a careful, "*Jambo, habari driva?*"

Goodbyes were lost in hurried departure in order to make their night stop before dark. Next day they would face another gruelling journey through Iringa and Mbeya in southern Tanganyika, some going further to Chunya and from there to the Lupa gold-fields. Elusive Gold, Susie said, finding it was like trying to catch sight of an aardvark.

Dodoma was the point at which our teachers relinquished their duties, losing no time in disappearing to the Church Missionary Society settlement some miles out of town.

Those of us remaining waited anxiously for supper, announced by a brass gong and a smell of fish. No, not of sardines, but a nutty aroma rising from lake fish fried in bread-crumbs. In the dining-room, each table was covered with a red and white gingham tablecloth, on which stood a cruet set and a bottle of Tomato Ketchup. Invariably it was sticky round the screw top, clogged within, and needed a thump on the bottom with foreseeable results, which we shared to diminish the mess.

"You shildrun O.K.?" asked the kindly Greek hotel keeper. "You not taking too mush ketchup?"

"No! no!" we shouted. "Is there any more fish?"

It was bought from his counterpart on the down train from Mwanza on Lake Victoria, never enough for our insatiable hunger.

Without Susie life had already begun to be lonely, though still to come was the experience of the evening train and the luxury of a berth with bedding and mosquito net.

During the night I was awakened by shouts amplified in the stillness of the stationary train.

"Charly! Charly!" two voices from a man and woman, shouting in unison. Presently I could hear conversation.

"My son must be on your train."

"Bwana, I have looked, he not being there."

"I tell you he is on the train, you must tell the driver to stop until we find him."

"But Bwana, I have list, no child with your name on list. He probably arriving next train on Thursday."

"It's you!" I said, waking up to the fact that there was a little boy in the compartment sleeping in his blazer on the bottom bunk.

Meanwhile the whistle had blown for the train to leave. I urged him to look through the window, hastily pushed down.

"Mum!" he shrieked as the figure of his mother went slowly past the moving train.

The parents shouted at the Guard who was still on the steps of his van, showing the driver the green side of his lantern. Coming abreast of the couple, therefore able to hear what they were shouting, and seeing Charly hanging rather far out of the window grasping the air where his mother had just been, he realised what was happening.

The whistle blew shrilly several times, bringing the train to a stuttering halt, brakes locked, wheels screeched, a few bumpers shuddered, clanking the chains.

Charly, losing no time, ran through the corridor, onto the observation platform, and jumped into his father's arms. I passed his belongings through the window to his mum, while he and his dad ran up to the guard's van for the trunk.

After the train was in motion once more, I left the compartment door open, knowing the Guard would want the last word.

"This boy say nothing about getting off," he complained when he came round.

"No, Mr. Singh, he didn't tell me either."

"Very good," a sigh of relief rose from the depth of his belly through the breadth of a chest filling the doorway.

"You'll remember to wake me in time for Lohumbo?"

"No worry, your name on my list."

It seemed only the interval between a hyena's laugh and his mate's answering call, before he wakened me, and I stood on the observation platform shivering in the twilight cold, peering at the three dots growing into figures as the engine drew into the one shack Station.

The Guard handed me over personally, "Hello, Mr. Kori, good morning Memsahib, here is your daughter, all well."

"Hello, Mr. Singh, thank you for looking after her. Train very full?"

"Oh yes, many childrun, much work, one getting off here, one there, much responsibility."

His white turban rocked with his head as he spoke. I liked Sikhs, they were always addressed as 'Mr. Singh' though in my mind they remained Sinbads with a pocketful of rubies.

"Mrs. Kori, I take your daughter to Dodoma after holiday," he reassured her.

"Don't talk about it, I've only just got her back."

"Goodbye, Mr. Kori, salaam Memsahib." For me there was a kind nod. I was only my father's daughter. He went to release my trunk to the porter.

After months of school life, reunion with my parents felt stranger than ever. These two people were alien whites. Everything about them, their short stature, exaggerated gesticulations, their Austro-German pronunciation, even their fluency in Swahili, was uncharacteristic of the average English person with whom I identified at Arusha.

Big Sir had taken Vati's place as my role model, a practising Christian, a disciplinarian, magnanimous, though no push-over, a cowboy-type under a cassock. I did not want the religious overtone, nothing sissy, you understand, but I admired his command of respect from all manner of men.

Despite my assumed toughness, I shivered with the dawn cold.

"You'll warm up with the walk, darling."

"Where's the lorry, Mutti?"

"Almost sold!" Vati made a gesture of rejection. "You know how I dislike it. Despite the overhaul at Vugiri it gives nothing but trouble. The local Chief wants to buy it, and I'm hopeful that he will relieve me of that undesirable burden of retiring an old horse."

"Yes but 'His Highness' wants glass above the doors, Hans."

"Let him visit Venice!"

We began our walk, the porter balancing my cabin trunk on his head, Vati in conversation beside him, in front Mutti and I sharing the hand luggage.

The endless dawn landscape undulated round us, breathing in and out in slight rises and dips, still slumbering under an orange sunrise. The cold wind penetrating my blazer gave no inkling of the heat to come.

Toughness was put to the test indeed. Where, I wondered wearily, was that rest-house?

LEADER

The Uzule dawn turned pink around us. As always the sun rose at an alarming rate. One could see it moving up into the sky until, moments later, its speed was no longer discernible.

The sudden warming lent wings to Mutti's heels whereas my father and I were sinking into fine sand, and the porter spread his toes to achieve a camel's tread.

"You see the young man walking at the back?" she said, lowering her voice. "Very cheeky. *Ach*, you have no idea, Putzimännchen, what I have to suffer;" it was a jocular phrase aimed at indicating Vati's failings. "Your father likes him, and asked me to train this recalcitrant youth. When I tell him to clean the corner of the room, he says, 'What for?' like a naughty child, and instead of telling him off, Vati only laughs."

"What do the other servants think?"

"Well of course it's unfair to them, they would not be permitted such forwardness. It shows the modern trend, Vati says I must allow the younger generation of African some backchat."

At last the outline of the rest-house, which had blended into the landscape like all mud and thatch dwellings, firmed to become three-dimensional. Another dip and rise, and we were there for a much needed breakfast on the verandah, half of which had been turned into my bedroom by means of a pole and grass partition.

My locally-made bed, a wooden frame woven with a warp and weft of rope, had a damask tablecloth thrown over it to contrast with the brown daub of the main wall. A colourful mat with dog-eared corners lay on the floor, a stick suspended across one corner awaited the hanging of my clothes. Bookcases had begun to mushroom in every part of the verandah.

When I greeted the servants, Saidi Kapota was among them reciprocating with his widest grin. Part of the district being his old chiefdom, he had come to work for my father as of old.

Once again, we were an oasis in the middle of nowhere. Sandy or stony ground crunched below our feet, the Uzule sky, filled with so much light that the blue faded, arched over us. The sparse scrub responded by shimmering in the increasing heat.

Fried eggs drained of fat, unlimited amounts of bread, butter and jam, tea by the potful, reduced my ambivalent feelings about being on holiday.

After breakfast Vati called for his bicycle, Government issue for messenger boys, I was told. He murmured something about his "novitiate", and rode away into the landscape leaving us to find a way of making the day interesting. At lunchtime the dogs rushed out yapping at the bicycle wheels as he pedalled slowly back across the plain.

"Now that one of the intelligent members of your family has returned, Hans," Mutti addressed him facetiously over lunch, "you might tell her about this novitiate you keep attending."

Although he would not speak about the ceremonies, except to say that he was undergoing blood-brotherhood, one fact had delighted him. Remembering the Makuyuni clay tablets, he had traced a copy of one of the murals in the sand, eliciting great astonishment that a white man should know about them. It was proof that Saidi's artistic efforts had been spot on.

Where he had his 'brothers', my immediate world was lonely without my friends whose faces loomed in my head, whose teasing laughter and ribald conversation rang in my ears. Mutti kept me busy extracting patterns from sheets sent with women's journals by the 'Lady'. I ran the pinking wheel over printed dots, dashes, stars, diamonds, and circles to extract them, piece by piece.

She approached the activity with pessimism, "Darling, I haven't got the sleeve, is it there? Probably lost in the printing. As usual."

I continued to run the wheel, "Here you are, the lost sleeve!"

"Didn't I say we would find it in the end, Putzi?"

"No you didn't."

There was no reply, engrossed in gathering the top of the first sleeve, she did not hear me, it was useless to argue. What would my school-mates say to such inane conversation? She sat turning the Singer handle for hours between visiting the smoky kitchen. Hand sewing was left for the evening, before Vati lit his after-supper pipe and suggested we play a game of rummy or bridge.

On my first night, bedtime brought an unpleasant surprise. The biggest brass trays were stood against the legs of my bed, and the rest at the entrance to my cubicle, "In case the leopard wants to come in."

"Really? What about Buyum? You said he was to sleep on my mat."

"Don't worry," shouted Vati from the inner bedroom, "a leopard would not dream of going past anything reflecting the flames of a lantern. Besides, remember he would only be interested in the dog."

I remembered our experience with Dachsi. The thought of hearing a dog scream, and being witness to our Buyum's murder was alarming. For extra safety I insisted on all the small brass ashtrays being stood on my side of the verandah parapet so that their glint might prevent the marauder from jumping in or out that way.

On further enquiry next day, the precautions turned out to be aimed at a specific beast. A man-eating leopard was terrorising nearby villages, attacking women on their return from water-holes, when they were handicapped by carrying a *debe* of water, or when they were gathering brushwood in thickets, and too preoccupied to notice the old animal crouching above their heads.

Twice the D.C. from Shinyanga came to make arrangements with headmen to have the leopard shot or trapped, paying us a visit at the same time. "Dear Lili, I have come to sample your delicious Viennese cakes," he admitted. "Hans, I hear you are dabbling in snake charming."

"Not quite, it is more in the nature of joining a club with a useful social function, and one which keeps going by remaining secret."

"I've heard of several."

"Oh yes! Their existence is well-known, but not their ceremonies. There are the *Bufumu* secret, religious societies, and then there is the *Buswezi*, which I participated in while I was on the Tanga Line. At present my novitiate in the *Buyeye* is going well.

"There's also a Porcupine society, and one, *Busambo*, a guild of thieves."

"Really Hans?" the D.C. looked quizzically at him. "That would be rather useful for the Police, you know."

"No, I am not turning informer, if that is what you mean. My entry into any of these groups depends on a rather nervous acceptance of my credentials as a semi-native, confirmed by one of my men, Saidi Kapota, who was my original mentor in these matters. Quite a lot of what I see and hear, therefore, has to remain outside the knowledge of the Administration. After all, my brief is Social Anthropology, I am fortunate in being no London 'Bobby'."

"You do realise you are an accomplice?"

"Now you see! You D.C.s only want litigation, what about

sociological aspects. In the Territory, as you well know, deformed children do not survive. Are you going to prosecute for murder, or accept that a way out of a debacle will remain as long as it's a necessity."

"I get your point. On another matter, do you believe that human sacrifice is continued?" The D.C. bit into his third doughnut unperturbed by the gravity of the subject.

"There are ingredients of magic medicine purported to be of human origin as no doubt they were once. Nowadays it is most likely that a piece of rag containing some sort of substance is sold by one magician to another, for the real thing."

"You're being judicious!"

Seeing the conversation was becoming too one-sided, Mutti poured more tea for the men, pushed the plate of doughnuts nearer the D.C., and rose with the excuse that it was time for us to take the dogs for a walk.

I felt resentful of the way men had their serious talk to keep them occupied and feeling important. We as females, like Mutti, contributed nothing to the topic except doughnuts! In fact she had admitted inferiority by dismissing us from the discussion.

I resolved not to be like her, playing 'wife', avoiding making statements of substance by saying, "Hans can tell you far better than I can." Her deference was not dissimilar to that adopted by black females, hardly able to open a mouth of sensible sentences by comparison with their menfolk.

Before it was time to return to school, the moon waxed full, and we were fetched each evening to join a royal audience.

"Lili, our daughter, the Chief and I, left our quarters night after night at twelve o'clock," wrote Vati, "and went to places where we attended one of the big Sukuma competitive dances held between neighbouring villages. Sometimes we had to walk more than an hour, and often we arrived back home at five or six a.m."

On these festive nights, bright enough to let us see our path, Saidi Kapota walked in front swinging a lantern to discourage the unpredictable leopard, one of the other servants carried the camp chairs, and one of the Chief's men armed with a spear brought up the rear.

The path wound on interminably, disappearing into moon shadows until the distant throbbing of drums, the smell, and finally the sight of a fire, hastened our tired feet to the mêlée of drummers, dancers, and a throng of ever-changing bystanders.

The Chief sat in the lee of the smoke, next to him my father, then my mother and I, both of us of minor importance except to the women, who looked at me, estimating my marriageability by the development of my breasts, all important for feeding a resulting infant.

The chill night air refreshed us from occasional wafts of smoke, and every now and then leading male dancers advanced towards us in a thunderous tattoo of stamping feet, and clashing ankle bells, their sweating bodies shining like polished hardwood. They beat up the dust, swirling the air about our heads with switches made of animals' tails, blew whistles, crouched and sprang, tensing and releasing their muscles as near to us as possible for our admiration.

We moved our chairs back from their line of attack, but when we were almost in danger of being mobbed by the enthusiasm of the performers, the Chief smiled, nodded his approval, and thereby allowed them an honourable retreat to the middle of the arena.

But not for long. A brief respite, a drink of water, a cigarette handed over for a few deep draws, and the drummers' hands began again, like the frenzied flutter of leaves in a rainstorm.

"The *ngoma* may take two artistic forms," Vati wrote, "in one, the music and dance play the chief part, in the other they are subordinate to words." On those nights it was all movement, showing off a male's power of muscle at speed, like the forward rush of a bull elephant.

Wildness emanated from them, especially at close quarters, exciting and overwhelming. Their sweat smell was strongly acrid, their eyes revealed the pleasure of their frenzy, a knowledge of the ability to arouse similar feelings in others.

Despite being denied participation, I throbbed and thrilled to their drive - in my chair.

Vati, with the advantage of a musical education, was excited by the tunes and their harmonies. "Listen to this," he hummed a snatch as we were making our way back, "can you hear this change of key, no?" I could not, my ears being as tired as my heavy eyelids, and heavier feet.

"It is almost like an African 'Emperor'," he could not tear himself from the subject. "You know, where it goes, mta-mta, mta-ta, m-mm, and then the horns, bah-bah-ah-ah, then very deep argh-gh. Very softly the piano comes in, tada-tas, several times, and then aha! - aha! - aha! - the orchestra."

I said, "*Ja,*" only to show my enthusiasm equalled his, though for what? He was at that moment in a world I did not know, mine was the African night giving way to dawn.

At Arusha only Mama Chui was interested in native culture, she pressed my father for information whenever he visited. "How interesting," she spoke with the additional inflection of the assumed cultured voice, "you must tell me more about girls' initiation ceremonies. You see, when I was working at the Berega Mission..."

"Why not come to visit us in the holidays?" Mutti had suggested, "then you and Hans can talk into all hours of the night about his favourite subject."

The first letter from home contained the sort of news I could offer for general interest, "My mum writes that our leopard is dead."

"Eh? What was that you said, Cocky?"

"I'll read it to you." I began to translate: "'The Hehe tribesmen who happen to be here, set a trap. They dug a hole into which they put a goat, and a gun set to be triggered off. At about two o'clock during the night, they heard a shot, and ran out only to see the leopard escaping, and then found the goat shot dead by the action of the gun. They reloaded it, left the dead goat there, and the *chui* actually came back to fetch it. When he disturbed the carcass, the gun discharged, and he paid with a shot in the head.'"

The description started the boys reminiscing about traps, each gruesome tale ending more dramatically.

"Hey!" I said, "there is more, listen: 'The *chui* was indeed a magnificent beast. I went to see the stretched skin at the home of our black heroes - huge! The grey background had large and small dots, I think he was already an old gentleman. The skin will be given to our European who supplied the gun.'"

At the end of her letter the up-beat description petered out, "Everything is sad, the whole of Uzule has changed its landscape since you left."

It was awful to know her so lonely, I had to resist my conscience by telling myself that she had had her day, mine was only just starting. My tenderfoot trials at the school were over, replaced by acceptance to membership of the core pupils. Cockiness had won the day, although having lived among adults for so long, I could not retrieve the lost days of being young among youngsters, therefore the only position I could occupy was that of one foot in each camp, with a constant sliding too far one way or another, resulting in the danger of doing the splits!

On my next holiday I found my parents moved into a rest-house on a minor diamond mine, "And not a diamond to be seen," Mutti had grumbled. "The manager, a Frenchman by birth brought up in America and married to a pretty South African, has offered to help Vati in turning the 'Austrian English' of his reports into language that might be better understood by the Dar administration."

The *banda* was homely enough, after Mutti's ornaments and Vati's books had found their usual places. In front of it grew the only tree in sight, a spindly pawpaw that could have competed with my mother, and therefore cast no shade for Mama Chui's tent.

We were drinking morning tea when she remarked that clock and calendar time were happily lost in the expanse of the East African plateau, stretching for mile upon mile around us.

Mutti, with a sigh from somewhere in her emaciated middle, added that if time was the subject, she had turned forty. Wasn't it awful?

"Age becomes you, Mrs. Kori - may I call you Lili? - and besides, you have something to show for it, a fine and eloquent offspring." Chui used big words in my parents' presence, and with an archness I put down to her spinsterhood.

She couldn't help it, could she? No intercourse for so many years, a dried *kweme* (oily nut) unable to generate a shoot. It was bound to make any person lacklustre. A woman needed to swell sometimes like a gourd, yes, round and satin smooth. Mm! Some had dents, and grew squiffy necks. I hoped fervently a man would have me some day, properly, without causing such ungainly results.

Despite being passé, Mama Chui was thoroughly nice, pleased to be on holiday. Vati, I could see, hated tea with two and a half females, but played host as best he could by asking about her morning walk.

"I like talking to the natives on the way, some of whom have had the influence of our Missionaries, enabling them to discuss the Lord

Jesus, but unfortunately many are still in darkness."

"I am sure they appreciate your timely intervention."

She accepted his remarks with good humour, ready to laugh at herself. On arrival, she had brushed aside my mother's apologies for not being able to offer more varied surroundings, with the assurance that she loved walking, no matter where.

I had once heard her addressing an African, in a form of Swahili presumably meant to be middle class, "*Jambo!*"

"*Jambo, mama,*" he said deferentially in consideration of her greying hair.

"Have you heard of Yesu Kristu?"

"I do not know him." You could see he thought it safer to deny acquaintance in case the person was sought for a criminal offence.

"He was a very good man, the Son of God. You must go to the Mission to hear about him. He makes the crops grow, and the rain fall."

Convinced that she wanted to sell him something, or was mentally unbalanced, he had smiled disarmingly, "I will go tomorrow, *mama.*"

As a Missionary seconded to a European school, financially semi-aided by the Administration, she was almost in the camp of British officialdom.

We were not quite there yet. My father had no contract with the Government, his salary resembled a hand-out to a student thought worthy of encouragement. Gradually, however, my parents were being drawn into their world.

They were a group of whites apart, the rulers.

At Rusegwa, we had been the 'Austrian plantation owners'. When adversity struck, we no longer existed for them. At Shinyanga my parents were tagged 'Austrian Anthropologist and wife', slotted somewhere into the descending scale that British officials imposed upon each other. It resembled the animal kingdom of Shabani's fables, in which the lion ruled supreme, giraffe and elephant, though slightly stupid, were respected for size, hyenas and jackals ranked low because they ate foul meat, and hares and tortoises were both respected and discredited, depending on the slant of the story. Despite such variations, and because they were mammals, these animals ruled the world to the detriment of insects, fish, reptiles, and birds, believed to be of such minor importance in the order of things that they were largely forgotten.

Whatever the ranking, Vati chose to ignore it, Mutti enjoyed being invited again, and Chui acted her classy status when we were asked to dinner.

The Amani experience prepared me for the evening's rituals, such as that of 'powdering your nose' after dinner, a euphemism for a combined withdrawal by the ladies to the main bedroom for the purpose of using the only lavatory in the house. The men, meanwhile, filed out of the bungalow into the dark, or moonlit night, as the case might be, and could be found on our return in animated conversation at the verandah entrance, the host attempting to usher them back in the Maasai-like exercise of getting cattle together before driving them into an enclosure.

There followed the awkward silence of integration over coffee.

Did the men, I wondered, stand out there within sight of each other, or did they commandeer a bush, not usually available in number. I would find out.

My chance came when one of the houses had a front-facing bedroom and window. Tongues wagged looser away from husbands, and when the ladies were absorbed in conversation, I sidled up to the curtains, and gave a tug for an observation slit. There was just enough light from the house to show up the meagre growth in the garden patch, on its perimeter a few figures stood face outward like sentinels in the night, well-spaced.

"It's nice material, isn't it? I brought it from England, it's called 'chintz'," curtailed my peeping. I was forced to join the women, and their talk about lawn, tulle, and crepe de Chine. Why were women so boring? Had I been a man, I would have been out there relieving myself in the cool night air, to return to 'Uzule tribal history' which Vati was still explaining when we joined the men.

During coffee, the spirit flame writhing in the agony of heating the over-sized bulbous percolator, talk turned to transfers. It was a standard topic. "The Darwins are at Biharamulo, did you hear, Lili dear? Poor Betsy is so fed up with the lonely existence there."

"Awful!" My mother knew about finding herself the only white woman in a place offering nothing but mirage memories of company. For husbands, she always maintained, it was different, they worked with African men, sharing common interests and problems, agricultural, veterinary, administrative.

There appeared to be no way in which she could have a satisfying conversation with black women. On our walks, if Mutti commiserated over the hardness of the ground they were hoeing, they stared incredulously at her; if she remarked about the failure of the rains, they remained silent. Admiration of ornaments was giggled at, and if Mutti asked which colour was preferred, the question was not understood.

Vati pointed out that silence could be due to the fact that Mutti spoke in Swahili, unintelligible to many women in the tribal areas, and that discussion involving abstract ideas necessitated not only a much larger vocabulary than both she and the African possessed, but also a shared cultural understanding.

Somehow where he had a way of bridging such difficulties, she failed, and gave up.

Chui's evangelical activities, which included studying the Bible, allowed my mother time to paint at the improvised easel, having found a winsome child in an Arab family living nearby.

Sent with a black minder, both were plied with cake, tea, soda, milk or juice, before the little boy was hoisted into a chair elevated on petrol boxes.

It did not take more than minutes before the wide-eyed astonishment of finding himself on the rickety chair wore off and he was squirming to get down.

"How are your dogs?" asked Mutti, to divert attention. Unable to hear the answer, she hardly paused before continuing, "Oh! I had forgotten you haven't any. What does *mama* play with you? Mm? I think she is too busy growing grapes."

She stepped back, shut one eye, lifted the pencil horizontally to take a monocular sighting of his nose. Alarmed, the boy jumped off. She caught him deftly, murmuring promises of little cakes, "Mmm, you like them, don't you? Or would you like a bit of *chokoleti*? Eh?" Drawing a quick outline as she held him, "Or soda?"

She called for it to be brought, and in softer tones, ready to promise the earth, told the child-minder both could earn a few cents if the boy sat still a little longer.

Realising what advantages were in store, the former lifted the child back onto his podium seat, with strong words about him staying put.

My mother, working on borrowed time, quickly resumed the lost conversation while working furiously to capture the child's likeness,

"And your sisters? How many have you?"

I could see his expression change to recognition of content, "Three!"

"Yes of course I remember now, five," she confused *tatu* with *tanu*, "Fatima? Salima? Er...?"

"No!" he screamed, determined to have his way at last, and climbed down.

The session over, Mutti continued to sketch from memory, her first concern "the windows of the soul". Noses might be off-centre, hair somewhat wig-like, the ear lobes merely indicated, but the eyes in her portraits not only looked at one, but sometimes followed one round the room.

She maintained to paint exactly what she saw, "That mauve shadow on the lobe, Putzi? Funny I can see it quite clearly. Mauve h-e-r-e, and a stroke of yellow, so!" Brown skin, she said, reflected all the colours of its surroundings, and the portraits actually resembled her sitters, though I had never seen a mauve lobe.

Chui was as fascinated by her work as she was in Vati's studies, flippantly she remarked, "We should take notice of how our tribal people know one 'art form' we would call 'mutual help'. Don't you think so, Hans?"

"It is not quite as you put it. You may think that Africans in their daily lives are following some innate goodwill, or a fund of practical knowledge. Nothing could be further from the truth!"

He explained that he had just started studying a system of customary law in regard to the inheriting of widows by the deceased's brothers.

I could see Chui, with her Missionary background, was ready to pounce. He obviously sensed the same.

"I mean levirate, and as you are an ex-Missionary you will know about the idea Europeans have, that widows are automatically taken over by the dead man's brother, as one of your 'help-one another' gestures."

"Yes, of course."

"You see!" he parried, "it's not like that. In the first place it is the widow who chooses the man she wants from among the deceased's brothers, or kinsmen, and they very often vie for her favours for a whole year before she makes up her mind.

"There are thirteen major clauses in my notebook at this moment pertaining to the subject, and one cannot relegate the custom to a mere act of practical kindness, it is far too sophisticated for that."

Chui was impressed, "I had no idea that our Africans have such refined laws. In fact, I always thought the wise old elders just meet, have a palaver, and decide on a verdict."

Her departure ended the spirited discussions which Mutti's new-found worry about reciprocal dinner parties could not fill.

She worried over the menu, was it the right time of year for wild spinach? If the market boy forgot to buy tomatoes, how could she make her Italian salad?

I could never make up my mind whether my mother was a superficial being, or a grass stem, dried and broken by the tropics. Her knowledge of European art and literature, her amusing letters, an ability to laugh at herself, confused the issue. I dearly wanted to be of help to her, but my discontent grew until the day of departure loomed like distant headlights to the driver out of petrol.

At school, removed from Mutti's Italian salad, I found my own nagging worries - despite the satisfaction of having been made 'Leader' together with Susie.

One was still the meaning of life, especially when one side of Meru lit up in the sunset, an old cone bathed in youthful glamour to make my chest contract with something Vati might have called sentimentality, Mutti, "the romanticism of a fourteen-year old", but I knew to be a pain that asked explanation.

Secondly, why could I not attract a boy? Tessi, so fragile, but displaying a will more granite than my sedimentary rock, had hordes scurrying after her.

My girl friends had problems too. Boys! Too many. We discussed every aspect, frankly, under 'our' tree, on weekend afternoons. Boys might visit the shady spot, only to hurry away again when they found the turn of conversation serious.

"What's love, Cocky! Is it different from sex?" It was Zambuk's question, she hated her nickname derived from sharing four letters with the proprietary ointment.

"It's probably all the same if you mean the emotion between a man and woman," suggested one of the older alabasters, who admitted she might have a husband chosen for her.

"Ah-ah," I said, remembering Mwana Idi, "it ain't like that at all. You can have sex made to look like young love, under a cloak of marriage."

"Gee, Cocky, you know a lot." Tessi, of all people, sounded envious.

Maura, younger than us, therefore not of the group, came sauntering along, a lanky cheeky girl, chewing a stem to show her contempt for what she knew would be our reaction, "Get that filthy cow-pat grass out of your mouth!"

She was renowned for her agility in climbing trees.

"Do you want a lesson, Cocky, or are you big girls sitting here all day swapping boyfriends?" Somebody lunged at her but she sidestepped smartly.

"C'mon then, Madam Cockroach."

I had to tolerate her as she was willing to be my instructor.

She led the way to the tallest tree on the playing field perimeter, jumped up to catch hold of one of its lower branches, pulled her lithe body onto it, and began to climb. "Cocky! if you don't do it today, you never will."

"My legs are too short."

She descended to lend me a knee for a step up.

Weeks later on a warm Saturday, when the Seniors were lying on grassy banks, the boys smoking behind the tool shed, I stole away to the tree, rolled a rusty oil drum out of the grass, and standing on it reached the lowest branch. The chance to prove myself had come. I was 'Cocky', supposedly fearless. If I met a lion in the bush, as my father had done one day when he was reading a book on his way to finding a private spot, and looking up found the beast sitting in his path, I would do as he did, turn round, and just walk away. But of course!

Logic told me that climbing such a high tree without practice was dangerous, on the other hand, school life presented no confrontations with lions - desire for adventure won.

I began to climb, finding myself getting tired, having to rest with arms encircling the main trunk, my cheek affectionately pressed against it. Peering at the ground made me dread retreating, as much as looking up showed me the extent of height.

When the trunk swayed under my weight, I had reached the top and a stupendous view. Almost at my feet lay the barracks of the King's African Rifles, beyond them, Meru's own island of green vegetation, studded with trees, thinning where it would meet the arid plain. There was no sound except the rustling of leaves. Nothing moved in the sleepy afternoon, it was all vast, and that question - the meaning of life - bore in on me.

As a breeze began to rock the crown, I felt the sweat cool, and knew the moment for my next test, the descent, had come. Maura's words of advice rang in my ears, "Concentrate on your hand and footholds, never look away."

Monkeying downward slowly, arms exhausted, tackies slipping off branches, I was panic-stricken. "Did you know, Cocky was found stuck up a tree, blubbing." That must never happen, especially not to a Leader.

I swung from the last massive branch, let go and gained the ground.

Once dared, the performance did not have to be repeated, or was it that the spaces of heaven and earth were too overwhelming, raising the question of what connected me to it all.

Mutti in her letters provided banal answers. She had another worry, the action of the Nazis in annexing Austria. Where would she find a niche now, I wondered, to whom could she attribute the Wiener schnitzel and strudel? And what was more, I was to be ashamed of being German, ashamed of being Austrian, who was I to be? Furthermore there was the question mark as to how the British administration would regard Vati.

The next concern was her sister in Vienna. A friend had written from Switzerland, conditions were terrible in Austria. Would my parents please do something about getting Erna and her husband out, by finding them work in Tanganyika.

My mother's letter sounded truly heartbroken. We were unable to help, she wrote, having nothing more than cash for a hand to mouth existence, therefore no capital to pay for a deposit to allow their immigration. What must her sister think? Vati's employment with the Government of Tanganyika would look like a certainty that he could pull strings, as did the corrupt officials in the Nazi administration.

The possibility of Erna being sent to a concentration camp began to haunt Mutti. I knew about them; their description had filtered through in letters sent by relatives who had emigrated to Belgium, Britain and America.

Instead of seeing my ancestors as founders of culture, I had to accept that their descendants were capable of more cruelty than the most pernicious slavetraders. Leader or not, where did all this leave me?

Vati had gone to Dar to explore the opinion of the Secretary for Native Affairs concerning his future. Although promised the Department's continuing interest, his salary did not stretch to staying at the Arusha Hotel in the absence of the Mayonnaises, when he passed through Arusha.

Susie and I found him sitting, cool and comfortable, in a wicker chair on the verandah of the Greek *hoteli*.

Being a Saturday we had permission to remain with him for the afternoon, an occasion, he said, for a little party. Mr. Andreu, the proprietor, was willing to provide as many sandwiches and cakes as we could eat.

"Do you really mean that?" I asked, worried about the bill.

"Of course, this is your tea party, please order but excuse me for a short while as I have a letter to post."

"Your dad's real nice, isn't he?" Susie was appreciative of his perception of our needs.

During his brief absence we came to an unanimous decision.

"Haven't you ordered?" he asked on his return, astonished at the empty table.

"Well, no. We were waiting to ask whether you really meant that we could have anything?"

"Of course."

"And if you can't order it?"

He looked slightly annoyed, "Now come on! There's no necessity for so much secrecy, you don't want a wedding cake, do you?"

"No, nothing of that sort, but Susie and I would like a tin of Bully Beef."

We looked anxiously at him for reaction. He was incredulous for a moment, recovered from his astonishment, and said pleasantly, "If that is all, certainly! I'll go out again to buy one."

We sat back relieved. That was what I liked about my father, no fuss.

A short while later, we moved round the wicker table covered with a white cloth, half the contents of the tin in front of Susie, half in front of me. Mr. Andreu had not minded at all, in fact he had personally opened the tin, and supplied plates and cutlery at my father's request. It was a memorable occasion. Nothing could have tasted better to our craving stomachs, nothing was so satiating.

Next day he left for Mtarawanda, telling me that he had received a telegram from Sefu, a shout for help. The Manager of Gomba was refusing to pay the contract money, with the excuse that my father's labourers had become one with the plantation's workforce. He would pack up our belongings, storing the figurines and his plant collection at Vugiri, and see what could be done.

Later I learned of the drama that ensued.

A great homecoming festivity took place, involving the old hands in the camp, whom he had known for about ten years starting with Rusegwa. Ramadhani, incidentally, had become cook to the Manager, Ariga was still with him and their small daughter was wearing the latest fashion, a dress.

After the feasting, drinking and singing, that is, once the men were sober again, Vati said, he held a meeting under the shade trees to explain a plan of action, welcomed enthusiastically by everybody.

At Tanga-Amboni he went to see an old acquaintance, the General Manager of one of the oldest and best-kept sisal plantations, with whom he concluded a contract in the name of Sefu bin Salim, who was to be paid for the labourers he would bring with him, as their overseer. The arrangement included transport, half a dozen lorries or so to pick up the families and men.

Our labourers packed, possibly for the last time. It had never been difficult for them to leave one camp for another, knowing they would be together again at the next.

The lorries arrived within the week, with them the moment for my father to settle the score. He described how he was able to surprise the Gomba Manager - a recently appointed man - with an announcement that his labourers were about to leave for another plantation.

Asked why, he told the man that his deceit, as reported by Sefu, who had never told a lie in his life, had forced the issue.

Of the incident Vati wrote: "I left behind me a semi-Nazi who produced a really Teutonic rage, but without any effect, as in true African business fashion, no contract had existed between me and his Sisal Company.

"The next day we arrived in Tanga-Amboni, where I said goodbye to Sefu and my people, and returned to my studies in Sukumaland."

In his decision to move the labourers, and in making the contract over to Sefu, my father lost a third of his income, my mother a stake in the Mtarawanda bungalow. Roofless, and dependent on whether the British Government would continue to employ an Austrian who could be regarded as 'German', Vati banked on making the Administration see the lasting importance of his Social Anthropological work.

It was an enormous gamble.

TRUST

The completion of new dormitories made us girls move lock stock and barrel from the old building. Thus, the squabbling household of the boarding school, one hundred and twenty children, presided over by Big Sir as substitute father, divided, becoming a mere coeducational establishment and he, increasingly, the conventional headmaster.

Sensing that the school fabric had suffered an irreparable tear, he was anxious to hold us together in mutually agreeable activities, such as a picnic near the foot of Meru, where some minor volcanic cones stood in the image of their mother.

A hired lorry bumped us along a track until boulders stopped our progress. The boys fetched wood, girls made a fire, Little Sir brewed tea in the safari kettle, and Chui rationed the sandwiches.

It was a lovely spot, leafy, next to a mountain stream, and some children lost no time in taking off their socks and shoes to cool their feet in the water. Laughter turned to hysterical screams when they found that the black mud clinging to their ankles was a mass of leeches.

After that discovery we agreed to a walk, collecting pebbles, and plant specimens to press between Bible pages. The older boys held a competition, throwing stones at specific target points on rocks.

Presently, in need of a convenient bush. I went off at right angles to the stream but although the ground began to rise steeply the cover wasn't thick enough for privacy, therefore forcing me to climb higher. When the bushes thickened, and knowing the area abounded in big game, elephants and rhino in particular, I was wary of coming face to face with a piggy eye on either side of a horn.

However, all was so quiet that the breathing of a large creature would have been audible. Continuing upward in the fun of being alone, one of my feet went through loose twigs. Teetering and grasping for branches to hold, I found myself on the edge of a crater, the sides of which fell away steeply to a lake lying far below. It was incredibly blue, not the blue of a heaven reflected, but that of my mother's sapphire pendant and equally round, the foliage growing on the crater's rim being its garland of emeralds.

There was no ripple on the water, no flight of a bird.

Opposite, where the wall sloped less steeply, allowing a growth of vegetation, a boat with one oar was tied up to an overhanging branch. It lay on the glassy surface like the husk of a peanut.

Clinging to a tree-trunk, I stood as close to the abyss as seemed safe, drawn to look down by the intensity of the colour. It was all so... so very beautiful, with the stillness of somebody holding his breath because of an intruder.

I looked and looked again, until something hostile made me uneasy. There was no animal about, no human either, nevertheless the feeling of not being wanted was strong.

Awed by the beauty of the lake, but upset by what seemed like its rejection, that hurtful attitude experienced in my first term, I fled pell-mell back, making enough noise to flush several small animals from cover.

"Have you been in MESS-o-POT-amia?" Garry asked.

"Don't be so crude, man, I've been two bushes away, too lazy to find a third - like you no doubt."

The lake had been a Sleeping Beauty, and boys of his calibre were not the Prince, besides, there was that sensation...

At the end of the afternoon, hungry again for supper, we packed up the empty tuck box, and piled back onto the lorry. The mellow time of day, the sun quickly rolling beyond sight for a few moments of dusk before it was night, affected each of us differently. Younger children looked sleepy, older girls and their boyfriends held hands, stole kisses. Most boys tried a surreptitious smoke, as did some girls.

As a Leader it was difficult to know what to do since it was the Seniors who were most involved. Susie and I refrained from commenting; it had after all been a lovely picnic.

To our consternation, one of the most Senior girls had been permitted to bring a man, her current admirer, resulting in a show of cuddling and kissing that the descending dark could not cloak.

At a *ngoma*, when men and women were entranced with dancing and singing, when the firelight flickered, the smoke wafted here and there in the currents of air made by the dancers, and the drums throbbed relentlessly, I had often seen a youth pull a girl towards the shadows at the back of huts. He was always determined, she reluctant, but yielding without much struggle. Her friends nudged each other, giggled, pulled a *kanga* over their heads and across half the face to signify that they had not noticed.

I had never seen an African making love to a woman, flirting was common, but not body contact in public. White girls and boys flaunted themselves as though they were showing off De Beer diamonds.

Susie and I, embarrassed by the necking performance, put on an impromptu act.

"Um, Mr. Kongoni (hartebeest), whisky? Cigarette?"

Searching in my blazer pocket I found a stub of pencil. Pretending to take it from her 'cigarette case', I lit it from her proffered match, a pen. My hand held the imaginary glass of liquor.

"Er, yes thanks old man, shot any big game lately?"

"Had an awfully good safari, Mr. Kongoni, my bearer handed me the gun just in time. You know how it is, one hesitation, 'Boomf!' the beast would've knocked my head off. As it is I have his to put up on the wall!"

When we had exhausted the tomfoolery, Susie, with her true voice, began to sing, quietly, others joined in. The lovers' kisses lasted longer, cigarette tips glowed in the wind.

Next day I was called to Big Sir's office to hear an astonishing tale.

"I'm informed that you, a Leader, did nothing to curb the smoking which was taking place yesterday on the bus, but what is really unacceptable is the fact that you had a cigarette yourself. I can hardly believe such foolhardy behaviour."

Neither could I, had it been true.

"But Sir, I didn't smoke." To explain the imitation cigarette would have sounded like an excuse. His voice and manner showed extreme hostility.

I looked him in the eye steadfastly, my conscience as clear as the lake. Surely he would see I was telling the truth.

"I've been told of the fact by reliable sources."

"I did not smoke!"

Inwardly I was as astonished about the allegation as I was about my calmness. Big Sir's inquisitions were famous, he could reduce boys to tearful confessions in no time at all.

"It is all the more regrettable that you can't find it in your heart to admit to a wrong, possibly committed in high spirits." His voice, icy, doused all the fire of my affection for him. I was devoted to Big Sir, had a lion charged him, I would have thrown myself sideways, and then hammered the beastly head with a rock.

"The staff have decided to demote you as from now. You may go."

My exit from his office resembled that of a sleepwalker finding her way to the dormitory block. I sat on my bed, meditating with a mind so shocked that I could feel little, and when asked what was the matter, could only shake my head, speech having been knocked from me as though physically assaulted. My throat felt constricted, my chest drawn together like a coiled spring, and eventually the tears that flowed were superficial because they could not well from the innermost anguish.

The unthinkable had happened, Big Sir, whom all admired for his leadership, his fair-mindedness, had fallen victim to the devil's tongue. The devil had scored! And who was the stronger now?

The imperfection of humanness was my most bitter lesson. I realised that people who seemed admirable were like fireflies in the night, glowing here and there, in grass and on bushes for the briefest moment, if I followed their light, they would suddenly be gone, made invisible in their own darkness.

The leader's badge was put to one side. Why should I return it, having in no way discredited its office?

School continued, I existed, nobody put questions, it was as if the pupils were sworn to ignore the matter. After some weeks a member of staff, offering no explanation, told me to continue my leadership. I asked for none, my trust in adults was broken and nothing could have mended it.

Vati, meantime, had begun the study of 'Law and Custom' with the elders and chief of the tribe, assembled to argue the minutiae of rules which he then codified and recorded in pencil in a notebook, I knew, having seen him do it.

Although his work brought chiefs into contact with us across Mutti's tea trolley, we hardly ever knew their main, let alone minor, wives. Therefore, "His *Ngole* came to the house yesterday in company with another beauty," was astonishing news from Mutti, at the rest-house in Kizumbi.

"They wished to learn how to bake bread. You know yourself how difficult that is. First, the making of the initial dough with the *Flörelin* mixture, then the second kneading, dear God will they be able to do all that? However their dear husband does love bread. So I taught them how to bake it. They, however, haven't got an oven. I wonder if they can follow my advice on digging a hole etc.

"Through Vati, the chief invited me to visit the *Ngole*, an honour I was not going to miss, and so I obeyed the royal invitation, arriving at a large European type, mosquito-proofed house, which had once belonged to an Official of the Tsetse Department.

"As I mounted the royal steps to this 'Castle', the *Ntemi* welcomed me in the most friendly manner, behind him his large and imposing wife.

"The interior was comprised of huge rooms housing most comfortable armchairs and sofas. Turning to the *Ngole*, I began by admiring them, but when she continued to look stupidly at me, I asked the *Ntemi* whether she spoke Swahili? - not a word! I had wasted my time trying so hard to talk grammatically.

"Before leaving the residence, the *Ntemi* asked me to come again to help her with dressmaking. She is a Christian brought up at the Mission, therefore able to use a sewing machine."

The sequel came some weeks later: "Yesterday afternoon I went there feeling like our old Fräulein Hebel," her mother's seamstress, "carrying needles, scissors, and paper patterns; but would you believe it, the *Ngole* was not to be seen, although on the previous day I had sent word of my intended visit.

"Her husband told me he had quarrelled with her, and she was sulking."

Well, if Mutti couldn't see why, I could. Had the *Ngole* not felt the ignominy of not being able to converse in Swahili? Then, the chief's personal insult of inviting the white woman to teach her sewing when she knew all about it!

Our household too was discontented. Rajabu, Mutti wrote, had left with the excuse that he was attending a sister's funeral. Shabani was upset because he had to return his 'lady love' to her husband, and Boma, full of his 'answer-back cheek', sulked for days because she told him off about the room corners filling with dust.

An urgent request had been sent for the return of either Mohamadi or Ramadhani from Makuyuni. Neither could be persuaded to come. The latter wrote that he now owned a field which he did not want to leave, and at any rate he wished to continue working for the Bwana *Manaja*. Mohamadi and Mama Panya were settled, happy with their plot, and obviously not desirous of joining our nomadic life.

Mutti was sad, then furious that the 'Nazi' was keeping her cook. On purpose, she maintained, to pay my father back for taking the labourers away.

Increasingly her letters turned to the political situation in Europe, and a possible conflict involving Britain which might result in our internment. Her knowledge of world affairs was derived from listening to a wireless, a battery set, installed by somebody called George, a young man addicted to her cake-laden tea trolley, as I discovered on my next holiday.

From four o'clock onwards we waited to hear the screech of brakes, after which she shouted, "*Chai!* (Tea!)" and Vati emerged from his studies to keep the young man company in the face of two females.

He was tall, slim, dark and not bad looking, especially as he always dressed in spotless white shirts and trousers, which bore the hallmark of a good *dhobi* in having permanent creases.

Though my senior by quite a few years, he was the answer to my daily craving for energetic exercise, a dash up and down the stony rises, or a long run with the dogs, who barked and jumped at us bewildered by the changed tempo in their lives.

When Mutti became tired, turning for home, when the sun was about to sink at that fast rate that it would assume at sunrise, and we sat on the surface of granite rocks, so hot that we had to test whether our bottoms could take the heat, he was prepared to discuss anything, from the morality of shooting antelopes to the possibility of a God-less universe. A companion after my own heart.

After a harum-scarum run, laughing from sheer exhilaration, my chest as dry as the inside of a calabash, and demanding a walking pace, George said, "I've got something for you." His charming smile expressed secrecy.

"Let me guess - it's chocolates, so I'll run less fast, and you can win." It was said jokingly, considering his long legs could have outdistanced a duiker.

"No it's not." His smile widened.

"No? I'll guess again, it's a penknife." It was just a hope. The boys at school prided themselves on having beautiful specimens, some finished off with ivory, or tortoiseshell.

"Wrong again. Here!" He struggled to pull a little wooden box from a pocket. How had I missed its bulge?

"Thanks, George, it's really nice of you to give me something to put my bits and pieces in."

"I made it myself."

"Then double thanks, you know how much I like handmade things." It was nice of him to realise my preference for the plain in place of the carved, sandalwood jewellery boxes imported from India.

Days later, out on a walk under a burning half-past four sun, the dogs' jowls drawn back, tongues lolling, my forehead hot, my tackies burning through my socks, George, by contrast, looked cool in his white togs.

Confronting me with a Prince Charming flourish, he offered another box.

"Would you like a ring?"

"A ring?" I echoed to gain thinking time.

"How about an engagement ring?" He flicked open the lid.

I looked, struck dumb. He was serious, yes, really serious, there was no doubting the warmth in his brown eyes.

"I want you to be my wife." He attempted to take my hand.

Somewhere, I had read of a similar scene, and smiled at its clichés: "...taking her small hand fondly in his, he said, 'You must allow me the honour.' The unmistakable warmth in his eyes, reaching deep into her soul, left her..."

Furthermore, it had taken place in a dell: "...flowers mingled their scent with resin, and the distant roar of the sea was lost in the moment of their awareness of each other."

This part of Sukumaland, this Kizumbi, more desert than savannah, a stick of thorns for a tree, was the counterpart setting. I saw it as an endless barren landscape, where a young male runs and runs to pursue his female, laughter disguising his desire to mate.

What a dreadful situation! I liked George, we had an afternoon friendship based on teas, teasing and talk.

"Thanks," I said lamely, "it's nice of you, but I don't want a ring."

"Why?"

"I'm not marrying at present."

"But couldn't you wear my ring and marry me in a year or two, when you've finished school?"

How did one go about not hurting a friend? Had I not been in that situation before? "Let's discuss it on the way home."

By the time we reached the rest-house, the matter was settled in favour of friendship without matrimony. Fortunately the holidays were at an end, George having sprung his surprise strategically on the last day for a quick promise.

Gossip was carried on the winds of Kizumbi. In the evening on Shinyanga Station, dimly lit, almost empty, my father began his teasing,

"A certain young man is to the damsel loyal,
As King George is to the nation royal."

Mutti laughed, despite the tears over my departure. I mustered an indifferent smile, glad to see George had not come, glad to see the searchlight of the locomotive streaming over the horizon.

In my empty compartment the white linen gleamed on the previously ordered top bunk. I could hardly wait to get into it, and when the whistle blew and the lantern turned green, I said a relieved goodbye.

One last wave at the trio, my parents and Boma lit up by their lantern, then I turned in, put on my pyjamas, mounted the bunk, switched on the mauve night light, wriggled under the light blanket, and felt the luxury of the night-ride to Dodoma.

There would, of course, be an interruption, first the Guard, then the Train boy. Shortly it came, a discreet tap-tap.

"*Karibu!* (Enter!)"

"Hello, I just jumped on the train!" It was George.

"Jumped on the train?" He was the last person I wanted to see, but he made it sound almost like the Wild West, a hold-up, masked men, pointing guns...

"Yes, just to see you." He was taking delight in his swashbuckling action. Already my hand was captured in his while he swung himself up easily onto the bunk with his long legs. His touch was like an electric connection, desire flowing in the attraction of opposite charges.

Hemmed in on the top bunk, dressed in my pyjamas, in immediate proximity of his bodily charm, it was extremely difficult to resist all the verbal offers and physical desires in a conflict in which I tried to keep the situation on a level of friendship that he was determined to convert into betrothal.

After what seemed hours, during which the absence of the Guard and Train boy was noticeable, the carriage gave a lurch, George jumped off the bunk. "This is where I get off." He peered through the window into the pitch dark, "Cheerio, I'll write."

Opening the door stealthily, he blew a kiss, and disappeared as I was still shouting, "No! Don't write! Don't you dare!"

The train slowed down without a station in sight, gave a few shuffles and puffs, then moved off smartly. There was no sign of a waiting vehicle.

My body felt drained, my mind exhausted. I fell back onto the pillows under the mauve light, too weary to care whether George had jumped off into a chasm, or had managed to land beside the track at the momentary stopping point.

At school, I was not the only one who was feeling my age - fourteen - as a result of my encounter; the old brigade having left, the rest of us had moved up a notch of maturity until Tim arrived.

"Cocky, there's an older chap just come to school. Eighteen I'd guess."

"Never!"

"He is, you know! Very polite too, doesn't talk like a kid."

"What's he come for then? What's the excitement? Is it Clark Gable, or Errol Flynn?"

He turned out to be a mousy-haired, hazel-eyed, freckle faced individual, neither boy nor man. Of medium build, a teenager in shape, his manner indicated that he had worked as an adult.

Leaning against the wall at the end of a row, he looked sheepishly around during lessons, making no attempt to join in.

Newcomers sometimes behaved strangely until they had overcome their embarrassment over being less familiar with school subjects than car engines.

In the second week, asked by Mama Chui to read, he still shook his head.

"You need not worry, Tim," she said encouragingly, "many pupils you see here could not read well when they first came and still can't! Read one sentence, and, tomorrow you might make it two."

"I can't read."

"Oh, hm, never mind then," she feigned indifference though we knew she was as shocked as the rest of us. "Next please."

We read, some faltering genuinely over "sastrugi" and "Apsley Cherry-Garrard", others pretended.

In the next period, Little Sir wrote sums on the board, and sat down to correct a pile of books. Every eyelash hid a surreptitious look at Tim to watch for his reaction. The tattered motor magazine was out again in his hands.

"What's the matter with you, Tim? Isn't it time you started doing something?" The staff had obviously decided that this was the day of reckoning.

"I can only count, Sir."

It was out, all we had suspected, the ogre of many of us 'white bush children', namely that like Tim, lack of education in Tanganyika in our primary years meant that we would never catch up. There was not one among us who was not truly sorry for him.

He was given special work which he did sitting outside our classroom on the verandah floor. Legs placed over the side in the rain drain, he copied letters from a primer.

Tim's fate faded into the background, replaced by an excitement concerning our own educational prospects. Big Sir, as always immaculate in grey worsted shorts, a cream-coloured short-sleeved shirt, and maroon coloured tie which we thought might have been his Welsh Rugby colours, strode through the classroom door bringing a wind of authority before which our lips closed like tent flaps in an imminent gale.

"Good morning everybody."

"Good morning, Sir."

"I'd be grateful if you could make up your minds straight away about a small matter."

We relaxed in response to his pleasant manner. Was it perhaps a question of starting pupils' gardens again, a few of my friends longed to have their own peanut plants.

"We out here have to register early for the Overseas Junior School Certificate Examination."

There was a sound of exhaled disappointment.

"Please Sir," Alex had his hand up, "what good will it do to pass them?"

"The immediate advantage is an entrance to the Prince of Wales for Boys, and the Kenya High School for Girls in Nairobi."

"And if we don't want any more education, Sir?"

"There's more to life than making a jalopy into a Buick." He left us laughing as Mama Chui entered, requested by him to make a list of candidates.

Carefully she tore a page from her notebook, selected a pencil from her bag, "Who is first? One at a time please." She obviously expected a stampede.

Nobody moved.

Relenting to an encouraging smile, "I'll take the names row by row."

The class sat transfixed, molten lava, suddenly cooled; I put up my hand.

"Right. Next?"

Betty raised hers, and Jerry trailed his in the air, at half-mast.

Chui looked round the poker faces, "Who else?"

No genet could have been more stealthily silent than our class.

"Very well then," she sighed deeply, and I knew that for a moment she felt wholly dispirited. All that work to show us the psychological reason for the death of Scott and 'Titus' Oates, all the explanation to bear out the earthly nature in Caliban as opposed to the 'aerial' spirit of his tormentor, and now, how many candidates?

"Well, then, you three had better see me after break for a plan of work."

"You twits!" I heard somebody whisper. "Wait until you get to those Kenya Schools, they're full of settlers' children who think they are white 'natives'."

It was loud enough to be heard all over the class, Chui began to laugh, the class joining in with relief.

In the following weeks, the other pupils lost no time in telling us that we were odd, mad or stupid to want more work.

I did not mind the banter, Vati had always talked of University-learning as a sort of initiation ceremony for life. That being the accepted direction in his family for becoming a working adult, my immediate task was to take the exam.

The only subject I could not fathom was Arithmetic which depended on magical manipulation, an 'add a one to the top, and a one to the bottom'. It was like Vati's entry into the snake charmers' society when each novice had to bring a cock with reddish-brown feathers, on which he had to spit and ask whether the omens were favourable for admission. The diviner cut off its head with one stroke of his knife, my father had to throw it in the air and, as he related, its body continued to move in convulsive jerks finally spread-eagling itself on the ground.

Its position was closely studied for different interpretations; had it landed on its left, he, as a novice, would have had to arrange a sacrifice to his paternal ancestor, in a right side landing, one for his maternal. By sheer chance, his cock's attitude showed ancestral pleasure with his intended entry. Sheer magic!

The Kizumbi rest-house having been scheduled for demolition, my parents had moved into tents further into the bush.

"Mondo, 26 miles from Shinyanga, is a steppe landscape which unfolds itself before us. Wherever one looks there is yellow grass, even a few trees - what a wonder - tamarinds and baobabs. Groups of gigantic rocks tower out of the earth. There are no villages as the inhabitants live at some distance from each other.

"Vati is working with the local *Ntemi* on Land Tenure because the allocation of plots differs from Shinyanga."

Apropos land tenure, he had already told us that acquisition was governed by tribal laws, often varying with a 'parish'. Even Administrative Officers, who knew about such matters from litigations in the Native Courts, questioned him about land rights. I had heard them, sometimes on their way in from the moon gazing: "Um, Hans, what happens when a bachelor wants a holding?"

"Let him marry first."

"Oh? No wife, no land?"

"No. But having one can make the difference in some situations."

Though jokingly said, it was the first time I had heard him admit to female usefulness.

Mondo seemed typical of the areas we had lived in since leaving Rusegwa: a big country asking for a big heart to encompass it. Vati did not seem to be affected by such a landscape, seeing in it only a network of tribal life. Mutti painted it in water-colour, badly, unless she had an inspirational day, because her brush strokes were more suited to oil paint, tubes of which had gone dry at Rusegwa.

In my holidays, I was touched by the enormity of a parched and empty land as helpless as I felt wanting within it. At other times it was so beautiful in its width of sky, the length of hills, the breadth of land, and the hue in which everything was bathed, that it took me over physically, a very sore and sad experience. Sometimes it cried out for attention, and not knowing what to do, I wanted to get away from it.

Africans had a simpler relationship with their land, seeing it either as a place of growth after the rains, or a shrivelled body in a drought.

There was further news: "That nuisance of a monkey has escaped, Shabani saw him sitting on a baobab tree. I can imagine what a wonderful feeling it must be, freedom, a chance to see the world. May we grant him the pleasure. He has much to see in Sukumaland, much to eat, peanuts, sorghum, and there is water here too. Fortunately there is no danger because wild animals and snakes cannot reach the tops of these tall trees."

It was the story of all our monkey pets. Mutti reared the pathetic babies to adulthood after which she could not get them to take to the wilds until one day when it suited them, they were off.

Wondering what I would do in Mondo on my next holiday, I was relieved to read of my parents' forthcoming departure to the west of Lake Victoria. It was surprising because Vati had only just started his meetings with the elders.

Years later the precipitated move was explained when he wrote:

"...I met a member of the Secretariat. We often walked together, and so I asked him one day about the reason for my transfer shortly after giving a list of all the work still to be done. I knew that he had been in the Secretariat at the time.

"He looked at me, and his face showed a mixture of amusement and embarrassment. Finally he said, 'Now look, don't be cross Kori, it was all my fault, I got your report, but I thought those pages at the end were an index, and I assumed you had finished your work.'"

Resigned to face more bush life, and homeless, my parents were in the middle of packing up after a night back at Kizumbi, when there was a call from outside the tent. It was a messenger, Boma said, and he had told him to wait. Was it urgent? No, it was only a boy. After a while, Mutti remembering Boma's inherent cheek, went out to see for herself. It was the child-minder holding a shallow basket with the customary cover woven like a hat.

"Go in safety and peace." He pronounced the words slowly, obviously having been rehearsed. "This is for your journey."

Under the cover, lying like a shell-ful of pearls, was a bunch of green grapes. My parents could not remember having tasted any since our departure from Europe. It was the most generous of farewell presents.

VICTORIA-NYANZA

At last during a half-term holiday, Josie's mother fulfilled her promise of taking us both to Nairobi to see a film.

"You'll looove it my darlings," she told us. "You'll fall for Ronald Colman, he's just gorgeous!" Her throaty voice was the drum to her dancing eyes as she winked coquettishly at an imaginary beau.

It was enough to sour the prospect momentarily, because it sounded like the stuff girls were supposed to like, all that "I am loving yououou..." à la Jeanette MacDonald. There was my reputation to think of, the one that declared me tough.

"Have you heard? Cocky went to Nairobi to see a film - she's nuts about Ronald Colman," was an unthinkable accusation.

Despite my misgivings it was a rare treat and Josie's mother so enthusiastic that we caught her infectious mood.

Her meeting with what I assumed to be the typical settler, a cigarette drooping from the corner of her mouth, pure whisky held in a tumbler by a shaking hand, and the shout of, "Hell-lo darling! How e-bsolutely super to see you," was exactly what I had expected.

Finally, primed with chocolate, we took our seats in a cinema. The lights went out, and the names of Ronald Colman, Douglas Fairbanks Junior, and Madeleine Carroll became etched in blinding flashes on a screen, announcing that we were about to see *The Prisoner of Zenda*. I sat forward not to miss anything but the longer the projector whirred, the more confusing became the story as scenes changed before their significance was apparent to me. The actors ran, jumped, fought with swords, talked in American English. Shafts of light from the projector flickered uncertainly like a car's headlights in the rain, and though it moved the images on the screen, they lacked substance in their greyness. It was such a disappointment, though the New Stanley Hotel never let me down in harbouring bizarre characters.

The next half-term started with the challenge of a Geography competition.

"I've been sent some work-books," Little Sir held up the specimens. "You may have one each. The most successful completion will earn a prize."

"What'll you give, Sir, a Bible?" Panya's question rang with cheek.

"No, I'll give the person an Atlas!"

"He's found a gold-mine in the holidays."

"Please Sir, do you prospect in your spare time?"

"He wouldn't know how to swirl the gold-bearing sediment in a *karai*..."

"Sh!" was all he could say, trying to look cross.

As ever, and like vultures at a kill, the class began to tear him to pieces verbally.

In the end only Betty and I took the competition seriously, and she won. My disappointment was acute, hidden in making a special effort to congratulate her sincerely, but when I saw her open a page at her Pacific Ocean, I felt envy draw at my stomach.

My inner voices called for daring and winning, they were an 'I' encased in a whirring generator without a turn-off switch. Other voices clamoured for virtues, another party shouted, "Hey, what about applying logic!" The conflicting din within me caused pain, at times as much as my Singida dysentery, but all over rather than in the bowels. The experience of broken trust added to the anguish with which I had to live until an unexpected remedy improved my condition.

"I've something new for you," Chui announced one day.

A leather bound copy, spine facing outward, lay at the edge of her table, a marker already in place.

A gasp rose from the class followed by protests, "There's a swastika on the book!"

"Don't worry, it's an ancient symbol for "sun" used by Rudyard Kipling. Settle down and listen:

> 'If you can keep your head when all about you
> Are losing theirs and blaming it on you...'"

I listened, enthralled. The sum total of my upbringing and aspirations, the me I wanted to be, was gathered up in the four stanzas of If, right down to the last line "And - which is more - you'll be a Man, my son!"

There it was, simply put though difficult to emulate, but I would try. Kipling's creed was for me. Knowing how I should conduct my life in the face of adversity took much of the hurting away.

My parents regarded my acceptance of school Christianity, and then *If*, with the same mild interest mustered for any of my ideas. To them I was a teenager who would mirror her environment like the toy kaleidoscope I had been sent at Rusegwa, finally coming to a stop at a particular pattern which would then have to be recognised as the adult configuration, still changeable but only by insignificant turns.

By the time the holidays came round, I had found some equilibrium, and hadn't Mutti promised a fascinating sight where my parents were staying temporarily?

The train rocked and rolled through the savannah, that land of yellow-yellow, occasionally bisected by a brown gravel road, and patterned with a cover of thorn bush, a scattering of umbrella acacias, and more sparsely, a studding of baobabs growing branches like kudu horns.

At stations the draught through the partially open window stopped, leaving my compartment oppressively hot. Further along from my coach, Asians lifted bundles, baskets and children up the steep steps, or through windows. Their din was no less than that of the crying children and shouting parents among the third-class African passengers, trying to find room on slatted bench seats.

In addition there was the tinkle of the sweetmeats vendor, made by shaking a coin in a small white and blue-patterned bowl.

I lay back on the bedding, and slept my way from stop to stop, wondering in my waking moments why I was so tired. It was like having sleeping sickness, prevalent in many parts of Tanganyika.

On the previous evening I had revelled in having the compartment to myself. A wash in the stainless steel basin under the table top that hinged to hook back on the wall, a change into my Fuji silk pyjamas made by Mutti for best occasions, and I was on the top bunk switching on the reading lamp. The familiar smell of the upholstery, the lilt of the wheels, the bar of chocolate I had saved, and *Jock of the Bushveld* to make my heart swell with the tales of his bravery, made the evening perfect. Then came the inevitable knock on the door.

"Memsahib Mdogo, how you are these days?"

I could never tell one Sikh from another. They all wore white turbans from which wisps of black hair escaped to tangle with their beard; they were all portly father figures; they commanded respect, being capable of ignoring insolence. Was this the one who had greeted my parents at Uzule?

"Thank you Mr. Singh, I'm well."

"I seeing your father only last week, he very well. Your family now in Mwanza. Your mother like Mwanza? Very good shops. She like I think."

I agreed, showed him the required Railway Warrant and settled back. Another knock, this time it was the head Train boy,

"*Jambo!* Mamsapu Mdogo. Is Bwana Kori well?"

"He's well."

"Is the Mamsapu well?"

"She's well."

"Tell Bwana Kori my brother died. He used to work for him."

The message would be conveyed I assured him, and anyway Vati would be at the Station to meet me.

"I will bring you tea tomorrow morning."

It was said with emphasis not meant for me personally, but as though he was mentally taking his deceased brother's place to serve the Bwana by replenishing his daughter.

I had no function. My position was that of a young white female out of reach for black males, of no interest. Had I been my father's son, ah yes, then I would have been the Bwana Mdogo, the young master.

Next day, as we approached the Lake Victoria region, the landscape looked like a playground where giant children had heaped rocks in competition to see which granite castle would stay upright. Every pile was huge, with bushes growing in clefts. Some stones, as large as houses, resembled hens' eggs more rounded one end than the other. Some, like those of snakes, looked rubbery, bulging with the weight above them, and everywhere there were boulders not firmly placed, about to roll off - which of course they never did, even when the locomotive rumbled past them.

The train slowed to a walking pace on approach to a natural gateway made by rock walls supporting enormous capping stones which, at one point, met over the line like two heads butting.

Excited now I looked for a sign of the lake. Still clanking cautiously between rocks, the train wound its way to Mwanza South Station, then picked up speed for a grand entry into Mwanza, "the place of the lake". I caught a glimpse of water shimmering between trees.

Collecting my things, I donned my topee, and was on the observation platform to greet my parents, looking shorter and more foreign than I could remember.

"Hello!" shrieked Mutti as we rolled past her before coming to a halt. Already she had broken into an ungainly trot on those high heels. Vati never hurried. A handshake from him, a hurried kiss from Mutti, knowing how years of derision from my father had made me dislike the custom, and we were reunited.

A small group of porters had gathered clamouring to be picked for their excellence of muscle.

"Ah, you!" Vati addressed one of the men, "aren't you Nyigombejo, the centre forward of the team that played for Mwanza last Saturday?"

"Your father," said Mutti with irony, "your father is even more football crazy than at Shinyanga. We'll leave him to his centre forward, and getting your trunk. Come! You'll be surprised to hear we haven't far to go."

Along an avenue of shady trees, we joined the throng of disembarked passengers carrying large bundles of household goods, *totos*, doing their best to balance something smaller on their heads.

Although women and girls carried most of the belongings, division of labour being an accepted feature of tribal society, small boys and girls were often treated alike until in growing older, physical differences split their paths naturally.

At morning tea parties, the black woman's position in terms of the beast of burden, the cow expected only to calve, the labourer in the field, sometimes aroused ladies to argumentative fury. When Mutti told my father about it, his comment was, "What *Quatsch* (twaddle)! Of course your ladies may not be aware of the history of 'hunters' and 'gatherers', neither do they seem to know that even up to 1910 there were still tribes skirmishing with German-led *Askaris*, and before that Tanganyika had a history of Arab slave-trading and tribal warfare reaching back into the distant past. Which of these white women, in such circumstances, would have taken up the spear to protect her load-bearing husband in case of an ambush?"

"Yes, yes, Hans, you've told us that often enough but they don't know it."

"Then don't act such a fool, tell them what you know."

Mutti made a wry face, I knew she preferred to bleat with the goats.

We turned into a shady forecourt to a stone-built bungalow behind a hedge.

"Two bedrooms, a dining-room, and as you see, a mosquito-proofed verandah which I have turned into a sitting-room. Unfortunately on train days it gets dusty from the passengers walking past, and on boat days we get it both ways."

From my external view of the wire gauze frames, assembled from roof to verandah parapet, the house resembled zoo cages in Europe for monkeys, apes and birds. I felt a twinge of embarrassment, was this accommodation all the Government had been able to offer us? The cotton curtains, strung round the lower part of the frames for privacy, were all very well during the day, but what of night time? Surely we would be seen sitting under the bright electric bulb literally like monkeys in a cage?

By lunchtime, Vati returned from having read some administrative reports, thought by the P.C. to be useful for his intended work on Land Tenure on the western side of Lake Victoria. Always the mention of the lake.

"But where is it, Vati?"

"*Na na,* not so impatient, something like that can run but only through pipes, it will still be there this afternoon, every afternoon, and long after Hitler has ceased to exist."

"I wish it were five minutes after the event," added Mutti, "that devil! I spit on him!" She was at it again.

Snotty noses and spitting, the supposed division between blacks and whites. But had I not seen some boys at school spitting when they were on the playing-field, despite their own oft-voiced disgust about "stinking, spitting blacks!"

"Let's go to lunch," Vati ignored her eruption, "we can't expect the hotel to keep our food hot."

Hotel! I was impressed, my parents must be earning a better salary. But no, it was only because the P.W.D. were lagging behind in painting our kitchen that they were getting the food bill paid.

The hotel verandah had a familiar look, easy chairs with khaki cushions, coffee tables littered with coasters advertising German Beers...

"Hello, hello! What a big girl, so much like her father, *nicht wahr*?" said a voice which awakened my memory of whooping for breath. It was the Manyoni hoteliers, she fatter than a calving rhino, he equally bald. My mother had kept their transfer of business to Mwanza a surprise. The food would be familiar too, sausages and bacon, pork soup for lunch, cured ham in the evening.

Before the meal, cooling down with a squash and soda, we were to witness a daily occurrence which became my favourite holiday fantasy. Briefly introduced and immediately indifferent to us, the hoteliers' daughter, Minna, sat a few tables away sipping her orangeade.

A tall blonde, she cut her hair short round a square face which looked like little Lotti's, grown up. Twiddling white rimmed sunglasses, and crossing and uncrossing her legs impatiently, she kept looking out at the road until a sports car swept into view. Minna reached it before it had even stopped, then waited for her suntanned 'Clark Gable' to jump out, run round and open the door.

She was a whirl of long legs, flared skirt, flip-flopping white sandals, as she threw herself into the bucket seat and exchanged greetings, lost in the roar of the engine when the car pulled away. The rest I had to imagine.

Her delicious looks, a complexion like mango, lips like ripe tomatoes, would have made any man want a taste.

"There'll be no happy ending," my mother once remarked, "she'll probably be recalled by Hitler - with those Germanic looks!"

In the late afternoon we took a walk to see the ship. Past the Station, the water I had glimpsed on my arrival was an 'arm', the body still to come.

At the Gymkhana club people were playing tennis; in the rugged landscape of granite rocks and vegetation a couple were hitting an invisible ball across cropped grass. Bungalows nestled at the foot of scrub-grown hillocks.

I lingered to look enviously at the players. A shout from Mutti who had gone ahead made me hurry to join her.

"There you are! And what do you say to that!"

A short way below us lay a foreshore to an expanse of water, round the edges of which were trees and rocks, and as we walked on and more came into view, there were inlets and headlands, beaches and promontories empty of habitation, a shimmering grandeur of blue water, disturbed only by the noise reaching us from the steamer being loaded at the pier.

"The Lake Victoria!" she announced with a flourish, as if introducing a prima donna. "Am I not right? isn't she beautiful?"

She was.

Descending to a road shaded by palm trees near the water's edge, we passed a tall family of granite rocks lapped by gurgling water. One had a cap shaped like a cone.

"The loaders have to finish by six," Mutti explained as we walked past sacks of maize, and piles of hides stiff as chapaties, stacked on the jetty. "In the cotton season, they go on until late illuminated by a big spotlight."

A net of sisal rope ensnaring a load of gunny bags, bulging to burst, was being hooked up to a chain dangling from a boom. Men shouted to us to get out of the way.

The donkey engines chuffed, the chain snapped taut with a resounding clank, and the bags were swept off as the cables swung the load and boom in-board, with the precision dictated by the stevedore who was communicating in sign language with the drivers on deck and the loaders below. On the bridge, like the giraffes that used to peer down at us, a white officer looked over railings, adding laconic directions when necessary.

Mutti for once in charge as though she had been a captain's daughter, led the way up the short gangway and along the deck to the stern, where Europeans were taking their drinks around tables under canvas awnings. Only persistent waving at the bar boy eventually brought him to our table for an order.

"These Kavirondo," grumbled Mutti, "are a law unto themselves. The whole ship's crew is the same tribe - an obstinate, haughty lot, though I hear that they are absolutely reliable sailors, being fishermen."

We sat looking over the deck rail at the water changing hue in the waning afternoon, the dogs exhausted by the hot walk lolled their dripping tongues. Mutti amused me with Shinyanga gossip, and I in turn related my temporary fall from leadership.

Gradually the water turned grey, then leaden. Cormorants spread their wings to dry, standing on the group of rocks.

"It's picturesque isn't it," sighed my mother. "I could live happily on Victoria's shores if it weren't for the worry about Erna. If only I could do something to get her away from the Nazis."

"Why don't you just invite her?"

"She won't leave the husband. They can't pay the fare, and we haven't the money either, nor the accommodation. Where would we put them, in a tent? Vati says neither Tanganyika nor Kenya will take an Austrian now unless he is guaranteed work out here." She pulled out a lacy handkerchief to wipe her eyes.

Under our feet the deck began vibrating, the loading had stopped. "She's going," said Mutti in the same vein, making statements of hopelessness.

A bell clanked to confirm her remark but made no impression on the sundowners.

"Drink up, ladies and gentlemen, we are about to sail," urged the officer rounding us up. There was no mistaking the Captain's voice, nor was there any doubt in the action of the burly Kavirondo, hands on the portable gangway.

The *Usoga* looked like a Noah's ark. On, the bridge the white officers with the Kavirondo helmsman; on deck, white passengers; below on the second deck, Asians with numerous children, and where the holds had been battened and the loading gear tied up, sat the black boat population, increased in volume by baggage, bicycles, and chickens in their open weave cages.

The ship hooted, the anchor was weighed, the hawsers, all but one, came off their bollards, black smoke belched from the funnel and the ship began moving away, though not without commotion, when some latecomers jumped the gap to land on the lower boat deck, and another man vacated by jumping the widening gap, back onto the pier.

Majestically the steamer drew away stern first until, at a command, the last rope was cast off. She glided into open water to start her turn. There was a moment's hesitation, the ship's lights came on, and she came about to move off smartly, a twinkling hull against the grey which was one part water and one sky. By the time we had watched the twinkle becoming as distant as starlight, everybody had gone, and the lake quickly joined night in its darkness.

From Mutti's letters I had heard about the couple who were about to share an afternoon's tea, anthropologists whom my parents had met at Shinyanga: "The man I was telling you about seems to be a likeable person. He told me that the Government is very interested in your father's work, some of the photos of the figurines made at Vugiri are to be sent to the British Museum. It seems that prospects are favourable."

Although in the first instance Vati was reluctant to divulge the existence of objects he had sworn to keep a secret, their future transportation as we moved from place to place, convinced him of their need for a permanent home.

Racker's Granny had been one hope of solving the problem when she had spoken of interesting her Basel Museum in the importance of the exhibits. My parents, entrusting Mohamadi with Mutti's coloured sketches of them, had sent him to deliver the parcel personally at her departure from Tanganyika.

Eventually hope died and the illustrations were returned.

This time, at the tea party, the subject of the figurines was broached again.

The man, as tall as Vati was short, sat forward, all eagerness, "Kori, I have been in contact with an old friend in London, and the next move is for me to send your photos with accompanying explanation to the Museum. Somebody there is interested in obtaining examples of East African culture, there being relatively little to show for it by comparison with the carvings and masks from West Africa."

Afterwards Vati looked pleased with renewed hope. Mutti was impressed by his wife, "You know, Hans, she's a professional in her own right, and so interested too."

The P.W.D. having finished the kitchen, Shabani had returned to cooking on the resident stove. The tin chimney, stuck through the back wall, drew well once the wood fire was lit, but until that moment, the smoke threatened to blacken the kitchen all over again.

When Mutti wished to do some cooking, she shouted through the gauze, "Has the smoke finished?"

I noticed that Shabani's options were either "yes" if he was ready to tolerate her, "no" if he wished to postpone her presence.

Towards the end of my holiday, we were settling down to the home cooked lunch, when Mutti asked her daily question about what was going on at the *boma.*

"Nothing worth mentioning, underhand dealings do not deserve the elevation of being reported."

"Oh?" - Mutti now all ears - "is it about the other Austrian lady, I've heard..."

Vati's silence was intimidating, I wished she would look up and see his grim expression, but she burbled on between helping herself to a quarter of a small piece of liver, "Did you say, yes or no, Hans?"

"No! and if you must know, our friend has been trying to steal the figurine photos."

Our forks and knives stopped their pecking of plates.

"*Wirklich*?" said Mutti incredulously. "But I can't believe it! That nice man! And his wife!"

A crisis seemed to have blown up like the storms for which the lake was renowned. Cosiness puffed away in a gust of ill wind. The comfort provided by the monkey box despite its exposure to public gaze, the security afforded my parents in Vati's Government employment even though, as he related with a smile, his name came low down on the civil list, only one line above that of Asian secretaries, all became void at that moment. I could see something terrible brewing up, and a consequent return to *banda* living.

Mutti looked stunned, Vati wore that mixture of expressions, a smile to hide the inward hurt, the eyes angry, and ready to do battle.

I began to wish myself back at the stalwart school.

"What can you do?"

"What can I do? Nothing more than anyone else would do in the circumstances. As soon as I heard that he had tried to appropriate the material by giving it his own name, I went straight away to him and said quite simply that he could do no such thing."

"What did he say?"

"He made the excuse that appending his name temporarily did not mean that mine would not be restored when the British Museum or whoever, agrees to house the collection."

"And what did you say to that?"

"I told him that not a single figurine would leave my boxes even though conceding the obvious, that his English name bore certain advantages over mine."

The ring of humour in his voice showed he had overcome his anger.

"And then?" urged Mutti almost breathless with curiosity.

"*Schachmatt!* (Checkmate!)" He began to smile broadly, "It is all like a game, I hold the King, he only has Pawns."

Vati's tone expressed an end to the matter, a turning to the next game whatever surprise that might bring.

Mutti could not bring herself to put the chess pieces away. "But who told you of the deceit in the first place, Hans?"

"Ah, there are some who are good friends, a Bishop or two..."

The Gymkhana club was exclusively for whites, mostly officials,

Asians having their equivalent elsewhere. Africans had their Saturday football, and their social life at the licensed beer shops in the township.

When we passed by, Mutti looked enviously across to the club's verandah where Mwanza officialdom could meet and socialise.

"Lili your wish is fulfilled, you two may visit the club from now on, order drinks, look into the *Tatler*, and I could possibly find interest in *The London Illustrated News*," was Vati's great news for us one day.

It put a spark of hope into my mind; where however would I find a partner to play my beginner's tennis?

"It appears," he continued, "that permission for our entry has caused difficulty. In view of the fact that my salary comes from the Secretariat I am a Government employee, but in that sense so is every Mr. Parek who transports firewood for the officials' kitchens."

My mother looked perplexed.

"How can we be like Mr. Parek, he is an Indian."

"Insofar as we are both contracted to do work for the Administration, with the difference of course, that he is not on the salary list."

"Yes Hans, but of course."

"And we are European!"

"Yes, of course." My mother was never able to detect the nuances of facetiousness in his conversation.

"Apparently the club committee were split on whether we should be regarded as Government officials. Operating in our favour was the fact that we are whites, and that the attitude of the P.C. and D.C. towards me has been appreciative of my work."

"Well that is very nice of them."

Vati, still tongue in cheek, continued, "I heard of even greater difficulties experienced by the committee. Do you remember the Indian lawyer I mentioned in connection with one of the penniless prospectors Mwanza seems to attract? Williamson by name. This particular Geologist who is looking for diamonds is being kept alive by the generosity of the Indian, a really nice man. He has a London-born wife, not only is she white but also a platinum blonde, the contrast is startling."

"Oh dear, she will have difficulties in this society."

With the advancing afternoon, the dogs were becoming restless. Teatime, however, was prolonged in order to enjoy my father's company, so often reserved for chiefs and tribal elders.

"Yes, she has shunned contact with the whites, but does not belong to the *duka* society either." I knew what she felt because we ourselves had to endure it, being like hyraxes, insignificant animals despite sharing a common ancestry with the noble elephants, the British. "Therefore it was decided to acknowledge her white descent by inviting her and the Asian husband for every New Year fancy dress party."

"Good heavens!" exclaimed Mutti, "and how does he come?"

"Disguised as a Maharajah."

"And she?"

"As his wife of course - dressed in a sari."

It was both funny and pathetic, so that our laughter was kind.

The first time that Mutti and I walked into the club, subjected to the gaze of a few members, was awkward. We seated ourselves round a vacant coffee table, ordered soft drinks from the bar, and made English conversation.

Thereafter we went quite often without meeting with any welcoming gesture, until my hope of being asked to join in a game of tennis was dashed. There was no way in which I could make use of the energy I had acquired from living a malaria-free life at school, except to demand that we walk further than my mother would have done on her own.

On one occasion, passing the old dhow harbour, where some wrecks still tangled with the reeds which I was told were the remains of a 'floating island', papyrus torn in chunks from river mouths in a storm, we walked to a cotton Ginnery, but there the road seemed to end. However, the dogs had found a track and nose down, were off to explore.

Mutti agreed to walk a little further round a few more bends until she stopped like a Muscat donkey, and brayed, "I'm not going on. We must turn for home." Calling the dogs, "I'm not following you, Putzi, not another step!" She was always doing it, just when the terrain became interesting, she sensed danger where I could smell adventure. I would see if the old ruse still worked.

"I'll go on by myself."

"All right then; you and your adventures! That's only in cowboy books you read at school."

Another bend, another and another, and to our mutual surprise we came upon a bungalow in the midst of palm trees near the water's edge. The place, backing onto rocks, seemed deserted, and strange too was the fact that although it was diagonally across the water from the harbour, we had not seen it from the ship's deck.

A late afternoon breeze moved the fronds with a "swish, swosh", the water lapped at stones set in the beach.

"Hello, were you looking for me?"

We greeted the lady, confessing our ignorance about the existence of her house.

"You must be new to Mwanza. Come in, have a sherbet, I haven't much to show you."

Sherbet! What a long time since I had heard the word. We drank her glowing liquid, my mother enthralled with the view, "It is like being in a villa on the Mediterranean."

"Come," the woman said to me, "your mother can go on admiring while I show you what's inside."

In a bare room a couple of tubs stood on the floor.

"Here you are."

I did not know what I should look at, besides, by this time logic advised caution.

"They won't bite unless you get your hand too near," she drew me towards the tubs.

In them a few baby crocodiles moved sluggishly in an endeavour to swim in a hand's depth of water.

"What do you do with these?"

"My husband sells them to zoos."

"And how does he catch them?" I wondered whether there was such a thing as a crocodile net.

"When he kills a female, he always brings the brood home." She stirred the water with a stick to give the babies simulated waves. "Your mother can see the ones we keep outside." We left the babies to their enforced turbulence.

"Hold onto your dogs," she warned us, "you've no idea how easily they get their noses bitten."

Hidden behind the trees were bath-tubs occupied from end to end by larger crocodiles, lying as if dead in water reaching just below their snout.

"Good heavens!" Mutti exclaimed, "What happens when they grow longer?"

"My husband kills them for the top class shoe and handbag trade. You see, they have no bullet holes nor spear wounds."

Keeping the creatures so narrowly confined seemed terribly cruel. Keep me lying in a bath for a few days, and I would be ready to lash my way out.

"Do you take them out when you have to clean the tubs?"

She laughed uproariously at my childish question, "No, dear, we take the plug out when the water gets too smelly. They get washed down with a couple of buckets of lake water and are happy as long as they get fed."

Taking a last look at the crocodiles which had not twitched a muscle, I drowned my welling pity in a fervent wish for their early conversion into shoes. How awful! No I did not mean the shoes, after all cow skin was turned into hide, it was the thought of inactivity, it made me run ahead with the dogs.

What an idyllic place the bungalow had looked - a crocodile slaughter house, of all things!

On our return we found Vati working at the old ironing table set up on the verandah. His reading of D.C. appeal cases had convinced him, he said, that the Chiefs of the 'Sukumaland Federation' were wise in demanding unification of their customary law.

"That will be my work at some future date, it'll mean a lot of *baraza* (court) work - getting the elders to come at specific times is difficult - and then the material will have to be collated." He was already working out the schedule in his mind.

"And, Hans, do you think the Administration will pay you for all this work?"

"*Aber* Lili! All you can ever think about is how many more tins of butter you could buy, never the interest of the work!"

How unfair they both were to each other, I thought. Of course Vati was right in demanding that she should place greater importance on his work, and she was right in worrying about paying the bills.

If ever I had a husband - not likely! The way boys treated me at school...

Sometimes our afternoon walk took us into the bazaar which consisted of one road like a trunk growing *dukas* on stems on either side. The stems were represented by planks over two drains, said to save Mwanza township from flooding in the torrential rainstorms.

Mutti willed herself to negotiate each short bridge with teetering gait, if the *duka* looked as though it sold what she required.

I loathed shopping, it was then that I found my mother as embarrassing as the Indian shopkeepers.

"You want this? I make cheap for you, very fine Manchester cotton, one shilling fifty per metre."

There followed the wrangling, degrading in the extreme. Should white people not set a standard, I asked myself, when purchasing cloth, as much as on the subject of truth?

My mother sounded like one of the local tribesmen, "Mr. Patel, this is cheap cotton, not worth the money."

"Oh but Memsahib, I hear Mr. Kori doing well, working in P.C. office these days. I sell same material to Memsahib P.C. yesterday."

"If the P.C.'s wife took it for shilling 1.50, I will take it for half because my husband does not earn as much," replied Mutti craftily.

"I will sell for 1.25."

"One shilling or I go, come along everybody," addressing the dogs as well.

Mr. Patel held up his hands in a gesture of defeat, "All right, I know Bwana Kori well."

A concession then. Smiles accompanied the presentation of the wrapped dress length.

I, for one, could not look him in the face.

All around us smooth, scintillating granite, piled high, split by thermal heat, begged for a foot to be placed in the cracks. Mine was willing, but my parents deemed it too dangerous for me to climb on my own.

Sensing my near depression Mutti suggested going to Capri Point beyond the club, at least a longer walk.

The track rose steadily, the lake visible below, above us the rocks piled high, glued with foliage.

A water tower reared into view, a metal tank supported on stanchions strapped by crossbars. A notice at the foot of a vertical ladder warned of prosecution for trespass, but no one had been behind us and no one likely to be in front.

Here was my chance to throw boredom down the well so to say; before Mutti could gasp with misgiving, I was up the first section and climbing, sight of the receding ground compensated by the lake's progressive expansion.

"Whew!" Reaching the platform beneath the belly of the tank, I stood looking at sky, lake, and land overgrown with masses of vegetation framing granite rocks, grey-white in the afternoon sun. Fish eagles circled at a lower level, otherwise there was no sign of life except my mother, a forlorn figure sitting on a stone, the two dogs waiting at her feet.

This part of the world was ages old, the granite a testimony to the welling up of magma. In the midst lay Nyanza, comfortably recumbent, cushioned against the horizon, a shade less blue than the water.

What was I in this vast order of things? What was this sadness I could feel emanating from vistas wherever I had seen them in Tanganyika? Was it the emptiness of big spaces, or was it that I had an empathy which made my inner ear hear the land cry out? And for what? My chest drew together again in the hopelessness of the situation, tears welled up. Through them the ground looked even further away.

Mutti called from below,

"I refuse to watch you, it makes me dizzy. Are you coming soon?"

No good shouting, she would not hear me.

Something could happen to the lake, an earthquake for instance. The waters would drain into a fissure leaving hills of islands, therefore valleys filled with mud. What a sight!

"Are you coming?"

I conjured up Maura'a face in my mind, "You're O.K., Cocky, keep looking up as you go down."

"I'm down," I called to Mutti, when I reached the bottom, tears having dried in the thrill of the descent.

Continuing the walk we reached a dead end overlooking the water between our peninsula and the mainland opposite.

"Putzimännchen," Mutti said casually, "I don't think you want to climb that tower again. Capri Point is rather picturesque don't you think, but also nice for leopards. We'd better not bring the dogs here."

We hurried home with not another backward glance.

The holidays were drawing to an end, Vati returning from the *boma* had brought my Rail Warrant.

"Any news about our transfer to the Bukoba region?"

"I met our friend, the purloiner of photos, he says we are going shortly."

"How does he know?"

"He is going too, and believes a certain amount of partnership in matters Social Anthropological is still possible."

"The man has a gall!"

"Not so bitter, Lili. He's after all British and in the Administration, whereas I'm only an Austrian from whom he wants to extract his occasional slice of 'gateau'."

"What! Again?"

"Hunger for good things has no time limit."

At Dodoma, being reunited with my friends was bliss after six weeks during which I had acted the young adult, sharing my parents' Austrian-German character and nationality, a sort of two-tone mat which allowed others to tread over us. At school, a pupil once again however foreign, I could fulfil the character of 'Cocky', and be that other side of me, the school child.

We settled into the new term as though we had never been away except that everyone had a holiday story. Susie's was after my own heart, about a memorable journey with a relative.

"Cocky! You should have been there. The jalopy stops dead, won't re-start. We get out and wait for the usual fiddle-with-this-and-that to get it going again. What do you think it was?"

"Petrol starvation."

"No such big word."

"Fan belt missing. No? Battery gone phut. Big end blown."

She kept shaking her head.

"A piston cracked? Now what was that thing that John mentioned last term? Cam shaft - shorn off."

"Go on with you Cocky! Where do you get all these words?"

"From John, I told you. I listen to the boys' tales about their dads' cars."

"To get back, we stand around in the burning sun, bonnet up, carburettor out, all its little bits lying on a hanky, then she puts everything together again..."

"What, a woman?"

"Yeah, listen, still no joy. The spark plugs get unscrewed, cleaned, put back. Still as dead as the warthog my dad shot. Next she..."

"I don't believe it, a woman?" Alex had joined us.

"Yeah, my aunt. If anything's wrong with a car she's got the bonnet up, her big hands in, and she's swearing like a trooper."

"Where is the 'he', all this time?"

"Arr, shut your bonnet, Garry!"

"Well what was it then?" I asked, sensing the story might get lost.

"She said a tiny God-damn wire connecting something to the distributor arm had come off. Were we glad she found it! In her words, she was beginning to hear the lions roar, that's what she always says when it's getting late."

We were impressed. None more so than I. At last I had found what I really wanted to be, a female car mechanic. Had I not listened enraptured to Africans voicing the most beautiful words: "deenamo", "faneebelti", "karbareta", "petroli kapi." Their hands wrought miracles with wire and string.

I knew my inner pleasure at the sight of metal sweating oil, hard-necked bolts refusing to accept their nuts, incontinent radiators, twitching rocker arms, and "boxi spanas" lying beside the inert engine they would coax into life.

The mists of my future cleared, like an exhaust once the cylinders were firing properly. I would go to the Kenya High School, then to University, finally becoming the sort of person who could lie under a car to tighten its sump nut without getting an eyeful of oil.

At long last my parents reached Bukoba on the west of Lake Victoria. There was a house for their headquarters, though for the moment they were back 'up-country' under canvas.

It was cold, rained daily, the tent poles had keeled over. Mutti, while writing the letter, was sitting in the kitchen with Shabani's 'wife' while all hands were restoring the intended roof over her head. Subsequently, Saidi Kapota, back as handyman, constructed a charcoal brazier to her design. Rain come shine, nothing disturbed Vati, away at a *baraza*, or sitting sheltered in the Chief's office.

Chiefs, in this part of Tanganyika, she informed me, were truly regal, ruling by ancient lineage, and so rich that every one had a driver to convey him in his Rolls Royce.

Next, they were in Ngera, Vati discussing with the secretary of the *Omukama* (Chief) Association, how, by changing custom from within the Bahaya tribe, they could effect an eradication of venereal disease.

Quartered in a 'beehive' hut on the edge of a bleak, rocky plateau with a view of the banana groves below, the wind had blown so fiercely that the bedroom tent could not be erected for fear of the main poles being torn out, and hitting them over the head.

In one of her rare happy moods, she added a P.S. "For we want to live, Vati to make the Bahaya well, Mutti to kiss her daughter welcome at Christmas... and if you desire so much to see the world, why not come to Bukoba?"

BUKOBA AND THE BEAST

When the hooter reverberated faintly round the granite-speckled hills, there was that familiar tickle of quivering timbers under the feet as the engines began to throb. I hung over the rail, listened to farewells sent back and forth across the water and watched as we churned our way round to face the open sea, leaving Mwanza to light its lamps at the going down of the sun.

At the end of the *Usoga's* deck, where railings divided the first-class cabins from the steerage passengers, vociferous Africans began making themselves at home for the night under tarpaulins stretched over the booms.

They had all waited on Mwanza pier until, the loading finished, the Captain had shouted orders for their embarkation organised by the Kavirondo seamen who thought them riff-raff, and treated them with rough justice. Any person arguing that he and his bicycle should be allowed up the gangplank first met with a rain of fast language and found himself bundled to the end of the queue.

From the second class deck below came the crying of babies, and a flow of admonition in Gujarati, followed by the howls of the recipient child.

The *Usoga*, fully loaded, was low in the water and dipping to a breeze.

At last the bell rang for dinner in the mess room where tables were set for the European officers and their white passengers. The Captain gave me a nod, "Your mother's anxious that we should bring you home safely. We'll do that all right! If I were you, I'd get to bed early for there's a storm brewing."

Taking the Captain's advice, I went for an early bath and returning to my cabin, found a fellow passenger already in bed, the door hooked back for fresh air.

During the night a feeling of levitation awoke me, I could see a wall of black water rising above the davit and its lifeboat which a second before had been silhouetted against a leaden sky. In the next movement the *Usoga* turned the other way leaving me with the same sensation of weightlessness, and the water disappearing from view.

Although the deck awnings had been removed to allow the storm an unhindered path, it swept audibly round the upper structure. A flash of lightning lit up the swollen sky, then came the crack of thunder, above the *Usoga* by the sound of it. The lifeboat, though fastened to its pulley, appeared to go up and up into the sky, stayed for a few seconds, and came down, down, down as if about to plunge into the sea, no doubt rising to meet it. It was a frightening spectacle especially as I felt in danger of sliding overboard.

"Oh my Gawd! Don't tell me we're having one of these God-damn lake thunderstorms."

The woman in the next bunk raised her head to have one look at the see-sawing lifeboat.

"Be a dear, will you? Shut the door before we get shot into the bloody mire."

I waited for a moment of equilibrium, made a dash, unhooked the door, and slammed it as the boat took another plunge.

The lady snorted her approval, "Good girl! Going to Bukoba? Well don't - oops - worry. Leave it to these *watu* (people), the Kavirondo know their waters, half of them are always away fishing. Sometimes all that's left of them in a storm is a fat crock sitting by bits of broken canoe."

A Kenyan! I had noted her flamboyant style at dinner when she cracked jokes with the captain. Her orange silk pyjamas encased thin arms, her face was still rouged, lips painted, fair hair and a fringe gave her a boyish look.

Relaxing in the belief that the tried seafarers would see to our safety, she tucked the sheet firmly round herself and turned to the cabin wall, her regular breathing becoming the soft accompaniment to the creaking of the lifeboat, and the receding claps of thunder.

At dawn I was awakened by a knock followed by the boy bringing a cup of tea.

"Mamsapu Mdogo, we are arriving at Bukoba."

Nothing could have woken the Kenyan.

Penetrating cold made me put on my school blazer. Outside there was calm, the sea reflecting blanket clouds. A tortoise hump on the horizon became an island.

As the boat drew nearer the coast, it detailed into an escarpment, rocks embedded in its upper edge like teeth in a gum. From the port side I could make out a steeple on a promontory, a small pier, then figures among whom must surely be my parents. Gradually, two whites became distinguishable between a few blacks, one figure waved. As we docked my mother shouted, "Hello! Hello! Have you had a good journey? Did you have a storm? Were you seasick?"

Her excited behaviour was embarrassing. Furthermore when I stepped down the gangplank she embraced me, and tried a kiss. I was back in my family's ways, my Mutti discreetly wiping her tears of happiness, Vati shaking hands - man to man - and Saidi Kapota, waiting to shoulder the trunk, ready with a smile among his many creases.

"Come along, darling, the Chief has put his limousine at our disposal."

"The Rolls Royce?"

"No, not quite. Hans! at your daughter's arrival you could surely stop talking to the natives and converse with her instead."

They laughed at his parting joke, it was one of my father's characteristics to be amusing rather than formal.

In the roomy limousine he talked of his work, a proposed project to codify Bahaya law. The P.C.'s wife was keen to collaborate with him.

But what of the Sukuma Federation which had thought of the idea in the first place, I asked.

"True," he answered, "but I'm like a dhow, blown where the Government wind takes me. At present it's Bukoba. Here I pick up whatever Social Anthropology they want. The next port might be Mwanza again, then I'll take up the unification of Sukuma law, some of which was completed during our stay in Sukumaland, but now I've been moved... *na ja!* As long as we keep afloat."

We turned into a drive at the side of a German-built bungalow with the usual mosquito-proofed verandah. Another round of greetings followed, Shabani now the head boy, nevertheless wore that shamefaced expression derived from an inherent shyness.

Buyum also claimed my attention. Mutti had informed me of Peter's death, sparing me the detail except to say that she had saved the younger dog with castor oil.

At breakfast I noticed a huge terracotta wall-hanging, edged with black triangles, the rest covered with a tiny horseshoe pattern. Vati called it a barkcloth.

I thought he was joking.

It was an ancient craft, he explained, the bark was stripped off the tree in one piece, beaten until fine enough to resemble cloth, and decorated with a mixture of black dye and clay. When the clay dried off, the dye was left on the material.

Were the tiny cylindrical baskets imprinted with similar triangles, standing on the verandah sills, also made by means of a Baron Münchausen method?

No, they were woven by newly-married wives who, by tradition, had nothing else to do for the first few months of their marriage but to excel in the craft.

"While they got used to their husbands," Vati added with a smile. "We're now in a very different part of Tanganyika, climatically and culturally. Even the Europeans are more friendly, I think the cool lake air has made them almost, what do you call it in English? 'Punch drunk'."

How literally true this was, I would soon find out.

The morning continued cold, the sky overcast, no wonder Kapota had made my mother a brazier for the tent. Just before four o'clock the sky cleared so suddenly that the sun was like a lamp re-lit. Leaves still dripping from a shower glistened in the rays, the grass in front of the house expanded into luscious lawn, Mutti's flowers picked up their heads relieved of the weight of droplets.

It was indeed a different world, nothing like the arid places of our previous homes.

When we set out with Buyum, the intensity of light gave each object a luminosity which made our hedge and the few trees between us and the lake, glow. A swathe of white sand in the bay threw its reflection at our squinting eyes, and the rolling waves deposited their scintillating foam on the beach. It was utopian.

"White 'horsies' today," my mother looked at the water with practised eye. I assumed she referred to hippos from the German *Flusspferde* (river horses), though 'white' was a bit farfetched. Whatever she meant, there was an upheaval of water, a family of five broke surface. They too became part of the radiant scene, the wet hides shining like polished shoe leather. "Huh! huh! huh!" they snorted to the accompaniment of a squeal from the season's baby.

"Come along," Mutti urged, "you can see them another day. Let's go to the *dukas* where I want to show you some dress materials. On the way back we can have a squash at the club."

A difficult task faced us on reaching the vendor's house, one belonging to an Asian lady, because not only was it filled with as many children as brass cooking pots, but with shelves of sari material, some breathtakingly colourful as others were delightfully pastel.

"How pretty! And let me see this one," an ultramarine with pink flower edging. "Oh how beautiful! Yes that one as well," a brilliant jade with a silver thread border. "Wonderful, really! And that?" Mutti pulled at another length. "Cerise, gorgeous, and this lilac is just what I used to wear in the Auguster Anlage, remember Putzi, in Mannheim?"

"Hardly!"

I thought it was time to call a halt, considering a mosaic of colour lay on the floor. Choosing a material for myself was not difficult: plump and short, I could not possibly look like the multicoloured butterflies we had seen on our walk flying up into the warmth of sunshine. Therefore it would have to be something less exotic in design.

Mutti agreed with the periwinkle blue costing Shs.20/- but with misgivings as to what Vati might say, money being shorter than ever now he was paying my school fees.

Asked how he liked it, Vati took a look, "Mm, expensive." Never a word as to how nice I might look in it. How differently he would have responded if I had been a boy buying a good quality football.

Each morning, the rain drumming on the roof, we settled to our sewing while Vati waited for his Government transport which conveyed him to huts in a banana grove. Mutti said he cooked with the Bahaya women. The very idea made me laugh until she qualified her statement, "The other so-called Anthropologist, remember he was coming here the same time as us, has this mad idea of making a banana nutrition survey."

"What's Vati got to do with it?"

"He goes with an orderly who weighs the food. Vati then writes down the quantity of bananas eaten, and the way to prepare them."

Seeing that Bukoba was so different, I was ready to believe anything, "Is he compiling a cookery book?"

"Not quite. Sometimes the bananas are wrapped in their leaves and cooked in hot ashes in the ground, sometimes more modern, the wrapped bundle is placed in a cooking pot. Vati says it is a most hygienic and nutritional cooking method."

Later in the week when I asked him about the project, he replied, "Finished, thank heaven. I have done my bit. The man can now write his report - and may he thrive on it! As Panzi would say."

It was his new name for my mother, and apt. When working in his study, he had become exasperated by the clip-clop of her heels, never so persistently audible when the ground had been under our mats, and had called her *Panzi*. Remonstrating that it sounded rude, she was mollified to hear that it was a grasshopper, and edible.

The name stuck, to my relief, because saying 'Mutti' had become embarrassing in front of English speakers. 'Mum' sounded equally alien.

On Christmas Eve, we wore our presents: mine the Cinderella gown with matching locket from Panzi's jewellery box; Vati his new black and white dinner suit. the matching bow-tie a present from us both; Mutti her extra high-heeled black shoes - an extravagance paid for by my father - to match the lemon blouse and black skirt which her friends had called "chic".

The night was cool. The lantern carried by the garden boy silenced frogs and crickets in the long grass, and hopefully warned grazing hippos of our approach.

African *totos* and their elders were already gathered outside the club to look through the windows at the colourful garlands, and the *Krismasi* rites of the whites.

Formal dress, black and white for the men, the latest fashion on those women who had recently shopped in London, and the sight of the buffet supper, added to the party mood. People were friendly although, when we had taken our plateful, and looked to find a spare table, it was obvious that the Administration had seated itself in order of rank, D.O. with A.D.O., the P.W.D. with the Prison Officer, but not with the Police Commissioner who favoured the neutral company of the German hotel owner who held a Belgian passport.

As soon as the food was cleared and the gramophone played the first tune, all the men disappeared into the bar from where, every now and then, their wives drew them out like a stone set in a catapult, ready to zoom back at the end of the dance.

Panzi and I sat, she hopeful that one of the D.O.'s might honour her with a dance, I acutely aware that we were interesting specimens in a cage as far as our black spectators were concerned.

Quicksteps and foxtrots were a new challenge I might have enjoyed if there had been young partners rather than avuncular men who were merely being kind. My mother kept saying, "Darling, do smile, you are frowning terribly," (my scar), but even if my teeth had been diamonds, there was nobody to dazzle.

After midnight when the ladies, accepting that the bar held greater attractions for their men, had begun to settle for second helpings of lemon meringue pie, and Panzi's chocolate 'hedgehogs' spiked with nuts, my attention was diverted by the bulk of the D.O.'s figure bending over Vati, "...Hans, you'd better come quickly!"

My father pushed away his plate, jumped up, and half ran through the bar door to emerge moments later, his short tubby figure looking comical between two tall drunks whom he was heaving apart. They in turn were arguing quietly but fiercely above his head, ready to come to blows. Others were ranged on either side of the combatants trying to calm the situation. Their pleading: "Leave it until tomorrow; not here now; let me take you home," being as ineffectual as the firebrands we had thrown on the *siafu* in the Manyoni camp.

Vati on the other hand was holding his ground, arms outstretched like the long horns of local *Ankole* cattle, until one of the men raised his fist. For a moment I thought he was going to strike my father, instead, letting it fall, he took closer scrutiny.

"My God, Kori, it's you! Mighty good of you, old chap!"

The other man's face took on a dazed expression.

"I recognise that the heat is greater at the level of your heads than mine," Vati joked. There was laughter, one of them asked him to have a drink.

"Very nice of you, but you see I have my young daughter here, you'll understand that her mother is anxious to put her to bed?"

"Of course, good night, Kori."

"Good night Kori," echoed the other man. Both seemed to have forgotten the tiff.

"Come along!" Vati called to us. Panzi and her friends Enid and Ella, locked in conversation, had been unaware of the shemozzle.

What if it had come to blows? I wondered. The black onlookers would have had a front seat watching their Administrators fight. How appalling.

Whatever our preoccupation - I was making a booklet of caricature figures, Panzi painting a portrait of an African girl for someone's birthday - there was always an interruption from a caller thirsting for tea, or coming to arrange an evening's battle of bridge. My parents had never had such a busy social round.

On Sundays a limousine brought a well-dressed man, black of skin but as un-African as chameleon is to lizard. A descendant of the Hamites who conquered the Bantu people in the north eastern regions of the lake, he had inherited their princely features, height, small noses, and haughty manner.

"Come in, sit down, breakfast is coming. Lili! The Chief is here," Vati called.

"Hello *Omukama*, how's the *Ngole*? And your children? All well? Do sit down, the boy will bring you a cup of tea in a minute."

It was surprising to hear my parents' deferential tone. He, in turn never lost his poise.

"We're having lemon tea," Panzi mentioned at the breakfast table on my first Sunday, "something to do with your totem, isn't it, *Omukama*?"

"Yes, the milk of a pregnant or striped cow is forbidden, also bananas that are joined together by their skin, and animal intestines."

The conversation turned to secondary totems which did not carry a taboo, and then to matters of religion. The chief was on his way to a service at the Catholic church on the promontory.

His long elegant fingers curled round the handle of the teacup, next, round the stem of a cigarette holder. Crossing his long legs for comfort, he leaned back in our P.W.D. chairs taking possession of them. Not for a moment were we allowed to forget that he was *Omukama*.

Behind our kitchen the cliff face thrust itself forward, grooved by clefts inhabited by hyraxes who let out occasional soul-splitting screams followed by shrieks from all the animals on the same ledge. A cacophony of sound. Their lairs looked as if they might be shared by bigger animals, and my parents would not hear of me climbing the rocks.

This left sewing, painting, morning teas and dinner parties, walks, an occasional picnic and dabble in the water, to fill the holidays.

Vati, finding us still sewing by teatime one day, exclaimed, "Still at the affairs of the *haut monde*? I can give you more down to earth news."

"Yes, Hans, we heard quite a bit at bridge this morning."

"No, no, nothing so ear raising, only that our friend the pseudo-embezzler is trying it on again!"

"What! Not that damn man." Panzi believed that in English, swearing was an acceptable expression of annoyance.

"He's taking over the entire V.D. matter."

"And what about all your work with the Chiefs?"

"The Government has voted a sum of money for dealing with the problem. Two doctors are to establish clinics, our friend will arrange for all administrative matters including meetings with Chiefs..."

"And you of course," concluded Panzi.

"No, but I may be asked to work on the sociological side."

"For the same paltry 400 shillings per month that we can't live on?"

"Would you rather be in Germany with your head inside a Nazi gas oven?"

The thought silenced her.

"What was your report, Vati?"

Relieved that the disturbed bees' nest was settling under the influence of his smokescreen he was only too pleased to elaborate. V.D. being thought a natural condition by the local population, one of the chiefs had come up with the idea that groups could be formed with a membership of healthy men, and an equivalent group for women, both made popular through their prerequisite health proved by examination in a clinic.

Panzi was dubious, remarking that the institution of clubs was surely European.

Vati reminded her of the societies in Sukumaland, "Some were no more than exclusive clubs - a sort of tribal 'Carlton'. Here it's not an unknown institution, there's one for ostracising professional thieves. All the Africans agree that it works with great effect."

My mother following her own train of thought, probably via clubs and sociability, changed the subject to remind him that the Caxtons were coming for 'pot luck'.

"*Ach!*" He waved exasperatedly in her direction. "You see how your mother considers parties more important than the subject of V.D."

Mostly, in the evening, Vati preferred to listen to the B.B.C.'s concerts on the newly acquired wireless, secondhand from the Police Officer. Panzi should not have cut him short. No wonder he did not converse much with her, a fact which made her complain that he sat in the Olympus while she wandered lonely and brainless on commonplace earth.

Our wanderings took us to the banana groves growing all over the scarp surrounding Bukoba. They were green, cool, dripping with the morning's rain, soft underfoot, filled with the rustle of fronds, and removed from the official world below. Here and there stood a beehive hut, the under frame made of flexible branches covered tier by tier with bundles of overlying thatch. Wisps of smoke rose through the top from the cooking of the evening meal abandoned in favour of seeing us pass, our approach having been announced by Buyum's barks.

"*Jambos*" exchanged, my mother introduced the possibility of making a painting of their home, via a compliment, "Your hut is very nice. Can I come and sit here to paint a picture of it?" She made appropriate gestures.

Children gaped, mothers sat unmoved keeping mum, old men smoked and pretended deafness.

"What shall I do now to make them understand?" She asked *sotto voce* as though they were German-speaking.

"Walk on," I suggested. "*Kwa heri*!" The group came to life reciprocating enthusiastically, our importance as curiosities having waned.

"These Bahaya!" Panzi grumbled. "Pretending they know no Swahili. I shall have to get one of Vati's orderlies to talk to them."

The groves were extensive, one leading to the next, and untidy; fronds lolled, trees leaned over with age or weak in root.

"There! A banana flower. Aren't the colours strong?" She stopped to admire.

From one of the boles a thin ridged stem curved down ending in a purple phallus, swollen and shiny. How could she not see the similarity? Waves of embarassment and then pleasure, rolled over me. The intensity of the stirring despite my pride in being inured to sexual images was shocking. I wanted to feel the petals, immerse myself in the satisfaction of touching but could not bring myself to do so in front of her.

"M-h!" I conceded, blasé, and we continued homeward.

The lake was losing its blue to an increasing grey. Hippos had disappeared though their nostrils must be breaking water for air. They would be back after dark to graze on Panzi's grass patch.

Vati was in conversation with Bwana Kahawa (Mr. Coffee), the Agricultural Officer who was enjoying the last sight of his dahlias before the sinking sun robbed them of all hue.

Panzi stopped to ask about his little girls.

"They're fine, Lili, thriving like my flowers, and even more beautiful."

"He's wonderful," she said afterwards, "spends his spare time playing and looking after them. I'm making them pyjamas for Christmas - you have no idea how good these people have been to us, and many others here."

It was a relief to hear her praises. I could remember how in Rusegwa she had laughed at Vati's jokes, without tears in her voice, and talked happily about our good quality sisal that would help to pay for Aunt Gretl's and Erna's holidays with us.

Bukoba had returned to her something of the old self, though each dinner eaten out was still in danger of being offered to the W.C. especially as she enjoyed a sherry or two, after which she lapsed into giggles if she failed to hear a question. I realised that Vati in refusing to take an alcoholic drink not only avoided paying for a round, but also achieved breaking the accepted social pattern. It gave him stature that he did not possess physically. Panzi preferred being one with a merry crowd.

Shabani's tipsiness could be equally delightful, a bit of an unsteady gait, more smiles than usual, singing and dancing in the kitchen.

Unfortunately *pombe* took hold of him increasingly so that even the long-suffering concubine refused to stay. When things became impossible in the kitchen - either nothing cooked or everything burnt - Vati's only resort was dismissal. When that happened he was re-engaged next day despite my mother's protestations that her "gall was overflowing".

Shabani and Panzi, at loggerheads so often, had moments of mutual understanding when conversation was low key, the kitchen tranquil, food simmered without her criticism.

"Shabani! Now watch this, a European dish I haven't shown you before."

"Very good, Mamsapu."

At other times their mutual help went further. "Shabani, I lost ten shillings from my bag, yesterday."

"No Mamsapu, I did not know, that is very bad."

"Our old boys would never do such a thing."

"No, they wouldn't."

"Is the oven ready? Let us put the pudding in to brown the top."

She left, knowing he had pointed out the thief.

When Kapota had returned to Sukumaland in mutual understanding that he had fulfilled his usefulness as dhobi, a local man replaced him.

Acting on Shabani's hint, Vati waited until we had gone out, to apply his 'method'. The boys assembled in a row, the Bwana walking up and down in front of them let off a thunderous furore. The innocent listened unmoved, the culprit became increasingly nervous until, with all eyes upon him, he confessed to his guilt. On our return the ten shillings had been cut from the wages owed to him on his dismissal.

In the belief that zebras keep each other's company, my parents hoped that Shabani would find a "tribal brother" whose character matched his own. Days later Dalmazius, Mission-influenced, came to work for them. Vati hoped he had regressed from Catholicism to indigenous faiths, despite his own respect for the White Fathers, always interested in their convert's customs. Mutti liked his grin and "honest eyes".

The parting from Panzi at the end of the holidays was particularly difficult. We knew it would be six months before my return, and despite all the kindness expressed by her friends, she was totally downcast.

Back at school I found that nobody had missed me as much as I had longed for them, nevertheless, my welcome was flattering.

"Hello, Cocky, back to crow?"

"Shut your own beak!"

Chui was still on leave, the bite missing, lessons flat, until the morning when Little Sir's smile was replaced by the grim set of his jaw.

His, "Be quiet!" instead of, "Good morning," had us shutting our mouths audibly like a crocodile's snap.

"I am glad to tell you that Tim, who as you might have noticed is not at school this term, has found employment with the Royal Navy. I'm sure I speak for all of us when I say that we hope he will do well, and conduct himself in a manner that will do him justice."

It was news indeed. The boys whispered, "Lucky bugger." "He

wasn't such a twit after all." "Wonder what ship he's on?"

"What ship's he on, Sir?"

Little Sir glowered. No answer forthcoming.

Betty cupped a hand over her mouth, "Bet he can't tell a ship's wheel from its rudder."

After the lesson uproar flared when the boys vented their envy, "I'm packing tomorrow! All this swot! 'Why haven't you done your homework?' - every morning."

"'Subordinate clauses'! They won't help me take over my dad's business!"

"What a damned swiz. Old T. gets into the Navy just like that!" - a snapping of fingers - "and my family tells me I'd better learn more than swimming to wear a sailor's cap."

"Wait a minute everybody, we don't know his ship's name. You go and ask Big Sir, Cocky."

"The *Ark Royal*, an aircraft carrier," I announced on my return.

"What? That poor kid who couldn't even read the name on a cigarette tin, flying! I'll eat my bush-hat if he ever does!"

We were flabbergasted; Tim endangering his life, crashing aircraft because he could not read a dial.

Jerry, always knowledgeable, shouted, "Hold on! You're all on the wrong tack, an aircraft carrier is big, absolutely huge, bigger than a hockey pitch."

"So what?"

"Well, he's probably the cook's *toto* on it."

That aspect calmed the boys.

John asked, "Don't they have Indians or some sort of wog to do that?"

"Absolutely not, it's all British personnel."

Tim, whom we had pitied so much, had beaten us all in getting a job on a Naval ship which to us represented British supremacy. England, that jagged piece of land on page five of the School Atlas, surrounded by blue on which the *Ark Royal* and similar vessels sailed round in never ending circles, now had Tim to help protect the nation.

I had another side of the coin in my mind. Britain might be protected but my aunt Erna and her husband Peter were at the mercy of the Nazis. No Royal Navy for them. Panzi had sent me his letter describing their desperate plight after losing his job. Gretl and her doctor husband were fortunate in having found employment in Beirut.

His anguish stopped any desire on my part to be Austrian as surely as Little Sir's wiping of our blackboard erased his attempts at drawing. No, I must not belong to that country, and not to Germany either, the only identity left to me was that of 'Cocky', and that would shortly be in jeopardy.

Chui had returned, filled with zest and new ideas, it was a pleasure to hear the highfaluting voice we had missed.

"Mother was fine and father talking of visiting Africa - the old dears."

"Cocky, how on earth can Chui still have parents alive when she herself looks like an old mealie cob?" Tessi asked between a change of teachers. Gary volunteered the answer, "Maybe the juicy bits have been gnawed off."

"Don't be disgusting, anyway you look like a screwed up skunk yourself."

We held our noses, coughed and pretended fainting.

In subsequent weeks we heard much about flowers and birds which abounded in every Englishman's garden, also about entertainment.

"I had occasion to see a Shakespearean play." Her tone indicated that the playwright ranked with Matthew, Mark, Luke and John. "It was *As You Like It*, and so extremely enjoyable that I promised myself we should stage it for the end of term concert. We have a marvellous Touchstone."

"What sort of person is he, Miss?"

"One of the most important in the play, he is Shakespeare's universal wise man, a clown. You wouldn't refuse that, would you?" Looking up I met the lively compelling eyes.

'Cocky the Fool' stuck. Not until Jerry, Betty and I walked out of the Junior Cambridge Exam, declaring the ordeal a pleasant experience, did I lose the derisive addition.

The last day of term, a final packing, the following morning cold, Meru hidden in cloud, goodbyes for friends waiting to go home on different transport, and the bus at last whizzing round the drive. The usual shove, push and occupation of a chosen seat, and we were off for the August holidays.

After six months away from my parents, their personalities were easier to remember than their faces.

"I will try not to fall over the side of the pier but I won't promise not to be excited, nor to refrain from a kiss. You must be patient with me," Panzi had written.

Request fulfilled at the pier, I was back.

At the house, we sat under a drum roll of rain.

"Mr. Konstantiadis," Panzi began, pushing away the slice of pawpaw glistening with the extra sugar she had sprinkled, "you know whom I mean?"

"Lili, eat!" urged my father.

"Yes, yes, Hansele. He's the Greek gentleman living up the hill in the old German house stinking of bats, and has a daughter about your age. I've already invited her to meet you when she comes on holiday. Now what do you say to that!"

It was cheering news, meanwhile I would have to bear the company of adults. Afterwards in the study, temporarily my bedroom, lined with our packing cases painted the colour of Panzi's prevailing scheme, I asked my usual question about Vati's work.

"Something interesting, I attend the High Court, presently sitting in Bukoba. The judge, with the aid of an interpreter, is presiding over a case of murder. You can imagine the confusion of British legal jargon translated into the vernacular. The accused, a young man of about twenty one, is supposed to have killed a goatherd."

It was sad to think of the youth, probably dressed in white shorts and shirt, sitting listlessly on a bench, and submitting himself to endless questions, futile in that the answers would seem self-evident to him.

His stoicism would be borne by the conviction that he was at fault: if he had committed the crime he knew his life was finished; if he had not, the ancestors must be angry with him for omitting some sort of propitiation, why else would they cause him to sit through the ordeal?

"What will happen to him?"

"It is expected that he will be sentenced to death."

"Why do you want to listen to such sad proceedings?"

"Whatever the aspects of the case, it's an opportunity for me to learn about a legal system. I have started compiling Haya tribal law for the book with the help of the D.C.'s wife, a very able lady even if your mother can see no good in her but the shape of her Aryan nose!"

Later that day, after our walk, Panzi hurried me back, "There's something on at about sixish, you will see."

This time the lake reflected its sky, losing out to the sinking sun, the beach without its dhobi white, hippos' backs like driftwood at the other end of the bow of the bay. An end of day atmosphere, quietly handsome, if only there were some young people with whom to share such poignant moments.

"Here we are," Panzi tied Buyum to a bush outside one of the lake-shore bungalows. "Hello everybody, you are here already Hans? Hello Enid."

"Welcome to our six o'clock tea-hour, dear. Here's a stool, squeeze yourself in next to your mother."

The verandah was filled with white Bukoba residents ranged on chairs round the walls. The tea trolley, angled to make more room, was presided over by Enid, straight-haired, fat, wearing thick spectacles, and pouting, it was her natural expression as she poured the milk, strained the tea, transferred slops from cups into a silver dish, replenished cups for the second and third time, and entrusted them to hands that passed them round the circle.

Conversation ceased as soon as her husband switched on the wireless for the six o'clock B.B.C. Overseas News. Bowed heads and still cups showed the visitors' concentration.

Everything was news to me: Mr. Chamberlain would go to the aid of Poland if she wanted to defend her rights.

"That's it!" exclaimed our host. "That's put the kibosh on it for sure."

"How dreadful!" Enid said quietly. "What about all of 'em at home?"

The men discussed the possibility of war, Enid wiped her eyes, Panzi asked me what the announcer had said.

The tea-hour had become a Bukoba institution at which the adults became increasingly distressed, and I, in my lack of youthful contact, increasingly depressed. At last came the day when the Greek family were back in residence.

Esme, their daughter, once out of her mother's view, changed into a keen rock scrambler though a trifle unwary. She was my age but bigger, sophisticated, at school in Greece, and had enough English vocabulary for our few forays.

Days later, we were sitting hot and tired behind the crags of the cliff top, rewarding ourselves with chocolate, when she pointed out a massive clump, split horizontally. The molar head was resting on its lower half but had shifted leaving a narrow ledge running along the side as far as another crack, this time vertical.

We agreed to try a traverse, I stepped onto the walkway with Esme following, finding that the further we went, the steeper became the drop to the ground where a tangle of thorny scrub warned us not to fall over.

Our goal was the vertical cleft where we would be able to turn. Edging along, our faces to the rock, the ledge narrowed alarmingly. My method was to go as fast as advisable, hoping the cleft would provide a resting place. Arriving well ahead of her, I stepped into the gap to find it was a shallow cave.

Something looked at me from the gloom within, a creature of my size with eyes so liquid brown and infinitely sad that I was riveted not only by the shock of the encounter but by their expression.

Our eye contact seemed to be that of two creatures recognising their common ancestry but questioning their meeting, though in split seconds I knew instinctively that the hairy thing before me could not be addressed with a "*Jambo*!"

Behind me, Esme, unaware of what was ahead, was giving a running commentary about heat. "My father's car it boils. He put in cold, I like that water for me."

Silenced by what I saw, I could not call out to her, especially when, after the few moments it took for my eyes to accustom themselves to the dark interior, two rounded animal ears became visible at each side of the head, which was broad at the top and narrowed...

"Leopard!" flashed through my mind. But then I saw a flicker of a movement, an arm! It was stretched above in the posture of a small person gripping a handhold above its head.

There 'it' was, and there was I, both facing one another across a dim space of mutual terror, and those eyes... looked out with an inner tragedy that touched my being.

"Back!" I snarled as quietly as possible over my shoulder at Esme who had just come up behind me. "Back, back!"

"Back? But I am not there for turning."

"Back, back!" I hissed, trying to sound inoffensive so as not to alarm the thing, but unable to move unless Esme was going to make her way backwards.

"Esme," I entreated, "please move!" Our retreat seemed interminable. My flesh crept with the expectation that the creature, whatever it was, would rush at me from the cave to defend its territory.

Had it been a recognisable animal, I could have whispered its name to Esme, cautioning her to hurry according to its expected reaction. A depth of thought in those eyes as I had only seen in persons and dogs, upstanding ears either side of a triangular head, and then the arm, made it an apparition in the flesh, and worst of all the eyes began to haunt me the moment I could no longer see them.

Esme, disappointed that I had stopped her from reaching the cleft, took her time. I clung to the rock, too frightened to make a sound until it was possible to jump off the ledge.

"Run!" I shouted, starting off at the fastest speed I could muster. My one instinct was to flee. Thrashing through the thorny scrub, I threw myself over minor rocks, and kept looking back expecting the grisly thing to come leaping after us, only to see Esme following at a leisurely pace.

"What's the matter with you?" she demanded crossly, catching up with me at the main road. "Was it a snake?"

"No, no, it was - some - thing," I panted, trying to catch my breath, "but I - can't tell you - now."

My only desire was to continue fleeing homewards to tell my parents. Bidding Esme a hurried goodbye, I ran and slid down a steep short cut that brought me out near the main road by our house, and still at full tilt bumped into Panzi helping the garden boy by our driveway.

"Hello! back already? *Mein Gott,* Putzi, look at your clothes!" Trying to convey their unimportance I waved an arm in Vati's gesture.

"And your arm, all scratched! What have you and Esme been doing?"

"I'll tell you in a minute, can I have an orangeade?" The sweat was running down my face, my throat was parched, worst of all I could not forget the look of those melancholy eyes.

When I related what I had seen, Panzi was unimpressed.

"Don't worry, it was probably an owl. You will have forgotten our 'Eulalia' at Morogoro, she had human-like eyes whenever she opened them below those tufts which looked like ears."

"But Panzi, she didn't have an arm to stretch above her head."

"Yes, funny really. Ask Vati when he returns."

"Animals look human when you look them in the eye, it's because we recognise ourselves in them," he suggested.

"Be serious, what do you think I saw?"

"A hyena, I don't want to make it sound sensational by calling it a leopard, as you imply."

"But the arm! Shouldn't someone go and have a look?"

"Only to shoot the poor creature? Let's leave it alone."

My parents remained dismissive of my encounter. It seemed to me that nothing ever stirred them except their own affairs. I for one knew that those eyes were as near to 'human' as mattered, the ears as 'animal' as I knew myself to be Homo Sapiens. So what was it? A chimpanzee? They existed hundreds of miles from Bukoba. An old crone disguised with animal skin to warn off would-be-intruders? Those eyes were not looking through a mask, I was certain of that. A leopard sitting near a tree-trunk which had made me think it was an arm? Not with eyes that could touch my heart. It was futile to conjecture, especially before falling asleep at night when the creature filled my imagination, although during the day too, it was there looking at me from inside my head, never to be forgotten.

My headlong flight had somehow spoiled Esme's friendliness. She was busy doing other things each time I called at the hill house until one day it was shuttered, and the family gone.

Realising how my hopes of companionship had been dashed, Mutti hoped to revive my spirits by offering to buy some material we could make into a dress for the sundowner to be staged by the Ismalia community in honour of the visit to Dar es Salaam of the Agha Khan.

Vati was incensed, "What? another expense! Have you forgotten, Lili, that we had a bill for Shs.240/- for her school fees?"

Panzi looked crestfallen, "Hans, we are in debt anyway, another few shillings will make no difference."

He sighed deeply, threw his serviette to one side, "Have you looked at your *duka* bill this month?"

"No, I thought it far safer for my state of nerves not to."

"Lili! Well, if we have nothing else, at least we can look forward to one hundred Shillings, one goat, two pieces of barkcloth, one hoe, two calabashes of *pombe*, and if we reside in the district of Ihangiro, ninety cowrie shells which Lili can hang round her neck for she won't have much else.

"I think with all this silly talk I need to get back to my studies of

Makula."

"Which is what, Vati?"

"Brideprice in Uhaya."

At the sundowner, Asians and Europeans squeezed onto the verandah of the Abul Karims. Unfortunately the Indian ladies, who had provided the two sorts of samosas, mouth-burning and mouth-watering, were out of sight in a back room despite our requests that they should emerge for a chat in Swahili.

Among the white guests there was a lady I wanted to meet because she did carpentry. A woman doing man's work, just the sort of person I wanted to be except in mechanical wizardry.

To my consternation her appearance was none too good, eyebrows too thick, Elleni would have offered her tweezers. Her hair was cut on the plain side, too masculine. God forbid that I should follow such fashion. Nevertheless, she was pleasant, admitting shyly that she did sometimes mend table legs.

"Hello, Kori," her husband greeted my father as we were leaving, "pleased with what the Hun is up to? *Jawohl!*" He clicked his heels in mock imitation.

Vati turned away with embarrassment. Later he asked Bwana Kahawa about him.

"What is he, Hans? Good question. A bloody little tyke if you ask me, a P.W.D. Assistant. Always yapping, and taking swipes at other people."

Next day while we were having our morning tea, Vati, who had gone off early while the heavenly watering can was still being filled rather than poured, made an unusual reappearance.

"I've thrown it away. That's done!"

"What?"

"My wartime pistol, down the boys' latrine hole. A worthy depository for a firearm, don't you think?"

I was utterly astonished. Never had I known him to keep anything for sentimental reasons. The matter was all the more strange considering he had always spoken against people keeping firearms. Having declared his views on life so strongly, a sort of black and white painting on which a smudge would diminish the value of the canvas, his lapse was deeply shocking. I saw that his iron principles could melt as much as my mother's heart softened, and how often had he made fun of that!

The crested cranes were back on the grass airfield, a tiara of golden plumes on their heads.

A man approached, plucking a repetitive tune on his hand-held marimba, a rhythm for walking.

Buyum, straining on the lead, pulled me up the path to the ridge forming the northern scarp of the Bukoba basin. Ahead stood our 'sentinel' in typical attitude, knee up, foot resting on the other thigh. It was a tree with a bent lower branch growing back upon itself, providing the illusion of the herd boy with raised knee, the sparsely leaved crown could have been his hair.

He was looking out over the Victoria-Nyanza, ahead the tortoise-shaped island dividing water from sky, to the side the scallops of bays edging the lake as far as we could see.

"Beautiful!" exclaimed Panzi. "When you go back to school, Phoebe and I will come up here to paint this magnificent view." It was truly beautiful and vast, like seeing a part of Little Sir's revolving globe peeled off, enlarged, and spread out; turquoise where the reeds grew in the river-mouth below us, sky-blue where the shallow water lay over a sandy shelf used by the hippos, deep blue with streaks of currents further out, and the scallops, hemstitched in dark green curving, curving, curving.

It was as still as a chameleon on guard, but what for? Its emptiness appreciated by artists, but who else? It had no future as it had no past, it was in a state of suspension, and at the sight of it my chest began to feel as though a python was constricting it.

"*Kush Dich* (Sit), Buyum!" Panzi's command interrupted my gazing.

From behind his ear she prized away several ticks bloated with blood. "He needs a bath." She ground them into the gritty soil, staining it red with the spurting blood. "Let's go, darling, Enid will be expecting us."

I could not move. Once again something inexplicable reached out to me from the vast scene, drawing me in, beauty spilling into sadness. I could offer it no comfort, being as it were one with it, equally in limbo.

"Come along!" Panzi shouted, halfway down the slope. "It's getting dark."

"I'm not staying in Tanganyika, I'm not! I'm not!" Almost

blinded by tears, I ran after my mother.

"There you are at last, dears. You're a bit late, aren't you? We've had the news," Enid greeted us.

"Is everything all right?"

"You could hardly say that, Lili," her husband butted in, "it's getting on if you ask me! Time we declared war on these bloody Germans, pardon my language."

"Oh how dreadful, you mean there really will be one?"

"Yep! Lili. The sooner the better!"

My mother looked shaken.

"Sit down," he said kindly, "Enid quick, give her a cuppa."

Vati was there as well, saying, "Lili, eat one of Enid's biscuits."

A moment later conversation continued with the inevitable pros and cons for conflict.

Near me an A.D.O. was asking Vati about a court case, "Hans, how can these people here believe that four years after a woman has had relations with a man, and subsequently gets married to another, her first born may have been fathered by the first beau?"

"It's all bound up with a superstition that the ancestors of the woman's family may take revenge if she does not confess to the deed once her first child is born. A custom has evolved to lift the threat, by her coming out into the open to declare it a *Mwana wa Bisisi*. There is no stigma attached."

"And what about the rules of succession?"

"A Bisisi child becomes the heir of its natural father."

"But, Hans, born four years late!"

"The African has no microscope, he does not have scientific means to prove biological facts one way or another. The Bisisi child is thought to slumber in the mother's womb, the word actually means a charred stick which is easily rekindled."

"Quite poetic, mm! I must tell Valery when I get home."

When we arrived back at ours, Panzi went straight to the kitchen to see whether Shabani had enough eggs for a fish soufflé. Coming from the W.C. I noticed him standing in the dark of the back verandah.

"Mamsapu Mdogo!" he called softly, "I have heard that there will be war."

"Yes, we too hear it on the *wirelesi.*"

"Whites will fight whites?"

"Yes, that will happen."

"Lo! Lo!" He was rooted to the spot. Not being of the generation of Mohamadi and Sefu, the possibility was incomprehensible to him.

Feeling the same I found nothing to say.

"Wadatchi have great strength." He was gone, back to the kitchen.

Near my bed, a camp-bed had been erected for Panzi in persuasion of a rest before taking off each afternoon like a true grasshopper.

During one of our siestas, Vati, instead of turning off the static-ridden transmission on the wireless in the verandah, was twiddling the control knobs to tune the B.B.C.

We must have dozed off, and simultaneously been woken by his call. He came into the room, a strange expression on his face as if he had heard news that was affecting him emotionally. Turning to me he said, "In years to come remember this moment when I just heard that World War Two has been declared. From now on we speak no more German!"

We rose hurriedly, running to the set to catch more of the news.

Before long a sharp "rat-a-tat-tat!" on one of the windows made us look up to see the head and shoulders of the P.W.D. Assistant.

"Hello!" shouted Vati, starting to walk towards the mosquito-proofed door. "Do come in."

Panzi asked me to tell Dalmazius to hurry up with the tea, and bring an extra cup.

Returning from the back door I was in time to hear, "...war is declared, you being an enemy alien I am confiscating your wireless."

My parents stood there as if they had just seen my beast from the cliff top.

No more Arusha School... no more friends... internment... flashed through my mind.

The man brushed past us, walked up to the set, and began fumbling with the battery connections.

"I will do it for you." Vati, regaining some composure, in turn fumbled until the leads allowed themselves to be parted from the terminals. The aerial, however, was not only fastened down on the window sill with bent nails but resisted being pulled off through the hole in the back cover.

Vati reached for the pliers kept on the sill, "Here you are. I'm never any good with these things, you'd better try."

There was the sound of a "snick", the set stood freed. Without another glance in our direction, the man carried it to the door held open by Vati too upset to remonstrate.

"*Chai tayari* (Tea is served), Mamsapu." Dalmazius set down the tray bearing four cups and saucers. An assortment of Shabani's cakes lay regimented round a plate.

The war had begun.

For Tanganyika it meant the loss of innocence. It was not Eva who ate of the forbidden fruit but Adamu by helping the white man in his war.

Before it would all happen Panzi had the last word.

"*Ach mein Gott!*"